GALAHAD SUNS

David Kimberley

First published 2017
Published by GB Publishing.org

Copyright © 2017 David Kimberley
All rights reserved
ISBN: 978-1-912031-61-0 (paperback)
978-1-912031-60-3 (eBook)
978-1-912031-59-7 (Kindle)

Cover Art   © Wendy Kimberley Art

GB Publishing.org
www.gbpublishing.co.uk

For my wife, Gina

Acknowledgement
Special thanks have to go to Gina for being unbelievably supportive through thick and thin, Wendy for coming up with fantastic art that always inspires, my family and family-in-law for believing in GS, GBP for helping make a lifelong ambition become reality, and to the wonderful Papworth staff who once mended a broken heart.

CONTENT

Map

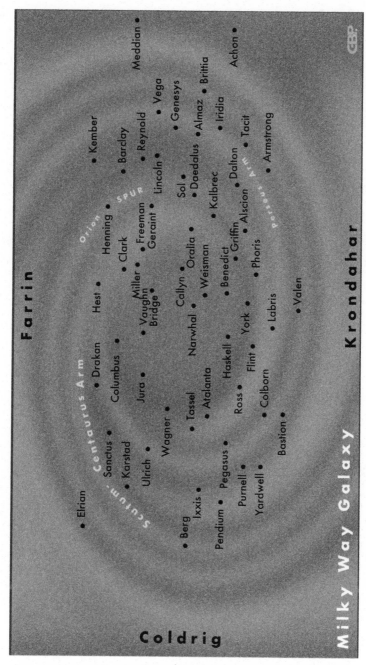

Kismet
Genesys system

There were too many obstacles.

Traversing the ruined streets of the outer colony would have been difficult even without the supply wars raging, but the constant ducking and diving to avoid getting caught in crossfire was slowing him down. He cursed Rane for bringing him to the ragged outskirts of Monarch City.

Leaning out from behind the remnants of a wall, Kurcher peered along the narrow street. Numerous life readings flickered to the left and right of the pock-marked road. He refocused his app on the only one moving away west from his position – three hundred and forty metres between them.

'He's getting away, Davian.'

Frost's ability to state the obvious annoyed him as it always did. 'I know. If I can just work out how to get to the other end of this street without getting my head blown off, I'll be able to close the distance again.'

'Rane managed it.'

Even through the comms app, Kurcher could tell Frost was smiling. He glanced up at the *Kaladine* as it began moving slowly west, the fading Genesys sun glinting off the underside of his ship. He imagined Frost sat at the controls, cigarette on the go as she watched him struggle with grim amusement.

'Why don't you come down here and I'll sit in the fucking comfy seat for once?'

'You're the enlister.' Her smile had definitely faded. 'I can see an alternative route for you but you'll have to make up time on Rane.'

'Fine. Where?'

'Look to your left. See the broken archway? Go through it and then take the first right down the alley. That'll take you round this street.'

Kurcher checked his revolver. He hadn't fired it since Frost dropped him on Kismet, but he had a feeling he might have to soon. One bullet into Edlan Rane's skull would suffice.

He sprinted for the archway and heard the crack of weapon fire as the colonists resumed their exchange. Following Frost's directions, he found himself in the alley and checked on Rane's position as he headed west.

'Shit, he's over four hundred metres away now. Can you get a bead on him yet?'

Frost sighed in his ear. 'He's too smart for that. I'll carry on tracking him as best I can, but he knows how to avoid us. He *always* knows.'

'Just give me a heads up if he deviates.'

'I will. By the way, watch out for a handful of colonists heading your way from the south.'

Kurcher could see a junction ahead, a dust-covered buggy seemingly abandoned on the road. He heard the colonists approaching as he reached it and crouched low for a moment as they charged past. He heard one man boasting about killing a Monarch guard who got in his way and another saying he would kill them all if he had the chance.

'I thought Sigma Royal said they would ensure no civil war erupted on Kismet,' remarked Frost.

Kurcher began moving west again. 'I wish they had. The last thing I need is to be gunned down by some colonist who just wanted a loaf of bread.'

Putting the war-torn street behind him finally, Kurcher noticed that Rane had changed direction and was moving south. He couldn't see the *Kaladine* either.

'Justyne, this is crazy. I can't gain ground on Rane like this. Can you tell where he might be heading?'

'I can take a guess.' The sound of smoke being exhaled whispered through the comms app. 'If I'm wrong though, then we'll lose him.'

'He's got a ship somewhere here. I reckon he'll head for that if it's nearby.'

'My thoughts exactly.'

Kurcher grimaced. 'Take your best guess then and point me along the quickest route.'

Frost was silent for several seconds. 'Left at the next junction, then follow the road until it reaches a plaza.'

Kurcher followed her directions once more, keeping close to the walls. As he neared the open space of the plaza ahead, there was a sudden explosion off to his right that sent masonry and dirt showering onto him. The impact caused him to stumble, but he managed to stop himself sprawling onto the broken road and continued into the plaza.

Three colonists appeared ahead, each armed with a basic Sigma Royal pistol. The weapons were standard colony defense equipment that the corporation provided and had all seen better days.

Kurcher did not intend on slowing down to deal with them, but it was not his lucky day.

'Whoa there,' cried one colonist, raising his pistol. 'Are you Sigma...?'

Kurcher's first bullet cut the question short as it entered through the man's

4

eye and out the back of his skull. The second and third bullets dropped the other two colonists before they could even react. Kurcher sprinted across the plaza.

'Where am I going?'

'He changed direction again,' Frost told him. 'Take a right and you'll be on a long strip that runs west as far as you can see. Rane is five hundred metres along that strip.'

'I'm losing him, for fuck's sake.'

The strip Frost mentioned was not so much a road now; more like a killing ground. Bodies were strewn along both sides, some from Monarch City, but most were part of the force who had attacked the colony; members of several smaller settlements who had banded together, driven by a need to feed.

'Fucking morons,' growled Kurcher, making his way past the dead.

A glimmer of hope appeared ahead as the *Kaladine* came into view, hovering over several buildings to the south of the killing ground.

'You got a lock on him yet?' he asked his pilot.

'He looks like he's heading for the storage facilities nearby. Hurry up.'

Kurcher checked the distance to Rane's life sign. Three hundred and eighty-five metres.

As Frost barked the directions, he followed them exactly, leaving the strip and darting between the silent buildings. At one point, Frost mentioned that the supply war was nowhere near this part of Monarch so only frightened colonists would be trembling behind the closed or broken doors.

Two hundred and fifty metres.

'Why has he slowed down?'

'The streets are like a warren here,' replied Frost. 'Plus he is likely trying to recall where exactly he left his ship.'

Kurcher's trigger finger twitched. The thought of finally catching and killing Rane gave him immense pleasure. The killer had always kept one step ahead of him, managing to escape and disappear through a jump point, leaving Kurcher and Frost to start their search all over again.

Rane had made a mistake coming to Kismet though. Despite Genesys being a Sigma Royal system, the jump point had a concealed Taurus Galahad monitor, which recorded Rane's arrival. He had hoped that Kurcher would not follow him down onto such a sorry world as Kismet, especially with Monarch City once again under attack over supplies, but the enlister liked proving him wrong.

'Are you not even curious about him?'

Kurcher laughed. 'No. We've been through this before. Rane has killed over forty people across five systems. Taurus Galahad want him eliminated and so do I.'

'After three years of hunting him down, you're not even slightly interested as to why he murdered those people? Besides, it was forty-one victims in 2615 so it's likely to be more by now.'

'Enough, Justyne. Rane is wanted by all of the corps except Impramed and I don't intend on letting one of them bag him.'

Frost was quiet for a moment. 'Seems apt he should meet his fate on Kismet then.'

Two hundred and seventy-three metres.

'Fuck this.' Kurcher activated the boost app and smiled as the small dose of Parinax entered his system. The aches he had started feeling in his legs vanished instantly and the kick of adrenaline spurred him on through the tight streets.

'Really?' came Frost's disapproving tone. 'There was a time you didn't need a boost of that shit to help you catch a crim.'

Kurcher ignored her and enjoyed the rush. Even the dust-stained buildings seemed to glow whiter under the now golden sky as he passed them. The underbelly of the *Kaladine* shone brightly as it moved overhead.

'Davian!'

Frost's sudden cry made him slide to a halt as he entered a long, narrow courtyard. The wall to his right exploded towards him and he reeled backwards, slamming into the opposite building. His boost numbed the pain.

Kurcher's heart sank slightly when the mech stepped into the courtyard. Its humanoid frame was painted black with a vertical red line on its front and the crown emblem surrounding the sigma letter was boldly displayed upon its shoulder.

'Pursuit mech,' came Frost's hushed voice.

'No shit.'

The mech's head swivelled in his direction, then all hell broke loose. Kurcher dived for cover behind a low wall as the mech's dual shrikes buzzed into action. Bullets hammered into the soft walls of the buildings alongside the courtyard, blowing them apart. Waiting for the distinct whirring of the shrikes cooling down, Kurcher leapt up and fired twice at the mech through the cloud of dust between them. Both bullets ricocheted off the reinforced frame and he hit the ground once more as it unleashed another barrage, this time destroying most of his cover.

'Get in there and kill him,' came a man's voice from behind the mech.

'Getting mechs to do your dirty work now, Beck?' called out Kurcher, his eyes looking for a possible escape route.

A laugh echoed across the courtyard. 'Just stand up, Davian, and do us all a favour.'

'Do you intend helping me?' Kurcher whispered to Frost.

'Nearly there. Just buy yourself some time.'

Kurcher reloaded his revolver as quickly as he could, cursing himself for preferring the feel of such an old-fashioned weapon. 'Listen, Beck. You and I may have had our differences, but I'm not here to harm Sigma Royal.'

'I know,' came the amused reply. 'You're here after Edlan Rane, and so are we. It was just too enticing to kill two assholes with one mech.'

Kurcher could hear the heavy thudding footfalls of the mech as it approached. 'You know what? I made a mistake not killing you back on Titan Station. Why don't you do yourself a favour and leave now?'

'Always the arrogant prick. Why don't you go fuck yourself?'

Kurcher pressed his eye up to a bullet hole in the wall. The mech was close and he could see two men dressed in black and red entering the courtyard behind it, razepistols in hand. He recognised Beck instantly by the enlister's size. Both Sigma Royal men were wearing light armour and protective helmets, which still made Kurcher smile. He refused to wear anything so demeaning and Taurus Galahad obliged.

'Hey, Davian,' called Beck. 'You can tell that pilot of yours I'll see to her once I'm finished here.'

Kurcher spotted a way into one of the nearby buildings and took his chance, sprinting into the ragged interior before leaping behind another wall with fewer holes in it. The shrikes tore into the building once more, but the mech's AI kicked in and it began flanking his position. If it managed to do so, his only means of escape was straight into Beck's line of sight.

'What the fuck is keeping you, Frost?'

'Thirty seconds.'

Kurcher focused on Rane's life reading. Three hundred and ninety metres.

'Just the two of you, Beck?'

Beck laughed again. 'We don't need the whole crew to take you down.'

'So the other three are tracking Rane then I guess.'

'Enough of your shit,' yelled Beck. 'Get out here and I'll make it quick.'

Frost's voice was music to Kurcher's ears. 'You might want to duck.'

The *Kaladine* descended on the courtyard and opened fire with both gats mounted beneath the cockpit. Beck and his fellow enlister dived for cover, but the target was the mech. It was blown sideways while trying to bring its

7

shrikes up to return fire, finding the gat spread too heavy. It staggered across the front of the destroyed building, too preoccupied with the *Kaladine* to notice Kurcher crouched just inside.

'That thing's not going down,' yelled Frost. 'I think I'm just pissing it off.'

'Save your ammo.'

Kurcher moved towards the mech, unsheathing his knife. As it lifted both shrikes to retaliate against the *Kaladine*, he slammed the blade into the thin gap between its head and shoulder frame then pulled sharply to the left. A spurt of oily liquid told him he had found his target as the mech juddered once before its arms slowly lowered.

'How'd you know where to hit it?' asked Frost.

'Sigma Royal pursuit mechs have that one design flaw.' Kurcher pulled his knife free. 'Their manufacturers thought that, since nobody could get near them to strike from behind, they wouldn't bother amending it.'

'You might want to look to your right.'

Kurcher raised his revolver as Beck and the other enlister rose shakily from their meagre cover, glancing up at the hovering *Kaladine*. Both gats were aimed at them.

Beck stammered as he threw down his razepistol. 'Your...your ship wasn't kitted...with...'

'New spec,' shrugged Kurcher, sheathing his knife as he approached them. He lowered his voice to speak with Frost. 'Rane's reading is sketchy. I think these idiots have delayed us too long.'

'If he's reached his ship, he'll be off-planet shortly.'

'I can take care of Beck. Go after Rane. If you can stop him, do so. If not, send a tracking probe and hope it gets a reading before he leaves the system.'

Frost hesitated. 'What are you going to do?'

Kurcher looked up at the *Kaladine* and smiled. 'Just go.'

He watched his ship turn and soar off across the outskirts of Monarch. The sky was a blend of gold and dark blue now as the sun dipped below the horizon. Shadows were creeping across the colony and a cool breeze accompanied them, but the Parinax still circulating in his body kept him high enough to appreciate the beauty of such a troubled world. When it wore off, no doubt he wouldn't give Kismet a second thought.

'So, you've stopped me from finally ridding this galaxy of Edlan Rane,' he said to the Sigma Royal enlisters. 'Not a clever thing to do.'

'He'll surface again,' sniffed Beck. 'Shit like him always does.'

Kurcher levelled his revolver with Beck's face. 'At this range, that helmet isn't going to help much.'

Beck unclipped his helmet and removed it, throwing it at Kurcher's feet. 'We both know you can't shoot me. Taurus Galahad wouldn't risk pissing Sigma Royal off further.'

'Tell me where your ship is.'

Beck frowned. 'Why should I?'

Kurcher swung his revolver right and shot Beck's silent colleague through the cheek, snapping the enlister's head back before he fell.

'What the fuck?' Beck's eyes were wide with disbelief as he looked down at the dead man. 'You can't do this.'

Kurcher stooped and picked up Beck's weapon while keeping the revolver trained on him.

'Do you know what damage a razepistol does to someone's face at this distance?'

'You're a psycho, Davian, a fucking psycho.'

'It's a simple question.' Kurcher pointed the razepistol at Beck too. 'Where is your ship?'

Beck looked around, hoping to see some way out of the situation. 'I'll take you there.'

'That's not an option. Tell me where it is and I'll let you scurry off into the Monarch City shithole.'

The larger man weighed Kurcher up for a moment. With a nervous glance down the barrels of both guns, Beck's shoulders sagged. 'Half a mile away to the north, near one of the monuments.'

Kurcher's comms app crackled. 'Davian? Rane's off-planet and heading for the jump point. The only way I can get the probe away is to break orbit.'

'Do it. Get the probe after him then come get me.'

'Understood.'

Beck shrugged. 'We could work together to catch Rane, y'know? If he goes to another Sigma Royal system, I could...'

The razepistol fired. Beck flew backwards, landing near the broken wall he'd first arrived through. Kurcher took the holster from the other enlister's belt and attached the razepistol to his own waist. As he stepped over Beck's body, he glanced down at the smoking wound and the smattering of blood on the ground. For a second, he pondered where Beck's head had rolled to or whether it had been vapourised. Then he headed north to look for the monument.

Beck had been telling the truth. Kurcher spotted the monument first: a stone crown held to the sky by a depiction of a colonist. It was no wonder Sigma Royal's colonies rose up against the corporation. Their higher

9

echelons would rather spend money placing several of these monuments in each colony instead of buying more supplies for those in need.

The enlister ship sat alongside the monument, looking like some gigantic black and red insect. While the *Kaladine* was unique in design, having been constructed in a merc shipyard to Kurcher's specifications, all of the Sigma Royal ships looked the same. A soft blue light emanated from the cockpit windows and the ramp beneath it was down, indicating that at least one of Beck's three remaining team members was outside the ship.

Night finally fell as Kurcher moved from building to building, circling the ship and gauging the area of open ground between himself and the ramp. When he looked up into the sky and saw only darkness, he realised his boost had worn off. His legs were starting to ache again and unwelcome doubt crept into his mind. He shouldn't have killed Beck and his partner.

The Sigma enlister had made their life as difficult as he could whenever they went after the same quarry, but Beck was a veteran and his death would raise questions. He may have been vain and abrasive, but the man had never backed down from a job, despite numerous run-ins with enlisters from all the other corps.

Reaching into his jacket pocket, he pulled out the two devices Frost had recommended he take just in case. The explosives were a new Taurus Galahad design, keeping the tubing small and light while apparently maintaining the same destructive power as the last model. It was a good time to try them out.

Kurcher began walking towards the ship, pocketing the explosives again and resting his hands on the two guns at his side. He could have taken the uniform after killing the enlister, to give himself a better chance of walking straight onto the ship, but he preferred not to hide behind some disguise.

'Cut it out,' came a woman's shrill voice from just inside the ship. 'Beck will be back soon.'

Kurcher glanced up at the name written along the outer plating and smiled. *Beck's Fire* was certainly apt.

'Come on, Den.' This time, a man was heard just at the top of the ramp. 'We've got time to kill and the ship to ourselves.'

'Piss off.' The woman's reply was followed by the sound of boots on a metal grating that faded into the interior.

Kurcher pulled his revolver from its holster as he reached the bottom of the ramp and, with a final look behind him, headed up into the *Beck's Fire*. As he neared the top, the dim light from within illuminated the face of an enlister who was leaning against one wall, a cigarette clenched between his

10

teeth. As the man looked up, Kurcher put a bullet in his brain and he crumpled to the floor. No point beating around the bush now.

He knew the layout of the ship well, having studied the designs when Taurus Galahad intel heard of the new-look vessels four years previously. It did not take long for him to locate the fusion cell that powered the ship's main weapon and he quickly attached one of the explosives, priming it for ten minutes.

'Hold it right there, fucker.'

Kurcher recognised the voice from before and turned slowly. 'Den, is it?'

She had her razepistol aimed at him, but her blue eyes were fearful. 'Take that device off the cell and disarm it.'

'Can't do that. Once it's primed, I can't stop it.'

'Who are you?'

Kurcher saw her weapon arm twitch. 'Listen, Beck is dead, as are two more of your team. If you want to join them then by all means stay here. I think you'd rather live though. Am I right?'

Den blinked. 'Dead? I don't...'

'Am I right?' Kurcher's firm tone jolted her. She was clearly green.

She nodded and lowered her weapon slightly. Kurcher lifted his and shot her between the blue eyes.

'Pity,' he mumbled as he stepped over her. She was one of the more attractive women he had encountered recently.

He swiftly left the ship and made his way back into the streets, turning to watch as the *Beck's Fire* exploded violently in a blaze of green and orange light. The monument was also blown apart and Kurcher drew some satisfaction in that.

'I'm back, Davian.' Frost's voice was almost robotic. 'Where are you?'

'See that ball of flame rising into the sky?'

'Yeah.'

'Head for that.'

The *Kaladine* landed briefly, allowing Kurcher to return to the security of his beloved ship. Only once they had left Kismet's orbit did Frost come to find him.

'Just what the hell were you thinking?' she asked angrily as he stored away his newly acquired razepistol. 'Destroying a Sigma Royal enlister vessel in a Sigma Royal colony on a Sigma Royal world? Do you want the bounty on your head to increase further?'

'On *our* head,' corrected Kurcher.

'Oh no, that was all *your* work.' Her hands were on her hips and her face

11

was reddening by the second. 'I assume you also killed Beck?'

'Do you know what happens to a human head if you fire a razepistol at it point-blank?'

Frost threw her hands up. 'Are you trying to start your own little war?'

'The corps have been at war for twenty-three years, Justyne. Taurus Galahad will welcome the elimination of another enlister team. Besides, Beck was just a merc pretending to be a Sigma Royal officer.'

'And what are you?'

Kurcher scowled. 'I've never hidden who I am behind uniforms. If you want to go back to being a planethopper pilot, then be my guest.'

Frost sighed and shook her head. 'Of course I don't. I just worry that all this is going to come back and bite us one day.'

'It will eventually. Whether it be one of the corps, a merc, a pirate or just a pissed-off colonist, someday we'll have to deal with retaliation. Until then, we do our job and get paid.'

'So what's next?'

Kurcher rubbed his sore eyes and could feel his muscles beginning to tighten up. He needed another hit soon. 'You got the probe away after Rane?'

'Yes. That little ship of his is quick. He must have something different that reacts with the helium-3. If we ever get a chance to find out what that is, I'm having it installed on the *Kaladine*.'

'I'd rather just blow him and his ship up when I get the opportunity. Check the tracking signal and head for the jump point. I'm not letting him go that easily.'

'Course already set.' Frost noticed the dark rings beneath his eyes. 'You should get some sleep before we jump. It'll take a couple of days to get there.'

'I know that,' he snapped. When he saw her expression darken again, he held one hand up in apology. 'Look, I'll go get some rest, but just keep an eye out for Sigma Royal fleet ships lurking nearby. The last thing we want is one of them intercepting us before we get to the jump point.'

'I've outrun assault ships before,' she reminded him. 'I'll see you in a few hours.'

Kurcher watched her leave the storage room and then put a hand to his aching head. He felt like shit and knew exactly why. He finished storing his gear, all but the revolver which he always carried with him, and headed to his quarters.

The small room was dark and quiet, which was perfect for him. He laid back on his bed and reached for the container beneath his pillow. One

Parinax Calmer ought to do the trick.

It was nearly a whole day before Frost saw Kurcher again. The enlister entered the cockpit behind her and lowered himself into the only other seat.

'Time to the jump point?' Kurcher peered out of the wide screen before them at the star-speckled darkness.

Frost focused on her pilot app display. 'Twenty hours. Good sleep then?'

'Not bad. I dreamt of throttling Rane to death.'

'I still can't help wondering why he does it.'

'Don't bother. He is a serial killer who enjoys torturing his victims before cutting their throats. I'm cold, but Rane is made of ice.'

'He never rapes the women though.'

Kurcher shot her a quizzical look. 'So? He doesn't rape the men either.'

'I don't know, Davian. The longer we spend hunting him down, the more questions come up. Why does he kill those specific people? Why travel light years to kill just one person? If he needed to satisfy some urge, surely he would just choose people who are close together.'

'Rane is a clever man.' Kurcher hated to admit it. 'He moves around from system to system so that we struggle to keep track of him and it works. He has had run-ins with enlisters from Libra Centauri and Sapphire Nova more recently but he still escaped. He's either very smart or fucking lucky.'

Frost smiled. 'He was lucky on Kismet. Had it not been for Beck, we might have caught up with him finally.'

They sat in silence for several minutes until Frost lit a cigarette. She always talked when she smoked.

'Rane came from Rikur, right?'

'Yeah. Born in Harper.'

'I hear that's a shithole.'

'It has been ever since the rig accident back in 2590. Sapphire Nova never managed to restore it to what it once was.'

'So that accident was what set Rane on a bad road, after his parents died?'

'Probably.' Kurcher shrugged. 'Who gives a shit though? Scum like him need to be eliminated.'

Frost glanced across at him and blew a cloud of smoke in his direction. 'Some people would say the same about you.'

'Not to my face they wouldn't.'

Frost studied her pilot app display for a moment, checking over the ship system updates that flashed within her vision. 'Gats need reloading. Other than that, the *Kaladine* is in good shape. No fleet ships nearby.'

'I'll sort the gats before we jump,' yawned Kurcher.

13

Incoming communication from Taurus Galahad assault ship Requiem.

'That can't be good,' grimaced Frost.

Kurcher stretched and leaned forward. 'Patch it through to the display here.'

Frost activated the ship comms display from her app and made a sweeping gesture with her left hand. A man's face appeared on the display in front of Kurcher.

'Davian Kurcher here.'

'Enlister Kurcher.' The Taurus Galahad officer gave him a curt nod. 'What is your current position?'

'I didn't catch your name.'

The officer flinched. 'Lieutenant Connolly. I repeat, what is your position?'

'We are heading for the jump point in the Genesys system.'

'Have you completed your mission?'

Kurcher found himself disliking this man already. 'Not yet. Edlan Rane evaded us on Kismet thanks to an encounter with Sigma Royal enlisters. We are tracking him though and will pursue until he is eliminated.'

'You have new orders,' stated Connolly bluntly. 'You are to jump to the Sol system and rendezvous with the *Requiem*, where you are to be given a new brief by Commander Santa Cruz.'

Kurcher shook his head. 'Surely this can wait. Edlan Rane has to be eliminated and I am...'

'Your new orders stand, enlister. Instruct your pilot to make the jump to the Sol system. The *Requiem* will await you near Neptune.'

'And what of Rane?'

Connolly turned his head slightly as if listening to someone just out of view next to him. 'Another enlister will continue the pursuit of Edlan Rane.'

'Why can't Santa Cruz just talk to me now?' Kurcher was aware his voice was louder than before.

'*Commander* Santa Cruz is indisposed at this time and will need to see you in person. You have your orders.'

Connolly's face vanished and Kurcher punched the display. 'Fucking unbelievable. I've been chasing him for this long and now they decide to reassign me? Jorelian fucking Santa Cruz better have a good reason for doing this.'

'Why him?'

'What?'

Frost didn't want to fuel Kurcher's anger more, but the question was sound.

14

'Why Santa Cruz? I thought he was special ops.'

Kurcher looked confused for a moment. He had not considered that. 'He is. I guess whatever it is must be important, but we were so close to Rane again.'

'Something tells me that Rane will still be out there when this new assignment is complete. So, what are your orders?'

Kurcher knew Frost would follow him even if he said to hell with Santa Cruz but, tempted as he was, there was only ever one option.

'Make the damned jump to Sol.'

Sprint-class vessel Basilisk
Genesys system en route to jump point

Rane was curious and that could only lead him into trouble.

Despite a great deal of static, no doubt left over from the Taurus Galahad firewall after his comms hacker had bypassed it, he could still make out the order that Kurcher had been given. Why now though? What was so important?

He stared out towards the metallic gleam of the jump point, fingers steepled on his lap. He was not sure he liked the idea of somebody new picking up the chase. It was an insult really as he knew the corporation would not have anyone quite as ruthless to send after him. Davian Kurcher was an opponent he enjoyed sparring with mentally.

He was rapidly approaching the jump point and knew he would have to slow the *Basilisk* down in order to enter the co-ordinates and pass through the wormhole.

'How close is the tracking probe?' he asked the computer.

Probe is 0.7 AU from the Basilisk.

He smiled. Those probes were almost as quick as he was. 'Download the probe's signal to a buoy.'

As the computer silently followed his order, Rane glanced down at the controls before him in the tight one-man cockpit. He imagined Kurcher's pilot seated at her controls, not having to utter a word of command as she accessed all of the *Kaladine*'s systems via her app. A simple brush of the holographic keys could bring up her star maps, telemetry, cargo manifest and so on. The human race had become lazy and the continuing app developments just made things worse. He remembered being offered a boost app back on Sullivan's Rest once by some merc junkie. The thought of implanting anything like that into his body sickened him. He would control his ship the old-fashioned way and he would get a natural high in his own unique way.

Probe signal downloaded.

'Release the buoy.'

There was a short, sharp hiss followed by a click.

Buoy released.

Rane made a slight alteration to his course, to ensure he would arrive at the jump point's nucleus. It was much larger in his display now and he always marvelled at the workmanship of each gate. One thing he had to give to the corps was that they were always efficient in building a new structure around a system's wormhole. Each of the five corps gave their own work distinct markings, of course. This one had the sigma letter emblazoned on it in three places.

He was glad that the concept of staffing the jump points with personnel had also been ruled out by the corps. There was ample room for a crew of five or six inside each structure, but it was simpler to automate the entire process and record jump data instead. Due to the corp wars though, most of the data wasn't even monitored, allowing fleet vessels to move from system to system relatively undetected.

Jump co-ordinates are requested.

Rane saw one of his screens flicker into life and he carefully input the numbers.

Please confirm that destination is the Almaz system.

'Confirmed.'

The screen went blank again and Rane watched as the structure lit up. The inner discs began rotating, slowly building speed to ensure the wormhole opened the moment the *Basilisk* arrived at the gate.

Would you like to hear data on the Almaz system?

'Yes.' He had heard it a thousand times before, but he always liked hearing the computer's soothing voice reading out the facts about his home.

The Almaz system is owned by Sapphire Nova.

The corp emblem appeared on one of his screens; the yellow sun encased in a blue gemstone. It was quickly replaced by a map of the Milky Way with a highlighted star.

Located on the edge of the Perseus Arm twenty thousand light years from Earth, the Almaz system consists of four planets.

An image of the system replaced the Milky Way.

Rikur, Ishar, Conis and Janus. Rikur was colonised in 2323. Ishar was colonised in 2324. Temperatures on Conis are too hot to sustain life due to its proximity to the Almaz sun. Janus is a gas giant.

Rane looked away from the screen as Rikur was shown in all its dark glory.

Rikur is a mining world with a population of six hundred and eighty thousand. Colonies were built surrounding the Planetbore Rigs that mine for silicon dioxide and...

'Stop. I've heard enough.'

As the *Basilisk* approached the jump point, Rane felt a momentary stab of fear in his gut. Of all the systems he needed to go to, he never expected to end up back in Almaz again so soon. If it hadn't been for the information he gleaned on Kismet, he would have never returned to Rikur. The old fool in Monarch City better have been telling him the truth. If he closed his eyes, he could still hear the man's whimpering as he realised his life was over. Then again, whenever he did close his eyes, he could hear *all* of his victims.

Entering jump point in ten minutes.

Rane shook his head clear of all thoughts about his home system and instead returned to contemplating Kurcher's reassignment. Something was going on amongst the hierarchy of the corporations and he wanted to know what. He had been following several levels of communications over the last couple of years and had been trying to piece together the facts. He knew that a number of Taurus Galahad personnel had vanished during this time: scientists, soldiers, explorers and agents. Was Kurcher to be next?

He also knew that Taurus were oddly infatuated with the Coldrig deepspace sector. The other corps had been too, but Sapphire Nova had shifted their attentions to the Krondahar sector while Libra Centauri had made every effort to get closer to Farrin.

The most recent communication he had picked up, and the latest piece of the puzzle, was a garbled message sent to someone in the Sol system on a protected signal that reeked of Taurus Galahad. He still recalled the only line he could decipher: *Apprehended in Geraint system. Rest of crew eliminated. Cargo jettisoned.*

Rane tapped one finger against his temple as his mind whirled. Were these strange corps activities linked to the war they had declared on each other or was it something else?

Tracking probe destroyed.

He had almost forgotten about that. Good, the buoy had done its job.

'Let's see you follow me now,' he said to the vast expanse outside his ship.

As the *Basilisk* reached the jump point, the wormhole opened like a yawning maw in space, drawing the ship in. A smile played across Rane's lips as he disappeared through.

Taurus Galahad Assault Ship Requiem
Sol system

Staring at the display screen was giving him a real headache, so he turned to gaze out at Neptune for a moment. The blue eye looked back at him from the darkness, Triton positioned as its pupil. It was somewhat unnerving.

Santa Cruz glanced back at the screen and frowned at the highlighted points that had been troubling him for too long now. There was no apparent pattern; nothing leading him to the answer he so desperately sought.

'Show me the most recent find,' he ordered with a sigh.

One point remained highlighted and he shook his head. Coldrig was vast. How could he hope to find his needle amongst a haystack of this magnitude?

'Let me see the report on the last find.'

Coldrig vanished and was replaced by a screen filled with data. He ran his eyes over it, studying the translations carefully. Perhaps his scientists had made a mistake and missed something. He hoped they had so he could hold someone accountable. The frustrating part was that it had been within his reach and now could be anywhere in the galaxy. The thought that the data could be in a system belonging to one of the other corps made his stomach turn.

'Show me the technical diagram from the most recent find.'

The image that had been haunting him appeared and he leant closer to the screen. He remembered the first time he had seen it, after the raw data had been deciphered. The sheer beauty of it had taken his breath away and he knew Taurus Galahad would lead the human race into a new era once they found it.

A message appeared via his comms app.

'Close files,' he told the computer. 'Lock using Santa Cruz restriction.'

He moved from behind his desk and paced across his quarters to the mirror. He straightened his uniform and made sure the command insignia could be seen clearly on his shoulder. He then stared quietly at the face looking back at him, dark eyes glinting in the dim light.

Finally, he focused on the message that refused to leave his vision. 'Yes, Connolly?'

'He's here, commander,' came the quick reply. 'Davian Kurcher.'

'On my way.'

'What about his pilot, sir?' asked Connolly.

'What about her?'

Connolly hesitated. 'She is here too and I didn't know...'

'Tell her to remain on the *Kaladine*,' interrupted Santa Cruz. 'They'll be under way again soon enough.'

'Yes, sir.'

Santa Cruz found Kurcher studying a small HDU in one of the meeting rooms. Connolly stood quietly watching the enlister.

'You're excused, lieutenant.'

'Sir?'

Santa Cruz glowered at him. 'Leave us.'

Kurcher looked up from the HDU and smiled as Connolly left the room with an expression of disappointment etched on his face. When he turned to regard the commander, he found the man's stormy eyes already weighing him up.

'I've wanted to meet you for some time,' began Santa Cruz, moving to stand directly opposite the enlister. 'You have managed to earn yourself quite the reputation within Taurus Galahad.'

'I have a reputation with the other corps too,' Kurcher remarked. 'Most of them want me dead.'

'All of them do,' corrected the commander, pulling his own HDU from beneath his jacket and glancing down at the screen. 'I can see from recent reports that you have not enlisted many into the ranks. In fact, you seem to prefer elimination.'

'Most of them need to die.'

Santa Cruz regarded him coldly. 'Indeed. Although Edlan Rane continues to evade you. You have been chasing him for some time now.'

Kurcher shook his head. 'I had him on Kismet, but those damned Sigma Royals got in my way.'

'I am assuming they regretted that.'

Kurcher knew from his tone that Santa Cruz was already aware of the outcome of his time on Kismet. 'Is that why you are reassigning me? Because I killed some Sigma enlisters?'

'You killed four out of a team of five. The only one left survived because he decided to leave the ship for a while to walk the streets. A lucky man.'

'Would you rather I let them kill me?' growled Kurcher.

'No. You are a valuable asset to us. More so now.' Seeing the confusion on the enlister's face, Santa Cruz continued: 'Your reassignment has nothing to do with your exploits on Kismet or with Edlan Rane. Another ship will hunt down the latter.'

20

'Good luck with that. He blew up the probe we sent after him.'

A thin smile played across the commander's face. 'You do not appreciate the resources we have at our disposal. Edlan Rane will be found and executed, just not by you.'

Kurcher's HDU screen lit up as fresh information began downloading to it. 'I'm all ears then.'

'Did you know Enlister Ged Cooke?'

The unexpected question made him hesitate. 'Sure. I met him once or twice in passing. He qualified as an enlister just after I began my training.'

Santa Cruz swiped a finger across his HDU, transferring an image to Kurcher's screen of the man in question, which was joined swiftly by three other faces and the schematics of a ship.

'Cooke had a crew of three who worked with him on their vessel, *Seeker*. They were a specialist team who chose to capture a number of targets before returning them either to be enlisted or to be executed. Their ship was equipped with eight cells, all of which Cooke would ensure were filled before they returned.'

'So something bad happened to them,' stated Kurcher. 'You're referring to them in the past tense.'

'Enlister Cooke and his crew had captured seven criminals. These were unusual targets to say the least but, needless to say, we were keen to have them out of the way. During his mission, Cooke unearthed a data file that Taurus Galahad have been seeking for a long time and he was ordered back immediately. Unfortunately, he realised the value of such important data and, in his infinite wisdom, told us he wanted a substantial increase in his pay. He then made the error of threatening to sell it to the highest bidder from one of the other corps.'

Kurcher leant forward. 'What happened to him?'

'Enlister Cooke realised his mistake and tried to go into hiding. He was tracked down in the Vega system and, when he tried to flee, he and his crew were killed.'

'I'm missing something here,' Kurcher said, frowning. 'You're telling me that one of us got too greedy and was eliminated. I don't see why you need me.'

'Knowing that he was going to be hunted down, Cooke decided to download the data file into one of the seven criminals he was holding. He then released all of them on Sullivan's Rest before fleeing to his demise.'

Kurcher stared across the table at Santa Cruz, trying to spot any emotion leaking through the commander's stoic visage. 'You haven't recaptured the

21

crims?'

'That's where you come in.' Santa Cruz swiped another series of images across to Kurcher's HDU. 'Six men and one woman. One of them has the data file we want, but the problem is Cooke implanted it without them knowing. The only way we can secure the data is to recapture all of them.'

Kurcher's eyes scanned across the faces on the screen. He knew one of them already and another was possibly the ugliest brute he had ever seen so would certainly stand out in a crowd. 'I can't capture all seven. The *Kaladine* only has three cells and I'm not about to let them bunk with me. Although this Tara Oakley isn't unpleasant on the eye.'

'Sleep with her and you'll never wake up.' Santa Cruz placed his HDU on the table. 'A new ploy is needed to deal with this group of criminals. I want you to enlist them; promise them work plus pay if they allow Taurus Galahad to utilise their individual talents. In exchange, they will no longer be hunted so relentlessly, allowing them to make a life for themselves once again.'

Kurcher went silent for several seconds. 'You really expect them to go for that? What if they would prefer a quick death instead?'

'We can't afford for any of them to be executed.' An urgency crept into his voice. 'If the one carrying the data dies, we lose all of the information.'

'I don't suppose you're going to tell me what the data package is exactly and why it is so important? It must be big to tempt Cooke into threatening to betray his own employers.'

'I chose you for this task because you don't ask questions. Perhaps I should find somebody else.'

Kurcher held a hand up. 'No. All I need to know is how much we'll get paid for this.'

Santa Cruz gave a half-smile. 'Eight thousand to you, four to your pilot.'

'Payment on completion?'

'If you need supplies beforehand, we can make arrangements to pay some now and the rest later.'

Kurcher rubbed at his unkempt stubble. 'I would need a few things. Nothing drastic.'

He looked back down at the seven faces on his HDU. 'I'll do my best to enlist them, but will have to incapacitate any who refuse.'

'How?'

'If the cells aren't enough to sedate them, I guess cryo would be the best option.'

'If the body is frozen, the data may become corrupted.' Santa Cruz glared at Kurcher, willing him to come up with a better solution.

22

'The only other thing to do is chain them up so they can't move. That's not easy to do when it's just me and Frost.'

'Then hire someone else for your crew.'

'No.' Kurcher was too quick to respond. 'I don't work with anyone else but Frost.'

Santa Cruz picked his HDU up and placed it back underneath his jacket. 'These details I leave to you. I want these seven found and brought back here as quickly as possible so we can determine who holds the data file.'

Kurcher knew the corporation wouldn't care about the crims as soon as the data had been recovered. It was likely that they would execute all of them afterwards. It should have left a bad taste in his mouth offering false promises in order to get what they wanted, but crims deserved everything they got.

'I suggest you spend some time going over their files,' Santa Cruz said, straightening his jacket. 'Some of them may prove a challenge.'

'There aren't too many places to hide on Sullivan's Rest.'

'They are resourceful. It's likely they will no longer be there.'

Kurcher shrugged. 'No matter. Crims like this will leave a clear trail for me to follow.'

'Then I won't keep you any longer.' Santa Cruz headed for the door. 'Bring all seven here to the *Requiem*. I will keep you informed if we move position. Any reports you need to make will be made directly for my attention, understood?'

'Understood. We'll be under way as soon as we've refuelled.'

Santa Cruz left the meeting room, issuing an order to a waiting Connolly to ensure Kurcher and his pilot received any supplies required. He then made his way to the interrogation cells two levels below the command deck and entered the only occupied room.

'He's still alive then,' he said with an almost disappointed tone.

The medic behind the monitoring station looked up at him with tired eyes. 'Yes, sir. He has not said anything since you were here earlier though.'

Santa Cruz circled the seated man in the centre of the room, eyeing the holographic images displaying his life signs. An erratic heartbeat echoed softly in the quiet room.

'Thought of anything else you'd like to tell me?' he asked the prisoner. 'Anything that could help us find them quicker?'

The man slowly raised his head and regarded Santa Cruz with hate-filled eyes. 'Go fuck yourself.'

Santa Cruz tutted. 'You enlisters have no regard for rank. I just met with

23

the man who will be bringing me your criminals and not once did he call me sir.' The commander's eyes darkened. 'Is there any reason I should keep you alive now, Cooke?'

'Stop toying with me and do it.'

'I don't take orders on my own ship.' Santa Cruz glanced up at the medic. 'Give me access to the app controls.'

The interface images appeared around Cooke and Santa Cruz immediately touched one. The enlister cried out as searing pain burned through his abdomen and his body tensed against the restraints. Another touch of the control ended the pain.

'Now, what else can you tell me about your prisoners?' Santa Cruz ignored Cooke's obvious discomfort. 'We have the reports that were logged by you and your team, but there are key pieces of information missing.'

'You murdered my team.' Cooke spat onto the floor. 'They didn't need to die. Your assassin didn't even ask questions.'

'He's not paid to ask questions. He did his job, unlike you.' Santa Cruz began pacing in front of the seat. 'You safeguarded the data file before implanting it in one of the criminals. What program did you use?'

'One that means your scans will never pick it up.'

'You'd be surprised how far we have come with our app technology. Mercenaries, pirates and smugglers have developed so many codes to protect their operations that we have had teams of researchers working around the clock to counter them. I doubt your program will keep the data hidden long.'

'Long enough.'

Santa Cruz came to a halt and loomed over the restrained man. 'You think you're clever, but all you have done is delay the inevitable. True, I could have done without the other corps being aware the data had been found, but Taurus Galahad will prevail.'

'You trying to pin the corp wars on me too?'

'Did you ever stop to wonder why the fighting started in the first place?' countered Santa Cruz.

Cooke's forehead creased. 'Domination. Nothing more than petty turf wars.'

'Data.' The word echoed around the room as Santa Cruz stepped back to regard the enlister. 'It is a volatile commodity.'

'Let's just get on with this.'

'I don't think you've told me everything,' stated Santa Cruz. 'Perhaps you need more of an incentive. Your wife and daughter live on Mars, right? Pioneer City, I believe.'

24

Fear edged into Cooke's eyes. 'Leave them be, you son-of-a-bitch.'

'You should've thought about them before making your threats. You can take a lot of pain, I'll give you that, but I doubt your little girl would last as long.'

'What more do you want from me?' Cooke's voice was only just audible.

Santa Cruz lurched forward angrily. 'I want the one piece of information that you refuse to tell me. Which of the seven has the data?'

'I don't recall.'

'Would you remember when your wife and daughter are begging for their lives in front of you? We are in the Sol system. It won't take long to get to them.'

Cooke gave a snort of derision. 'For all I know, we're right across the other side of the galaxy. Look, we both know that I'm dead no matter whether I tell you or not.'

'I have interrogated hundreds of people,' Santa Cruz told him. 'Most were criminals, but some were innocents who just got caught up in events. To be honest, I didn't give a shit about any of them. My job is to extract information for Taurus Galahad and to find data such as the file you managed to discover. If you tell me where it is, I will have no need to go after your family but, if you choose to keep quiet, I will make sure you watch them suffer a slow, painful death.'

'I don't think you're listening to me,' said Cooke, meeting the commander's gaze. 'I'm not giving you or the fucking corporation anything. I know what the policies are and, while *I'm* expendable, citizens loyal to Taurus aren't. As an enlister, I read the small print surrounding civilian casualties during missions. You're a commanding officer in the Taurus military so you have to adhere to the regs too. *Sir.*'

Santa Cruz now wore an expressionless mask. 'Usually, yes, but the parameters changed when you found that data. *That* is my priority now.'

The commander swiped at the control interface over Cooke's head, sending a burst of pain into the enlister's skull. He stepped back with arms crossed and watched as Cooke writhed in his seat.

'Sir, I wouldn't recommend longer than...'

'Quiet,' snapped Santa Cruz, glowering at the medic.

Blood ran from Cooke's nose as he convulsed violently and Santa Cruz wondered if this was how it must've looked when criminals were given the electric chair back on Earth. He had studied various interrogation and execution procedures from human history in detail, finding them both fascinating and insightful.

25

Cooke's heart monitor flashed as it flat-lined, filling the room with a high-pitched drone.

Santa Cruz swore beneath his breath before gesturing to the medic. 'Revive him.'

'He may not respond this time, sir.'

'Do it.'

The medic activated the defib app, ensuring the interface Santa Cruz was using was offline. Cooke's body shuddered once but remained still. It took two more hits to restart his heart.

'Don't die on me yet,' ordered Santa Cruz, leaning on the side of the seat as he spoke into Cooke's ear.

The enlister struggled to raise his head. With one eye open, he tried desperately to refocus. The blood from his nose dribbled down over his lips and off his chin.

'Commander, I'm not sure he will be coherent enough to talk,' the medic stated nervously. 'In fact, he may well never be coherent enough after that.'

Santa Cruz knew he had made a mistake and let his anger get the best of him, but he had to see it through. 'He brought this on himself. At least it will show all the other enlisters what happens if they defy Taurus Galahad.'

The medic mumbled something but bowed his head. Santa Cruz moved around to where Cooke's one good eye could see him and gripped the enlister's head with both hands.

'Tell me where the data file is. Which criminal has it? What safeguards did you place on it?'

Cooke opened his mouth, emitting an incoherent grunt. Behind his station, the medic shook his head.

'Last chance, Cooke. Tell me something of use or I'll watch you die again and this time there will be no revival.'

Cooke's eye focused on Santa Cruz, but it was clear the damage had been done. The commander sighed in frustration and cursed the fact that it was now more akin to putting an animal out of its misery.

'Shall I end it, sir?' asked the medic, his finger hovering over the app interface on his station.

Santa Cruz reluctantly nodded, letting go of Cooke's head. A moment later, Cooke jolted once before his eye rolled back in his head and his body was still again. The spikes of the weak heartbeat descended swiftly on the monitor and Santa Cruz grimaced at the flat-line.

Now it was down to Kurcher.

'Connolly.' His comms app woke up.

26

'Yes, sir.' It sounded like his lieutenant was in the room with them.

'I need to speak with Saul Winter.'

'He returned to Earth at the request of the Taurus board.'

'Then send a message to the board telling them I need him back on the *Requiem* urgently.'

Connolly hesitated. 'Yes, sir.'

'Once you've sent that, take us to Mars. I have business to attend to in Pioneer City.'

Enlister-class vessel *Kaladine*
Sol system

'No matter how many times you explain it to me, there is no fucking way I'm having them wandering the *Kaladine*.'

Kurcher weighed Frost up. Her hands were on her hips – never a good sign – and she seemed much taller for some reason. 'Last time I checked, this ship was mine.'

'It's a registered vessel of Taurus Galahad, actually.'

'Don't get smart.' His head was starting to hurt. 'Do you have a problem with all seven of them or just the psychos?'

Frost scowled. 'Where do I start? Not only are we talking about catching the man who started the Echo pirate operation and persuading him to enlist into Taurus Galahad, we're also looking at having to share this confined space with a schizo, a biomech freak and an escaped killer who just so happens to have a penchant for rape.'

'So you're fine with the other three then.'

Frost spun sharply and paced across the rec room. 'What if we put the three who pose the biggest threat in the cells?'

Kurcher gave an amused snort. 'And which three would that be?'

Frost turned to study the data on the rec screen. 'Bennet Ercko for one.' She found the man's image unnerving. 'He likes women a little too much, plus he spent ten years in Rockland.'

'So?'

'Anyone working the Aridis mines will have physical strength and he managed to overpower the guards on that transport. I wouldn't want to end up alone in a room with him.'

'He had help. Ercko wasn't the only one to escape.'

'And how many of his accomplices survived?' Seeing Kurcher's expression, Frost continued: 'The report says Ercko likely sacrificed his fellow inmates in order to get away.'

Kurcher rubbed his temples. 'Speculation. I'm not defending this guy, but we don't have many solid facts about his escape and subsequent capture by Cooke. Ercko is dangerous though, I agree. Who else?'

Frost returned her gaze to the screen. 'Angard. He's unstable, which is an understatement.'

Kurcher looked up at the brute's image and shrugged. 'The bigger they are, the harder they fall. He's got a face only a mother could love and no doubt he won't be the most intelligent of this group.'

'Have you even bothered reading their files?' cried Frost, jabbing an accusing finger at the enlister. 'Angard is insane thanks to the tech they kept pushing into his brain, but he is not stupid. He killed twenty-two people on Temple and eighteen at the research facility on Shard before Cooke caught him. In between those two bouts of killing, he spent eight years alone on a quaran before managing to seize control of a survey vessel.'

Kurcher held his hands up in submission. 'You got me, Justyne. I hadn't got round to reading his file yet. Sounds like a real genius though, battering his way across a station and a lab before getting himself caught. If he was smart, he wouldn't have wrecked the survey ship after it landed on Shard.'

'Thought you hadn't read his file.'

'Look, I agree that Angard is a concern. Having someone like him roaming the *Kaladine* is just asking for trouble, but I'm guessing there is a way to sedate him.'

Frost shook her head. 'Cooke didn't have to. Angard relies on a cocktail of drugs to keep him going, all of which are automatically released when needed by his apps. When Cooke arrived, Angard was running dry and didn't put up a fight.'

'Yes, but he will have been refuelled, or whatever the right term is, so won't be as compliant when we find him, I reckon. We need an app specialist who can hack his biomechs.'

Frost realised what he was getting at. 'You think Maric is the one to do that? He was going to be my third choice for lock-up.'

'Not Maric. Choice.'

'Same person.'

'Same body, different person.' Kurcher shrugged. 'Apparently Maric Jaroslav's alter ego is an app genius. The perfect solution.'

'You have an odd definition of perfect. The man's a killer and another unstable one at that.'

'You'd be unstable if you went through what he did. Those revenants are sick bastards.'

Frost lowered herself onto a seat opposite the screen. 'Well, they've all got their issues and we'll have to find a way to subdue them somehow.'

'I never said it would be an easy task,' Kurcher said, closing his eyes as pain rifled through his skull again. 'We'll make sure that access to the cockpit is restricted to just the two of us, plus storage will be locked down. They will be given access to the rec room and I guess the cargo hold, which makes the

29

perfect sleeping quarters for them.'

'I doubt Tara Oakley will want to sleep in the same room as six men... seven if you count Maric twice.' Frost laughed and the room seemed to warm slightly.

'I doubt the men will want to share a room with her,' Kurcher stated. 'We can make other arrangements nearer the time.'

'What about the corridors? Is it best to restrict their movement as much as possible?'

'We'll see. Depends how much trouble they cause.'

Frost reached for a cigarette. 'At least we got some money upfront this time. Makes it easier if we need to bribe our way out of any situations again.'

Kurcher watched her light up. He always enjoyed the moments when she fell silent long enough to savour the smoke. For all her concerns and trepidation about the task at hand though, Frost would help him get the job done and he knew she wouldn't take any shit from the crims once they were on the *Kaladine*. There was nobody else he would want at his side.

'You feeling alright about going back to Sullivan's Rest?' he asked her, trying to ignore the familiar itch gnawing at the back of his brain.

Frost blew a cloud of smoke into the air. 'I didn't think we'd be going back there quite so soon. I'll be fine though, just as long as I don't bump into those fuckwits again.'

'You won't.'

'You don't know that.'

'I do.' He offered her his best winning smile. 'They're dead. Each man shot once in the head and once in the heart. Sounds like their killer was a real pro.'

Frost's cigarette smouldered in her grasp as she stared open-mouthed at him. 'You didn't need to do that. You could've got in trouble with Fortitude.'

'I'm already disliked by most of Fortitude. Three dead drunken mercs were never going to be missed. I can't have my pilot getting molested by men like that during a mission.'

'That's possibly the most romantic thing anyone has ever done for me,' chuckled Frost.

Kurcher tried to laugh, but his head was pounding. 'Once we jump to Vega, we need to decide on our approach to Sullivan's Rest. The crims were all dropped there by Cooke, but odds are against us finding them still nearby. If we're lucky, one or two might still be in hiding on the station, but locating them is going to prove tricky. I'll need to be at my most charming.'

'Do you want me to check out the latest wares when we get there?'

30

'Not alone, no.' The itch was getting worse. 'I think it's best if you stay on the ship while I ask around about the crims. I'll contact you once we have some leads. Just make sure you lock the *Kaladine* up tight.'

Frost looked as though she was about to argue, but then simply nodded and leaned back in her seat, gazing at the screen through her smoke. She could talk a good game, but her run-in on the station had shaken her up more than she let on. The less time she could spend on Sullivan's Rest the better.

'You should give those up,' Kurcher told her.

'You give up the Parinax first and I'll consider it,' she snapped back, keeping her eyes locked on the data.

The mention of the drug made him flinch and he began heading for the door. 'So can I assume that you're on board with this task now?'

Frost shrugged. 'I don't have a choice really, do I? Good pay and I get to spend most of my time locked in the cockpit instead of having to speak with them. Sounds fine to me.'

He stopped at the doorway. 'The toughest thing will be enlisting them when my instincts are screaming at me to blow them all out the airlock.'

Frost looked over her shoulder and gave him a wry smile. 'Guess that's why the corps chose you then. If you can't enlist them, nobody can.'

Kurcher disappeared without another word and Frost listened to his footsteps fade. She imagined him reaching for the Parinax as soon as his door was closed and locked. The last time she had questioned him about it, he had threatened to find another pilot who could keep their thoughts to themselves. It was a prickly subject, but one that still troubled her, and the fact they were on their way to Sullivan's Rest amplified the concern. There were too many drug-runners and dealers on the station who could sniff out users, whether it be for Parinax or something much more potent.

She shook the thoughts from her head and stubbed the cigarette out before studying the rec screen once more. She avoided looking at the image of Bennet Ercko and instead read the profile data on Sieren Broekow. He seemed the least psychotic of the seven and was not unpleasant to look at, but looks could be deceiving. He was still a trained killer – a corps sniper who for some reason killed a bunch of Taurus officers.

She moved on to Jaffren Hewn and her stomach knotted. He would be trouble, she just knew. All pirates were and he was a veteran of the trade. It was likely that Hewn would already be back in the Echo Expanse. If so, there was no way she would risk taking the *Kaladine* in after him.

The only other crim she hadn't looked at much was Regan D'Larro. His image was the epitomy of innocence; a youthful face and charming smile.

31

Still, Frost could see something in his eyes that unsettled her. The youngest of the seven, D'Larro was seemingly fascinated with death and this had led him to abuse his position as a medic, resulting in the demise of many people. When Cooke had apprehended him, D'Larro was a member of a trauma team looking after those injured during the colony wars on Amity. It was unclear how many patients they lost thanks to his handiwork.

A message flashed up in the corner of Frost's vision letting her know that the *Kaladine* was not far from the jump point. As she headed for the cockpit, she made a mental note to store a weapon close to hand before their guests started arriving.

Earth
Sol system

The satisfying crack of bone ended the revenant's struggle and Winter was glad that this particular one had such a weak neck.

He held the body for a moment longer, making sure that all life had seeped out of the wretch, then quietly lowered it to the ground. He caught sight of the dead eyes staring out from behind the crude mask, so rolled the corpse onto its front.

As he began making his way back to his gear, Winter glanced around the ruins. London had seen better days, that was for sure. This part of the city seemed to have suffered the most during the Revenant attacks. Buildings were nothing but broken husks and the roads that had taken so long to build were now cracked and being slowly taken back by nature.

A chilling wind hit him as he darted into the remnants of a church and he pulled his overcoat tighter across the body armour beneath. Moving around the piles of debris, he made his way to the back of the structure and up the old staircase, keeping his footfalls as quiet as he could. It seemed odd to him that the leader of this particular Revenant force would use these local ruins as his base of operations and yet avoid the church, but they were unpredictable. Nobody really knew what was going on in the crazed minds of these lunatics.

He arrived back at his camp in one of the upper rooms and peered out of the window, looking down to where he had just killed the wretch. It was easier to take the man out than leave him scouting the area. Winter had taken too long setting up his traps for one lone revenant to trip them.

Settling back into his waiting position by the window, he checked the time. Night would fall soon and he knew that, while he would be able to move around easier in the darkness, he would not be the only one stalking through the ruins.

He passed the time by releasing the ammunition from his rifle and pistol, then reloading them. It was the fifth time he had done so, but it put his mind at rest. He stopped once to listen as the wind howled through the window and passed through the cracks in the walls. All was quiet out on the dead streets of London.

Just after night fell and the moon began rising over the city, a message alert flashed in Winter's vision. This was most unorthodox as he had given orders not to be contacted unless it was related to his current mission. He

33

could see it was text-only so opened the message and began reading.

Message from Commander Jorelian Santa Cruz. You are ordered to the Requiem for a new assignment as soon as current mission is complete. Requiem will be in orbit of Mars.

This pissed him off. He had just finished one mission for Santa Cruz and now he would have to go back and put up with the arrogant prick again. He wouldn't rush his current task for anyone though. Santa Cruz would have to wait.

It wasn't long before he heard the sound he had been waiting for as one of his proximity sensors activated at street level. It indicated there was a group of eight heading his way and amongst them would be his primary target.

Winter grabbed his rifle and positioned himself at the window once more, this time leaning the barrel of the weapon on the ledge as he aimed down to the street below. He activated his sight app, forming the scope as it linked with the rifle. Dull heat signatures appeared to the south, flagging the approaching Revenants. He waited silently, keeping his scope locked onto the junction ahead.

His first explosive activated behind the Revenants and the church shuddered. He watched as all eight ran towards an adjoining street, reeling from the blast. The second explosion knocked three onto their backs, but it had the desired effect and the other five changed direction again, this time running for the scoped junction. Noting that two of the fallen Revenants were gingerly getting to their feet while the other was still, he saw the marker appear in his vision around one of the five heading towards him. He took a deep breath and held it.

As the Revenants appeared at the junction, he fired one shot that took his target through the forehead. Winter pulled back and laid his rifle quietly on the floor. Outside, he could hear cries of shock and a woman's wail as she realised her master was dead. He turned his head so the heat signatures re-appeared and, satisfied they would be preoccupied with their insane mourning of the false prophet, he gathered his belongings and headed for the stairs.

Once he was far enough away from the church, he deactivated the app and his vision cleared fully, which was always refreshing. He swiftly made his way deeper into London's shattered remnants, making sure to be vigilant as he went from building to building. As he headed for his pick-up location, Winter began wondering what Santa Cruz wanted with him. Military officers only ever called when they didn't want to dirty their own hands and his previous mission had certainly left its mark. It was the first time he had been ordered to apprehend a Taurus Galahad enlister while ensuring the rest of the crew did not survive. It was also the first time an enlister team had gone rogue, to his knowledge.

A cold rain started to fall, quickly soaking Winter and darkening his mood. Hopefully this next assignment would take him to a warmer climate.

Sullivan's Rest
Vega system

The station seemed dirtier than last time he had visited.

Kurcher had made his way deep into the grimy interior of Sullivan's Rest, leaving the relative safety of the *Kaladine* far behind. As soon as he had stepped out onto the docking pylon, his senses were attacked. The smell of sweat and metal was heavy in the air, and the chill of the docks nipped at his skin. A buzzing Fortitude mech had hovered near his face, trying its best to blind him as it scanned for weapons and valuables. Unable to penetrate the protective suit he was wearing beneath his usual clothes, the mech blinked its one blue eye and flew off to pester someone else.

He had counted sixteen ships docked at their pylon, ten of them bearing the clenched fist of Fortitude. The other six were either pirates or smugglers. Most of the ships had seen better days. The *Kaladine* stood out amongst them. He knew that would attract interest. While not painted in the grey, white and black of Taurus Galahad or bearing the corp crest, those who claimed to run the station would recognise its unique design.

The number of people wandering the walkways increased the further in he went. He recognised members of Fortitude straight away. The mercs acted like they were part of some official corporation, even wearing crude uniforms with their emblem emblazoned boldly on puffed-out chests. They seemed to believe they were untouchable and, to a degree, that was the case. Corp vessels all tended to shy away whenever they encountered Fortitude ships, even Taurus Galahad. There was a clear reason for this though: the mercs used powerful but unstable fusion weapons. Their fusion beams punched holes through corp ships as if they were made of paper, but it was when a Fortitude ship was critically damaged that caused the most concern. The unstable cells had a habit of turning an exploding merc vessel into a deadly weapon, emitting intense bursts of fusion that could wipe out an entire fleet if within range.

Kurcher also saw members of Jericho's Bold roaming the station, their tattooed faces giving them away. He always avoided pirates where possible; the Bold were particularly known for their vicious streak.

The rest of the men and women he passed were a blend of merc, pirate and those who fell into neither category; people who had found themselves on Sullivan's Rest for one reason or another. Some had the look of addicts, no

36

doubt there to score a hit of whatever floated their respective boats. Some were clearly working on the station, trying to earn a living amongst dubious company. He even saw a family heading for one of the pylons, likely off to catch a transport to some colony. It didn't matter who you were – at some point in your life you passed through Sullivan's Rest.

As Kurcher approached the central hub of the station and the cacophony of noise that told him the infamous black market was in full swing, he saw a familiar face heading in his direction accompanied by two armed mercs.

'We have unfinished business,' grinned Coyle. 'Can't say I expected to see you back here so soon though.'

Kurcher glanced at the raised pistols. 'Those for me? I'm flattered.'

'Well, let me see.' Coyle scratched at his greying beard. 'You killed three Fortitude men last time you were here, so I'd say you're lucky we haven't already gunned you down.'

'Three Fortitude men who assaulted my pilot,' corrected Kurcher.

Coyle leant closer. 'One of those men just happened to be the nephew of Morton Hurst.'

'Why should that matter to me?'

'Hurst is a major honcho in Fortitude and you should...'

'I know who he is,' Kurcher interrupted. 'And I don't care. Has he put a bounty on my head?'

Coyle sniffed. 'No. He didn't really care for his nephew.'

'So would you mind lowering those pistols?'

'I should still take you in for the murder of three men on my watch.'

Kurcher sighed loudly. 'Firstly, there are murders on Sullivan's Rest every day. The place is so fucking big that anything could be happening in the filthy areas you're too scared to patrol. Secondly, you don't really give a shit what happens as long as you have a healthy money flow coming in and I'd wager that most of the traders here are lining your pockets.'

Coyle grimaced and gestured to his men. They reluctantly lowered their weapons. 'You're packing, right?'

Kurcher nodded. 'Everyone is.'

'So who are you after this time? Edlan Rane hasn't been back here.'

'Not Rane. Can we talk somewhere away from prying eyes and ears?'

Coyle nodded, spinning on his heel and heading away towards the main hub. His two mercs quickly followed. Kurcher strode after them.

They passed through the outer edge of the vast central hub and, had Kurcher not known where Coyle was already going, he would have got lost easily. Even on the edges of the market, the crowds were staggering and he made sure he kept a hand on his revolver just in case some thief tried his luck. Old neon signs mixed with the latest holographic ones in a colourful spectacle unrivalled across the galaxy. Sullivan's Rest truly was a world unto itself.

After dodging several relentless traders who had been unlucky enough to find themselves on the outskirts of the main throng, Kurcher dived through a doorway and jogged up the nearby stairwell, catching Coyle and his men up as they entered watchpoint D.

'Out,' Coyle barked at the five mercs loitering in the room. 'Go patrol the market perimeter.'

A couple of the men gave Kurcher sneering looks as they gathered their equipment and filed out. The two who had accompanied Coyle took up positions outside the door.

'You do have some sway here then,' Kurcher said, pulling his HDU from beneath his jacket. 'I'm impressed.'

Coyle stared out of the wide window that overlooked the market hub, his face illuminated by several of the nearby signs. 'If certain people knew I helped you, my life wouldn't be worth living.'

'I'm not asking you to be my informant. If you're so scared of Fortitude, why bother working for them?'

'Just for that reason.' Coyle turned to face him. 'They can sense fear amongst the corps and so they're getting bolder. Did you know that a squad of Fortitude soldiers landed on Kismet and fought against Sigma Royal, aiding the colonists?'

'I did notice, yeah. I was in Monarch City not so long ago, chasing Rane.'

'We usually steer clear of colony wars so it makes me wonder whether Sigma Royal is being targeted. Then again, even your corp are acting strangely at the moment.'

Kurcher shrugged. 'I don't get involved with their ops.'

'No, you just get rid of their trash.'

'Are you going to help me or not?' asked the enlister, holding out the HDU.

Coyle snatched it from his grasp and looked over the data. 'You're shitting me, right?'

Kurcher gave him a wry smile. 'My thoughts exactly. You know them?'

'Maybe.' Coyle grinned. 'Maybe not. Hard to say really.'

'Are we really going to do this?' Kurcher groaned. 'Okay, how much this time?'

'You couldn't afford it,' replied the Fortitude man. 'So what did this lot do?'

'They were in the custody of another enlister until he decided to release them on your station a few weeks back. Taurus want them recaptured.'

'Or dead,' added Coyle.

Kurcher chose to ignore that. 'If they were let loose on Sullivan's Rest, you or one of your colleagues must've seen them. Your damned scanning mechs buzz round those pylons all the time, so one must've logged them.'

Coyle rubbed at his beard again, then scratched his head. 'One of our mechs went offline a couple of weeks back. Lost the little fucker out on the pylons. Maybe your crims didn't want to get noticed.'

'They aren't exactly your usual visitors to the station. If you've seen them, I need to know.'

'Look, I don't want your money this time around.' Coyle handed the HDU back. 'Some of them look familiar, but I'd have to access the logs to find out more.'

'So do it.'

'Not until you do something for me.'

Kurcher laughed. 'I knew there was a price. What could a corp enlister possibly help a Fortitude merc with?'

Coyle crossed his arms. 'I need someone iced and it can't be traced back to me.'

Kurcher was genuinely surprised. 'Who?'

'A week ago, this guy arrives on Sullivan's Rest and straight off I knew he was trouble. Shifty looking little shit who came in on a transport from the Brittia system. He gets scanned but comes up clean. Next day, we find Kindred symbols painted on some of the walls in one of the residential arms.'

'The Kindred are here?'

'They weren't until this guy showed up. Since then, some equipment has gone missing and I'm getting worried that they are planning something.'

'You really think they'd blow up the station and risk the wrath of every merc and pirate organisation here?'

Coyle shrugged. 'Maybe. They're fucking crazy. Anyway, this guy's name came up on the scan as Jenson Cassius, which is no doubt an alias. I want you to find him and get rid. Then I'll help you. Deal?'

'Sure. I'm already hated by every other organisation, so why not add the Kindred to the list? You know where this Cassius is?'

'Last seen leaving Carly's, a questionable establishment in residential arm K near the cargo bays. Usually a hangout for the warehouse workers and a whole bunch of whores. He hasn't booked anywhere to sleep since arriving

39

according to our info.'

'Anything else I should know?' Kurcher was eager to get it over with. 'This guy got any friends he hangs around with?'

'Not that I've seen.'

Kurcher's eyes narrowed. 'You wouldn't be setting me up here, would you, Coyle? If what you're saying is true and Cassius is one of the Kindred, he is likely to be a very dangerous individual. One sent on a mission on his own is usually not expecting to return, if you get my drift.'

'I'm not setting you up,' growled Coyle. 'It wouldn't exactly do me much good getting a corp agent killed.'

'Show me the way down to arm K then.'

After downloading an image of Cassius to his HDU and memorising the route, Kurcher left the watchpoint and headed down into the bustling hub. He wasn't about to try making his way through the centre of the market so instead he circled it, keeping close to the walls. It took him nearly an hour to reach the door Coyle had mentioned and he slipped through, finding the elevator a moment later.

Luckily, nobody else got on so it gave him a chance to check his revolver was ready to rock when he found Cassius.

The long descent to the bowels of Sullivan's Rest gave him time to think and a couple of things Coyle had said played on his mind. The increasing boldness of the mercs was going to be a real pain for him. He didn't want to start running into Fortitude during a mission just because some gullible colonists had put all their combined money together to pay for protection. If Fortitude were growing in confidence then surely the same could be said for the other organisations. The galaxy was likely to implode if things got too out of hand.

The other concern was the Kindred. Those freaks were cold, emotionless and cruel. If Cassius was one of them, he would need to make sure he didn't underestimate the man. While most branded them as terrorists, Kurcher saw them more as mindless automatons programmed to wreak havoc by whoever brainwashed them. Hopefully one day, someone would stamp out the Kindred for good.

Carly's was everything he had expected, and more. He knew certain areas of the station never slept, but to find the place packed at this time spoke volumes. The music playing in the bar room was loud and offensive to his ears. Women in various states of undress writhed on platforms in each corner of the place, leered at by a group of horny drunks. Trying not to breathe in the toxic blend of alcohol and body odour, Kurcher pushed through the

40

crowd to reach the bar. He beckoned to one of the serving girls. She approached looking thoroughly exhausted, her skin glistening with sweat, but tried to manage a smile for him.

'What can I get you?' she shouted over the music.

He showed her his HDU. 'You seen this guy?'

She squinted at the image. 'Nope. You wanna drink then or what?'

Kurcher shook his head. Before he could say anything else, she disappeared to serve a paying patron. Already getting pissed off, he grabbed one of the other girls and showed her the HDU too. She hadn't seen Cassius either.

He turned and leaned back against the bar, looking out into the throng. Tapping his HDU, he uploaded the image of Cassius' visage to his sense app and hoped it would pick him up amongst the revellers.

'You looking for someone?'

Kurcher gave a sideways glance at the man who had suddenly appeared next to him. He was middle-aged and balding, a fixed smirk wrinkling one side of his face. The ill-fitting shirt he wore showed off a hairless chest and he smelt like he had bathed in the most pungent perfume he could find.

'What's it to you if I am?'

'The name's Pask.'

'Did I ask for your name?'

Pask laughed and leaned against the bar alongside him. 'Maybe I can help you find who you're looking for. I know most of the people who come through here.'

'And why would you help me? What do you want in return? Drugs or several drinks, I suppose.'

Pask laughed again. 'You always so suspicious?'

'Yes.'

'Look, I run one of the storage bays near here and I also help the owners of this place keep track of certain people. Long story short, they take all sorts in here but some just need to be watched.'

Kurcher turned to face him. 'You're with Fortitude?'

'I work for them, but I'm no merc.' Pask grinned. 'You on the other hand look like a freelancer. If you're after someone dangerous, it's in my best interest to help you get rid of them.'

'So I'll ask again, what do you want in return?' Kurcher's throat was starting to hurt from shouting.

'A finder's fee.'

'Can we talk away from this fucking noise?'

41

Pask winked and lightly patted Kurcher's hand before beckoning him away from the bar. When they were in a small private room at the back of the place, Kurcher grew even more uncomfortable as his new friend stroked his arm.

'In here, we can do what we like,' stated Pask.

'Good.' Kurcher's hand gripped him by the neck and slammed him against the wall as his other hand raised the HDU in front of Pask's shocked face. 'This is the person I'm looking for.'

'What're you doing?' gurgled Pask.

'Making sure you don't touch me again. I need information and that's it.'

'Okay, okay.' Pask raised his hands. 'You asked me what I wanted in return for info.'

'And you said a finder's fee.'

'I didn't mean money.'

Kurcher threw him down onto one of the stained seats and handed him the HDU. 'Seeing how you take such an interest in men, have you seen this one?'

Pask rubbed at his neck as he looked at the image. 'Yes. Why are you looking for him?'

'Where is he?' demanded Kurcher, ignoring Pask's curiosity.

'He came in here a couple of times, bought some drinks and left. He had no interest in the wares on show, if you know what I mean.'

'And?'

Pask frowned. 'I also saw him in one of our storage bays. Yes, he has a locker there.'

'How often does he use it?'

'I've only seen him there once, but my guys tell me he comes back every four or five hours to put stuff in his locker, which is odd.'

'When is he due to be back then?'

Pask checked his watch. 'Couple of hours maybe.'

'Anything else you can tell me?'

'Not really. Is he dangerous, this one? He looks it.'

Kurcher snatched the HDU back and returned it beneath his jacket. 'Tell me where the storage bay is.'

Pask started rising from the seat. 'I can take you there.'

Kurcher thought for a moment. Perhaps this man had his uses after all. 'Fine, let's go.'

'What about my finder's fee?'

'I just told you...'

42

'This time I mean money,' scowled Pask.

They left Carly's and Kurcher was glad to find the storage bay was closer than he had anticipated. A few twists and turns along the labyrinthine corridors was all it took before Pask opened the door and welcomed him to his humble workplace. It was no surprise to find most of the vast chamber was hidden in shadow as the lighting only ever came on in whichever areas were occupied. A hundred racks must have lined the bay, each filled with a number of metal crates.

Pask led Kurcher to a room off the main chamber. It was smaller but still lined with hundreds of lockers of varying sizes. The lights were always on in there it seemed.

Pask checked a nearby screen. 'Five six two,' he said eventually.

Kurcher noted the position of the locker and looked around the rest of the room. 'No other exits?'

'None. One way in, one way out.'

'Good. Easy to corner him that way.'

Pask wrung his hands nervously. 'Look, why don't I help get his attention for you?'

'How? You planning on coming on to him too?'

'Of course not,' snapped Pask. 'I only go for grizzled mercs with a chip on their shoulder like you.'

'Just tell me how you can get his attention.'

'I run this bay most of the time, so what if I approach him and ask some standard security questions about his frequent locker use? We'll be by his locker so you can enter behind us.'

Kurcher glanced back at the entrance. 'This guy isn't just some thief. He's more likely to stab you through the eye socket for just talking to him.'

Pask paled slightly but remained resolute. 'I can handle myself. Anyway, I doubt he will get much of a chance with you nearby.'

'You realise I'm not here to apprehend him, right? I'm putting a bullet through his deranged brain the moment I see him. It's likely to make quite a mess of your lockers.'

The thought of the finder's fee seemed to dictate Pask's response. 'I understand. People like him are better off dead.'

Something in the back of Kurcher's mind warned him to be wary of trusting someone like Pask. The only person he truly trusted was waiting back on the *Kaladine*. He didn't really need Pask, but he might be useful in distracting Cassius long enough.

'Fine. Just make sure he is facing his locker and get the fuck out of the way when I walk in. I don't want your blood on my hands too.'

Kurcher left the locker room and took up a position amongst the storage racks. When the lights flickered on above him, he cursed and made sure he was hidden from anyone who might be entering the bay. He checked his revolver and kept it in hand beneath his jacket.

His comms app clicked. 'Davian, you there?'

She always had such good timing. 'I'm busy.'

Frost ignored that. 'I was just checking in if I hadn't heard from you, like you said.'

'Great. I'm still alive, if that's what you were wondering.'

'Why are you down in arm K? Did you find a lead?'

'You don't need to keep track of me.' He wished he had deactivated his app so she couldn't monitor his position. 'I'm doing a job for Coyle as payment for information.'

'*You're* doing Fortitude's dirty work? I hope you got the info first.'

He groaned loud enough for her to hear. 'As soon as I'm finished here, Coyle will access his data and find out what happened to our crims. That's the deal.'

'Pretty shitty deal. You can't trust him.'

'You're stating the obvious again.'

'So what's the job?'

Kurcher glanced around to make sure nobody was nearby. 'Someone's causing them concern. I'm just waiting for the target to show up.'

'Watch yourself then. If it's not a corp target then it could get messy. I'd hate to have to bail you out if you get into trouble.'

'How's the ship?' Kurcher changed the subject.

'No problems here. Nobody seems too interested.'

'Well stay on your guard. This place is crawling with pirates and mercs just looking for an opportunity.' Kurcher peered around the storage rack. 'By the way, that other matter has been discussed with Coyle and dealt with.'

'That simple?'

'He wasn't best pleased, but I talked him round. Turns out one of the men who accosted you was the nephew of Morton Hurst.'

'Who?'

'Exactly.'

Frost sighed quietly. 'Did you get the impression Coyle knew something about the crims?'

'He had a flicker of recognition in his eyes when I showed him their data. He knows something. I'm just not sure how much. He...' Kurcher hesitated.

44

'Everything okay?'

He lowered his voice. 'We'll speak later. My target just walked in.'

Even from his position, Kurcher recognised Cassius as soon as the man entered the storage bay. He wasn't exactly impressive to behold, but members of the Kindred never were. He was short and wiry, with long lank hair that drooped down over his eyes. Kurcher noticed he was wearing a coat that looked too large for him and that meant one thing: he was hiding something underneath.

Cassius disappeared into the locker room, prompting Kurcher to head after him. He pulled his revolver out as he moved quickly towards the doorway. The Kindred never used guns, so he felt secure in using the direct approach.

He heard Pask's cheerful voice as he entered and hoped his helper was holding Cassius' attention. He saw them ahead; Pask pointing at the locker as he asked for an inventory check and Cassius glaring at him silently. As Kurcher lifted his revolver, his target grabbed hold of Pask and positioned him as a human shield. A long knife with a serrated edge appeared at Pask's throat. All Kurcher could see of Cassius' face was one eye watching him from behind the fringe. That eye flickered with app data. This would be more difficult than he had hoped.

'Help,' croaked Pask, struggling to breathe as Cassius' forearm held him in place.

'Care to tell me why the Kindred are on Sullivan's Rest?' Kurcher asked Cassius.

The man simply dug the blade slightly into Pask's skin, drawing a trickle of blood and a muffled yelp from his captive.

'I forgot that your fucked-up lot aren't big on talking.' Kurcher took a step closer but Cassius moved back, dragging Pask helplessly with him. 'No matter what you do, you're not leaving this room alive. Just drop the knife and accept that you made a bad decision coming here.'

The hollow eye set in the gaunt face seemed to hold no emotion. If anything, Kurcher found it difficult to look away from.

'Fine,' Kurcher shrugged, not seeing even a waver in the man's resolve. 'Sorry about this, Pask.'

He lifted his revolver and fired one shot. The bullet passed straight through the right hand side of Pask's neck and struck Cassius in the collar. As Cassius staggered backwards and slammed into the lockers, he released Pask who fell to the floor with a gurgled whimper.

Kurcher strode across the room, firing two more shots into Cassius' chest.

45

A flicker of doubt crossed his face as his target refused to drop, instead reaching beneath his coat for something, and Kurcher remembered what someone had told him once: Kindred refused to die unless by their own hand. He had dismissed it as bullshit.

His fourth bullet took Cassius through the eye and lodged in the man's brain. That did the job finally.

'Fucking freak,' muttered Kurcher, kicking the corpse.

He opened Cassius' coat carefully and found several devices inside one of the pockets. He didn't have to be an expert to know they were illegal explosives, made out of shoddy materials. If he had hesitated, it was likely his internal organs would now be sliding down the dirty walls of the locker room.

'Help me... please.'

He had forgotten about Pask. The bay worker was clutching his bullet wound as blood ran between his fingers onto the metal grating beneath him. As he crouched down next to him and reholstered his revolver, Kurcher saw two of Pask's fellow workers enter the room nervously.

'You'll be fine,' he told the injured man. 'No artery was hit so you may lose some blood but not enough to kill you.'

'You... shot me.'

'Yeah. Had to.' Kurcher beckoned to the two workers. 'You'd best get Pask to a medic pronto.'

He stood back as the two men lifted their co-worker and carried him out. Kurcher heard Pask mumble something about a finder's fee as they left the room. Not giving it a second thought, he went back to the corpse and gathered the explosives before placing them in his own pocket. He then checked the rest of Cassius' pockets and found just the locker keycard, which he took. Coyle could deal with the contents of the locker and with the clean-up operation. With a final glance down at Cassius and the serrated knife he had used, Kurcher pulled his revolver back out and put another bullet into the dead man's skull. Best to be sure.

He didn't waste any time in heading back up to the station's central hub, glad to be away from the murky depths of arm K. He found Coyle almost exactly where he had left him.

'Cassius is dead,' he announced. 'Left his body in one of the storage bays.'

Coyle smiled. 'Fuck me, you don't hang around.'

'You tend not to when you're an enlister. Thought you might want these too.' Kurcher handed over the explosives and the keycard. 'I wasn't about to

46

touch his locker. It's probably rigged.'

'These what I think they are?' The merc held one of the devices up to the light.

'Nasty little bastards, I'd wager. Probably pack more punch than you'd think. The problem is that these weren't made by Cassius. He was supplied by someone on Sullivan's Rest.'

'How'd you know that?'

'Because these were components for something bigger. If he truly was a member of the Kindred, then they don't go in for pissy little devices like this. Those explosives would've been part of a bigger bomb he was building. It probably took him the time he'd spent on the station just to find a supplier.'

'Great.' Coyle kicked at the seat to his left. 'The last thing we need here is homemade explosives being sold to the likes of Cassius.'

'He was using an app too. Saw me coming without even turning.'

'How the hell did he get his hands on a sight app like that? We don't sell them on the market.'

'Hacked apps are the work of pirates usually. Schaeffer's Nine spring to mind. The Templars aren't against using them either. Seems your black market has some unofficial traders working outside the hub.'

'Explosives and hacked apps. Cassius knew the right people it seems.'

'Well, he's one you definitely don't have to worry about anymore.' Kurcher nodded at the console in front of the Fortitude man. 'I helped you, so it's time to reciprocate.'

Coyle thought for a moment. 'You could help us find those making these explosives.'

'You asked me to ice one man and I did that.' Kurcher raised his voice. 'I'm not here to work for you or your organisation.'

'Pity. You're a ruthless son of a bitch. You could always ditch Taurus Galahad and join Fortitude.'

Kurcher felt a slight itch at the back of his skull. He knew his last Calmer had been a smaller dose than usual. 'Yeah, mercs make for great employers. The data, Coyle.'

'That's all the corps are. They're all mercenaries in their own way.'

'Enough.' Kurcher slammed his hand down on Coyle's desk. 'Are you going to help me or have I just wasted my time acting as your personal assassin?'

Coyle rubbed at his beard as he regarded the enlister. 'Fine. I looked into the records while you were down in arm K and I don't think you're going to like what I found.'

47

'Just tell me.'

'Of the seven crims you're after, only one remained on Sullivan's Rest as far as I can tell. The rest disappeared.'

Kurcher tried to scratch the itch at the back of his brain. 'Which one stayed?'

'As far as I can tell,' Coyle repeated, 'Sieren Broekow. Checked himself into one of the sleepers in the residential sector of arm F and apparently never checked out.'

So the sniper was the first. Kurcher had hoped he'd be one of the easiest to enlist, but nothing was straightforward any longer. 'What about the other six?'

'I told you. They're gone.'

'You don't know where?'

Coyle gave him an incredulous look. 'People come through here every day. We're not in the business of noting down who boards which ship and heads off to whatever system. As long as those people trade here and spend their money, Fortitude is happy.'

'I'll remember that when the Kindred blow you to shit.' Kurcher shook his head. 'So you don't know anything else. No movements for the crims during their time here?'

'They stayed below the radar. Jaffren Hewn wouldn't have wanted to stay here long now, would he? Echo aren't too popular amongst the other pirates. Hell, Jericho's Bold would have jumped at the chance of ridding the galaxy of such a massive pain in the ass as Hewn.'

Kurcher studied the merc's face for a moment. The returned grin told him Coyle was not hiding anything more, for once. 'Then I guess I'll be visiting arm F next. Can you send Broekow's location to my HDU?'

Coyle did so without question, but spoke as he handed it back. 'So your plan is to grab Broekow, take him back to your ship and just go?'

'Something like that, yeah.'

'How will you find the others?'

'Fuck knows.'

Kurcher left Coyle's watchpoint without so much as a farewell. He couldn't wait to be off the station and back on the *Kaladine*. As he located an elevator down to arm F, he activated his comms app.

'Justyne?'

'Ah, you're alive.'

'I've located Broekow. He's holed up in a room down in the residentials, apparently. The rest of the crims are long gone, according to Coyle.'

'You believe him?'

'As far as he is aware, they've not been on the station for some time. Hate to agree with that asshole, but they wouldn't have stuck around here.'

'So why did Broekow?'

'No idea. Maybe he found work, maybe he drank himself into a coma or maybe he's dead. Wouldn't be the first war crim to off himself.'

'Need some help?'

'Not this time. Just get the ship ready to leave as soon as I get back.'

'Understood. What happened with your previous job, by the way?'

'Target was a member of the Kindred and was making some sort of bomb. I think Fortitude may have some problems arising in the future with those bastards.'

'Easy kill?'

Kurcher recalled the creepy eye watching him from behind the long fringe. 'Five bullets.'

'Shit.'

'Yeah. Listen, our only lead to the other crims is Broekow, so I'm hoping he knew what happened to them. If he doesn't, our task is going to be difficult.'

'Like it already wasn't. Watch your back down there.'

Déjà vu hit as he left the elevator. Arm F was frighteningly similar to K and he half expected to see Pask appear around a corner any minute asking for his fee. As he headed into the residential sector though, things started looking different. He passed numerous sleepers, blocks of rooms where people would pay to use the quarters either to rest or entertain. Other doors lining the corridors led to larger quarters for those who had made a home on Sullivan's Rest. It was quieter down there and he already liked that.

He arrived at his destination, fully-loaded revolver in hand. He couldn't take any chances with the man he was seeking. Coyle's data had shown that Broekow was in room F185. He soon found the right door along a silent hallway. He should have asked Coyle to furnish him with a sleeper skeleton key.

Kurcher tapped the intercom screen on the wall next to the door. 'Sieren Broekow. My name is Davian Kurcher and I need to talk with you urgently.'

Silence fell once more. He paused before trying again. 'I'm going to be honest. I have been sent to find you by Taurus Galahad, but not to apprehend or eliminate you. I have been asked to enlist you and to ask for your help in finding the six others who were held by Enlister Cooke when he captured and subsequently released you.'

49

The screen remained blank. Kurcher bit at his lip. It had been a while since he had enlisted anyone and he felt rusty. 'Look, Broekow, this is a one-time offer. The alternative is that the corp continues to pursue you relentlessly no matter where you go.'

The thought dawned on him that he might have been talking to an empty room beyond the door. He tapped the intercom once more. 'We have a ship docked above and can be off station in...'

'Why the weapon?'

The voice sounded almost metallic through the intercom.

'A precaution.' Kurcher holstered the revolver. 'There. Now can we talk?'

'You really think I'd work for Taurus Galahad again after what they made me do?'

'Look, I don't like talking to a door. Let me in and I'll explain everything.'

'Piss off. There's no way I'm falling for a ploy like this.'

Kurcher needed a better approach. 'I get that you don't like Taurus. I hate the bastards too, but they pay me to do what I'm good at. I know your father died in their service during the civil war on Cobb. I was there too and can tell you that too many died on that planet, all thanks to Taurus. They are responsible for a lot of shit that happens, but they're also powerful and that makes them dangerous enemies to have. I'm offering you a way to appease them while utilising your particular skill set.'

For a moment, the intercom was silent and grey. Then it flickered and an unshaven face appeared, glaring at Kurcher with exhausted eyes.

'What else did they tell you about me? Do you know what my crime was?'

This was a step forward for Kurcher. 'You shot and killed three of your commanding officers during a mission debrief in 2616. You then managed to flee but were apprehended by Cooke eventually in the Reynold system.'

Broekow laughed and shook his head. 'Taurus records claim that I shot and killed those officers in cold blood because of a *disagreement*. Nobody gives a shit about the truth.'

'Of course not. The corp only cares that you killed three of their own. You did shoot them, right?'

'Yes.'

Kurcher shrugged. 'Then you're the crim in their eyes. Why don't you try me though?'

Broekow pushed his fringe back. 'You work for them. Why would you believe me?'

'Because I told you that I know exactly what the corp's capable of. Some

50

of the people I find for them aren't the murderous psychos they are made out to be.'

'Okay.' Broekow leaned closer to the intercom so his face filled the entire screen. 'They used me. They sent me after targets claiming they were war criminals or people in charge of enemy operations. It wasn't until the last target that I realised they'd lied to me and that the people I'd killed were innocent.'

'Why would they get you to kill innocents?'

'Because they were in the way of Taurus' plans in one way or another. The last guy I killed was apparently a member of the government on Valandra. The data I received said he was supplying military specs and numbers to the other corps, telling them what Taurus was up to on Bayos. I did my initial homework and saw the target often travelled between the two planets, visiting military depots on Bayos. I went to Valandra, found him and did my job. He made it easy for me, standing on a balcony at his home one evening. No sooner had I blown his brains out, his wife and children appeared. I packed up my gear and left.'

Kurcher frowned. 'So how did you know he was innocent?'

Broekow's head bowed slightly. 'Because something seemed off afterwards. The reaction of the local community when they heard of his death was staggering. They all mourned him as if he were a family member and his funeral had the biggest turnout I've ever seen. Then accusations started flying, blaming Sapphire Nova and Libra Centauri. It sent the entire community into uproar and threatened to get out of control. I managed to get off Valandra eventually but, rather than go straight to my debriefing, I chose to visit Bayos. It was there that I uncovered the truth.'

Kurcher wanted to tell him to just skip to the end of his story. The sooner he could get off Sullivan's Rest, the better. 'Taurus had fucked you over.'

'I spoke with several officers at the depots on Bayos. Turned out that the man I killed was opposing a new weapon prototype and had filed an official request to hold a review of the tech behind it, thus delaying production. I went to my mission debrief after that and confronted my commander with the info. He denied it to begin with, but eventually admitted they wanted the target out of the way so the weapon production could begin. When I noticed two others enter the room with rifles in hand, I didn't even think. I just opened fire and fled. They would have killed me to keep me quiet.'

'Perhaps, although you don't know that. Listen, I'm not here to dwell on the past. I'm here to offer you a better future and one that doesn't involve you hiding away in some shitty room for the rest of your life.'

51

Broekow's brow creased. 'What, so all is forgiven? Come work for Taurus Galahad again and they'll just forget I killed three men?'

'If you work with me to find the other six, the corp will leave you be.'

'But I only have your word on that. For all I know, you'll put a bullet in my head the moment I leave this room or the corp will after I help you.'

Kurcher felt the itch again. 'What other option do you have? You're going to have to trust me. You're a talented sniper and I could do with your skills as I go after the others.'

'My apps were disabled by the corp,' Broekow said in a venomous tone. 'I don't have the sight or sense I had before.'

'I can get them reconnected,' Kurcher told him. 'Once we are on my ship, I'll contact Taurus.'

Broekow watched him via the intercom for a moment then disappeared from the screen. A moment later, the door opened and Kurcher stepped inside, grimacing at the stale odour that greeted him. Broekow stood in the centre of the room, pistol in hand and aimed at the enlister.

'You're not wearing the Taurus colours and I don't see any sword logo.'

'I do things my own way.' Kurcher cast his eyes around the small quarters. 'Is it the maid's day off?'

'You look more like a merc,' Broekow stated, looking him up and down.

'I get told that a lot. Look, I'm not some officer in the military or a lackey brown-nosing the hierarchy. I'm an enlister who was reassigned from chasing a serial killer to come here and find you. I'm tired and I just want to get back to my ship and get off this fucking station. If you choose not to come with me, I walk out that door and don't come back. You should expect others to come knocking though and they won't be as amiable as I am.

Also, Fortitude know you're here and that'll make them nervous.'

Broekow's arm wavered slightly. 'And you want me to do what exactly?'

'Help me track down the six crims you were released onto the station with. They are all to be enlisted.'

'You're joking, right?'

'Unfortunately not.'

'Do you know who they are?'

Kurcher nodded. 'I know it isn't going to be easy so some may need to be subdued but, with your help, we can do that.'

Broekow laughed. 'I saw what these people are like and what they are capable of. The last thing they'll do is allow themselves to be restrained and thrown in some cell. What happens when, or should I say if, you persuade them all?'

52

'Those six would be taken off my hands for briefing and ultimately integration into the corp's merc ranks,' lied Kurcher. 'You're different though. After your briefing, you'll be given a choice. If you prove your worth to me, I may well request you become part of my team.'

'Why me?'

'Because you're not like them. I've read your history and it was quite familiar. Plus, I don't trust people either, especially the corps.'

Broekow blinked and his shoulders sagged, betraying his exhaustion. The pistol slowly lowered. 'If your offer is genuine then I guess I'm on board. I'm tired of rotting away on this station.'

Kurcher wanted to smile but managed to stop himself. *One down.* 'Good decision. Gather whatever possessions you need and let's go.'

'Look, I'll level with you.' Broekow's finger was still wrapped around the trigger. 'I know where three of the six went. As for the others...'

The itch in Kurcher's head turned to an ache. 'We'll talk when we're on the ship and I'm watching Sullivan's Rest vanish behind us.'

It didn't take Broekow long to find what he wanted to take. He bundled some clothing into a bag, put on his belt complete with holster and then grabbed a sniper rifle that had been leaning against the bed.

'I thought you would have discarded your weapons,' remarked Kurcher. 'May draw a few looks as we head to the pylon.'

Broekow opened a small locker and pulled out several rounds of ammunition for his rifle, which he pocketed. 'They've been the only trustworthy things in my life recently. I'm short on ammo though.'

'Don't worry about that. I'll make sure your apps get reinstated too when we leave Sullivan's Rest, as promised.'

'No.' Broekow gripped his rifle tightly. 'I don't want them back. I want to be free of Taurus tech.'

Kurcher shrugged. 'Up to you. I'm not cutting the implants out though. You wouldn't be much use to me then.'

'I'm ready,' Broekow said. 'I take it I can clean up when we get to your ship?'

'Yeah. You look like you could do with a shower.'

They made their way back up to the station's central hub, avoiding the still-bustling market as best they could. Anyone who glanced at the rifle slung around Broekow's shoulder was met by a steely glare from the sniper. Kurcher wanted to tell him not to make eye contact with anyone but, after so long residing in the depths of the station, Broekow had clearly become paranoid. An itchy trigger finger was not the best trait for a sniper to have.

53

Coyle appeared ahead, moving to intercept them. Kurcher told Broekow to let him do the talking. What did the bastard want now?

'This Broekow then?' the merc asked.

Kurcher noticed there was no hint of the man's grin. 'Did the rifle give it away?'

Coyle looked Broekow up and down quickly before turning angry eyes on the enlister. 'You didn't tell me you shot one of my fucking people.'

'Sounds like Pask survived then.'

'I'd appreciate it if you stopped shooting members of Fortitude,' Coyle growled. 'He has been shouting his head off about what you did so I ordered the medics down there to sedate him for as long as possible. I don't want to end up getting grilled by those above me, asking why one man got away with murdering four people and wounding another during two visits to the station.'

'I killed Cassius for *you* and Pask isn't even a merc. He just works for you.'

Coyle shrugged. 'If you come back here any time soon, I'll have to have you arrested. Understood?'

'What makes you think I'll be coming back to this shithole?' Kurcher pushed past the merc.

'Something always brings you back, Davian,' Coyle shouted after him.

As the two men headed to the docking pylons, Broekow broke his silence. 'So you're not exactly on good terms with Fortitude then.'

Kurcher shook his head. 'You could say that.'

'You killed someone for them though?'

'In my line of work, information often comes at a price,' muttered Kurcher. 'I plan on giving this place a wide berth from now on, as should you.'

He forgot who he was talking to for a moment. Still, best to keep up the facade.

The *Kaladine* was right where he had left it. Frost met them as they stepped through the airlock and Kurcher gestured at the pistol she was holding.

'You won't be needing that. Sieren Broekow, this is my pilot, Justyne Frost.'

Broekow forced a smile. 'He's right. You don't need the gun. I'm not here to cause you any trouble.' He glanced at Kurcher. 'I didn't have much choice but to join you.'

Frost hesitated then saw the look in Kurcher's eyes and holstered the

54

weapon. 'Fine. Just don't step out of line. You're not the only good shot here.'

'Show him his quarters,' Kurcher ordered. He headed along the corridor. 'Then get us off this station.'

'Which direction are we heading?' Frost's tone was sharp.

Kurcher didn't even bother looking back. 'Just put some distance between us and Sullivan's Rest. Head for the jump point. Broekow, clean yourself up. Then we'll need to know where to find the others.'

As the enlister disappeared around the corner, Frost regarded their guest. Her hand remained close to the pistol.

'Does he often leave you alone with criminals?' Broekow asked, offering her another smile.

Frost found herself wanting to return the smile, but managed to keep her resolve. 'The last crim who tried something with me ended up getting his balls blown off.'

Broekow's smile vanished. 'I didn't mean... I wasn't...'

'Head to the end of the corridor and down the stairs,' she told him, allowing herself to smirk finally once he had passed her.

By the time Broekow had been given a tour of the makeshift quarters in the hold and safely stowed his weapons away in storage, Kurcher had returned. Frost shook her head at him before making her way to the cockpit.

The *Kaladine* departed Sullivan's Rest and the station swiftly vanished into the void behind them on Frost's display. She liked watching it disappear, but also had to make sure no ships were in pursuit. She wouldn't have put it past the pirates or even some of the mercs to try taking the ship. The *Kaladine* would be quite a trophy. Once she had punched in the course to the jump point and linked her app to the ship, Frost lit a cigarette and headed for the rec room, where she found Kurcher and Broekow silently staring at the data for the other crims.

'Makes for good reading, right?' She poured herself some of the disgusting coffee they used on board, wishing that just once Kurcher would pay a bit more for some quality goods.

'I still don't think you grasp how dangerous these people are,' Broekow said.

Frost took a sip of coffee, then took a long drag on her cigarette. The smoke took away the bitter aftertaste and made it bearable. She glanced at Broekow, taking a moment to study him as his focus was on the screen. He hadn't yet shaved and looked like someone they might have seen begging on the streets of some starving colony, but he had a strong jaw beneath the beard and no doubt a toned body beneath his clothes. Military men always did. She found herself gazing at his torso and random sordid thoughts began invading her mind. It had been too long.

'Don't forget that you're one of these dangerous people,' she said, forcing herself to remember who this man was and what he had done.

Broekow turned his head towards her. 'I'm *nothing* like them. I killed people because that was my job and what happened during my debrief will haunt me for a long time. I may be a criminal now, but these six are something altogether more inhuman.'

Frost was held momentarily by his angry eyes. Broekow seemed much older than he was, but that may have been down to his current state. He was only two years older than her, yet he carried much more personal baggage. She noticed Kurcher watching them from across the room and so took another drag before shrugging at Broekow and turning to the screen.

'Tell us about them then,' Kurcher said. 'We've got time.'

Frost glanced at the enlister. Kurcher seemed to know what she was thinking a lot of the time and that was still unsettling. If he knew she found Broekow attractive, he would likely ensure they never went near each other. Not out of spite or jealousy, but just because it would jeopardise their task and she couldn't let him down like that. As she relaxed back onto one of the seats, she wondered whether Kurcher did have any pangs of jealousy. He was not unattractive, but she could never look at him like that. She knew how fucked up he was.

Broekow approached the screen as an image of Maric Jaroslav appeared. 'Before I begin, I just wanted to say that I fully expected to get a bullet in the brain or to be thrown into a cell the moment I walked onto your ship. I appreciate being given this chance, but it still seems strange that Taurus would want to enlist these people.'

'I'm just doing what they're paying me to do.' Kurcher exchanged knowing glances with Frost. 'You help us find them and we'll see about getting you onto the *Kaladine* permanently. Besides, Taurus probably wants them for various reasons. Oakley would make a good spy, for example, and imagine what they could do if Hewn started working for them. They would be able to control Echo.'

Broekow nodded, keeping his eyes on the screen. 'Trust isn't an easy thing to come by anymore.'

Frost wondered if he knew his weapons would only be released by Kurcher's authorisation. There was no way they would let any of the crims carry a weapon around with them while on board.

56

'Shall we start with him then?' Kurcher waved a hand at the screen.

'Bearing in mind that I spent most of the time just watching and listening when I was in Cooke's custody, this guy was the only one who actually tried to engage me in conversation. My advice? Don't let him get under your skin.' Broekow pointed at the solemn face before him. 'This is how he looks when he is Maric. *He's* not the one you have to worry about.'

'You're talking about Choice?' asked Frost.

'Yeah. Whenever I saw or heard him as Maric, he was harmless. Fucking crazy but harmless. He would spout all sort of religious crap, preaching to anyone who would listen, but he never got violent.'

'He was brainwashed by Revenants,' Kurcher stated. 'Unfortunately, Choice was a result of the trauma he underwent.'

'Well, Choice couldn't be a more different person. It was like having two separate people in the cell next to me. If Maric is crazy then Choice is insane. He sounds friendly enough but he always has a hidden agenda. Just don't disagree with him. He hates being challenged and won't stand for being proven wrong.'

'How often did he switch personas?' Kurcher felt it was a valid question.

'Maybe two or three times a day. He woke as Maric every day though. Listen, just be aware that he is a very clever man. Choice knows pretty much everything there is to know about apps and would tell me how he worked to create his own versions of the technology before getting caught.' Broekow shook his head at the screen. 'You can't control this one. I'd recommend throwing him in a cell.'

'Do you know where he went?' Kurcher asked.

'After Cooke freed us onto Sullivan's Rest, I heard Choice announcing loudly that he was catching a transport to the Almaz system.'

Kurcher pondered that for a moment. 'Most transports heading into that system go to Rikur. It'd be a dangerous place to lie low considering how hostile Sapphire Nova are at the moment.'

The image changed to Jaffren Hewn.

'I don't think I need to tell you much about him, right?'

Kurcher was smiling as the effects of his latest hit of Parinax lingered nicely. 'Unless you know where he went.'

'No idea, sorry. Wouldn't he have gone back to the Echo Expanse?'

'He'll make his way back there in time, but I'd expect him to hide out somewhere else for a while. He's going to be a bastard to find.'

'I didn't really have any interaction with Hewn,' Broekow remarked. 'He was the last to be caught by Cooke and just kept to himself. Even on the

57

station, he simply disappeared before anyone could talk to him.'

Kurcher hoped the pirate had not yet made his way back to the Expanse. He was loathe to take the *Kaladine* into such a dangerous region of space, although the thought of not having any solid corp presence there was an enticing one.

When the next image appeared, Frost tutted and stubbed her cigarette out.

'Another one I would lock up straight away,' said Broekow, noting the pilot's reaction to Bennet Ercko's face. 'He's an evil fucker. No morals and no fear. Not the brightest though. He got caught by Cooke because he couldn't stay away from a certain region on Val... Valandra.'

Kurcher heard Broekow's voice falter at the mention of the planet and could see the turmoil still behind the sniper's eyes. 'He likes the women.'

Broekow blinked. 'He has a thing for Valandran women it seemed, yes. Although I doubt even he would be stupid enough to go back there again.'

'I agree,' piped up Frost. 'Ercko should be locked up. None of the other crims are convicted rapists.'

'We have to find him first.' Kurcher gave a dismissive wave of his hand that pissed Frost off. 'I know that Ercko will be trouble, but I'm sure we can persuade him to play nice.'

'If not, you can always blow his balls off,' Broekow said, looking back at Frost with a wry smile. 'But again I don't know where he went.'

An angelic image came up next, looking out of place among the crims.

'Any info on her?' Kurcher had an eager edge to his voice that made Frost tut again.

'Now Oakley I can help you with,' said Broekow proudly. 'She's gone back to Cradle and she took Angard with her.'

This drew surprised looks from the other two. Frost was first to ask the obvious question. 'Why would she do that?'

Broekow shrugged. 'Protection. Pity. I'm not sure. What I do know is that she and Angard seemed to develop this bizarre bond when they had cells next to each other on Cooke's ship. It began when Angard went berserk one day, pounding on the walls and roaring like some crazed animal. I heard Cooke's team rushing past saying they needed to kill Angard as he was a real danger to the ship. Oakley intervened and managed to subdue Angard just by talking to him.'

'Beauty and the beast.' Kurcher's remark was apt.

'It was she who told Cooke that Angard needs a supply of drugs to survive. His going berserk was basically him having a fit as the drugs began wearing off. If he hadn't had a fresh dose, he would have died. Just one of the

58

side effects left over from what they did to him on Shard.' Broekow saw Kurcher's frown. 'I overheard them talking one night.'

'But taking him to Cradle would be a massive risk,' Frost pointed out. 'If she was going back to be under the protection of her family, I doubt they'd agree to having Angard there with them.'

Kurcher looked at her with a raised eyebrow. 'You know how the wealthy think, do you? The Oakleys have more sway than a lot of people realise. They have their own forces down on Cradle, as do the other wealthy families controlling the system. They might welcome a brute such as Angard as a bodyguard to their precious killer of a daughter.'

'A *criminal* like Angard,' corrected Frost. 'He's killed a lot of people.'

'So has Oakley. Not as many of course.' Kurcher looked back at the image. 'Her family has links with criminal networks anyway. It'll be nothing new to them.'

'So how exactly do you plan on getting to her then?' Broekow asked. 'If she is hiding behind her own personal force then reaching her will be impossible.'

'I have something up my sleeve,' Kurcher smiled.

Angard's face appeared on the screen.

'You'll need a way to neutralise him,' Broekow stated. 'He won't go quietly and the last thing I imagine you want is a bloodbath on Cradle.'

Kurcher weighed up his options. 'We go after Maric next then. I know he's unstable, but he may be able to help us subdue Angard. If Choice creates his own apps, maybe he'll know how to build something that can take Angard's offline for a while.'

Broekow nodded his agreement. 'Good thinking. Just make sure Choice doesn't build something that can take your ship offline instead.'

Kurcher turned to Frost. 'We'll make the jump to the Almaz system and make for Rikur. Just keep an eye on what Sapphire Nova has in the area. I expect they'll have ships in orbit and a considerable presence on the surface. We need to stay under their radar for as long as we can.'

'Okay.' Frost went to pull another cigarette out, but decided against it. 'I'm assuming we'll be jumping to Oralia afterwards?'

'Yeah.' Kurcher glanced at the screen as the final crim's image came up. 'So what about him? Know anything?'

'Very little.' Broekow scratched at his beard. 'He kept very quiet. Nervous type, but there was something quite cold about his eyes.'

'They called him Tranc,' said Frost, rising from her seat. 'Something to do with the fact he liked to sedate his patients before killing them. He may be

59

the youngest, but he's a killer, just like the rest of them. Just like the both of you too.'

Kurcher yawned. 'Sometimes it takes a killer to catch a killer.'

Frost noticed Broekow grimacing as he rubbed at his eyes. 'Looks like you could do with some rest.'

'I've had headaches ever since the corp took my apps offline,' the sniper sighed. 'They get worse when I'm tired.'

'Well, we've got some time before we get to Rikur,' said Kurcher. 'I'll be needing you to help me find and catch Maric when we get there, so I'd rather you were focused.'

'Are there any negotiations on the sleeping arrangements?' Broekow asked. 'I'd rather not sleep in the same room as the others.'

'They're not on board yet, so the cargo hold is all yours.' Kurcher smiled. 'But no, there aren't any negotiations.'

Taurus Galahad Assault Ship Requiem
Sol system

'I think the commander has forgotten his place in the hierarchy.'

Santa Cruz clenched his jaw, willing himself not to rise to the bait. Before him, the four members of the nine-strong board waited patiently to see how he responded. It couldn't have been that serious a matter if five of them couldn't be bothered to attend.

'Why so quiet, commander?' asked Fraser Lenaghan, peering at him from the screen.

Lenaghan was the highest-ranking member present. He had an air of arrogance surrounding him, Santa Cruz could tell. Despite the fact that the overweight asshole was on Earth, Lenaghan's stare still unsettled the commander.

'With all due respect, the four of you have never been in the military.' Santa Cruz glanced from screen to screen, gauging each member's reaction. 'The task I need Winter for is of utmost importance for Taurus Galahad as a whole. I'm sure that General Mitchell would understand my reasons.'

'The general isn't here,' bristled Lenaghan. 'The fact is you pulled Winter away from his current assignment for your *task*, so going over our heads in the process. We're still waiting for an explanation of what exactly you need him for.'

Santa Cruz noticed one of the others shaking their head and thought he saw a flicker of contempt for Lenaghan's words. 'As I said before, Winter performed a mission for us recently tracking down and apprehending the rogue enlister, Cooke. His work was flawless and I need him now to help me track another enlister.'

'Another rogue enlister?' This time, it was Solomon Rees who asked the question. 'One I can just about get my head around, but two?'

Rees was the highest-ranked judicial officer for Taurus and often sent the enlisters out after known crims. He was also a highly suspicious man.

'No, sir,' replied Santa Cruz. 'As you know, Cooke let seven criminals loose on Sullivan's Rest. Davian Kurcher has been sent after them and I want Winter to follow him.'

Rees frowned. 'Why not just have Winter track them all down and eliminate them?'

Santa Cruz had to choose his words carefully. 'Kurcher is one of our best enlisters, is he not? I want Winter to follow as a safety net. Something clearly happened out there to make Cooke suddenly turn against the corporation and I don't want it happening again.'

Rees narrowed his eyes. 'It seems a waste of Winter's time, don't you think? His talents would be better used taking care of the Revenant infestation on Earth.'

'Exactly my thoughts,' nodded Lenaghan, crossing his arms.

'Winter has just docked with my ship,' Santa Cruz told them. 'What would be a waste of his time is if I sent him away again now. I intend on continuing with my plan to send him after Kurcher and, if you don't like that, I suggest you convene the entire board and put it to a vote. Comms off.'

The screens went dark and Santa Cruz stood silently for a moment at the centre of the room before letting out an exasperated breath. He wasn't about to tell them the real reason he wanted Winter to go after Kurcher. The safe return of the data implanted in one of those crims was his priority. Once he had the data, then the board would understand.

He left the private comms chamber and made his way to the meeting room where he had met with Kurcher just a few days before. This time, it was Saul Winter who was waiting for him.

'Good to see you again,' said the commander. 'Sounds like you've been busy since the last time we met.'

Winter did not turn, instead preferring to remain looking out at the view of Mars. 'You could say that, commander.'

Santa Cruz moved alongside him and looked out at the red planet. 'Our ancestors would be shocked if they were to see how the colonies down there turned out. Pioneer City has become overpopulated, leaving many homeless. Dantes and Phoenix aren't much better.'

'Is it not the responsibility of Taurus Galahad to sort it out then?'

'It is.' Santa Cruz shrugged. 'There are more pressing matters though. I need you for another assignment and again this is all highly confidential.'

'Every assignment I perform is confidential, commander. What is it you need?'

'I have sent an enlister by the name of Davian Kurcher after the criminals that Ged Cooke released. I want you to follow his ship to ensure that the task is completed and to intervene if necessary.'

'Intervene?' Winter's eyes still did not move from Mars.

'If we have any problems with Kurcher as we did with Cooke, I want you close by so the matter can be dealt with quickly. I'm hoping this won't happen, but I'm not taking my chances this time. The other reason for you following

62

them is to assist if they get into trouble.'

This time, Winter swung his gaze towards the commander. 'But remain out of their way, I assume.'

Santa Cruz found it hard to look into the agent's icy blue eyes. His name certainly suited him. 'Correct. They may well be heading into systems owned by the other corps or into merc and pirate territory. I need you to make sure Kurcher completes his assignment and I know you're adept at keeping to the shadows.'

Winter turned back to the planet. 'I understand, commander. Just relay their co-ordinates and I'll be on my way.'

'That's the thing,' said Santa Cruz. 'Kurcher is unorthodox and all attempts by Taurus to place a marker on his ship have failed. He prefers to work without being monitored. Luckily, we requested an update and received a blunt message from the pilot that they are on their way to Almaz.'

'That's it?'

'Afraid so. I take it you're still piloting the stalker?'

Winter nodded slowly before turning from the view. 'Send me any data on Kurcher, his pilot and their ship. I will review en route to Almaz. Is that all, commander?'

'If you're noticed, do not engage them in conversation. I don't want them starting to ask questions.'

'I won't be noticed,' Winter stated. 'Anything else?'

'Do what you must to ensure their assignment succeeds.' Santa Cruz looked him in the eye. 'Nobody gets in the way, understand?'

'Yes, commander.' Winter headed for the door.

'And one last thing,' called Santa Cruz. The agent looked back. 'You report only to me during this assignment. No other comms with Taurus.'

Winter regarded him quietly for a moment. 'Understood.'

When Santa Cruz was alone, he gazed out at Mars once more. The Sol system was falling apart planet by planet. With Earth ravaged by the Holy Revolt and the corps still fighting the Revenant cockroaches across the world, he had hoped Mars would thrive. All of the people who fled Earth and hoped to find sanctuary in one of the Mars colonies were now struggling to survive once more, but just on a different planet. He wondered how long before the Revenants found their way onto Mars or managed to reach one of the outer colonies in the galaxy. Perhaps Winter *was* better suited to extinguishing them.

He turned away from Mars. If he had his way, he would wipe the planet clean of all life. Best to let them die and just recolonise. A wry smile crept

63

across his lips as he imagined having the power to order the destruction of an entire world.

He just had to be patient for a while longer.

Enlister-class vessel Kaladine
Almaz system

Kurcher studied the image of Rikur as he leant on the headrest of Frost's seat.

'Four guardians orbiting one planet,' he muttered. 'That seems excessive.'

Frost shrugged. 'Must be a meeting or something.'

'Maybe.'

The four silhouettes of the guardian-class vessels belonging to Sapphire Nova could just be made out on the screen. They were larger than those of the other corps and no doubt packed enough firepower to swat the *Kaladine* as if it were a fly.

Also orbiting the planet were two vast mining transports and Kurcher wondered whether they were waiting to head down to the surface or whether they were loaded up with cargo and due to make their way slowly to the jump point soon. The former would offer a possible way to get onto the barren world, as long as the *Kaladine* could stay hidden for long enough. The last thing they needed was to be picked up by the guardians.

'Do we know which ships those are?' he asked Frost.

'Does that matter?'

'It might. I've had run-ins with a handful of Sapphire ships in the past.'

Frost checked her app display. 'Can't tell from this distance. I should have more info when we're on approach.'

'Guardians have excellent scanning range,' he reminded her. 'They'll be able to pick us up quite a while before we get anywhere near Rikur. The conflector better work properly this time.'

'It got tweaked the last time we had the *Kaladine* repaired. It should mask our arrival.'

'I don't like *should*.' Kurcher moved to the vacant seat. 'Especially when we risk facing off with four guardians.'

'Jesus, have a little faith,' snapped Frost. 'I know what I'm doing.'

Silence fell in the cockpit. Kurcher kept his eyes fixed on the dark sphere that was Rikur. Two of the guardians glistened as the Almaz sun reflected off their hulls while the other two were momentarily blotted out by a transport passing in front of them.

It didn't look important, but Rikur was one of the largest mining worlds in the known galaxy and Sapphire Nova protected it viciously. Attempts had been made to sabotage the planetbore rigs in the past but it still remained unclear what had caused the largest of the drills to be destroyed in 2590. It had taken over a decade for the rig to be repaired and rumour had it that Harper had suffered greatly during that time, especially as the colony was so heavily reliant on all trade brought about thanks to the mining operation.

'Broekow is still asleep,' Frost said suddenly.

Kurcher glanced across at her. 'How do you know that?'

Frost smiled. 'I set up a camera feed in the hold. I was just making sure he wasn't doing something he shouldn't.'

'Sure you were. Good idea though.'

As the *Kaladine* edged closer to Rikur, broken circles of light could be seen on the surface. From afar, the colonies gave an otherwise lifeless world an enticing look. Glistening rings dotted across the dark planet would have been a beautiful sight was it not for the fact that everyone knew they were simply artificial lighting illuminating the various structures surrounding the planetbores.

Frost engaged the conflector before Kurcher could remind her again and the soft, almost inaudible hum of the machinery swiftly became background noise. Kurcher just hoped that Sapphire Nova hadn't developed scanners clever enough not to be fooled by the conflector's false readings.

'Keep a close eye on those guardians,' he said after a lengthy silence. 'If they leave orbit on an intercept course, we're not sticking around. Luckily, they aren't ones I've come across before.'

'Okay.' Frost frowned as something flickered at the top of her vision. 'There's a garbled message coming up from Rikur.'

'Can you clear it up so we can hear?'

'Hold on.' She swiped at several commands brought up by her app. 'Seems the message is aimed at the guardians and is coming from Harper on a corp-only channel.'

Kurcher leaned forward, his interest piqued. 'Play what you can.'

The hiss of static filled the cockpit. Through the white noise, a voice could eventually be heard.

'Nobody will be permitted in or out of Harper following the incident, until the culprit has been found.' The static crackled again. 'Transit stations to the other colonies are also closed until further notice.'

'Fucking typical,' said Kurcher, appreciating the irony.

Frost waved her hand at him. 'Hold on. There's something else.'

The man's voice came through almost robotic this time. 'Acting Head of Security Devlin will be leading the investigation. Report to follow.'

'I wonder what happened to Portman,' pondered Kurcher. 'He's the one running Harper's security teams usually.'

'What do you want to do then? If we can't get into Harper, maybe we should leave Maric for now?'

'No.' Kurcher's reply was quick and sharp. 'It's no coincidence that Maric goes to Rikur and suddenly Harper is shut down. He must be there and we need to get to him before the corp sec do.'

'We can't get into the colony though. I could land, but what's the point?'

'There must be more than one way in. Harper is a big place and Devlin's sec team can't be everywhere at once. We'll set down at one of the quieter docks and go from there.'

The *Kaladine* approached using Rikur itself as cover from the patrolling guardians and Frost held her breath as they entered the mining world's orbit. When it looked as though the conflector had done its job well enough, she exhaled and took them down into the upper atmosphere.

As the dark surface grew ever closer, Kurcher appeared with his HDU and showed her a basic schematic of Harper.

'This dock,' he said, pointing at the screen. 'It's used by couriers and supply ships mostly but is ample distance from the heavily populated areas.'

'If it's used for deliveries, won't there be a big security presence there?'

Kurcher smiled. 'Like I said, there must be more than one way in.'

The glint in his eye told Frost that he had a plan. He always had a plan.

The lights of Harper soon came into view on the horizon. Several small vessels circled the colony like insects drawn to the artificial glow. The *Kaladine* swooped towards it, passing over one of the transit lines which stretched off across the surface. The line was shrouded in darkness; intelligent lighting only activating when one of the trans-shuttles would approach.

Frost checked the time. The Almaz sun wouldn't rise over Harper for several hours, thankfully. Even then, the sky would remain a hazy mix of grey and beige, giving pilots limited visibility.

Rikur certainly wasn't an attractive world. It was a partially dead one, lacking in vegetation and only of interest for the minerals beneath its harsh surface. Frost didn't like planets whose atmosphere wouldn't allow people to walk around outside. Sapphire Nova were reported to have executed people by sending them out onto the surface. That was a death she hoped she never had to witness.

As they passed over the vast crater that Harper encircled, the planetbore rig came into view below. Frost usually only had a thing for the *Kaladine* when it came to machinery, but even she had to admit that the drill was an impressive piece of kit. Multi-tiered and multi-armed, the rig worked day and night with relatively minimal human interaction. It was connected to Harper via several enclosed walkways and elevators, allowing the coming and going of workers as they ended one shift and started another. The planetbores really were the mechanical hearts of the Rikur colonies.

Following Kurcher's directions, she set the *Kaladine* down at a dock on the southern side of the colony before joining him in the storage room.

'Keep the conflector running,' he told her as he holstered his revolver. 'And make sure the ship is ready to get the hell out of here at a moment's notice.'

Opposite them, Broekow was checking the ammo clip of his military pistol. 'Care to divulge how exactly we're getting in? Those security doors are locked down tight.'

Kurcher opened one of the nearby lockers and pulled out two breathing masks, throwing one to the sniper. 'There's a reason I wanted us to land specifically in this corner. Between the *Kaladine* and the edge of the dock, there is a hatch that leads to maintenance tunnels running beneath this part of the colony.'

'Won't that be locked too?' asked Broekow, frowning.

Kurcher felt his latest Calmer hit starting to work and smiled. 'Not for long.'

Frost stepped close to the enlister. 'If you're discovered by Nova's sec teams?'

'Things will get ugly.'

'I'm being serious.'

'So am I. If they realise a Taurus enlister is poking around their territory, they'll shoot first and ask questions later.'

'Just like you.' Frost shook her head. 'This could go bad very quickly. Maybe I should take the *Kaladine* some distance from Harper once you're inside.'

'No. Stay here and keep an eye on what they are doing if you can. If things do go bad, then you get off-planet.'

Frost grimaced. 'I've got a feeling you'll be saying this to me a lot over the coming days.'

Kurcher glanced at Broekow. 'You ready?'

'Sure am.'

'Follow my lead though. We locate Maric, grab him and get back here fast.'

68

'You don't have to tell me twice.'

'I do.' Kurcher's eyes darkened. 'Because one fuck-up from you and the whole task is in jeopardy. Understand?'

Broekow glanced at Frost then nodded. 'Affirmative.'

As they headed out of the storage room, the pilot pointed at Broekow's face. 'Decide to keep the beard then?'

He grinned. 'Yeah. Figured it would help hide my identity for the time being.'

Frost watched as the two men headed for the airlock. She preferred Broekow with the beard, but couldn't possibly tell him that. She had to keep reminding herself that he was one of the seven crims. His life would likely be forfeit when they returned them all to Santa Cruz and that left her with an annoying sense of regret.

Kurcher and Broekow left the ship and headed for the maintenance hatch, shrouded nicely in shadows cast by the lights dotted around the edge of the dock.

'Didn't realise the wind was quite so bad on Rikur,' Broekow remarked, his voice echoing inside the mask.

'Save the talking until we're inside.' If Kurcher hadn't been stimmed up on Parinax, his response would have been harsher.

The hatch looked secure enough. The heavy-duty metalwork had several pock marks across it but had been built to withstand the Rikur atmosphere and weather. Kurcher crouched down next to it and grabbed a device from inside his jacket.

'You sure you're just an enlister?' Broekow asked. 'I thought bypass tech was banned.'

'Perks of working for Taurus.'

After a couple of minutes of fine tuning, the device linked with the lock system and Kurcher peered through his foggy mask at the screen, making sure that the bypass signal avoided any alarm trips. The signal wound its way through the circuitry maze without detection and, with a mechanical clunk, the hatch slid open. Lights flickered on below to show them the way, which made their descent much easier.

Broekow glanced back up as he followed Kurcher down the ladder, watching as the hatch slid quietly shut behind them. 'So what now?'

'We head north. There should be an airlock we have to pass through under the colony that means we can take the masks off after. Once we are through that, we head for one of the small storage rooms nearby and hope that someone left their uniforms in their locker.'

'How do you know so much about this place?'

Kurcher reached the bottom of the ladder. 'Last time I was here, I made a point of getting hold of schematics showing ways in and out of Harper. Never know when you might need them.'

Broekow snorted. 'Lucky for us, I guess.'

Kurcher led the way along the narrow tunnel north, lights continuing to flick on as they approached. All they could hear was the constant thrum of distant machinery along with their own breathing. After passing several junctions and the occasional ladder ascending back to the dock, they arrived at the airlock. Once inside, they waited patiently for one door to seal before the other opened.

'Doesn't anyone work in these tunnels?'

Kurcher removed his mask as he stepped from the airlock. 'Not many on this side of the colony.'

Broekow pulled his mask off and took a deep breath. 'Smells like shit down here.'

'Sewer system runs nearby. Quite a few of the workers on this side of the colony are here to make sure the shit runs smoothly.'

'Nice. Which way now?'

As they traversed the labyrinth of tunnels, machinery and stairwells, Kurcher occasionally glanced at the sniper. Broekow had surprised him by embracing the idea of working as an enlister, but he wondered what the man was actually thinking. Unlike a couple of the other crims he had to find, Broekow had a keen mind and a part of him must have been thinking that the offer to work for Taurus Galahad again was too good to be true.

Kurcher also found himself wondering whether the all-important data implant was actually right next to him. If he could locate a scanner that could determine whether or not the sniper had the data, he could save himself the trouble of finding the others. *If* it was in Broekow. Knowing how such things work, it would be in the last crim he found.

They located the storage room eventually and Kurcher allowed himself a smug smile when they found several maintenance uniforms hanging on the wall. The only downside was that they all had the Sapphire Nova logo emblazoned on both front and back of the rust-coloured all-in-one suit.

'Find one that fits,' he told Broekow. 'Keep your weapon out of sight.'

As they stepped into their respective uniforms, a man's laugh echoed along the corridor outside followed by the sound of footsteps approaching.

'Fuck.' Broekow quickly fastened the uniform. 'What now?'

'Act like you're supposed to be here.' Kurcher focused on the data from his app. 'Three of them heading our way. Let's go. Hopefully they won't try to speak to us.'

Broekow followed him out of the room and away from the approaching men.

'Hey there.'

The call made Kurcher swear beneath his breath. He looked over his shoulder to see one of the men waving. 'What?'

The three were of similar stocky build and had a dirty look to them. The one who had called out was scratching at his beard.

'You on shift?' he asked.

'Yeah.' Kurcher kept it abrupt.

'Nobody told me we had two newbies starting. Welcome to the too-early crew. If you hang on, we'll get suited up and join you.'

Kurcher was already getting impatient. 'I'm no newbie. I work on the north side but got roped into showing this one the sewers.' He poked a finger at Broekow. 'He'll be joining you real soon.'

The two other workers shrugged and disappeared into the storage room, leaving their companion alone in the corridor. 'What's the word from the north side then?'

'Everyone's stretched thin as usual,' replied Kurcher, his tone confident.

'That's not what I mean.' The worker crossed his arms. 'I meant have they found out who did it yet?'

Kurcher shrugged. 'Don't know.'

'Don't get me wrong. I hated Portman as much as the next man, but what a way to go.'

'So what did you hear on this side then?' Kurcher asked him, feeling a sudden sense of apprehension.

The worker stepped closer to them. 'Just the leaked info like most about how he died and that everyone needs to be careful with a murderer on the loose.'

The enlister had met Portman twice before. The head of security was disliked by all because of his reluctance to get his hands dirty and always got his teams to crack the skulls when need be. In his younger days though, Portman had been dynamic and was a member of the team who investigated who or what was behind the rig disaster twenty-eight years ago.

If Choice was the murderer, why would the schizo pick Portman and draw so much attention to himself? Something just didn't add up.

'How did he die?' Broekow suddenly asked the worker. 'I only heard rumours.'

'Heard he was stabbed several times. Stomach, chest, neck and eyes.'

'Look, we'd love to stay and gossip,' said Kurcher, holding his hands up. 'But I'm running out of time and need to get this greenhorn sorted or it'll be my ass.'

They turned and walked away before the worker could say anything more, finding the nearest stairwell and heading up to the colony proper.

'Sounds like Choice's M.O.,' Broekow noted as they ascended. 'He likes using a knife.'

'Doesn't make much sense though. He's released from custody by Cooke along with the rest of you and the first thing he thinks to do is come to Harper and murder one of the most powerful men in the colony?'

'I did warn you about him. Choice is fucking insane.'

'Well, Devlin's now the head of security. That's not good news. Portman was easily swayed for the right price, but Devlin won't take any shit. He'll have his men combing Harper looking for the killer and is likely to execute him on sight. He's like Sapphire Nova incarnate.'

They emerged from the maintenance network into a barely lit corridor and Kurcher checked the schematics on his HDU before leading Broekow north-east. He also took a moment to upload Maric's image to his sense app. He couldn't afford to let the man walk straight past them in a crowd of people.

'So we just circle around Harper until we get to the north side?' Broekow looked over his shoulder as they made their way through the all-too-quiet colony.

'Harper's highest population is in the north, with the main hubs located there. The only reason it's so silent here is because most people are still asleep.' Kurcher nodded to a number of identical doors along one wall. 'This part of the colony looks like it did when first built, but you'll be surprised the nearer we get to the north side.'

Broekow patted his side to make sure the pistol was still in place. 'Can't wait.'

Carson Freight Station
Geraint system

Santa Cruz approached the Taurus Galahad military offices, prompting the soldiers outside the door to snap to attention. He didn't bother acknowledging them and strode past. Behind him, his own personal guard made sure they kept pace.

Akeman was waiting in the usual room on the third floor. The spy was just as gaunt and sickly-looking as the last time they met, but Santa Cruz noticed a new angry-looking scar over the man's left eye.

'Wait outside,' the commander ordered his guards, closing the door behind him.

'Good to see you again, sir.' Akeman's voice was rough, as though he had just smoked his way through a pack of cigarettes.

Santa Cruz pointed at the scar. 'Where did you get that one?'

'The Knights Templar,' replied Akeman, venturing a crooked smile. 'They don't much like me it seems.'

'I hope you got some useful information for me then.'

'Yes, sir.' Akeman gestured for the commander to sit as he fetched two bottles containing cloudy orange liquid. 'Picked this up for you at Temple. I know how much you like their brand of whisky.'

Santa Cruz nodded his appreciation then glanced up at the thin window above them. The *Requiem* could be seen docked at one of the VIP pylons, overshadowing the other ships moored nearby. He enjoyed looking up at his own ship, admiring its sheer size and power. That was one of the reasons Akeman always met him in the same room.

The spy placed a small glass of the whisky before Santa Cruz then raised one himself. 'Here's to Commander Rolan Cairns.'

Santa Cruz sipped the potent beverage, feeling the pleasing burn as it hit the back of his throat. 'Care to tell me why we are toasting one of the most hated men in the Sapphire Nova hierarchy?'

Akeman sat down opposite. 'For giving you such an opportunity, sir. Cairns is due to arrive at Temple one week from today, where he will be spending a considerable amount of time with a lady who is certainly not his wife. The Knights Templar have agreed for him to use their station for his dirty little affair.'

Santa Cruz couldn't help but smile. 'What about his ship and crew?'

'Off somewhere in the Vaughn system while their commander takes some well-earned leave.'

'I take it by the scar that this information was not offered by the Templars out of kindness.'

'It took me a while, but I eventually found one of the mercs who hated Sapphire Nova almost as much as we do. I got the scar simply from a drunken fight with a few of the Knights.'

Santa Cruz sat back and took another sip of whisky. 'So I would likely run into resistance if I show up at Temple.'

'Nothing the *Requiem* can't handle, sir,' grinned Akeman. 'They wouldn't dare try fighting the flagship of the Taurus fleet.'

'We're not the flagship yet, but we will be.' Santa Cruz swilled the remaining alcohol around his glass. 'So what else do you have for me?'

'There are rumours that Libra Centauri and Sigma Royal are growing much more interested in Aridis. I heard that one Libra spy managed to make it down onto the surface but my source was less than reliable.'

'They pride themselves on having the best spy system, so there may be some truth in it. Aridis has long been of interest to the other corps. What else?'

'An Impramed med-ship was attacked by Jericho's Bold on the edge of the Benedict system. It was carrying supplies destined for one of their colonies stricken with some disease.'

'Did they leave anyone alive this time?'

Akeman finished his drink in one gulp and poured himself another. 'A handful survived. Apparently the Bold took several doctors along with all the medicine. They killed the rest.'

'You ever thought about cutting back on the alcohol?' Santa Cruz asked him sharply.

'No, sir.' Akeman grinned. 'It helps me focus.'

'We could get you a boost app implanted. Parinax is a much better way to focus.'

'I'd rather not get hooked on that shit.'

'Continue then.'

Akeman thought for a moment. 'Libra Centauri traffic to the Elrian system continues to increase. Most of their explorer-class ships are there now.'

Santa Cruz was somewhat unsettled by this news. Of all the other corporations, Libra Centauri were the ones more likely to get in the way of his operations in Coldrig. There was also the possibility that they might unearth new material or data in the depths of Farrin too.

Akeman noted the commander's distant look. 'If I may, sir, I managed to glean some information from a freelancer who had been searching some of the uncolonised systems near Elrian. Thought Taurus Galahad may find it useful for further expansion plans.'

'Excellent. Send it to the *Requiem* once we've finished here and I'll take a look later. The sooner we can set up a base nearer to Elrian the better.'

'Cenia has upped material supply to Meta,' continued Akeman. 'That little snowball of a planet seems to have much better resources than we first thought.'

'Sigma Royal know that they have to build more fleet vessels, especially with Sapphire Nova frequently moving against them.' Santa Cruz glanced up again at the *Requiem*. 'Any further news about Nova?'

Akeman shrugged. 'Same as before for the most part. They are getting more aggressive across the entire galaxy, picking fights whenever they find another corporation sniffing around their systems. There was even a skirmish out near Armstrong between a small Nova fleet and three ships belonging to Schaeffer's Nine recently. Only one pirate ship got away.'

Santa Cruz frowned. 'Schaeffer won't forget that in a hurry. Nova will find themselves surrounded by enemies eventually.'

'That's all I have for you today, sir,' Akeman stated, finishing his second drink. 'Is there anything else you need?'

'The whereabouts of all ships belonging to the other corps would be useful,' replied the commander with a smirk.

'And I thought you were going to give me a hard assignment.' Akeman shrugged. 'I'll find out what I can.'

Santa Cruz placed his glass down and rose from his seat. 'Then I thank you for your help as always and wish you good hunting. Your payment will be transferred shortly.'

Akeman remained seated. 'Don't forget your bottles, sir. Oh, and do give Commander Cairns my regards when you see him.'

Rikur
Almaz system

The lockdown lifted as Kurcher and Broekow entered the main concourse, prompting a rush of bodies as those who were waiting to catch one of the trans-shuttles out of Harper made a dash for their rides.

Kurcher gave himself a quick boost of Parinax to counter the concerns creeping into his mind. If the lockdown had ended, did that mean Choice had been caught?

Broekow tore his eyes away from the bustling neon streets of Harper's northern section long enough to notice the enlister's expression. 'That can't be good for us, right?'

Kurcher didn't answer and instead sought out one of Harper's news screens. He immediately saw the image of the late Portman displayed at the top and began reading the text beneath.

'It says Devlin and his team searched the entire northern side of the colony to quickly find the killer, unearthing vital evidence that led to the arrest of a drug dealer named Simeon Hayk.' Kurcher glanced at the smaller image of a bald man with a tattoo of some kind inked across part of his face. 'Well that's not Choice at least.'

'Someone with a vendetta against Portman then I guess,' said Broekow, pulling at one sleeve of the maintenance uniform.

Kurcher carried on reading. 'A weapon caked in Portman's blood was found in Hayk's quarters. This was used to immobilise the...'

Broekow heard him hesitate. 'What is it?'

'It says Portman's hamstring tendons were severed to make sure he couldn't get away. Then the murderer tortured him by stabbing and cutting certain parts of his body to inflict maximum pain, going as far as to take one of his eyes.' Kurcher turned away from the screen and looked around the concourse. 'Then he cut his throat.'

'Nasty piece of work. Do they always go into such graphic detail on these bulletins?'

'Sapphire Nova don't censor material like other corps do.' Kurcher read the text again and shook his head. 'Hayk was framed.'

'How do you know that?'

'Because this is the M.O. belonging to someone else. I've seen it too many times before.'

76

Kurcher stood in silence for a moment, watching the Harper citizens wander past. One of the neon signs above him glowed with a hazy green light, softened by the drug coursing through his veins. His initial thought had been that Rane's presence there would be a serious problem, but it dawned on him that perhaps fate was giving him another chance to bag the serial killer.

Broekow shifted uncomfortably. 'So who killed Portman then?'

'Edlan Rane.'

'That sick fuck? Jesus.'

'It gives me a great opportunity though.' Kurcher was smiling. 'A chance to finally end Rane's killing spree before we leave with Maric... or Choice... or whoever he is when we find him.'

'So why did Rane kill the head of security for Harper?' asked Broekow, his brow deeply furrowed.

'He kills, frames someone else then moves on to the next world. He never bothers to let me know why he does it. Insanity, vengeance, boredom... I don't really care. The outcome is going to be the same for him no matter the reason.'

Broekow peered along the concourse. 'I can see a church down there. Maybe we can ask there about Maric.'

Kurcher laughed. 'A church in this god-forsaken place. Even after the Holy Revolt and the appearance of the Revenants, people still believe in some divine fucking power. Let's see what they have to say then.'

They headed off along the concourse, passing a variety of shops and bars. Narrow alleyways snaked off the main street, all of them illuminated by groupings of small signs. Even the brothels had neon images displayed outside, some more explicit than others.

Broekow occasionally found himself wondering how a colony could look so different from one side to the other. The south was a labyrinth of narrow corridors, low ceilings and basic chambers, whereas the north had been built to resemble a small city. It was easy to forget that it was still surrounded by thick metal walls to protect against the Rikur atmosphere.

The church was no different to the other buildings, apart from the neon cross over the entrance. The main interior chamber was lined with benches, all of which had seen better days, and a shoddy-looking altar stood at the far end. The only light inside came from a number of candles, but the way they had been positioned caused the corners of the room to be shrouded in darkness.

'This place is fucking sinister,' muttered Kurcher as they looked around for any signs of life.

'Cursing is not appreciated here.' The voice echoed from the back of the room. 'Kindly leave if you plan on exhibiting profanity again.'

Kurcher rolled his eyes. 'We'll gladly be on our way once we ask you some questions. Care to step into the light?'

'Very well.' A man appeared near the altar, his face pale in the candlelight. 'I am Anton and this is my church. How can I help?'

Kurcher and Broekow approached warily. Something felt off about the place.

'We're looking for someone,' said Kurcher, pulling his HDU from beneath the stolen uniform. 'We thought he might have come here as he is quite the religious type and I doubt there are too many other churches nearby.'

The priest moved further into the light and they could see that he was dangerously thin, with receding hair and sunken cheeks. 'If I can help then I will.'

Kurcher held out the HDU, showing him the image of Maric. 'Recognise him?'

One of Anton's eyebrows lifted. 'I do. He came here several days ago seeking refuge, but I turned him away.'

'Why? I thought you priests accepted anyone into your flock.'

Anton ignored the remark. 'He needed to find himself. He was struggling with his identity and I simply didn't trust him.'

Kurcher snorted. 'Struggling with his identity? You have no idea. Do you know where he went?'

'Why are you seeking him?' asked Anton, eyeing the two men with sudden suspicion.

'Because he's a lost soul and needs to be rescued.' Kurcher was beginning to lose patience. 'Do you know where he went or am I wasting my fucking time?'

The priest glanced at Broekow, who simply shrugged. 'He is sometimes seen preaching on the concourse near the medical centre. That's all I know. I'd like you to leave now.'

Without another word, Kurcher obliged. Broekow caught him up as he headed further along the street towards the large green and red sign of the med building.

'If a priest pisses you off, I don't think you're going to get on with Maric,' commented the sniper.

'Fine by me,' snapped Kurcher. 'I don't have time for anyone who still believes there is a god. That belief has killed millions of people.'

Broekow looked back at the church. 'Well, if there is a god, he well and truly screwed up when he made us.'

As they neared the med centre, a security team was leaving the building. Kurcher couldn't see their faces behind the dark visors, but he wasn't taking any chances so turned his head as they passed. Broekow chose to gaze at the floor.

It was too much to hope that Maric would be standing in plain view on the concourse. After scanning the people wandering past for several minutes, Kurcher pointed at an alley opposite the med centre.

'Go wait over there and keep an eye out. I'll stay here and hopefully he'll show his face.'

As Broekow nodded and made his way across the concourse, Kurcher found himself watching the streets instead for Rane. He didn't care what orders he had been given. If he just happened to cross paths with Rane, so be it. The thought of finally being able to put a gun to the killer's head and pull the trigger made him very happy. The Parinax probably had a hand in his elation too. The only downside was that Rane was probably already trying to find a way out of Harper. He still had his own sick rules: find the victim, immobilise, torture then kill them, frame someone else and get the hell out.

After two hours of tedious waiting, Kurcher's app highlighted a face among a wave of people. Maric was calmly walking towards the med centre, a smile on his face as though he didn't have any concerns. The man's striking trait was a streak of silver through his otherwise dark hair, plus he walked with a slight limp.

'Got you,' mumbled Kurcher as his app implant logged Maric's features, making him easier to track.

Maric broke from the people around him and approached the med centre. He then waited near the entrance, producing a small book from inside his dusty-looking jacket which he began to flick through.

Kurcher met Broekow halfway across the concourse. 'I'll approach him and get him to lead me to a quieter area where we can talk. You follow at a distance. I may need you when I decide to take him down.'

'Be careful,' warned Broekow. 'The man you see there is Maric. If Choice decides to show his face, you'll know about it. He's probably got a knife under his jacket somewhere.'

'Just be ready.'

Kurcher headed for his target, undoing his maintenance uniform slightly so he could easily reach his revolver. He hoped all of the other crims he had to find were as bold as Maric. As he got nearer, he saw a man and woman exit the med centre, prompting Maric to burst into voice.

'My friends, the doctors inside can heal your wounds. But I can help to heal your souls.'

The couple veered away from him. He did not give up. 'I only ask that you pray with me. Pray for your souls to be cleansed and for our Lord to keep you safe in these dangerous times.'

As the couple hastily shuffled away from Maric, Kurcher realised what Broekow had meant earlier. The priest at the church was bad enough, but here was a man who got in peoples' faces to preach God's will. He watched him for a while longer, talking at anyone who entered or left the med centre.

There was a strange innocence about Maric, with his warm smile and an accent betraying his origins. It seemed odd that this preacher had been a member of Taurus Galahad, joining them when he was still a teenager because of his aptitude for apps and electronics. He had managed to get away from the horrors of the Holy Revolt in Central Europe only to make the mistake of trying to visit his sick mother six years ago and getting himself captured by Revenants. They were to blame for what happened next.

'This book has helped me on many occasions.' Maric tried to get the attention of some other people who had left the med centre. 'It can help you too. Believe in the power of God and welcome Him into your hearts.'

'I want to believe.' Kurcher felt sick saying the words as he approached. 'But I have seen terrible things. How can I trust in a God who lets them happen?'

Maric weighed him up for a moment then waved the book in the air. 'Your question is on the lips of many people. You simply have to trust in the wisdom of our Lord.'

Kurcher pushed the ruse further. 'I have heard you before and have only now found the courage to speak with you. I truly do agree with some of the things you say, but I need to know more.'

'You are a maintenance worker here?'

'Yes. South side mainly.'

'You are unique then because most of your fellow workers tend to mock me instead of listening to me.' Maric stepped close and laid one hand on his shoulder. 'But one man can change the views of many.'

'I'm Callum.' It was the first name that came to mind. 'What do I call you?'

'My name is Maric and I shall help you, my friend.'

'I would feel more comfortable if we could speak away from prying eyes.'

Maric gazed deep into Kurcher's eyes for a moment, as if trying to read his mind. 'Very well. I know a place. It is quieter and I would gladly discuss God's will further with you there.'

'Please. Lead the way, Maric.'

Kurcher made sure he gave Broekow a knowing glance as he followed the preacher across the concourse and into one of the alleys. With a number of people still moving around nearby and the glow of the signs above, Kurcher knew he just had to be patient before he made his move.

'It is only recently that I have seen you,' he said, preferring to sound keen rather than walking in silence. 'Where were you before?'

'Different places,' came the soft answer, barely audible over the sounds of the women calling to them from a nearby brothel. 'Most recently Sullivan's Rest, but I was keen to leave that place.'

'How come?'

'It is a disgusting place and best avoided.'

Kurcher noticed that the ceiling was getting lower the further they walked. They were heading into a network of corridors and backstreet establishments. 'Harper is not exactly the nicest place to live.'

Maric did not look back at him. 'How long have you been here?'

'Most of my life.'

'So why not leave if you dislike the colony so much?'

Kurcher had to be careful not to get too wrapped up in his false tales. 'Some day I'll leave. When the time is right.'

'God will help you to understand your place in the universe.'

Kurcher gauged Maric's strength as he followed. The preacher was shorter and thinner, plus his limp would hinder his movement overall. Still, he was only twenty-nine years old and his reactions were likely to be reasonable.

The old jacket he wore gave no clue as to what he might have been concealing. As Broekow had said, Choice favoured a small blade when he went about his business. That gave Kurcher some satisfaction knowing he had range on his side.

'Where are we going?' he asked Maric's back.

'Not much further,' came the calm reply. 'As you can tell, this part of the colony is quieter at this time. There is a place around the corner where we can talk.'

Kurcher reached beneath his uniform and gripped his revolver. He hoped that the appearance of the weapon would not cause Choice to surface. Maric would be much easier to handle.

In the corridor ahead was a small security post, manned by four armed

81

men. Kurcher swiftly pulled his hand away from the revolver but realised the security team were hardly even paying attention to any passers-by. Still, they were all carrying rifles manufactured by Sapphire Nova and those things packed a real punch. He tried to look as casual as possible, keeping a reasonable distance behind Maric.

The preacher suddenly stopped next to the post and Kurcher's gut clenched.

'Please help me,' Maric called to them. 'This man following me has a gun and is threatening to kill me.'

Four rifles swung up to aim at Kurcher, who immediately lifted his hands in the air.

'On the floor now,' yelled one of the team, stepping forward.

Kurcher's mind raced. 'I don't have a gun. I'm just a worker here.'

'A worker who has apps designed by Taurus Galahad,' added Maric from behind the security force.

'I said get on the floor or we'll shoot you,' growled the guard from behind his visor.

Kurcher caught sight of Maric but the preacher was wearing a different face and gave the enlister a wicked grin before disappearing along the corridor. At the same time, Kurcher's sight app shut down, making him blink in surprise.

'Things were going so well,' he muttered, kneeling slowly. 'You security types are always so keen to point those rifles at someone. Do you ever stop to think or are you programmed to be complete assholes?'

The leader of the security team stepped forward and struck Kurcher across the face with the back of one gloved hand, sending him sprawling onto the metal floor. With his vision swimming, Kurcher cursed himself for his poor choice of words. All he was trying to do was buy some time.

As one of his colleagues began speaking into a comms device on his wrist, the sec leader loomed over Kurcher. 'Anything else you want to say?'

'Yeah.' This was such a bad idea. 'Turn around and walk away before you and your team get hurt.'

'Can you believe this fucking guy?' the leader asked his men, chuckling.

As he raised the butt of his rifle, looking to land a knockout blow to the centre of Kurcher's forehead, a loud crack echoed in the corridor. The sec leader fell backwards and landed heavily before his dumbstruck men, a smoking hole through his visor.

Kurcher's revolver was in his hand in an instant. He fired three times before leaping up and sprinting back the way he had originally come. Two bullets missed as the sec team dived for cover behind their post. The third took one man in the leg, shattering his kneecap.

Broekow fired two covering shots as Kurcher slid around the corner to join him. 'What happened? I only lost sight of you for a moment.'

'Choice happened,' grimaced the enlister, spitting blood from his split lip. 'Nice shot by the way.'

'They're calling in reinforcements,' Broekow told him as he peered back at the sec post.

'We've got to get after Choice, but he scrambled my tracking.' Kurcher could see a line of data at the very top of his vision giving him an error code. 'We've got to get past that sec team now. Can you take care of them?'

Broekow hesitated then nodded. Checking his ammo clip, he drew in a deep breath before stepping around the corner and walking calmly towards the post. One guard glanced out from behind his cover and got a bullet through the brain. The one with the shattered kneecap was trying to drag himself to safety and had dropped his rifle. Broekow ignored him for the time being. As he approached the post, he heard a sharp intake of breath ahead, giving away the position of the last guard. As the man jumped up and sprayed a wild arc of bullets along the corridor, Broekow crouched behind the low wall of the post and waited. As soon as the last shot rang out, he rose instantly and fired once. At such close range, the guard's skull blew apart with a grisly crack.

As Kurcher joined him, Broekow stood over the wounded guard who had started pleading for his life. 'And that was without your apps,' noted the enlister.

'Yeah.' Broekow was staring down at the doomed man. 'The more Nova men we kill, the worse it will be for us.'

Kurcher could see doubt spreading across the sniper's face. Pushing Broekow to the side, he shot the stricken guard once in the head. 'No time for thoughts of morality. Kill or be killed.'

Broekow moved to pick up one of the rifles. Kurcher shook his head. They didn't need to be weighed down with heavier weaponry.

'How're we supposed to find him now?' asked Broekow as they began searching the maze of corridors beyond the post.

Kurcher didn't have an answer. He hadn't seen the change in Maric back on the concourse. Choice was an app genius so would have known what data-infused eyes looked like, even those with minimal reflection.

'How would he have known it was Taurus Galahad tech unless he had a way to recognise the coding?'

'He'd developed his own apps, don't forget,' Broekow reminded him. 'He's probably been working on new ones since Cooke released us too.'

'My sight app needs rebooting. Good job he didn't shut down any other apps.'

'What do you mean?'

Kurcher really wished he thought before speaking sometimes. 'Nothing. We should check any nearby tech stores or...'

Something rolled into their path, but they were too slow to recoil. The pulse grenade activated, sending out a small but powerful shock wave that blew both men off their feet and sent their weapons flying.

A moment later, four sec guards were standing over them. They couldn't make out what was being said, although they could probably guess.

'More Nova goons,' groaned Kurcher, his own voice sounding distant. He hadn't intended saying it out loud, but the situation was already dire.

The guards began talking to each other, with one of them seemingly wanting to execute Kurcher and Broekow right there. The others pushed his rifle away. Another guard started speaking into his comms device.

Kurcher knew he was screwed. If they weren't both shot in the head now then Devlin would certainly want to interrogate him to find out why a Taurus Galahad enlister had crept into his colony along with a wanted man. He couldn't even contact Frost as that would surely seal her fate too. He thought about how she would try to flee Rikur and how the guardians orbiting the planet would simply destroy the *Kaladine* in an instant. As the effect of the pulse grenade began to abate, he could hear the guards much clearer and the sound of Devlin's furious voice was crackling from their comms. It seemed the new head of security wanted them alive after all.

'Fuck it.' Kurcher banged the back of his head against the cold floor for getting himself caught, although the pain didn't register thanks to the Parinax.

One of the guards suddenly cried out, his yell turning into a strange gurgling noise. Kurcher lifted his head in time to see a flash of steel from behind the guard standing over him. A spray of blood doused both Kurcher and Broekow as the guard's head spun into the air and landed several feet behind his body.

Kurcher reacted first, leaping up and retrieving his revolver. When he turned back, wiping the blood from his eyes, he saw a lithe figure darting from one side of the corridor to the other, towards the only guard left standing. The other three were most definitely dead. The one who had wanted to shoot Kurcher and Broekow straight away had a gaping wound in his belly. The one who had been speaking into his comms device had had his

84

throat opened.

A rifle shot rang out and Kurcher saw the agile killer take a bullet to the arm, spinning him round violently as he approached the guard. He also saw the sword in the man's other hand lash out and slice across the guard's throat, cutting through the reinforced uniform as though it were paper. Blood spattered onto the wall and the guard crumpled to join the rest of his team.

Kurcher strode forward, raising the revolver at his wounded saviour. 'Not exactly how I expected our first proper conversation to begin.'

Edlan Rane crouched down and wiped the blood from his blade, wincing at the pain in his arm. 'I didn't expect to have to rescue you, Davian. Seems you don't make friends too easily.'

'I don't care what you just did,' Kurcher growled at him. 'I've waited a long time to end your sick killing spree.'

'And how many people have *you* murdered, Davian? A lot more than me, I'd wager.'

Broekow appeared alongside Kurcher. 'We don't have time to wait around here.'

'He's right.' Rane nonchalantly sheathed his sword beneath his long jacket. 'Shall we go?'

Kurcher tasted blood in his mouth, but couldn't tell whether it was his or not. 'There is no *we*. *You* end here.'

'Not if you want Maric.'

Kurcher desperately wanted to squeeze the trigger and watch Rane die, but he found his finger frozen in place. 'What are you talking about?'

Rane laughed as he stepped over a pool of blood congealing at his feet. 'I've been keeping a close eye on our schizo friend since arriving here. I know where he will go.'

'Why are you doing this?' Broekow asked.

'Because I know why you're after Maric and I decided to help you catch him.' Rane smirked at the expression on Kurcher's face. 'Plus I felt it was time that you and I met properly. I know you can't just let me go once we find him and I'm not expecting you to. I can help you, Davian.'

'You're a fucking serial killer,' spat the enlister. 'I've chased you across worlds and systems, getting myself in trouble with other corps in the process. What makes you think I won't just blow your head off right now?'

'You know you don't stand a hope in hell of finding Maric before Devlin's sec forces find you and they'll be here in a few seconds.'

Kurcher's mind raced as he tried to comprehend what was happening. 'You can't possibly know why we're here. You're a liar, Rane. Those people you framed can vouch for that.'

'He's one of seven.' Rane's emerald eyes glinted. 'As is Sieren.'

Kurcher and Broekow exchanged bemused glances before Rane continued. 'You're going to need my help, trust me.'

'I don't trust you.' Kurcher studied the killer's face, but found no answers there. 'Why come here, kill Portman then help us?'

Rane looked over his shoulder as if he heard something. 'I have my reasons and will gladly explain more later. Right now we have to leave. I swear that, once we find Maric, I will surrender my weapons to you and leave with you on your ship.'

The sound of heavy boots on metal grating could be heard. Kurcher flicked his revolver to gesture Rane away and, with one last look down at the dead guards, followed. Once they found and apprehended Choice, he would still put a bullet in Rane's skull and next time wouldn't be deterred.

~

Frost tapped at the console as she smoked her fourth cigarette in twenty minutes. Not hearing from Kurcher always made her nervous, even when she knew comms silence was necessary.

The cockpit was a disgusting shade of beige thanks to the morning atmosphere. It was a windy day; clouds of dust and debris blew horizontally across the *Kaladine*. Once or twice, a stone bounced off the hull and made her jump.

Frost grew more anxious by the minute. Her eyes scanned the sky for signs of approaching Sapphire Nova ships. She felt exposed now that the morning had arrived, plus their ship was sitting well away from the others on the docking platform. She tried to distract herself by guessing what the four ships sharing the platform were doing there. The largest was approximately the same size as the *Kaladine*, but was emblazoned with a Nova emblem plus the name *Herald*. She surmised it was a courier vessel, transporting various goods from one Nova world to the next.

The next was much smaller and a deep green colour, plus it had no helium-3 drive. It looked worn out and no doubt was an engineer's nightmare, giving the impression that it was simply based on Rikur, perhaps to move material from colony to colony.

The other two ships were harder to read. One was possibly a planethopper, designed to go between Rikur and Ishar, as it was similar to the sort of ships she used to fly before joining Kurcher. The other looked like a decommissioned gunship, with obvious welds where weapons once sat.

There was no name on it, leading her to believe it was a private vessel now, belonging to someone at Harper with the money to run it.

Her mind drifted back to her first assignment after qualifying as a pilot. Taurus Galahad made her a co-pilot on a rickety transport that only shuttled passengers back and forth on Earth. She recalled the way it took her breath away as the transport touched the edge of space before descending once more into the atmosphere. Back then, the sight of the stars and the infinite void had been the most inviting thing she had ever seen. Four years later, she had to take the controls of a planethopper after the pilot had been killed during a pirate attack. She had guided the damaged vessel to Titan Station and still remembered the look on the faces of the engineering team who came aboard to fix it. They had told her it should never have made it to Titan.

Those times seemed so long ago now. It felt like she had been at the controls of the *Kaladine* all her life and just parting with the ship made her nauseous. At times, her implanted pilot app made her feel like she and the *Kaladine* were one. It was an odd sensation, open to ridicule often from Kurcher, but she liked it.

A shadow flitted across the cockpit and Frost leaned forward to peer out into the beige. Above Harper, two small ships had begun circling. A blinking blue light on them told her they were security vessels. Her anxiety intensified further. They were looking for something and she hoped it wasn't her. The *Kaladine* wouldn't remain unnoticed forever.

~

The tech store was one of the smallest Kurcher had ever seen, with one flickering sign above the door stating that beyond was an app wonderland. He doubted it would live up to such a boast.

'This is his usual haunt?' Broekow asked Rane as they approached.

'Yes. When he's Choice, that is. I'm not sure the store owner is still alive though.'

'Let's go get him then, so we can leave this fucking colony.' Kurcher urged the two men forward but Rane turned to face him, finding a revolver placed against his temple again.

'You have apps, Davian, as does Broekow.'

'So what?' Kurcher's Parinax was wearing off, but he was trying to wait until returning to the *Kaladine* before boosting again.

'Yeah, my apps are offline,' added Broekow.

Rane smiled. 'I don't have any apps, so there's less chance of me being affected by any traps he may have set up in there. Let me go in and draw him

87

out.'

'Why would I let you do that?' Kurcher found Rane's arrogance unbearable. 'For all I know, you're working with Choice to get me out the way.'

'You're such a pessimist, Davian.'

'Stop fucking calling me that.'

'It's your name.' Rane shrugged. 'You must've read up on this guy. You know how he reacts when someone questions his genius. If he has taken over control of this store and aims to sell standard apps to fund his own work, let me go in to haggle with him. I'm sure I can get him to dislike me.'

'He's not one to mess with,' Broekow said.

Rane flashed the sniper a look of pure amusement. 'Neither am I.'

Kurcher gestured at Rane's arm. 'That's going to cause problems.'

'I've been shot before. It won't slow me down.'

Eventually, Kurcher gave in. He knew this was their one chance to get hold of Choice before they were run down by security. The sounds of distant alarms could still be heard somewhere behind them.

Rane entered the store, clutching his wounded arm. The injury gave him an obvious reason to engage with the madman who dwelt within. It was not long before he appeared.

'Hey, what're you after today?'

Rane knew straight away that this was not Maric. He could see the tiny square of light in the man's right eye, no doubt an app interface. 'As you can see, I've hurt my arm.' He feigned a pained expression. 'In my job, I seem to pick up injuries like they're going out of fashion and I need some sort of med app to keep the pain at bay.'

Choice grinned. 'I've got just the thing.'

It was not long ago that the man had led Kurcher into a trap, yet here he was acting the innocent shopkeeper. Rane wondered whether he was even aware of the double personality. Something told him he knew full well what he was doing.

'Haven't I seen you on the concourse?' he asked as he was led to a particular section of the store.

'Probably,' chuckled Choice. 'I'm often there.'

'I've seen you outside the med centre sometimes. You're a preacher, right?'

Choice froze for a split second before shaking his head. 'Not me, friend.'

'No, guess not. Must be someone who looks a lot like you.'

'Here.' Choice swept his hand out and several images appeared before

88

them. 'A selection of med apps, and all at competitive prices.'

Rane gave them a cursory glance. 'No, I need something stronger to last longer. These are mediocre at best.'

Choice's tone became sharper. 'Have many apps, do you?'

'None yet. What else do you have?'

Choice's eyes narrowed. 'What job did you say you did here?'

'Maintenance mostly. Odd jobs around the colony.'

The false shopkeeper stared at him for a moment, weighing up whether or not to take Rane at face value. 'If you need something stronger then I can probably custom-build an app for you.'

Rane gave a surprised look. 'I thought building your own tech is illegal. Surely you'd have to bastardise corp tech to do that.' He paused for effect, then continued to manoeuvre the conversation back to where he wanted. 'I knew people who used homemade apps. There were always side effects or malfunctions.'

'They clearly never used my tech,' bristled Choice. 'I've been working on this stuff for a long time and never had any complaints.'

Rane knew that was a lie. Choice's victims were testament to that. 'Can you show me something?'

Choice took him to a counter and produced a small box from under it. Inside was an implant that looked disturbingly like some tiny parasitic bug. 'This is a powerful med implant that'll keep you at peak fitness throughout your working hours.'

'Says you.' Rane sniffed. 'You show me something that looks like it was made a decade ago and just expect me to accept it is what you tell me?'

Choice's lip twitched. 'This is a unique device. You won't find it anywhere else.'

'No, just in some grimy store hidden away in Harper's depths.' Rane bent down and examined the implant closely. 'I'm not going to part with my money without knowing more.'

'You asked for something more powerful,' cried Choice, his eyes darkening. 'This is it. Either buy it or get the fuck out of my store.'

'You haven't even offered a demo. That speaks volumes.'

'You don't deserve my tech.' Spittle flew from Choice's snarling mouth. 'You came here wanting an app and I gave you the options. My apps are the best you will find anywhere, but you're too fucking stupid to see that.'

Rane smiled. 'You do have a short fuse.'

Choice stormed to the door and smashed his hand against the switch to open it. 'Get out.'

Rane crossed his arms and held his ground. 'What makes your apps so damned special? I need to understand what I'm looking at.'

Choice bit. 'I designed that one with increased operational capability, using Sapphire Nova tech and blending it with a reactive agent that stimulates adrenaline. It is a natural high that means you don't feel any pain and your stamina increases. I can't go into more technical jargon as you wouldn't understand.'

'You need to work on your sales technique.' Rane glanced around the small store. 'Come to think of it, I recall walking past this place not so long back and there was a different man working here. What happened to him?'

'He went out of business and I took over.'

'That was quick. Surely it takes time to request your claim on the property to the authorities?' Rane's arm was throbbing so he decided to bring their unpleasant conversation to an end. 'From what I've seen here today, I reckon you're a charlatan trying to sell dodgy wares to the unsuspecting public. I wouldn't be surprised if you've got the true owner tied up in the back... or worse. If I implanted your tech, it would probably poison me.'

Choice looked ready to explode but managed to hold his resolve, pointing at the door. 'I said get out. I won't tell you again.'

This time, Rane brushed past him but stopped in the doorway. 'I'll see what Harper security has to say about this.'

That pressed the right button. Choice was quick as he lunged angrily forward but Rane was quicker, grasping the app specialist's arm and hurling him out into the corridor. It came at a price as a searing pain coursed through his own injured arm. Despite Choice sprawling to the floor outside the store, he was back on his feet instantly with a knife in his hand.

'People like you just don't appreciate my work,' he snarled at Rane. 'My apps will change the way...'

Kurcher's revolver struck Choice hard across the back of the skull, knocking him unconscious.

~

'Shit, shit, shit.'

Frost's pulse quickened as the conflector flat-lined. She tried twice to bring it back to life via her pilot app. Leaping from her seat in the cockpit, she raced down to the engines and crawled into the tight space where the conflector had been fitted. She could smell the burnt wiring before even opening the cover.

'Useless corp bastards,' she muttered. Her eyes scanned the exposed

90

entrails of the machine.

Conflector tech was known for being temperamental and for struggling if used for an extended period of time, but this latest version was supposed to have back-up systems to take over when the primary power began to die. It seemed as though the automatic switch to the auxiliary system hadn't even occurred so the conflector had simply burnt out into scrap parts.

Frost shook her head. She had a decision to make: break the comms silence and contact Kurcher to let him know he had to get out before the security ships returned, or wait. Either way, they risked being discovered. She shuddered at the idea of Sapphire Nova getting their hands on her.

She made her way back to the cockpit, expecting to see a sec force already bearing down on the *Kaladine*, but instead the dock was quiet. She opened up the link to Harper's comms traffic. The first voice she heard was that of Devlin. The acting head of security had ordered another lockdown and she hoped it wasn't due to Kurcher.

A number of small rocks ricocheted off the *Kaladine*, whipped up by the frequent winds. Frost's heart leapt and she cursed the bloody planet again. Rikur was fast becoming her least favourite world to visit and she hoped there would never be a reason to do so again.

After several minutes of listening to the chatter, she picked up enough information to know there had been a *serious incident* leading to the death of several members of Devlin's sec team. There was a full-blown manhunt on within Harper's walls and it would only be a matter of time until they turned their eyes to the docks.

'Time to leave.' Kurcher's voice cut through the comms noise suddenly. Relief flooded through Frost's body, but something in his tone warned her something might not be right.

'Airlock's open. How many should I expect?'

There was no reply, so she checked her pistol was by her side as she headed for the airlock. Five minutes later there was still no sign of the enlister or Broekow. The thought crossed her mind that perhaps Kurcher had been forced at gunpoint back to the *Kaladine* so that Devlin's men could get at her. She momentarily toyed with the idea of locking the ship up again.

'We need two cells prepped.' Kurcher sounded pissed off. 'And we're going to need the med supplies too.'

'Two cells? Who else did you...'

'Just fucking do it.'

By the time the airlock opened, Frost had everything ready as ordered. She watched as four men entered the ship, all wearing breathing masks.

91

Kurcher and Broekow were carrying an unconscious Maric. Behind them, the fourth was clutching his arm. As he removed his mask, Frost couldn't hide her disbelief.

'Get Rane into a cell,' grunted Kurcher. 'Then get us the fuck off this planet.'

Frost marched the ashen killer into one of the small cells at gunpoint. The door locked and Rane slumped down onto the uncomfortable bed, forcing a pained smile. Kurcher and Broekow dragged Maric into the adjacent cell. Frost was relieved that both men made it back alive. When the sniper gave her an exhausted wink, she felt a rare warmth in her cheeks and quickly made her way back to the cockpit.

A simple command through her app and the *Kaladine*'s engines were fired up by the time she got to her seat. A moment later the ship rose into the hazy sky, fighting against the strong winds howling above Harper. Frost was made aware of three sec ships heading in their direction from the other side of the colony. There was no chance of seeing them with a naked eye in the shitty atmosphere, so she had to rely on the *Kaladine*'s sensors.

'Trouble?' Broekow appeared behind her and she instinctively aimed her pistol at him.

'You shouldn't be in here. Where's Kurcher?'

The sniper raised both hands. 'He went to his quarters, I think. Choice crashed his apps and he needs to reset them. I just thought you might need a hand.'

Frost had no time to weigh him up. 'Just sit down and shut up so I can get us out of here.'

Broekow lowered himself into the other seat and Frost, still with pistol levelled at him, issued her command to the *Kaladine*, sending the ship hurtling over Harper and rising sharply into the upper atmosphere.

As the sec ships were left in their wake, Frost caught some chatter coming up from the surface and grimaced. 'I don't know what you did, but Nova are pissed off.'

'Choice got us noticed by Devlin's men. Thanks to Kurcher and Rane, we managed to get back to the maintenance tunnels. But quite a few died down there.'

A warning flashed in Frost's vision. 'Shit. Best hold on.'

'What is it?'

'The guardians have been alerted and one is on an intercept course with us. One hit from them and we'll be orbiting debris.'

Broekow peered out of the screen. All he could see was pitch-black. A

92

moment later, tracking systems kicked in, highlighting the approaching guardian just beyond one of the long transports they had seen when arriving at Rikur.

'It'll be in range soon.'

'I know.' Frost had all of the data she needed lurking at the edge of her app. Pushing the engines as far as she dared, she let out a frustrated cry. 'Let go of us, you bitch.'

Broekow could feel himself being pushed back into the seat. 'What's wrong?'

'Rikur's fucking gravity well. Now shut up and let me do my job.'

The guardian vanished for a moment behind the transport, reappearing a few seconds later. All of her gun ports were open. There was no comms hail aimed at the *Kaladine*. That was a bad sign.

As Frost felt the pull of the gravity well subside, a sense of dread crept up her spine. Guardian vessels may have been slower than other classes, but they were designed to protect worlds and their weapon range was much better than that of an assault ship. The *Kaladine* could outrun them easily, but she knew the Sapphire Nova ship would get one or two shots off before they were at a safe distance.

As they made a break for it, a sudden burst of light made Frost and Broekow grip the arms of their seats. The transport listed to one side as an explosion ripped through its hull, sending black fragments spinning out into the void. As the guardian swooped beneath the floundering ship, it was forced to veer violently away to avoid a collision. By the time it had manoeuvred back into position, the *Kaladine* was long gone.

~

Winter watched the crippled transport trying to recover from the explosion and could imagine the panic the crew must have been experiencing. Once Sapphire Nova had a chance to examine the damage, they would see it was caused by a weapon. But he would be far from the Almaz system by then. Besides, he doubted they would know what that weapon was. Only his ship was fitted with such a device.

As his slender stalker silently left Rikur behind and picked up the *Kaladine*'s signal, he wondered what the Nova reaction would be to Kurcher's somewhat messy visit to Harper. The enlister's subsequent escape would certainly have them calling for blood.

He began preparing a message to send to Santa Cruz, warning him of retaliation. If he would have to intervene on every world Kurcher visited, sooner or later he himself would be noticed. He had thought Kurcher to be much better at operating under the radar. Finishing the message, he sent it immediately on secure comms to the *Requiem*. He could imagine the commander's reaction when he learnt what had happened on Rikur, but confronting Kurcher would only highlight that Santa Cruz had sent someone after him. He wondered who would be the unfortunate soul on the receiving end of the commander's fury this time.

Temple
Lincoln system

Santa Cruz watched the flashes of lightning streak across the surface of Kalvion. Mixed with the dark grey cloud cover which seemed to stretch across the whole of the visible side of the planet, he found it almost beautiful. He knew though that below the clouds was a world eager to tear itself apart. How that biomech freak, Angard, had survived for eight years alone on Kalvion still vexed him.

'Need I remind you that Lincoln is our system?' he asked sharply, looking back at the merc sitting uncomfortably behind the table. 'We tolerate your presence here but you're in no position to refuse, especially when you're playing host to a Sapphire Nova officer and his secret affairs. This isn't a request, Flynn. Give me access to Cairns and the Knights Templar can look the other way.'

Flynn stroked his thick black moustache as he regarded the commander, who had turned back to gaze at Kalvion. The merc then rose slowly from his seat, the patches of chain mail rattling beneath his shirt.

'And when Sapphire Nova come asking about their war hero?' Flynn's voice was deep and resonated off the walls of the small meeting room. 'Do I just tell them that I let you walk in and take him?'

Santa Cruz turned to face him and smiled. 'Who said I was taking him? You simply tell them Commander Cairns and his whore upped and left on a transport. You might even say that he was dangerously high on the drugs he is so fond of.'

Flynn crossed his burly arms. 'So we're just expected to clean up your mess?'

'Exactly.' Santa Cruz rubbed at an ache in his head. 'I'm not really in the mood for discussing this further. Either give me what I want or we'll dismantle your beloved *Temple* piece by piece. I should think you would stand to lose a lot of money while rebuilding the arena.'

Flynn clenched his fists. 'No need for that. I wouldn't want our understanding with Taurus Galahad to come to an unfortunate end. I'll give you Cairns, but I have one request in return. Take him off the station before you kill him. Hell, take him down to Kalvion for all I care. Just don't leave a blood trail here.'

Santa Cruz thought for a moment. He knew his actions would either end whatever deals the Templars were undertaking with Sapphire Nova or at the very least put them on hold. It wasn't his problem though. The mercs prided themselves on working with all of the corps in one way or another, using their vast station as a base of operations, so they would have other funds coming in.

'Fine. As long as he doesn't know we're coming and start firing at us, I promise no blood will be spilled here.'

'Oh, he won't know you're coming,' grinned the merc. 'I doubt he's even crawled out from between her long legs to take a piss yet.'

Santa Cruz shook his head. 'If you really lived up to the name of your organisation, you would have already imprisoned or executed him yourself by now. He is a dangerous man.'

'Aren't we all?' Flynn headed for the door. 'I'll send word to my men to grant you passage straight through to Cairn's love nest. Then I'll give you the directions.'

'One more thing,' called the commander. 'Why Kalvion?'

Flynn flashed him a confused look. 'Why not?'

'You're in our system, don't forget. Last time I passed through Lincoln, you were nearer to Shard. Why go through the pain of moving Temple here?'

'Better clientele.' Flynn's reply was honest. 'If we're near to a Taurus Galahad planet, we tend to get Taurus employees and mercs. Orbiting a quaran, away from your military, the other corps and organisations come out to play. Can't say I blame them for not wanting to get near enough to feel the heat of your razepistols. Besides, those on Shard who enjoy the arena still get some action at our operation on the surface.'

'Are the Templars still growing as an organisation?'

Flynn's eyes narrowed at the question. 'This is the heart of our operation.'

'I keep a close eye on all the merc organisations where I can.' Santa Cruz tapped the window. 'For instance, I know you've tried to establish a base on Kalvion twice over the last couple of years but failed due to the storms. I know you deal illegal apps from Temple. I also know Templars have been seen in the Mars colonies and on Cobb recently.'

'Our people move around all over the place on business,' sniffed Flynn. 'We're not causing any trouble to Taurus.'

'Not yet.' Santa Cruz shrugged. 'Listen, our agreement with the Knights Templar is a mutually beneficial one, but I don't trust you. Why would you be on Cobb? The planet is a wasteland with depleted resources and a dying population.'

'A wasteland you created,' snapped Flynn, instantly regretting the

96

outburst. 'We thought there might be some salvage left on the surface, but the people had to use what they could find just to survive. You left your own settlers there to die and you talk to me about trust?'

Santa Cruz knew he should leave it there, but he wanted the disgruntled merc to understand. 'Cobb is still in a Taurus Galahad system, but those people you speak of turned against each other and against us. They caused the civil war and the massacres that followed.'

'I know what happened. Everyone knows.'

'We left those people there because they turned their back on those who gave them that life on a new world. We merely gave them the independence they so clearly desired.'

Flynn shook his head. 'Whatever. Shall we just get on with this Cairns matter?'

'What else did your Templars see there?' pushed Santa Cruz.

'Old ships.'

The commander frowned. 'You mean the planethoppers we gave them?'

Flynn grinned. 'Nope. These had weapons on them. Style was old, but definitely merc-owned.'

Santa Cruz made a mental note of this. If mercenaries were on Cobb, were they delivering supplies for a price? Perhaps they were selling weapons to the people in preparation for another brewing civil war. Some of the mercs were like parasites, latching on to the weak to drain their last remaining resources. He would look into it when there was time to do so. He had a more pressing matter to attend to.

Flynn was true to his word. As Santa Cruz and his armed escort made their way through the station, the templars turned their backs or disappeared into the shadows. Behind the stoic mask he wore, the commander was extremely relieved. Of all the merc and pirate organisations roaming the galaxy, the Knights Templar were, in his eyes, the best fighters. While the likes of Jericho's Bold were wild and unpredictable, the Templars were calm and measured. Most of them were trained to handle a variety of weapons, both ranged and close combat. They were not to be underestimated. However, Santa Cruz would have had no qualms about destroying Temple and Flynn knew that.

The suite that Rolan Cairns had been given was in a quiet corner of the station, away from prying eyes. As they approached the door, Santa Cruz pulled his HDU from under his jacket.

'We take them alive,' he said quietly to his men. 'But if Cairns opens fire, kill him.'

As they raised their rifles, the commander used the passcode Flynn gave him and the door slid open. His men rushed in, securing an empty lounge. Santa Cruz calmly entered the suite as he swapped the HDU for a pistol. From behind a door to their right came a woman's cry. Santa Cruz smiled as he waved his men forward.

Cairns was so busy pleasuring his mistress that he didn't even hear them enter the bedroom. The dark-haired woman suddenly let out a piercing scream as she noticed the armed men standing at the foot of the bed. It wasn't until she pushed Cairns off and recoiled into the numerous pillows that the Sapphire Nova commander turned.

'Is this a bad time?' smirked Santa Cruz.

Cairns made a clumsy attempt to grab for the weapon under his pile of clothes. Two Taurus men rushed forward and struck him with the butts of their rifles. Cairns sprawled unconscious on the floor, giving Santa Cruz an eyeful he could have done without. The woman screamed again.

'Shut her up,' ordered the commander. 'Get both of them to the *Requiem*.'

'His clothes, sir?'

Santa Cruz turned away with a smile. 'Leave him naked.'

Cairns was as vocal as expected when he came to, just as they were carrying him along the boarding pylon. The Nova officer was a strong man, but Santa Cruz had chosen his men wisely and they easily subdued him. Once on board, the *Requiem* disembarked from *Temple* but remained in orbit around Kalvion.

'Those fucking traitorous Templars,' spat Cairns as he and his unconscious mistress were deposited in one of the cold airlocks. 'And you, Cruz. What the fuck do you think you're doing? You've signed a death warrant for your whole crew.'

Santa Cruz waved his men away as the inner airlock door closed, then opened the intercom. 'I'll forgive your tone and the fact that you still can't get my name right. Tell me, Rolan, if this situation were reversed, would you not be doing the exact same thing?'

'I probably would've found you with some boy rather than a woman.'

'Ever the charmer. Listen, if you tell me what I need to know, I won't kill you. I'll drop you on Kalvion and you can spend your days hoping someone rescues you before the planet kills you. Or you can spend your time fucking that whore. Up to you really.'

'You don't need her,' Cairns said, casting a fearful glance at the naked woman lying next to him. 'Leave her be.'

'Call her a bargaining tool. Now, why don't you start by telling me what

98

Sapphire Nova are up to? I know you're spying on various Taurus facilities and systems, but I want to know the names of your agents on our worlds. I also want to know where your fleets are.'

'Are we making you nervous?' Cairns was trying to stand as proud as one can with his manhood on show. 'Worried we're going to uncover more remnants before you and beat you to the prize?'

'Not really. You started searching Krondahar hoping you'd find something like we did in Coldrig, but I imagine it hasn't worked out too well for you so far.'

'What makes you think we haven't found anything?'

'Your tone. Oh, I'm sure you've found plenty over time, just nothing significant. Nothing that would lead you to believe you could be the dominant corp in this galaxy.'

'Taurus may have more ships and resources, *Cruz*, but Nova have the better firepower.'

'Perhaps. If you're not going to tell me about your men and ships, explain to me what your orders are from Straunia.'

Cairns shrugged. 'There are no orders yet. I'm on leave, remember.'

'Of course. I'll make sure to let your wife and children know where you were. They are based on Straunia, aren't they?'

'Fuck you.' Cairns pointed at his mistress, who was beginning to stir. 'Take her out of here and then do what we both know you're going to do.'

Santa Cruz sighed into the intercom. 'I didn't really expect you to give up Nova's secrets. You're too loyal for that. Obviously not to your wife, but I guess the corp means *everything* to you.'

Cairns moved to stand before the inner airlock, glaring at Santa Cruz through the small circular screen. 'When they find out what you did, Sapphire Nova will hunt you down. Nowhere will be safe for you. You are bringing about the end of Taurus Galahad if you kill me, you do realise that?'

'You think too highly of yourself.' Santa Cruz straightened his jacket and cleared his throat. 'Commander Rolan Cairns, you are guilty of numerous war crimes against Taurus Galahad including the destruction of colonist vessels bound for the Haskell system, killing some three hundred and forty-five innocents. You have also destroyed three other Taurus vessels during the last five years consisting of an explorer-class and two assault-class. You yourself shot and killed Commander Anders McCall during a firefight on Cobb in 2602. For these crimes, you are sentenced to be executed.'

Cairns glanced back at his mistress. 'Let her go first.'

Santa Cruz pressed the outer airlock release, then stepped up close to the reinforced screen. For a second, the two commanders stared at one another until Cairns stepped back to the woman and knelt down next to her. Santa Cruz saw him whisper the word *sorry*.

A moment later, the outer airlock opened. While she was thin enough to be sucked straight through the gap in the doors cleanly, Cairns was not so lucky. As he hit the airlock, it tore his shoulder open, nearly wrenching his arm off. Then he too was gone. Santa Cruz could see Kalvion's torrid colours roiling beyond the airlock and he found himself gazing at the sight for some time. When he eventually made his way back up to the command deck, he had decided that the planet was indeed beautiful after all.

Enlister-class vessel Kaladine
Oralia system

'I'm not buying it.'

Rane cocked his head to one side. 'Which part?'

'All of it.' Kurcher ran one finger along the flat of Rane's blade. 'You ever wondered what your victims felt like as you cut them with this?'

'I know what it feels like.'

The two men were facing each other in the cramped confines of the cell. Rane had remained seated as Kurcher began his questioning, claiming to still be feeling the effects of the painkiller Frost had given him.

'I do one of two things with criminals,' said Kurcher, his eyes still on the sword in his hand. 'Enlist or eliminate. I'm not going to enlist you.'

Rane smiled. 'I know what your job is, Davian. I also know that Taurus Galahad have got you right where they want you.'

Kurcher raised an eyebrow. 'Yeah, so you said. You base this sweeping statement on the fact you've been intercepting messages on coded comms signals. Signals that are designed to be deciphered only by corp tech.'

'Dated tech. Once you know what you're listening out for, it's easy to break the code.'

'This is how you knew about the crims I'm chasing, right?'

'Yes. A message from Commander Jorelian Santa Cruz to one of his contacts. Probably the same person who killed Ged Cooke and his team.'

Kurcher studied Rane's face carefully. How could he possibly trust anything this killer said? 'So, when you realised I had been reassigned, you decided to go to Rikur and *help* me get hold of Maric?'

'Like I said, there is more at stake here than you realise. The data you're looking for dooms everyone who gets too near to it. Taurus have been making people disappear. Scientists, researchers, explorers... and enlisters.'

'Cooke discovered the data though, so how could anyone else be involved?'

Rane rolled his eyes theatrically. 'You're not looking at the bigger picture here. The corps have all been upping activities lately in the unknown sectors. Sapphire Nova in Krondahar, Libra Centauri in Farrin and Taurus Galahad in Coldrig. They found something in Coldrig back in 2594, something the other corps got wind of and wanted in on. Did you never wonder why the warring between corps started in the first place?'

The Parinax coursing through Kurcher's veins made the light in the cell pulse, emitting warm halos of energy. The edge of his mouth twitched. 'Okay, if you're so fucking smart, what did they find?'

Rane's eyes narrowed. 'I don't know, but they all wanted a piece of it. One message mentioned *several* finds, along with a list of names. They were the explorers who first made the discoveries along with scientists, doctors and researchers who formed project teams to study whatever it was. Those people then began to disappear.'

'And was Ged Cooke's name on this list?'

'You're not an idiot, Davian,' sighed Rane. 'Stop acting like one.'

Kurcher stepped forward and the back of his fist struck Rane across the face. 'You're a prisoner. *Start* acting like one.'

Rane managed a wry smile, despite the red mark on his cheek. 'I gave myself up so I could help you. You have my weapons and I left my ship on Rikur. If you want to kill me, fine. If you want to keep me locked up, fine. Just listen to what I'm saying.'

'Another thing that doesn't make sense. Why help the man who's been sent to kill you?'

'Because the data file you're looking for may well be the key. It holds answers as to what the hell is going on with the corps.' Rane could see the unimpressed expression appearing on the enlister's face. 'People are going to keep pursuing me for as long as I live, sent by the corps. I figured that helping you was the best thing to do. If they get their hands on this file, it would be bad news not just for us but for everyone in this galaxy.'

Kurcher laughed, shaking his head and pointing Rane's own sword at the killer. 'You are just an attention-seeking murderer who clearly has some hidden agenda and I think I might just run you through with this right now. Nobody will mourn Edlan Rane.'

'Ged Cooke had a family,' Rane stated loudly. 'Why would he turn against Taurus and risk everything?'

'Greed. He knew the data was important but thought he could get a nice payout from it.'

'Cooke is the one who found the data accidentally. He found out what it really was and decided that giving it to Taurus was a bad idea. That's why he implanted it into one of these crims, that's why he let them all go and that's why he was killed. Now the corp are desperate to get their hands on it before Libra, Nova or even Sigma. I think it's the key to becoming the dominant force across the galaxy, but I don't much like the idea of Taurus winning the war and making others disappear... on a grander scale.'

'This is all bullshit,' growled Kurcher. 'I'm going to find these crims, deliver them to Santa Cruz and be on my way with a nice fat pay packet. I'm going to keep you locked up in here until I decide how best to execute you.'

As the enlister opened the door to leave, Rane stood up. 'If you were going to execute me, you would've done it by now. Don't deliver that data to them, Davian.'

Kurcher threw another punch, knocking the killer back onto his ass. 'Keep giving me a reason. I enjoy beating pieces of shit like you.' He stepped out of the cell. 'Why kill Portman?'

Rane looked up at him and shrugged. 'Seemed like it might cause the biggest distraction and give you the time you needed to find Maric.'

Kurcher stared at him in silence for a moment, then snorted. 'More bullshit.' He closed the cell door and after storing Rane's sword away, called for Broekow and Frost to meet him in the rec room.

By the time they arrived, Kurcher was leaning against one wall with the sullen-looking Maric seated at the table before him, hands cuffed behind his back.

'How long?' the enlister asked his pilot.

'Ninety-two hours. Thanks to that shit conflector, tracking beacons will have picked us up the moment we entered the system.'

'Once we've finished here, send the message.' Kurcher noted Broekow's confused expression. 'The Oakleys aren't just going to let us walk in and take their precious daughter. As soon as we approach Cradle, their ships will block us. If we have a different route down onto the planet, it'll make our task slightly easier, and the Palerska family just so happen to hate the Oakleys. They'll see this as an opportunity too good to pass up.'

Broekow shot Maric a wary glance. 'So what're we going to do with him?'

Kurcher took a seat across from his captive. 'It's a good question. First, I need to know who the hell I'm actually talking to.'

Maric lifted his head, regarding Kurcher with sad eyes. 'I am sorry that you had to restrain him. Did he hurt you?'

'You sound like the preacher now. How can I be sure? Choice does a very good impression of Maric, it seems.'

'You have suppressed his apps. If you were speaking with him, he would not be so calm right now.'

Kurcher glanced at Broekow. 'What do you reckon?'

The sniper shrugged. 'Hard to know.'

'Thanks for your input.' Kurcher leant across the table. 'From what I've

103

seen, Choice is a coward and tends to hide behind Maric. Right now, he's probably sulking because we put an abrupt stop to his Harper activities. I guess we'll start without him.'

'My book.' Maric's expression was almost pained. 'Do you have it?'

'Along with that knife of yours.'

'It's not mine.'

'Whatever. That book made for interesting reading.'

There was a flicker of concern in Maric's eyes. 'It's my bible. I've had it since my time on Earth. Please, allow me to have it back.'

Kurcher leaned back again. He had flicked through the dusty tome Maric had been carrying, expecting to find it full of religious writings. Instead, it contained mostly manic scribbles that could only have been made by Choice. They were the words of a troubled mind struggling to get to grips with reality, yet it seemed to hold real meaning to the preacher.

'I'll consider letting you have it back. First I need you to understand why we were sent to find you.'

Maric turned his head slowly to look up at Broekow. 'I understand why. We are to atone for our sins by helping you. Why else would this man be allowed to walk around your ship so freely?'

'Not so freely as you might think,' Broekow told him.

'You were once a Taurus Galahad man,' Kurcher stated, drawing Maric's eyes back across the table. 'They are willing to forget your crimes if you agree to work for them again.'

'Forget but not forgive.' The hint of a smile appeared on the preacher's thin lips. 'The crimes you speak of weren't mine though.'

'Let's not play this game. You may not have been in control when you murdered those people, but it was still your body.' Kurcher tried to bite back his anger. He was still pissed that Choice had duped him so easily. 'You are a talented electronics specialist. Your alter ego is even more talented. If you help us now, Taurus will wipe your slate clean.'

'A chance at redemption.' Maric thought for a moment, then shook his head. 'No, you cannot trust him. I can try to subdue him for as long as I can, but he is a danger to you and to the corporation.'

Broekow moved to stand next to Kurcher. 'This is the only chance you're going to get. I took the opportunity and would advise you do too.'

Kurcher glanced up at the sniper. Broekow was being very bold standing alongside him like he was a true part of the crew. While he didn't like it, perhaps it would have the desired effect on Maric.

'We understand Choice is a dangerous individual.' Not the best word

104

Kurcher could have used. 'The unfortunate fact is that we need his expertise too. Besides, I doubt you could control him.'

'It is easier in the quieter times,' said Maric softly. 'Why would you want his help?'

'Do you remember Angard?'

Maric's eyes shifted to Broekow for a moment. 'I do.'

'We're on our way to Cradle, where we hope to *persuade* Tara Oakley to join us and accept the corp's offer of enlisting. Angard left Sullivan's Rest with her so we believe he is somewhere on the planet too. He is volatile and will be extremely hard to subdue.'

'Unless you have a way to disrupt his apps,' nodded Maric. 'You need to incapacitate him.'

Kurcher watched the preacher's eyes closely. 'Yes. If Choice disrupted my app so efficiently, I'm hoping he can modify his tech to affect biomechs too.'

Maric pursed his lips. 'I fear that lost soul cannot be saved. If you are hoping to enlist Angard too, I'm afraid you will fail. The best thing for him is to be cleansed... body, mind and soul.'

'Kill him, you mean.' Broekow shrugged. 'Might be the kindest thing.'

'We're not killing him,' snapped Kurcher. 'He is seen as an asset to the corp, just as the two of you are. If he won't come quietly, he gets locked in a cell until we get him back to Taurus.'

'And you really believe Angard would stay locked up?' Maric asked the enlister.

Kurcher pushed himself up from his seat. 'Either you help us or I'll lock you up too. Or maybe I'll let you share a cell with Edlan Rane.'

Maric flinched. 'That man is *evil*. You should not have brought him on board.'

'You're a saint then?' Kurcher laughed. 'Just because you preach the word of God, that doesn't make you innocent.'

'You should all welcome God into your...'

'Quit the religious bullshit. Will you help us with Angard?'

As Maric fell into quiet contemplation and Kurcher's patience drained from him, Frost took a gamble. 'Redemption comes in various forms. A man of God with a past as dark as yours must surely seek out opportunities when they arise.'

All three men looked at her with similar surprised expressions, but it was Broekow who spoke up quickly.

'She's right. This is your first step on the road to atonement.'

Maric's gaze moved from Frost to Broekow and finally to Kurcher. 'You all speak of redemption and atonement, but my conscience is clear. It was not I who committed these crimes.'

'I've had enough of this shit,' snarled Kurcher, reaching across the table and dragging Maric onto his feet by the collar of his jacket. 'You're going back in the cell to think about this.'

'Take your fucking hands off me.'

Kurcher allowed himself a smug smile. 'I hoped that might bring you out, Choice.'

'Fuck you.' The suddenly wild eyes looked nervously around the rec room. 'Where is that piece of shit, Rane?'

Kurcher shoved him back down into the seat. 'And here we were thinking we'd been talking to Maric all this time.'

'Most of the time you were,' smirked Choice. He looked up at Broekow. 'So you sold out to this company lapdog then.'

'I didn't want Taurus hunting me down anymore,' the sniper stated. 'Continually looking over your shoulder gets tedious pretty quickly.'

Choice turned his gaze to Frost. 'Looking at this is better, eh? Was it the promise of having your crimes erased that convinced you or did this enlister sweeten the deal by whoring out his assistant?'

Frost held his leering stare as she took out a cigarette and lit it. 'Your file said you liked to talk. Personally I'd rather listen to that *Bible*-basher spout some more shit about God.'

Choice opened his mouth, ready to make another crude quip. Kurcher grabbed his jaw roughly with one hand. 'If you've been listening to our conversations with Maric, you'll know why we didn't just kill you on Rikur. You'll help us by creating an app that can disrupt Angard's biomech implants, giving us time to apprehend him. You do that and Taurus Galahad will consider enlisting you for your expertise.'

'I've killed a lot of people, enlister. We both know the corp aren't going to enlist me back into their ranks. I'm too high-risk. I'd be dead minutes after helping you capture that freak.'

Kurcher released his grip. 'I know you don't like to be wrong. You like to think you're so much smarter than everyone else. Well in this case, you *are* wrong.'

Choice rubbed his aching jaw. 'Really? What happened to Enlister Cooke after he let us go, pray tell?'

Kurcher weighed up the benefit of being honest. 'Cooke is dead. He turned against Taurus and was subsequently killed when he tried fighting them.'

'So the corp are prepared to kill someone who tries to leave their service but are willing to forgive us our misdemeanours after we murdered some of their own?'

'Would you rather be hunted down and executed?' Broekow asked. 'Or rot in some cell?'

'Clearly he would,' muttered Frost.

'I don't need all three of you trying to play bad cop here,' grimaced Choice. 'It's giving me a headache.'

'And you're giving me a headache.' Kurcher wrenched him to his feet for a second time – assuming it hadn't been Choice the first time. 'You and Maric can go back in the cell. If you agree to help, I'll see that you get the components you require to create the app, but we'll monitor you to make sure you're doing just that. If you don't help, we'll throw you to Angard as a distraction and then capture him as he pulls your arms off.'

Before Choice could blurt out anything else, the enlister marched him out of the rec room. Broekow leaned on the back of one of the seats and shook his head.

'I'm exhausted just listening to him.'

Frost blew a cloud of smoke into the air. 'He has a sharp tongue, but Davian will probably rip that out before we get to Cradle. Speaking of which, I'd better go send that message.'

'So am I allowed back in your cockpit if I behave?'

She stopped in the doorway and glanced back. 'We'll see. Just remember, I'm no deal sweetener.'

Cradle
Oralia system

Despite her time amongst the stars, she still found the night sky of Cradle an amazing sight. The full moon was so bright that she could see for miles across the verdant landscape surrounding the estate, as far as the eastern mountains. Even though there was a thin veil of cloud, the stars were still visible, as were the satellites as they moved silently in orbit of the beautiful world she called home.

The warm breeze whispered across the balcony, strands of blonde hair tickling her face. She shook her head gently before taking a deep breath of the night air. It was so peaceful that she found it easy to forget why she was there.

The peace was disturbed as a pair of patrol ships swooped over the estate and disappeared north, their engines making a deep humming noise that reverberated through her body. It was an almost erotic sensation that made her smile.

'Will there be anything else, Miss Oakley?'

She turned to face the guard and enjoyed watching him fight to keep his eyes from drinking in her lithe form beneath the partially see-through gown. He had served his purpose though for now.

'No. Return to your duties and make sure I am not disturbed.'

As she watched him walk away, she could feel no satisfaction. Sure, he had been an okay lay, albeit clumsy and nervous, but it was more the fact that she had let him live. Not many men got to see the next morning after sharing her bed.

She had to control her urges while at the estate. Her parents had hidden her away at the small holiday retreat for a reason and the last thing she wanted to do was let them down again.

Turning back to the moonlit view, Tara leaned on the edge of the balcony and pondered her next move. Should she stay at the estate, protected by her family's loyal guards, and just hope that nobody came looking for her? Or should she try leaving Cradle? The latter option left her with a bad taste in the mouth. She was, after all, the one who had come back home for protection, knowing her parents would not turn their back on their daughter, no matter what she had done. If only they knew how many men she had killed. Would they be so understanding then?

No matter how serene the retreat was though, she couldn't settle. Even though her parents had sent twenty guards with her, she still didn't feel safe. She felt isolated and alone, waiting for something bad to happen and the holiday home near the western coastline of Gamal was starting to feel more like a prison than anything else.

In the distance, the crimson lights of the patrol ships arced across the sky, keeping low to the treeline. She watched them for a while longer and then headed inside, taking a seat in front of the tall oval mirror before brushing her hair. She struggled to look at her reflection though, avoiding staring directly into her own eyes and instead focusing on her long hair. Anyone who didn't know her would gaze into the blue eyes flecked with green and see great beauty. All she saw was the monster she had become. Her last victim had called her a *succubus* before she had cut his throat – an apt description.

She tried reading one of the books her mother had given her before they sent her away, but the pompous nature of the author annoyed her. Most things written by men tended to get lost in bravado or falsehoods. Another book spoke of the history of Gamal, detailing how the Oakley and Palerska families had originally carved out their respective niches on the biggest continent. It was a story she was too familiar with as her father spouted it as gospel whenever they were in the same room. If he had wanted a normal daughter, maybe he should have been there to stop those mercs raping her.

As the moon moved across the heavens, she found herself wide awake. She always slept better when the man sharing her bed was lying dead alongside her. As she began heading once more for the balcony, there was a soft knock at her door.

'I asked not to be disturbed,' she said angrily.

'Miss Oakley, there has been a message arrive for you.' The voice on the other side was hushed but deep. Definitely not the guard from earlier.

'I've had nothing appear on my personal comms.' She double-checked that the screen was indeed blank.

'This was sent by courier. A letter for you.'

A smile spread across her lips. 'Fine, come in then.'

The guard who entered was taller than the last and his muscles were well-defined. Beneath the ill-fitting protective hood, she could see a strong but unshaven jaw. This one seemed to defy protocol and she liked that.

'Sorry to disturb you so late,' he said, keeping his eyes on the floor.

'How long have you worked at the estate?' she asked, knowing that he had not been one of the twenty sent with her.

The guard glanced up at her. 'A few weeks.'

Oakley gave him her most-wicked smile as she saw his hungry eyes. 'You don't look much like the type to take up such a boring post. Shut the door, will you?'

By the time the guard had closed the door and turned back, she was sat on the edge of the bed. Her legs slipped out from beneath her gown as she crossed them.

'Now, let me see this letter.'

He approached the bed boldly, producing an envelope from beneath his jacket. As he handed it to her, she lightly brushed his fingers with her own. Her name was emblazoned on the envelope, but she didn't recognise the handwriting.

'Someone likes the old-fashioned methods of communication,' she remarked, noting the guard take a couple of steps back and once again look down at the floor.

As she read the letter within, a frown began to form and her mouth opened slightly. When she looked back up, the guard had removed his hood and was standing with his arms crossed.

'The information on that paper is from a report ready to be sent to Taurus Galahad,' he stated. 'Unless you play ball, Tara.'

'What the hell are you talking about?' Her mind was reeling.

'I'm here to enlist you as a Taurus agent. Help me to find and subdue Horsten Angard, then the corp will take you into their ranks. If you refuse, those facts about your family will be sent to several of the Taurus hierarchy. They'll be very interested to know that the Oakleys have been forming alliances to build their own rival organisation, even going so far as to start work on a small fleet of assault ships and guardians. Taurus are very good at stamping out potential problems like this.'

Oakley stood and this time his eyes looked her up and down. 'Typical blackmailing approach.'

'You may be a cold-blooded killer, but you still care what happens to your family.'

'So what happened to Enlister Cooke?'

'He died. You get me instead now.'

She took another look at the letter and the source of the data leak became apparent. 'How much did you have to pay the Palerska family for this?'

He shrugged. 'They gave it free of charge once they knew we were here for you. Seems they still don't like the Oakleys very much. They clearly hoped I would give this info to Taurus no matter what so they could take full control of Gamal.'

'How do I know you won't just send it anyway?'

'You just have to take me on my word.'

Oakley threw the letter down on the bed and ran a hand through her hair. 'I suppose some unfortunate guard was forced to give up his uniform for you.'

The enlister held his arms out wide, as though he might step in to embrace her. 'No, you have the Palerskas to thank for that too. Their spies knew exactly where you were and they lent me the clothes.'

Oakley eyed him warily. 'So you got in, but how exactly do you expect to get out when there are more than thirty guards in the estate and several patrol ships in the area?'

'That depends whether or not they value their lives. The guns on my ship will make light work of anyone who tries to stop us.' He scowled. 'And there are only three patrol ships. We do our homework.'

'Perhaps we can come to an alternative arrangement.' She stepped forward. 'What's your name?'

He grinned. 'I know all about your *alternative arrangements*. Unlike all those mercs and officers you bedded then shredded, I have willpower.'

Oakley gave her best hurt expression. 'I was just thinking that I could help you with Angard, but then you might consider letting me slip away. I doubt I'd be suited to taking orders from Taurus Galahad anyway.'

His grin faded as he gave a deep sigh. 'Why can't you crims just accept that things have to be this way?' A revolver appeared in his hand. 'You tell me where we can find Angard, we both get on my ship and then you coax the brute out of hiding. Once that's done, I take you both with me for debrief with Taurus Galahad. The alternative is that I put a bullet in your brain right now.

'I'm guessing that you made sure Angard would receive his drugs so, with you gone, he'll run out eventually and go on another rampage. Even if the authorities here don't kill him, he'd run out of juice and die anyway. Besides, I can see in your beautiful eyes that you seem to care for him for some reason, so you wouldn't want him to suffer.'

Oakley could tell that her chances of seducing her way out of the situation were slim. This enlister was not like Cooke. He was harsher and more arrogant, plus there was a cruelness in his eyes that concerned her. He had all the bravado of a merc, but she could tell he had hurt people and had probably enjoyed it.

'I need to know that file won't reach Taurus,' she said softly. 'Please. My family mean everything to me and I'll do what I can to keep them safe.'

111

'If you come with me now, Tara, I swear the file will not be sent. I will, however, keep it just in case you decide to try killing me or escaping.' He raised the hood. 'So, what's it to be?'

Cobb
Kalbrec system

Cal Fuller watched as the assault ship slowly left orbit, then pulled his tired eyes from the screen. The grainy feed from the satellite cameras always gave him a headache.

'About time they went on their bloody way,' came a woman's voice from behind him.

He hadn't even heard her enter the tiny room. 'Jesus, Marie. You trying to give me a heart attack?'

'Which ship was it?'

'The *Requiem.*' He shot a glance at her silhouette in the doorway. 'Only one reason why they would have visited. Rumours are circulating.'

'Yeah, well rumours could get us all killed,' she muttered.

They left the room together and began negotiating their way through the network of corridors towards the main storage bay. As they walked, Fuller occasionally glanced at his head of ops. He still recalled the day when Marie Butler had first been shown off by her proud parents. The days that followed had been some of the happiest times for him. Eight years later, Marie was made an orphan when both parents were killed in the initial strikes during the civil war and it was left to him to help raise her along with the other survivors. Now, she was helping him oversee the resistance work in the murky bunker beneath the remains of Jefferson. Of all the colonists who signed up to the movement, she was the most driven to find ways of getting back at the corps for what they did to the people of Cobb. Taurus Galahad was at the top of her shit list.

As they entered the main storage bay, he quickly surveyed the work that was being carried out. Ships of all shapes and sizes lined the bay. Some were being fitted with weaponry while others needed full overhauls. He knew it was a big ask to get all of their meagre fleet ready, but they were running out of time. Supplies were dangerously low and even the merc shipments had slowed, most likely due to corp activity in the system.

As he and Marie made their way slowly around the bay, talking with each set of engineers and getting status updates where they could, Fuller could feel doubt eating away at him. He had imagined himself as some sort of modern-day Robin Hood, using the resistance to plunder corp supply depots on different worlds and returning to share the spoils with the starving people

113

of Cobb. The reality of the situation was that he would probably lead the ragged fleet out on their first skirmish only to have them all wiped out by corp defenses before they could even get close to the depot. Marie of course saw it a different way and would have called him a foolish old man if he had voiced his thoughts. She saw that, with the support of the mercs, the resistance had surprisingly strong firepower and the element of surprise. He would have liked to have had the help of the Knights Templar, but their alliance with the corps was of great concern and he was certainly not going to ask for the help of Jericho's Bold. So, it had really come down to Fortitude to help them get the resistance off the ground. He knew they had their own agenda for supporting a small army of disgruntled colonists. Fortitude was an organisation seemingly on the rise and would benefit from the disruption of the corps.

'Pick up the pace, Cal.' Marie had strode ahead as he meandered along with his thoughts.

When he caught up with her, she was giving an engineer a piece of her mind about some shoddy plating he was welding to the hull of an old decommissioned cargo vessel. By the time they left the storage bay, she had reduced several men to nervous wrecks.

'You keep busting their balls like that and they may rebel against *us*,' he said, seeing whether he could force a smile out of her.

'We don't want these ships falling apart before we even get out of orbit. Someone has to keep them in line.'

That seemed like a personal dig. 'I'm doing my part. Now we have Taurus sniffing around again, it may make things a bit more difficult but we'll be ready.'

Marie tutted. 'We have to. Cobb's fast becoming a dead planet.'

'Maybe we should focus our attention on finding a new home for everyone then,' Fuller remarked. 'Somewhere with resources. Somewhere that they can survive, even if something were to happen to us.'

'Maybe. Whatever we do, Taurus are likely to take an interest and not in a good way.'

Fuller nodded to several colonists passing them. 'Once this meeting is out of the way, I'm going to spend some more time studying the charts and giving more thought to forming an alliance with Impramed.'

'That again?' Marie rolled her eyes. 'None of the corps are trustworthy. I don't know why you want to get into bed with them.'

'Impramed are the smallest. They need all the allies they can find, otherwise the other corps will wipe them out over the coming decades.'

114

They entered the meeting room and the ten people sat around the crude metal table stood to attention simultaneously.

'Give me a break,' smiled Fuller. 'I'm not an officer. You'll be saluting next.'

He took a seat at the head of the table, with Marie choosing to stand directly behind him. As the others lowered themselves back down, their faces were etched with concern.

'First things first.' Fuller rested his elbows on the cold metal. 'The ship that has been in orbit for the last few hours is the *Requiem*, a Taurus Galahad assault vessel. It recently departed, thankfully. Yes, this is a concern, but the fact they didn't bother sending anyone down to the surface speaks volumes. My belief is that they heard some rumours and chose to stop off and check us out. Luckily the tech our merc associates gave us seems to have shielded us from any scans, but this visit by Taurus may be the first of many.

We need to get this operation under way as soon as possible and I want reports on the status of everything. People, ships, resources, supplies, weaponry, ammo... *everything*.'

Fuller looked around at the expectant faces. 'My friends, we are the Cobb Resistance and we will end the plight of those left here to die.'

Cradle
Oralia system

A herd of shellboars squealed and scattered in all directions as the group pushed their way through the foliage.

'You'd think that a planet like this would have some sort of intelligent life on it,' Choice commented. 'But no, just pigs, avians and insects... plus a few fish.'

Broekow cuffed him round the back of the head and prodded him forward with the barrel of his rifle. 'Shut your mouth.'

Choice glanced back over his shoulder and gave the sniper an amused smirk. 'What's the point of threatening me? You need me to activate this app. No one else can do it.'

'I said shut the fuck up.' Broekow looked across at Kurcher. 'Any way we can gag him?'

The enlister was peering through the trees ahead, revolver in hand. 'Quiet, both of you. At this rate, Angard will hear us coming a mile off.'

In front of the three men, Oakley was pushing through the undergrowth and stooped to pass beneath a thick branch. Kurcher noticed Broekow and Choice both staring at her backside. He couldn't really blame them. Even a brain-fucked schizophrenic had to appreciate something like that right in front of his eyes.

Flanking Oakley were the three guards from the retreat who he had insisted accompany them. They were the ones who had taken shots at the *Kaladine* as it hovered over the estate and, for that, Kurcher armed them only with stun prods and ordered them to protect Oakley on their trek into the wilderness. Naturally they needed some persuading and one of them still had a swollen eye. He didn't want to waste too much time on them though. They were simply there as fodder.

'This really is a beautiful world.' Choice was choosing to ignore his warnings. 'And the view from here is amazing.'

Kurcher found his patience wearing thinner than usual thanks to the persistent ramblings of the man... or men. The sun was beginning to dip behind the trees, turning the clouds orange and pink. The boost surging through the enlister's veins emphasised the colours while giving strength to his tired legs. He considered giving himself another shot just before they encountered Angard, to keep his reactions sharp.

116

His sense app being offline just supported his need for the drug. The damage Choice had done couldn't be fixed by a reboot, so corp support was needed at some point.

Choice had continued talking and Broekow was also getting to the end of his tether. The sniper gave him a shove and sent him tumbling to the ground.

'Do that again and I'll slit your throat.'

Broekow took a moment to calm himself. 'Whatever. Get moving.'

Kurcher watched the exchange and noted the contempt in the eyes of both men. He wondered whether one of them was the unwitting carrier of the implant Santa Cruz wanted and part of him hoped it was in Choice. The carrier would die slower than the others.

He also wondered whether he had made the right decision in giving Choice the components he needed to create an app capable of disrupting Angard's tech. It hadn't taken the crim long to put it together, but the fact he had ensured only he could use it still grated on the enlister. Choice was too smart to make himself surplus to requirements. Bringing him down onto Cradle was the last thing Kurcher had wanted to do, but time was of the essence. Oakley's parents would have been aware of their daughter's capture by then and had no doubt sent the authorities across Gamal to try getting her back. Frost had been insistent that she didn't want to engage in a fight with Oakley-owned ships, but that outcome was a possibility.

Thinking of his pilot prompted him to check in. At least his comms app was still working. 'Justyne?'

'Everything okay?' Her voice was loud despite the distance between them.

'So far. You still tracking us?'

'No, I thought I'd go on a jaunt across Gamal. Take in the sights.'

'No need for the sarcasm.'

'When you need me, I'll be there.'

'Any sign of Oakley's rescue party yet?' he asked, lowering his voice.

'Not yet. Destroying the comms at her retreat bought us time, but those patrol ships will have got the message through by now.'

'We should have destroyed them.'

Frost's sigh hissed in his ear. 'Killing anyone on this planet is a bad idea. It'd start a war.'

'Would it? The Oakleys may be planning to start their own organisation, but they wouldn't want to take on Taurus. These people aren't fighters.'

'All I'm saying is you don't have to start a war on every planet we visit.'

Kurcher saw Oakley signal. 'We're here, Justyne. Be ready.'

The abandoned storage depot was not quite what he was expecting. He had imagined a small building covered with greenery, with broken windows and holes in the walls. Instead, they found themselves standing before a long metal structure which was devoid of any windows and had withstood the elements well. It had clearly been built to last. Still, the forest had tried claiming it back. Vines had wrapped themselves around the walls and moss had grown all over the tall roof. The walls were dirty and streaked with water marks.

'You sure you can coax him out?' Kurcher asked Oakley as he moved up alongside her.

She nodded but her expression was blank. 'He'll get edgy when he realises I'm not here alone.'

'Just get him outside and we'll do the rest.'

As the light of day began to fade, causing the shadows around the depot to grow larger, Kurcher, Broekow and Choice moved to the corner of the building nearest to the door. The three guards hid in the shadows further along the front, each man clearly still harbouring thoughts of trying to turn the tables on the enlister as they glared at him. Oakley walked to stand before the heavy door and drew in a deep breath.

'Horsten?' she called, her voice echoing. 'It's Tara.'

Silence fell. Even Choice was quiet, his eyes wide as he watched.

'Horsten.' Her tone was harder this time.

From somewhere within the structure came a loud crash of metal upon metal. A moment later, the door scraped open slowly.

Oakley smiled at the face that appeared from the darkness within. 'See. It's me.'

'So who are the others skulking in the shadows?' The deep voice bounced off the metal walls, giving it an almost robotic edge.

Kurcher swore beneath his breath. Things were never simple.

'They're guards in my family employment,' Oakley replied. 'Can't let me out of their sight, so I agreed they could accompany me here.'

The one clear eye regarded her from the doorway. 'I have enough juice, so why the visit?'

Oakley crossed her arms and raised an eyebrow. 'Can't I visit a friend just to see how he's doing? You don't exactly have much to keep you entertained out here.'

'I keep busy. Your guards going to come out in the open where I can see them?'

Oakley thought for a moment. 'If you wish.'

118

Kurcher swore again. 'Get the app ready,' he whispered to Choice. 'You two stay here.' With that, the enlister strode out to join Oakley. At the same time, the three guards came out of hiding too.

'There.' Oakley held her hands out. 'Happy now? Come out here where I can see you. These men won't harm you.'

'They have stun devices and that one has a gun,' came the rumbling voice.

Kurcher could detect a sadness in the tone. If Angard was suicidal, it might make his job extremely difficult.

'They're *guards*, Horsten,' countered Oakley. 'They're here to protect me.'

Angard pushed the depot door open fully and took a step out into the partial light. While Kurcher kept his expression calm, the three guards all took a step back with looks of horror on their faces. The enlister dared a glance at the two crims hidden behind the corner and could see Choice shaking his head at Broekow. What was the matter now?

'Why don't you come inside, Tara?' Angard asked, holding out a huge hand. 'We can talk in private then.'

'Listen, Horsten.' Oakley took a step closer to the brute. 'There's a very good reason I have come here and I need you to remain calm.'

A frown appeared on Angard's brow, making the deep scar across his shaven head even more prominent. Kurcher took a moment to study the man. Standing at just under seven feet tall, he was like some creature out of folklore. His left eye had been damaged by the relentless efforts to fit him with biomech technology and was now a cloudy orb, but his right eye was bright. Part of his skull over the dead eye had been replaced with a metal plate and Kurcher knew the biomech implants would be lurking underneath. Angard's thick, powerful arms were covered with brandings. On one arm were a series of numbers and emblems given to him by the scientists on Shard during their research. On the other was emblazoned the logo of the Knights Templar, who bought him after Shard had chewed him up and shat him out.

Kurcher could even see a number of unnatural protrusions and scars beneath the ill-fitting shirt Angard was wearing. It was no wonder he had gone back to kill those who inflicted such suffering on him.

After the long pause, Oakley continued: 'You and I are in danger.'

Kurcher gripped his revolver tightly. If she chose to try killing them by using Angard, the whole situation would get out of hand fast.

'There are people here on Cradle who want you dead and who are quite

119

happy punishing me for bringing you here in the first place.' Oakley bowed her head. 'I'm sorry, but I tried so hard to hide you somewhere nobody would find you.'

Kurcher relaxed slightly. She was quite the actress. He noted that a hushed exchange of words was occurring between Broekow and Choice though.

Oakley looked back up, tears glistening in her eyes. 'So I've come here to ask you to leave Cradle with me.' She pointed at Kurcher. 'This man will take us away from here and has come to me with a solution that I believe is our only hope for survival.'

Angard eyed Kurcher warily. 'A merc?'

'Of sorts. If we leave with him now, Taurus Galahad will give up chasing us, but only if we agree to work for them.'

'No.' Angard's response was so abrupt that it caught even Oakley by surprise.

She took another step closer. 'If we stay here, we're dead. My parents can't protect me any longer. We need to leave Cradle and this is our only option. Enlister Kurcher has sworn that Taurus will no longer hunt us down and will welcome us into their merc ranks, me as an agent and you as... well, muscle.'

'No.' The clear eye was fixed on Kurcher. 'Enlisters lie, corps lie, everyone lies. We leave with him and he'll execute us.'

Oakley shook her head. 'He could have killed me back at my retreat but didn't. He's a man of his word and we need to trust him.'

Angard's lip curled. 'They want to take me back to the labs on Shard. I won't go back there, not again.'

Kurcher noticed Broekow trying to attract his attention, but he didn't want to give away the sniper's position. 'My orders are clear,' he said to Angard. 'I'm not here to harm you or Tara, nor am I here to take you back to Shard. If you stay here though, you'll die one way or another. Tara will leave with or without you and nobody will be around to replenish your *juice*.'

'I survived for eight years on Kalvion,' growled the giant. 'I could survive here.'

'I don't know how you managed to survive that long on a quaran,' shrugged Kurcher, trying to reply as quickly as he could. 'But there you didn't have men trying to kill you. If you stay here, you'll end up like Frankenstein's monster.'

That seemed to confuse Angard, who glanced at Oakley. 'Stop him talking. My head is hurting.'

120

She reached out for his hand. 'Horsten, please. Come with me. I still need a protector.'

For a moment, his shoulders sagged as he looked down at her and there was a calmness behind his eye that only she seemed to induce.

Then a voice called out. 'My brother, heed the words and join us in glorious redemption.'

'Fuck,' groaned Kurcher.

Angard turned suddenly and saw Maric standing at the corner of the building, holding his hands aloft. The calmness vanished instantly and the brute let out an anguished roar.

'What's this?' he bellowed. 'The psycho preacher. This is all a lie. You're hunting us all down, enlister, just like before and you're making Tara lie for you.'

Oakley squeezed Angard's hand. 'Calm down. This is not like before.'

The massive hands scooped her off the ground and placed her gently behind his hulking frame. 'Stay there.'

Kurcher glanced first at Maric, who was trying to wrestle free of Broekow's grasp, then at Angard, who turned to face him with a look of genuine hatred. As the giant's eye rolled back in his head for a second, heralding the activation of his biomech apps, Kurcher snorted in disbelief.

'Fuck it. You three, do your job and protect Oakley from that freak.'

The guards looked at each other in confusion. When one snapped his stun prod into action, the other two followed and they moved forward nervously.

Kurcher made to run for Broekow and Maric but Angard charged forward like a drug-addled bull, his teeth clenched and eye wide. A jab from a prod got his attention though and Kurcher heard the guards call for support as they became the focus of Angard's rage.

'You choose now to take over?' Kurcher yelled, grabbing Maric. 'You have to activate the app.'

The preacher shook his head. 'As I was explaining to Broekow, Choice created that app. I had nothing to do with it and wouldn't know how to activate it.'

'Well you'd better find a way.' Kurcher looked back to see the three guards lunging at Angard with the prods, desperately trying to dodge his flailing fists. 'Do I have to get Choice's attention again? Is he such a coward that he hides behind you?'

'Allow me to talk to Angard,' offered Maric. 'Reason with him.'

Kurcher slapped him across the face. 'Choice, get out here you piece of shit. Don't leave Maric to fight your battles for you.'

121

A pained cry drew their attention and they turned just in time to see Angard wrenching one guard into the air while swatting another away. The dangling guard tried kicking out. Angard caught his leg and swung the man violently in an arc, striking his head against the nearby wall with such strength that the side of his skull blew apart. Blood and brain spattered against the metal, narrowly missing Oakley.

'See that?' Kurcher knew their time was running out. 'If you don't activate the app, he'll do the same to all of us.'

Maric's eyes lingered on the lifeless body of the guard as Angard dropped it and pounced on the other two. 'I... I told you that I can't. I trust in God and he will help me calm this poor soul.'

'We should just shoot Angard,' suggested Broekow, hefting his rifle. 'A shot to each kneecap might bring him down.'

'No.' Kurcher slapped Maric again. 'Maybe Choice doesn't believe his app will work so he's gone into hiding.'

Angard's fist slammed into the face of a guard with a sickening crunch, sending the man sprawling to the ground several feet away. The final guard jabbed his prod into Angard's groin. With a howl of fury more than pain, the powerful crim snatched the weapon while catching the man by the throat with his other hand. As he tightened his grip, the guard gasped for air. Spittle flew from Angard's lips as he drove the prod into the guard's mouth, stabbing it through flesh and bone to protrude out the back of his head.

Dropping the body, Angard glanced at the injured guard who was lying on his back, blood running from a smashed nose and torn upper lip. The hate-filled eye then turned back to Kurcher, who cursed again.

'Don't do this, Horsten,' came Oakley's cry. 'Stop.'

He didn't pay her any heed this time and charged the three men at the corner of the depot. Such was his surprising speed that Kurcher threw himself backwards as Broekow, who for a split second considered trying to fire on Angard, decided to dive for cover too. Maric looked up at the approaching brute and once more raised his hands to the heavens.

'Allow God into your heart, brother. He is... He is...' Maric twitched as Angard bore down on him. 'Shit.'

Just before he ploughed into the preacher, Kurcher saw Angard's head flick upwards and his one good eye roll again. Then the giant crim stumbled and fell, his momentum carrying him into the stricken schizophrenic. Both men landed among the foliage and silence fell once more on the scene.

'Seems Choice does have a sense of self-preservation after all,' Broekow remarked, picking himself up. 'Albeit a touch too late.'

Kurcher made sure Oakley was still by the door and was pleased to see her crouched down in the shadows, seemingly shaken by Angard's actions. He dusted himself down and activated his comms.

'It's time, Justyne.'

As the *Kaladine* swooped in from the south and began descending towards the small clearing in front of the depot, Kurcher and Broekow managed to drag Angard's unconscious bulk from the foliage. Both were sweating profusely. He was as heavy as he looked.

Choice was limping behind them, muttering about the fact his app worked perfectly and pissed off that Broekow had caught him slowly trying to escape into the wilderness. Oakley had emerged from the safety of the building to gaze up at the lights of the *Kaladine* in the darkness, occasionally giving a concerned glance towards Angard.

Kurcher helped get Angard onboard and secured in the third and final cell, with Choice complaining loudly as he was thrown back into his cell next to Rane. The enlister then returned outside.

'Davian, we've got ships approaching from the west.' Frost's tone was calm. She knew they would be away by the time the Oakleys' rescue ships reached the depot. 'You done?'

'Nearly.' The amplified adrenaline rush he had experienced thanks to the Parinax was wearing off as he strode across to the only guard who had survived Angard's onslaught. The man was trying to roll onto his side to spit blood and teeth, having only just started to come to his senses. Kurcher's bullet took him in the temple.

As he walked back to the *Kaladine*, he looked up at the cockpit screen and could feel Frost's disapproving glare. It was too risky leaving a single witness and she knew that. Sure, the Oakleys would be pissed off, but three dead guards and a missing daughter was a small price to pay to stop Taurus from wiping them off the surface of Cradle altogether.

Taurus Galahad Assault Ship Requiem
Tacit system

Santa Cruz stood at the shoulder of his comms officer, peering down at the data flashing across the monitor.

'I want to know their names, corporal,' he said, impatience edging his voice. 'I need to know which ships we are about to encounter.'

The officer finally looked up, relief etched on his face. 'The Libra Centauri ship is the *Delphin* and the other is Sigma Royal's *Pegasus*, sir.'

Santa Cruz glanced at the main screen. 'Both assault-class. Guess they couldn't spare any explorers. Time to co-ordinates.'

'Ten minutes, sir,' came the eager response from his navigations officer.

In the top-left corner of the screen, Aridis hung in the void. Akeman had been right. Both Libra and Sigma were sniffing around the mining world, but this time the two ships had run into one another. There was no love lost between the two corps. Libra continued to operate a well-organised spy network across the galaxy and had focused their efforts on gleaning as much information from the Sigma data records as possible during recent years. Most likely, this was in preparation for some kind of takeover – one never knew with Libra Centauri. They preferred to strike from the inside rather than risk the direct approach. Even Santa Cruz had to admit he was puzzled by what their agenda actually was.

'Status of the two ships?' he asked the command officers around him.

Connolly was the quickest to answer. 'Based on the initial scans, the *Delphin* has only sustained minor hull damage. The engines of the *Pegasus* are failing.'

Santa Cruz looked across at his lieutenant. 'Sounds like Libra are winning the battle then.' He walked back to his command seat. 'Bring the weapons online and tell the *Ravenedge* and the *Mantheus* to do the same.'

As the officers carried out his orders, Santa Cruz activated his personal screen, bringing up both port and starboard images. The two assault ships he had enlisted as support were keeping speed with the *Requiem*. Both had been stationed in the Kalbrec system so his detour to check out Cobb had been worthwhile after all. The commanders of the vessels were known to him and he hoped to send them on to join the rest of his growing fleet after they dealt with the trespassers in Tacit space.

As his eyes returned to the main screen, one hand straightened the four sword pins beneath his insignia stripes. Aridis vanished off the edge of the screen and he found himself wondering whether the other corps had managed to land any agents among the mining communities on the surface. He doubted Sigma would attempt it, but Libra wouldn't hesitate. He also hoped they had steered clear of Rockland. The prison was not a place to be tampered with, but he could imagine that Libra would relish the chance to wreak havoc by causing an *accident* on the station and setting the prisoners free. Only the worst offenders were sent to Rockland and they were all just waiting for some opportunity to escape.

'Sir, we are approaching the co-ordinates,' announced the navigator. 'What are your orders?'

Santa Cruz looked round at the grey, white and black uniforms surrounding his central position. 'Open comms to both ships. When I have finished speaking, have the *Ravenedge* and *Mantheus* open fire on the Sigma vessel. Fusion only, no missiles. Tell them to aim for the engine ports.'

There was a moment's hesitation, then the room burst into action. When comms were open, Santa Cruz stood once more and stared at the two ships that had loomed into view on the screen. The red and black *Pegasus* was listing to one side, displaying the Sigma letter and crown directly at the approaching ships. Only a dim light could be seen glowing from the engine ports. The green and white hull of the *Delphin* was scarred by fusion beam fire, but she looked healthy other than the cosmetic damage.

'This is Commander Jorelian Santa Cruz of the Taurus Galahad assault vessel *Requiem*. You are trespassing in our system and I demand to know why. I order you to power down your weapons and surrender to us. There will be no second warning.'

'Commander, your orders...'

He cut Connolly off quickly. 'Stand.'

A moment later, the two Taurus vessels carried out their orders. Twin fusion beams struck the engine ports of the *Pegasus* and there was a flash of bright light before the rear of the ship disintegrated, sending the rest of it into a violent spin.

Santa Cruz watched the doomed ship then signalled his comms officer. 'Again.'

The *Mantheus* fired three seconds before the *Ravenedge*. The first beam pierced the *Pegasus* hull and punched a hole through it. The second tore it in half. A chain reaction of explosions throughout the broken interior of the Sigma vessel reached the fusion cells and one half of the *Pegasus* was obliterated as it silently rolled away.

125

'Open comms to the Libra ship.' Santa Cruz waited for the signal. 'To the commander of the *Delphin*, the same fate will befall your ship and crew if you do not explain your presence in our system. If you try to run, we will destroy you. If you try to fight, we will destroy you. You have one minute to reply.'

'I don't understand why they didn't flee as soon as we entered the system,' said Connolly, looking to his commander for the answer.

'Would we flee if the roles were reversed?' Santa Cruz nodded at the *Delphin*. 'We would stand our ground defiantly and give a solid reason for entering their space. Some commanders are cowards. Not this one.'

A voice came through from the Libra ship, right on cue. 'This is Commander Warden of the *Delphin*. The *Pegasus* had been undertaking illegal activities in one of our systems and we were in pursuit under direct orders from Libra Centauri. When they fled through the jump point, we followed and ended up in Tacit. Our aim was to destroy the *Pegasus* and return to our own space. As you have completed our task for us, we have no reason to remain here and can be on our way.'

Santa Cruz watched the screen in quiet contemplation. Pieces of the *Pegasus* were floating away in all directions. There could well have still been people alive in the remaining half of the ship, but they would perish shortly. Emergency seals wouldn't help when life support was gone. It would just turn the remnant into one large tomb.

'Commander Warden, you will go to the jump point and leave Tacit immediately. We will escort you there. We do not expect to see you in Taurus Galahad space again.'

The reply was muttered. 'Understood.'

As the *Delphin* began turning, Santa Cruz walked to the console of his weapons officer and studied the display.

'Do we follow, sir?' asked the navigator, poised to access his pilot app.

'Hold. Tell the *Ravenedge* and *Mantheus* to follow.' He gestured at the screen. 'Bring up the port view.'

The scarred hull of the *Delphin* came into view as it eagerly began moving past the *Requiem*, close enough for the command officers to see the galaxy swirl and scales emblazoned over the assault vessel's name.

Santa Cruz watched the screen with his crew for a moment then reached down to the console. The fusion cannons mounted on the port side of the *Requiem* burst into life and the barrage blew a jagged hole in the hull of the *Delphin*. The jaws of the command crew dropped open, especially when they saw several people sucked out of the breach. Two unfortunates were catapulted into the side of the *Requiem*.

'Commander, you told them they could leave,' remarked Connolly, his voice wavering.

'A lie to counter their lies.' Santa Cruz sent another barrage into the Libra ship.

The *Delphin* listed, but still had momentum. Santa Cruz ignored the expression on the face of his weapons officer and swiped a command on the display. Missile ports opened on the side of the *Requiem* and two fusion explosive devices launched, slamming into the *Delphin*. The resulting explosions rendered the assault ship dead in space.

'Have the *Mantheus* destroy what's left,' Santa Cruz ordered, returning to his command seat. 'Then put us in orbit of Aridis.'

As his shell-shocked officers returned to their duties, the commander gazed at the green and white fragments spinning in the void among debris and bodies like some morbid dance. Having two fewer rival assault ships roaming the galaxy put him in a good mood.

Enlister-class vessel *Kaladine*
Benedict system

'You can't keep him locked up.' Oakley stood over Kurcher as he spooned another gelatinous lump of food into his mouth. 'He won't react well when he comes to and finds himself in such a small cell.'

The enlister grimaced at the foul-tasting gruel. 'We really need to get something better to eat than this shit.'

Oakley glanced at Broekow. '*You* understand, right? You've seen what Angard is capable of.'

Broekow shrugged. 'Not my call.'

She threw her hands up and paced to the back of the rec room. 'Look, I told you where D'Larro went and I didn't kick up a fuss about coming with you. All I ask is that you take Angard out of the cell and put him in the hold so that, when he wakes up, he isn't restricted.'

Kurcher ate another rank spoonful. 'Why don't I just throw you in the cell with him so you can look after him in there? For the fifth time, you don't get to give me orders on my ship. I'm not sending a message to your parents telling them where you've gone and I'm not letting Angard out of his cell until I'm certain he can behave. Hell, you're lucky I'm allowing you access to any rooms on the *Kaladine*, even the toilet. I mean, for all we know, you'll seduce Broekow and cut his throat.'

The sniper looked nervous. 'Thanks for giving her the idea.'

'Don't worry, you're safe,' Oakley assured him. 'Believe it or not, I don't just kill for fun. Kurcher on the other hand...'

With a sigh, the enlister put his spoon down. 'You may be a wet dream to most men. I don't give a shit. I'm glad you happened to recall D'Larro's plan to head to Summit, but that doesn't make us colleagues. You are a murderer and I would've usually blown your brains out by now. Taurus see something special in you, so my hands are tied.'

Oakley raised an eyebrow. 'If only.' She headed for the door. 'I'm going to check on Angard.'

Once she had gone, Kurcher continued eating. His head was starting to hurt. He knew he had to use his drugs sparingly as he was running short and hoped he might be able to find somewhere on Summit to replenish his supply.

'I don't think you'll have much of a problem with her,' Broekow stated.

'But I worry about Choice and Angard.'

'They stay locked up,' mumbled Kurcher through his gruel. 'Although I may free up Rane's cell soon.'

'So what happens next?' Broekow lowered himself into the seat opposite.

'When we get to Summit, I'll speak with the Impramed reps and explain that all I want is D'Larro. They'll allow me down onto the surface where I'll head to Tidewell and track him down.'

'So you don't need my help this time?'

Kurcher didn't want Broekow thinking he was becoming a companion for these frequent visits to different worlds. 'No, you'll stay here and keep an eye on the others, apart from Frost. She can take care of herself.'

'Don't I know it.' Broekow smiled. 'She's quite the pilot too.'

Kurcher could see how comfortable the sniper was getting on-board the *Kaladine* and that worried him. He may not have been the cold-blooded murderer that the others were, but he was still a dangerous man.

'Don't get any ideas. Frost is off limits.'

Kurcher finished his food, flinching at the bitter aftertaste. As he stood to get rid of the bowl, Broekow tapped his fingers on the table nervously.

'Were you on Cobb for the entire war?'

The question caught Kurcher off guard. 'I was brought in three months before it ended.'

'I didn't realise any units were brought in towards the end. Then again, I wasn't there of course.'

Kurcher kept his back to Broekow for as long as he could. He didn't like talking about his time on Cobb with anyone, even Frost, so he hoped his silence would end the conversation. Besides, the mere thought of what he had to do there still made him nauseous fifteen years later. He could still see the faces of the women and children vividly when he closed his eyes; could hear them pleading for their lives. They had to put a stop to the war somehow and his team had specialised in that kind of strategy.

'My father was a corporal,' continued Broekow, realising he wasn't going to get an answer. 'Died in 2602 but we never knew how. Never wanted to know really.'

'And your mother?' Kurcher knew he needed to engage with him in some way, at least to keep up the façade.

'She was a field medic for a time. That's how my parents met. She works at a military hospital on Galt now. Guess I was always destined to be in the military too.'

'Parents have a lot to answer for,' Kurcher said quietly. He could still see

129

his mother crying into one of many bottles, blind to what was happening around her. He shuddered when he remembered her pale face, dead eyes staring up at the ceiling and vomit crusted on her lips. Suicide was never a pretty sight. Selfish bitch.

'Were your parents in the military?' Broekow continued.

Kurcher turned back to face him. 'No, they weren't.'

The sniper seemed to be feeling particularly curious. 'So did you become an enlister once the war had finished on Cobb?'

'Not straight away. Taurus always wanted me in one system or another, running their errands.' That was a wholly unsuitable word for what he had done for them. 'Guess I'm still doing that now.'

Broekow leaned back in his seat, stroking his beard thoughtfully. Kurcher was finished with the conversation. He didn't need reminding about his military service and he certainly didn't want to dredge up those years between Cobb and beginning his enlister training. He cursed himself for thinking about it in the first place and rubbed at his eyes, trying to get rid of the screaming ghosts in his head. He suddenly needed another shot of Parinax badly. It was the only thing that kept the dead at bay.

Frost strode into the rec room, cigarette on the go as usual, and broke the uncomfortable silence. 'Rane keeps asking to speak with you. Why don't you just go put that bastard out of his misery?'

Even the thought of dealing with Rane was better than dwelling on the past. 'Fine. He's outstayed his welcome long enough.'

As the enlister left the room, Frost watched him go. She could see he was hurting about something. When Broekow didn't volunteer a start to any conversation, she grabbed a glass of water and waited patiently.

'He doesn't like talking about himself, does he?' Broekow asked finally.

'No, and I'd advise you not to keep asking questions.' The water tasted strange thanks to the smoke.

Broekow looked up at her and smiled warmly. 'So what about you? What's your story?'

Frost toyed with the idea of walking out of the room to avoid the conversation, but found herself answering. 'Not very exciting. I became a pilot on Earth, which my parents frowned upon. They wanted me to work with them at Taurus headquarters. That just wasn't me. Eventually I upgraded to planethoppers, working in Sol, Geraint and Lincoln. Finally got myself noticed and signed up as an enlister pilot.'

'Pretty lonely existence though, isn't it? I mean, you get to interact with people but they tend to be just like Rane or Choice.'

'Or you.' She gulped down her water then took a long drag on the cigarette. 'I haven't forgotten that you're a crim too.'

'At least I have morals though.' Broekow shrugged. 'Guess once you're branded as a crim, it's hard to be seen as anything else. Listen, if I'm going to end up working with you and Kurcher longer term, I don't want you thinking of me as scum.'

Frost bit at her lip. The others could rot in hell for all she cared, but something gnawed away at her saying that Broekow didn't deserve what was waiting for him once they had completed their task. She stubbed the cigarette out and headed for the door.

'I never said I thought you were scum.'

Broekow gave her one of his best smiles. 'Glad to hear it. Maybe when this is all over, we could have a drink together.'

Frost opted not to respond and headed back to the cockpit. Broekow's words stuck in her head and she felt a pang of regret. When this was all over, she would move on to the next mission with Kurcher and nobody would ever hear the name Sieren Broekow again.

~

Winter checked the reports again, making sure he hadn't missed a key piece of information. It wasn't quite what he had been hoping for, but any lead was worth knowing. Once he had finished, he glanced at the tracking report. The *Kaladine* was still en route to Summit, making a direct approach it seemed. No doubt Kurcher would appeal to the good nature of Impramed in finding Regan D'Larro, which would hopefully make the task relatively easy, and then Winter could make a visit to a couple of the names on the reports.

He downed the last dregs of the coffee he had been enjoying, savouring the taste one last time. He had managed to grab some before leaving Earth and it always reminded him of home, bringing a nostalgic smile to his lips. It didn't matter that his last few visits to Earth had involved killing off a number of Revenant leaders. He always liked being back on terra firma.

Knowing that he didn't want to be away from the task at hand long, he considered the options before him. A significant proportion of his informants placed Jaffren Hewn somewhere in the Perseus Arm. Some believed that the pirate had travelled to the Alscion system, but he doubted Hewn would go anywhere near the Sigma Royal headquarters on Meta. Other reports placed Hewn as heading towards the Iridia system, which Winter could believe. The pirate's Echo organisation had history with Libra Centauri, so perhaps they

131

had arranged a hiding place for him until he could get back to the Expanse. Three reports mentioned the same name of a pilot working for Libra who had arrived in Iridia some time back and was still lingering in the system. Seemed an odd place to wait.

Winter brought up his navigation display and found Iridia. It was a small system out on the edge of the Perseus Arm with only three planets in orbit of the star. Ember was a gas giant, named because of its fiery appearance. Nikara was a dead world with no atmosphere and minimal resources. Tempest was a quaran world, designated as such by Libra in 2577 due to the instability of its weather systems and violent tectonic shifts.

As he pondered these three very different planets, his display indicated that he had a new message. Bringing this up, he saw it had been sent from Solomon Rees. He was intrigued. The judicial officer didn't often contact him.

After reading through the brief text, Winter sat in quiet contemplation for a moment, letting it sink in. He knew the Taurus board saw Santa Cruz as somewhat of a loose cannon, but his actions were clearly worrying them. Why else would they let him know that the commander had destroyed two assault ships in the Tacit system? If Rees was hinting for Winter to spy on Santa Cruz, he had not made it very clear. Perhaps the board wanted him to remain abreast of the situation so they could call on him if the time came to remove the commander from his post. Whatever the reason for the information, it was clear that the destruction of Libra and Sigma vessels would not go down well. All it needed now was for Kurcher to piss Impramed off and Taurus would have a full set of angry corps baying for their blood.

Winter gave the tracking data another look and hoped the enlister was more subtle in his approach this time round.

~

Kurcher pressed his revolver hard against Rane's temple.

'I don't know why I brought you along. It's time you answered for your crimes.'

Rane kept his eyes locked on the enlister's. 'You know why, Davian. You realised that there is something in what I told you before. I'm sure it's been playing on your mind.'

'There's no truth in what you said.'

'Then pull the trigger and get rid of me,' Rane said, impatiently. 'If you're so pig-headed, go ahead and find the remaining three crims. Sign your own

132

death warrant.'

Kurcher's finger twitched. He would enjoy seeing the killer's brains all over the cell wall and ending what had been his longest pursuit yet.

'I always considered you a worthy opponent,' continued Rane. 'But now I see that you're just like other corp-owned zombies. Money is your priority and you clearly don't care who loses their lives as long as you get paid. Even poor Frost.'

'Shut the fuck up.'

Rane rubbed at his aching arm. 'Have you considered what will happen to her? You deliver these crims to Taurus and she will be dead within a few hours. Not really fair, is it?'

Kurcher willed his finger to pull the trigger. His digit refused. Perhaps it was the comedown from the drug, but his head was swimming. Rane's words were echoing in his skull and his mind didn't help by conjuring up an image of Frost lying dead at his feet, amid seven other bodies. Maybe Rane had gotten to Cooke too and that was why the dead enlister had turned on Taurus. After all, Rane was a master of getting into people's heads and manipulating them.

'Enlist me, Davian.' Rane turned so that the revolver was aimed between his eyes. 'Let me help you find the remaining crims and then we can work together to determine what this data is and why it's so...'

Kurcher's fist struck him square in the face, knocking the killer back against the wall. As Rane reeled, the enlister stepped forward and slammed the revolver against the side of his skull. This time, Rane crumpled to the floor.

'Maybe that will shut you up,' growled Kurcher through gritted teeth.

He then realised that Rane wasn't getting back up and knelt down to check for a pulse. He cursed when he found one. Holstering the revolver, Kurcher turned the unconscious killer over and saw blood running from his broken nose. It would be so easy to strangle or suffocate the life out of him, yet Kurcher found himself leaving the cell and locking the door.

'Lover's tiff?' Oakley was leaning against the door to Angard's cell. 'Sounded rough.'

Kurcher walked to the next cell and peered inside. The eyes of the preacher looked back at him.

'Enlister, I am myself again now.' Maric's voice was muffled without the intercom open.

'Is that so?' muttered Kurcher, more to himself than anyone else.

'If you let me out of this cell, I will make myself useful,' promised Maric.

'I will not cause you any trouble.'

Kurcher opened the intercom. 'It's not you I'm worried about. Until you show me proof that you can control Choice, you stay in there.'

Before Maric could respond, Kurcher walked away and approached Oakley. He glanced inside the last cell and saw Angard sitting on the bed, which looked more like a child's beneath him.

'He's calm... for now,' Oakley said. 'Whatever Choice did seemed to kerb his anger. He looks like he's in a daze at the moment.'

Kurcher hoped Angard wasn't claustrophobic. 'If you can keep him this way, I'll consider letting him out. I can't have him jeopardising my ship though. Will he need more drugs any time soon?'

'Not for some time.' Oakley looked at the enlister with tearful eyes. 'You know it's not his fault, right? If those bastards did the same to you, you wouldn't exactly be stable.'

'True.' His torture had been very different to Angard's. 'Just explain the situation to him again and tell him he would already be dead if that was what Taurus wanted. Okay?'

Oakley nodded, but there was suspicion behind those beautiful eyes. Kurcher needed a hit before they got to Summit and to hell with the fact he was running short. He brushed past her and headed for his quarters, feeling the shadows once more creeping into the edge of his vision.

He couldn't keep the charade up much longer. D'Larro, Hewn and Ercko had to be found quickly, otherwise he might go mad having the others festering on-board, tainting his ship with their mere presence.

Alone in his quarters, he fell into a warm slumber thanks to the Calmer, eager to experience the drug-induced painless dreams one more time. Soon though, the pleasant visions were invaded by the sound of Rane's voice, repeating his warning over and over. *Sign your own death warrant.* As he fell into a deep sleep, Kurcher dreamt of a sword standing vertically against a horn-shaped constellation of stars: the Galahad Suns. As Rane's words echoed one last time, he reached out for the sword but it suddenly fell from the stars, arcing downwards to impale him through the heart.

Taurus Galahad Assault Ship Requiem
Tacit system

Santa Cruz made sure to keep eye contact with the general as he repeated his report for the third time.

'And you feel that you were justified in destroying both ships?' Mitchell asked, leaning forward so his entire face filled the screen.

'I do, sir. My actions were necessary. We cannot allow Sigma Royal, Libra Centauri or any other corporation to wander through our systems unchallenged. They will find any weakness they can.'

The general's eyes narrowed. 'I know this, commander. The fact is that your actions over the recent days have pushed us closer to a major conflict. Sapphire Nova are threatening retaliation for Enlister Kurcher's mess on Rikur and now think we're behind the death of their head of security too. On top of that, Nova are missing an officer who you decided to blow out of an airlock.'

'Sir, Cairns was a war criminal and I had the opportunity to get rid of him. As for the Rikur incident, that was unfortunate but again necessary.'

'Listen to me very carefully,' said Mitchell, furrowing his brow. 'You were put in charge of overseeing the Coldrig teams and given command of a small fleet to make sure our finds were kept secure. I even gave you the nod in getting Cooke under control. What I didn't expect was for you to jump from one system to the next, acting as some sort of executioner and driving us towards open war.'

Santa Cruz lifted his chin. 'With all due respect, general, we are already at war. I was simply tipping things in our favour. You told me to protect our finds and that is exactly what I'm doing.'

'You're one of the best interrogators I know,' Mitchell sighed. 'Plus you were there when we found the schematics, so you know what's at stake. You have to understand though that I have Rees, Lenaghan and the rest breathing down my neck to rein you in.

You pull Winter from his assignments on Earth to traipse after Kurcher, you continue to use Akeman as a point of contact despite his dubious connections, you drag Cairns and his mistress naked from their beds just to execute them, then you take the *Requiem* to Cobb for some Godforsaken reason before heading to Tacit, where you destroy two assault vessels and kill over two hundred people. I don't recall agreeing to any of these actions,

135

commander.'

'As mentioned, sir, I went to Cobb to check out rumours of armed ships being seen on the surface. I felt it was worth looking into, but we didn't find anything. Better safe than sorry.'

Mitchell leaned back again, glaring at Santa Cruz from beneath greying eyebrows. 'I want you back in the Berg system. You will take the *Ravenedge* and the *Mantheus* with you. Once there, resume your duties overseeing the Coldrig teams and I also want you to ensure we are on schedule with the shipyard construction.'

Santa Cruz pursed his lips. 'General, I don't...'

'This is an order.' Mitchell's voice carried a warning with it. 'I don't care if it's on the opposite side of the galaxy to your current interests. Get to Berg now and protect our assets.'

The commander nodded. 'Yes, sir. What of Enlister Kurcher's mission?'

'As long as he doesn't blunder again like he did on Rikur, he will finish his assignment. Have him report to you as agreed but at Berg. Your previous orders stand. Find and extract the data then clean up after yourself.'

'Understood.'

The corner of Mitchell's mouth twisted upwards. 'Try to remember your orders, commander. I don't expect to have this conversation again.'

When the screen went blank, Santa Cruz swore. He didn't need to go back to Berg and to that tiny rock Minerva, but he had pushed his luck as far as he could for now. Still, perhaps he could gain something positive from travelling nearly eighty thousand light years to the border of Coldrig. There were other ships he could take with him, ones that Mitchell wouldn't miss immediately. If he explained to the ship commanders that they were to join his small fleet as protection, how could they refuse?

As he made his way back to the command deck, Santa Cruz pondered which vessels he could enlist. The *Tucana*, the *Exodus* and the *Arcturus* sprang to mind, as he knew the officers well. Perhaps six assault ships, including the *Requiem*, would be enough. Minerva also had two guardians in orbit which could prove useful.

He felt something akin to guilt that the general had been fed only specific pieces of information. Mitchell had spoken for him after all at the hearings in 2611. Without the general, Santa Cruz may well have ended up working the mines of Aridis with the rest of Rockland's inmates. Taurus Galahad wanted results and he had delivered. The cost of that delivery had been in question, but Mitchell had always vouched that the commander's interrogations were a necessary evil.

The general would be proud once Santa Cruz delivered Taurus Galahad the entire galaxy and nobody would dare question him then.

Summit
Benedict system

Tidewell was impressive. There was no denying that.

Kurcher hadn't visited Summit for a long time, yet he had to admit that Impramed had done very well in creating a spa world that was arguably the most popular vacation destination in the galaxy. It must have been bringing in a huge profit too for the smallest of the corps and he was starting to think that perhaps Impramed were richer than they let on.

As the *Kaladine* had descended to Tidewell to drop him off, he and Frost had sat in silence watching as the verdant greenery appeared below. Lakes of various sizes and shapes dotted the landscape, each surrounded by spa structures. Tiny boats could be seen bobbing across the sapphire blue waters.

Tidewell itself shone white in the Benedict sun; a clean city of pale buildings, glass spires and canals that weaved throughout like a system of veins. Directly to the east of Tidewell sat the beautiful coastline, where people frolicked on the white sands and swam in the azure ocean.

The *Kaladine* had been ordered to land at a special docking pad away from the rest of the air traffic and Kurcher had been met immediately by representatives of Impramed who were very quick to offer their assistance in finding Regan D'Larro. It was clear that the idea of a killer being on their perfect world scared the shit out of them. Luckily, Summit was open to members of all corps, but that law would certainly change quickly were there to be any incidents.

The enlister now found himself being escorted to the Tidewell data library where Impramed recorded all arrivals and departures on Summit. If D'Larro was on the planet, they would hopefully be able to point Kurcher in the right direction. The crim wouldn't have even been able to get away with giving a false name as his face would be on record too. Impramed were very thorough and Kurcher was glad for that.

'You say that this man was a Taurus medic?' asked one of the Impramed officers walking in front of him.

Kurcher had seen the three crosses on the officer's white and red uniform when they first met, denoting his senior rank among them. 'That's right. Started out on Titan Station then skipped to Amity for a while. Now apparently he's here.'

'Skipped?' The officer glanced back with inquisitive eyes.

'Yeah, when he was identified as the murderer of eighteen patients at the station infirmary, he released some type of nerve gas to mask his escape. Clever bastard then managed to get off the station somehow and catch a ride to Amity.' Kurcher saw the officer exchange concerned looks with another man. 'What did you say your name was?'

'Aman Saib.'

'Sergeant, right?'

Saib nodded. 'You know, your ship would have been safe remaining on the surface.'

'My pilot gets twitchy on the ground.' Kurcher recalled the *Kaladine* lifting off mere seconds after he had departed. He didn't blame Frost for wanting to be careful this time, plus there would be no temptation for the crims on-board to try taking a wander.

As they entered the data library, the men marching behind Kurcher remained near the door, leaving only Saib and one other officer to escort him deeper inside. The relentless heat and humidity of Summit was replaced by cool air and Kurcher breathed a sigh of relief.

Saib continued to pry. 'So why did he kill those people on Titan Station?'

'Only he knows that. Most of them were sick or wounded so their deaths were not suspicious, but then he killed a Taurus officer who was misdiagnosed. They thought he had picked up some lethal disease from a visit to a quaran world but, just as they determined it wasn't quite so serious, the officer died and the investigation pointed straight at him.'

'What happened on Amity then?'

'He volunteered as a medic during the colony war, but ultimately got himself noticed again when his patients started dying.' Kurcher noticed the apprehension creeping across Saib's face. 'I'm thinking he may have come here to help in one of your facilities.'

That didn't help subdue the sergeant's concern. 'We run checks on our staff. He wouldn't have been able to slip into the system unnoticed.'

Kurcher shrugged. 'Like I said, he's a clever bastard.'

When they arrived at the secure data vault at the heart of the library, Saib accessed the main console and brought up files on all arrivals going back several months. Kurcher pointed out that was going back too far, but was told they were just making sure. Thorough indeed.

Eventually, the enlister sat down before the screen and watched as a list of names began scrolling on the left while the faces of men, women and children appeared on the right. The names quickly ran out and Saib grunted.

'No Regan D'Larro, as expected.'

Kurcher's eyes were fixed on the faces. 'Try Tranc.'

A minute later, the console emitted a ping of recognition and a name was highlighted. Saib squinted at the screen. 'Trank Regarro?'

Kurcher smiled. 'Maybe not that clever then.' An image came up next to the name. 'Yep. That's our guy.'

'I don't understand,' blurted out Saib. 'It says he passed through the scans and headed to the Pale Sands Resort in the northeast corner of Tidewell. If he is a wanted man, we should have picked that up.'

'These crims are resourceful, believe me,' Kurcher told him as he stood up from the console. 'He could've masked it with some illegal app or maybe he bribed his way through. Either way, I need to get to this resort now.'

The sergeant scowled. 'No one would have accepted a bribe, enlister. We don't work like that down here.'

'If you say so.' Kurcher headed for the door. 'Most men have their price though.'

~

The *Kaladine* was quiet. There was no sound of Kurcher beating on Rane, no grumbling as Angard muttered to himself or to Oakley and no engine roar. The latter told him that the ship wasn't back among the stars and was more likely somewhere in the upper atmosphere of Summit.

Choice stretched as he lay on the uncomfortable bed, staring up at the mundane ceiling of the cell. Kurcher was down on the planet looking for his next target, leaving the feisty pilot in charge. Now seemed as good a time as any to test his latest creation.

Swinging his legs off the bed enthusiastically, he tried to activate his library app and wasn't surprised when the data failed to appear in his vision. As he stood, a flash of pain shot up his left leg. Luckily, Angard hadn't broken it when he fell on him. It would still take a while to heal.

As he peered through the small window in the door, he tried activating his customised disruption app. Again there was nothing. A smile passed across his lips as he recalled using it on Kurcher and the priceless look of confusion on the enlister's face.

'You like to think you're so much smarter than everyone else,' he mimicked, trying to copy Kurcher's voice.

He activated the app he had built to interfere with Angard's biomechs. Only a small square of static appeared which tickled the back of his eyes. The tech Kurcher had used to subdue his apps was quite good, but there was more than one way to skin a cat. His vision swam for a moment as he accessed his hacker app, a modified version of the bypass app that the corps used. Several seconds later, the flickering commands appeared having managed to squeeze past Kurcher's tech. Their resolution had been weakened – he had expected that. His trusty hacking tool managed to give him access to the data blocks that made up the biomech disruption app and he gave a quiet snigger as he opened the hidden file he had placed inside during the build.

'I *am* smarter than everyone else,' he whispered.

Inside the file, he found the crude app which he had designed to talk to certain types of corp tech. He had come up with the concept a long time ago; the incessant chasing by the enlisters had put his plans to create it on hold. It was sweet irony that allowed him to use the tech Kurcher gave him to create a bastardised version of the real thing.

The *Kaladine*'s systems were complex and he knew his app wouldn't be able to link in with the more heavily-firewalled ones. It didn't matter. He was a genius and soon Kurcher and the others would realise that. He took note of the comms system, which branched off into external and internal routes, then tracked the latter wiring through to the cell intercoms. That would come in handy too later on. It was what was next to the intercoms he had been looking for. He issued the command, which took a moment to travel through the *Kaladine*'s inner workings. Then the cell door opened.

He had to be quick to stop the ship's systems from alerting Frost via her pilot app and marvelled at the speed of his latest creation.

Slowly, Choice edged out into the corridor, checking left and right. He knew that the cockpit and the airlock were to his right, along with the access point to the solo lifeboat the ship carried. To his left were the rec room, storage, the quarters belonging to Kurcher and Frost, and the way down to the hold.

He slunk to the right and looked into Rane's cell. It seemed the killer was sleeping off the effects of Kurcher's fist.

'You'll wait,' Choice mumbled softly.

He headed for the storage room, noting that Angard was wide awake in his cell. Choice found the giant intriguing. He would love to get his hands on the apps the scientists implanted so as to make Angard the way he was. What wonders he could do with that sort of tech.

When he reached storage, he tried ordering the door to open. His app ran into a very stubborn blocker that refused to budge. As much as he wanted to get his hands on his knife and book, he knew he wasn't getting inside. Disappointed, he moved to the edge of the rec room doorway several paces along the corridor and peered inside. A lonely-looking Oakley sat at the table, staring into a glass of water. She looked so vulnerable, but that was how she lulled her victims in; long lashes, mesmerising blue eyes, cleavage on show and the look of innocence. She was damaged goods though and he had no intention of getting close enough to become another of her victims, despite the lustful feelings he was experiencing.

He peeled away from the doorway and headed back past the cells. He had to be direct. There was no other option as Frost could take the *Kaladine* back down to the surface to pick Kurcher up any moment. At the cockpit door, he accessed his app again. There was another blocker in place for this door, but it wasn't as strong as the one protecting the storage room. He managed to wear it down gradually, proving to him that his own tech was superior to that developed by Taurus Galahad.

As the door slid open, Choice felt excited at the thought of taking command of the *Kaladine* and imagined Kurcher's face when he realised his beloved ship had left him behind. He moved inside quickly, aiming to grab Frost before she realised what was happening, but a strong arm suddenly wrapped around his neck and wrenched him backwards.

'Bad move,' Broekow remarked.

As Choice struggled to break free of the sniper's grip, Frost appeared from her seat.

'You didn't think it'd be that simple to get in here, did you?' she asked.

Choice groaned. 'Auxiliary alert system.' He had been so intent on breaking down the blocker that he hadn't considered a back-up alarm.

Frost raised her pistol as she approached and placed it against his forehead. 'Time to go back to your cell.'

'Does Kurcher know you allow *him* in here? Betting not.'

'Come on.' Broekow pushed him towards the door and Frost followed them out into the corridor, keeping her gun trained on the escaped crim.

'Think about this opportunity,' Choice said to the sniper. 'No enlister. His pilot wouldn't be able to stand against us if we took this ship. This is our chance to get as far away as possible and she would be an excellent hostage.'

'I *am* right here,' snapped Frost.

As Broekow shoved him back into the cell, Frost moved to close the door.

'Try getting out again and I'll shoot you in both knees,' she told Choice before locking him up. She then turned to Broekow. 'How the fuck did he manage that?'

'It doesn't surprise me that he found a way to bypass corp tech.' Broekow gave her a knowing look. 'You know he'll just keep trying.'

'Well I meant what I said. I won't hesitate in crippling him to keep him

142

where he belongs.'

'Maybe we should just do that now and save time.'

Frost gave a weak smile. 'Davian would string me up. It's bad enough that I allow one crim into my cockpit.'

'Listen, I'm not going to do anything that would jeopardise my being enlisted. It's not worth becoming the hunted again. I'll stand guard here for now, to make sure he doesn't get up to no good.'

'Thanks. I'd better go restore the firewalls he broke through.' She hesitated. 'For what it's worth, I believe you.'

Broekow grinned and nodded his appreciation. It took him by surprise when she planted a sudden kiss on his cheek before disappearing back to the cockpit.

In his cell, Choice rolled his eyes and slouched back onto his bed. No wonder she allowed the sniper access all areas. Closing his eyes, he began working on a new plan.

~

'Get the fuck out the way.'

Kurcher's cry seemed to turn people to stone rather than spur them into motion. He cursed at them as he weaved between the spa visitors and staff, occasionally seeing D'Larro through the throng as the medic tried to flee. All it would take was for one of them to stick out a leg and trip the crim up.

He missed the data from his sense app at times like this. The life readings and face recognition tech had saved him a lot of time in the past but now, thanks to Choice, he had to rely on his naked eyes. It was making him realise just how much he had become dependent on the app.

The two men sprinted along the main concourse of the Pale Sands Resort, with Kurcher several paces behind the sprightly D'Larro. Ahead, the glass wall at the front of the spa was getting closer and the number of people in their way was starting to thin. D'Larro darted out of the main entrance, bouncing off a new arrival and knocking the man to the ground. This gained Kurcher some ground but, as the enlister headed out into the street, the heat hit him and he knew the pursuit was only going to get tougher.

Seeing that D'Larro was heading south, clearly hoping to evade his pursuer among the crowds of Tidewell, Kurcher considered using up his remaining boost. The drug would ensure he didn't tire, but it still wouldn't gain him any ground, plus he would then be reliant solely on his Calmer supply. It wasn't worth it.

He saw the medic glance back at him. D'Larro looked much younger than his twenty-six years, but Kurcher could see there was something slightly off about him the moment they met. D'Larro had been laughing with two of the Pale Sands medical staff when Kurcher had entered the infirmary. However, he had seemingly clocked the enlister straight away. It was some feat how he had managed to integrate himself with the med team at the spa in such a short space of time. Kurcher suspected though that the staff there were stupid enough to accept such an innocent-looking man at face value, especially when he explained his credentials, obviously leaving out the parts where he murdered his patients. Moments after their eyes met, D'Larro fled. Kurcher was still wondering quite how the medic had known. He also wondered whether Cooke had found the same thing on Amity.

D'Larro veered off the main street, disappearing down a narrower walkway. As Kurcher turned the corner, he considered contacting Frost and getting the *Kaladine* down to help track the medic. The fact he had one ace left up his sleeve quickly made his mind up though and he switched to a more local comms channel.

'On Escabar, about to reach fountain plaza.'

Ahead, as D'Larro headed past the gleaming marble statue of a man pouring water into the cupped hands of children gathered below, several figures in white and red pounced on him and dragged him to the ground. A smug-looking Sergeant Saib watched on.

'We'll accompany you back to your ship,' he said as Kurcher approached.

'Not necessary.'

'Policy, I'm afraid. We need to make sure he leaves Summit.'

Kurcher shrugged then switched his comms back to the usual channel. 'Justyne, meet you back at the landing pad shortly.'

'Any problems?' asked his pilot.

'No.' He saw D'Larro being pulled back to his feet, a guard on each arm. 'Hoping this one will see sense and won't have to share a cell.'

'Okay, on my way down.'

Kurcher turned to D'Larro, who was wide-eyed and sweating. 'Don't try running again. These guys have a soft touch compared to me.'

'What happens now?' the medic asked him.

'First, I check you don't have any weapons on you or any of that nerve toxin you're so fond of.' Kurcher patted him down, finding a scalpel in one pocket and a wallet containing five small capsules in another. 'My ship will be landing shortly. Once we're on-board, I'll explain what happens next.'

'Are you going to kill me?'

Kurcher smiled at the question. 'Not unless you misbehave, Regan.'

144

D'Larro seemed to flinch at the sound of his name. He didn't say anything more, instead bowing his head as he was marched away by Saib's men.

The heat of the day was waning thankfully as the entourage entered the plaza leading to the landing pad. The *Kaladine* was waiting ahead, gleaming in the afternoon sun. Kurcher and Saib walked in front of D'Larro and the guards, weaving a way between the rubberneckers in the plaza.

'They act like they haven't seen a crim before,' Kurcher commented.

'We don't see many here,' admitted the sergeant.

Kurcher found Saib's response amusing but kept his laughter contained. There were probably a number of petty criminals roaming the streets of Tidewell, keeping under the radar of the guards protecting the city. It was no wonder Impramed were mocked by the other corps. They were naive.

As they approached the bottom of the stone steps leading up to the landing pad and the number of people in their way diminished, Kurcher saw a group of men enter the plaza to their right. The expression on their faces were grim, eyes fixed on the enlister. Glancing left, he saw another three men heading towards him and he reached for his revolver.

'I take it they aren't more of your men come to see us off.'

Saib followed Kurcher's line of sight. 'Definitely not. Do you...'

The sergeant was cut short as a shot rang out, sending the plaza into chaos. People fled, desperately trying to seek some safe hiding place. The Impramed guards looked around for a moment before drawing their stun guns.

Kurcher saw one of those on the right who had been moving towards him now lying on the ground, a spatter of red on the white stone behind him. Revolver in hand, the enlister reached back and grabbed D'Larro's arm before dragging him towards the steps. The dead man's colleagues gave each other confused looks before raising their own weapons. The sight of the razepistols and submachine guns spurred Kurcher on.

'Drop them now.'

Saib's command fell on deaf ears as some of the men opened fire on the Impramed officers. Another shot echoed across the plaza from the hidden sniper, blowing through the skull of a man on Kurcher's left.

'Find that fucker,' yelled one of the men, who then drew a bead on Kurcher.

The enlister shoved D'Larro forward, sending the medic stumbling to the bottom step. As the attacker fired his razepistol once, Kurcher dived to the ground. He felt the searing heat pass over him, singeing his hair. He responded with two shots to the chest that blew the man off his feet. Quickly standing again, he looked back to see two of Saib's men lying dead and the

145

sergeant himself ushering his remaining men towards cover at the edge of the plaza. A burst of submachine gun fire snapped his attention to the left and he threw himself backwards to avoid being peppered by bullets. Another shot from his revolver struck the gunner in the forehead.

'Get to the ship,' he called to D'Larro, who was lying where he had left him.

As Kurcher turned, he saw the man he had shot twice getting back up and adjusting his protective vest. It seemed they had come prepared. He then caught a glimpse of a familiar emblem beneath the man's jacket and suddenly the attack made sense.

'Justyne, we've got Sapphire Nova goons here trying to take me out. Can you cover with the gats?'

'Not from this position,' came the hurried reply. 'I can take off to get a better shot.'

'No, stay there. We're on our way.'

As D'Larro ran as fast as he could up the steps, Kurcher locked eyes with the Nova agent he had shot. They must have been sent to track him down after Rikur. If that was the case, these men wouldn't show any mercy – so neither would he. When he saw another Nova man fall to the sniper, Kurcher glanced around the buildings surrounding the plaza. If he had more time, he would've liked to know who exactly was coming to his rescue without being asked.

With three Nova agents moving around the edge of the plaza, seeking any sign of the sniper, and two keeping Saib pinned down, that left the final three to take down the enlister. Razepistols and a submachine gun fired, tearing holes in the immaculate stone of the plaza and prompting Kurcher to dive for cover once more, this time lying flat on the steps. As the barrage eased, he checked on D'Larro. The medic was nearly at the top. Kurcher returned fire, missing once but his second bullet passing through the calf of one agent and dropping him. That was his cue to leave and he followed D'Larro, taking two steps at a time. Behind him, the crack of the sniper rifle heralded another dead Nova agent and razepistol fire scorched the steps he had just leapt over.

At the top, he found D'Larro staring nervously at the *Kaladine*'s open airlock, where Broekow stood waiting for them. Footsteps came up behind him and Kurcher pushed the medic into Broekow's grip. As the two men disappeared into the ship and the engines began to roar in anticipation, Kurcher reached the airlock and spun as the Nova agent he had shot twice appeared, letting off a shot at the *Kaladine* which blackened the hull. Kurcher fired and his shot hit the agent in the hand, causing him to drop the

146

razepistol.

'Quick burst,' he said into his comms.

As the gats swivelled towards the lone Nova merc, Kurcher gave him a quick salute before heading into the *Kaladine* and closing the airlock. When the gats burst into life, what was left of the man landed at the base of the steps.

~

Winter watched the *Kaladine* soar into the sky and immediately moved from his position. The roof had sufficed during the panic of the initial firefight, but now the remaining Nova men were closing in and he didn't have time to wait around.

As he headed along the roof, he looked down into the plaza. He had killed five men, one shot each, and Kurcher had taken care of a couple more. That left seven in total, including the one the enlister had wounded. He could see the Impramed guards trying to use their ineffectual stun guns against the two Nova agents, both using razepistols. He should just leave them be. More security forces would descend on the scene shortly. As he went to move away, he saw one of the Nova men step back and holster his razepistol before pulling something much deadlier from a hidden holster. Winter had seen boomers in action before and he didn't care to see that again.

Kneeling down, he hefted his rifle and took aim at the man with the boomer. As his finger brushed the trigger, he heard movement behind him and glanced back. Two heat signatures were clambering onto the roof nearby with a third approaching the base of the building. Cursing quietly, he rotated his position.

As one of the Nova agents stood, Winter's bullet took him through the eye and out the back of his head. The second merc was halfway onto the roof when his colleague tumbled over the edge, making him hesitate. As the stunned merc finally hauled himself up, Winter's knife stabbed deep into his neck as the Taurus agent's other hand covered his mouth. Winter waited until all life had drained from the man's eyes then checked on the position of the third, who seemed to be staying put against the wall below, no doubt concerned having seen one of his team plummet back to the ground. Recovering his rifle, Winter stalked to the edge of the roof. Not wanting to stick his neck out, he linked his sight app to the rifle scope and held it over the edge. He waited patiently as his scope lined up over the thermal image of the hidden merc then held his breath and pulled the trigger. The bullet struck the merc in the top of the skull, passing straight through and out of his jaw

147

before ricocheting off the ground. Winter then went back to his previous position.

Unfortunately, he was just in time to see the results of the boomer as one of the Impramed guards took a shot in the shoulder. A second later, the bullet exploded and tore the poor man's arm clean off as well as making a mess of his torso and one side of his head. Boomers were the weapon of choice of particularly sadistic mercs and Winter found their use abhorrent. Before the Nova man could use it again, Winter put a bullet through his brain.

A swarm of Impramed guards entered the plaza, this time armed with more than just stun guns. The two Nova men left standing were told to lay down their weapons. Winter was pleased when they refused. As another firefight broke out, he fired one last shot from his rifle, killing the one Kurcher had wounded in the calf. It was best that the Sapphire Nova force was wiped out in its entirety.

By the time the exchange was over, the other two Nova men lay dead too and the sergeant who had been accompanying Kurcher came out from cover looking ashen, his once pristine white and red uniform covered in blood and dirt.

Winter left as the Impramed forces tried to make sense of what had just happened on their peaceful world. It was more likely they would blame it on D'Larro, believing the Sapphire Nova mercs had been there to kill him. They wouldn't suspect it was all down to Kurcher.

As he made his way back to his ship, he considered his next port of call. He needed to get to Iridia as quickly as possible, but dodging Libra Centauri would be tricky. He toyed with the idea of simply relaying some anonymous message to the *Kaladine* telling them to check out the Iridia system; Kurcher's penchant for drawing attention to himself was a concern. Winter also couldn't help but wonder where exactly the enlister would take his trail of destruction next.

Enlister-class vessel Kaladine
Callyn system

Kurcher purposefully delayed his arrival in the rec room. His head ached and his limbs felt heavy. He felt like his legs were going to buckle any moment and even walking along the corridor was difficult. The Calmers weren't really helping now and even his supply of those was running low. There had been a second of panic when he had tried to activate his boost app only to receive an alert that he was out of Parinax. So here they were, heading through one of the most dangerous systems to meet with the *Nomad* and her greedy captain to kill two birds with one stone. At least, that was what he hoped.

He groaned when he saw how many people were gathered in the rec room. It felt wrong having them there and he couldn't wait for Taurus to take them off his hands so he and Frost could get back to normal, or as close to normal as possible.

'You look like shit,' Oakley stated.

He ignored the comment and poured himself a bitter coffee, hoping it might take the edge off. He then turned and looked around at the expectant faces, preferring to focus on Frost rather than the crims.

'Found the *Nomad* yet?'

'Yeah, three hours away.' Frost had her arms crossed and a cigarette hanging from her lips. 'Had to talk our way past two Fortitude ships already so our presence here is probably the talk of the town by now.'

'Let them talk. No merc ship will take a shot at us unless we provoke them.'

'You really think Hewn will be here?' asked Broekow, who was in his usual position leaning against the wall. 'Not sure the mercs would like the leader of Echo hiding among them.'

Kurcher swilled the coffee round his mouth for a moment then swallowed with his usual grimace. 'Hewn won't be here, but my contact will know if he passed through on his way back to the Expanse.'

'Sounds like a long shot,' said Oakley, glancing at the brooding giant standing next to her.

'Well if one of you has any miraculous insight into the whereabouts of these last two fuckers, I'm all ears.' The tone of Kurcher's voice made Angard glower at him. 'Didn't think so.'

149

He had agreed to let Angard out of his cell shortly after he got back with D'Larro, mainly to avoid him going berserk being cooped up. Oakley had told him over and over that her apparent protector would behave while she was nearby, but seeing what he did to those guards back on Cradle kept Kurcher vigilant around the crim.

As he carefully considered his next words to the room full of killers, the enlister found himself thinking about Rane and Choice. Why Rane was still alive was a mystery even to him, but his head started pounding whenever he recalled their last conversation. Hearing about Choice escaping his cell had really pissed him off. At least Oakley, Angard and D'Larro had agreed not to rock the boat, albeit reluctantly. Choice would likely continue pushing his luck and Kurcher found himself between a rock and a hard place. He needed Choice's biomech disruption app in case Angard got out of control again, but he also wanted Maric to subdue his alter ego. He cursed Santa Cruz for giving him the assignment in the first place.

'Your job here is very simple,' he began finally, addressing everyone except Frost. 'You sit here and wait while I track down Ercko and Hewn, then we all get to go see Taurus. Unless you have any info that could aid me and get the job done quicker, I suggest you enjoy the fact that you're all sitting here in my rec room rather than being stuffed in one of the cells.'

'And what if you need our help?' asked D'Larro, who had been sitting silently at the table.

'Sometimes Broekow assists me, but that's it. Truthfully, he's the only one I trust not to stab me in the back.'

The medic continued to push his point. 'What if you get hurt? Who else could patch you up?'

Kurcher nearly sprayed coffee as he laughed. 'You think I'd let you anywhere near me with your record? Most of your patients end up dead.'

D'Larro looked hurt. 'You saved me back on Summit so I knew you were telling me the truth when you said you were there to enlist me. I'd be an idiot if I tried killing you or anyone else now.'

Kurcher glanced at Frost and noted how she couldn't look at the medic. 'You were an idiot to kill anyone in the first place, Regan.'

'Please don't call me that,' D'Larro pleaded. 'I don't go by that name anymore. Reminds me too much of home. You can call me Tranc now if you like.'

'Well whatever your name is, your past isn't easy to ignore.' Kurcher downed the rest of his coffee. 'I don't intend on getting shot any time soon anyway.'

150

'I'm still not buying it.' All eyes turned to Angard. 'We're just supposed to trust you and the corp?'

Kurcher knew he had to tread carefully. 'I don't think trust is the right word. I certainly don't trust any of you and I never expected you to completely trust me. I'd hoped you would realise that this is a better alternative to being hunted down and killed.'

The sarcasm wasn't lost on Angard. 'I'm the only one who didn't agree to this.'

'Would you rather be in the cell, big guy?' Broekow asked, drawing a look of pure contempt from the giant crim.

'You've since agreed to behave though,' Kurcher said. 'Look, this isn't exactly a perfect situation for any of us.'

Angard reached out with one huge hand and patted Oakley's arm. 'I'll play along cause she needs me. Just a warning though, enlister. If the corp try taking me back to Shard or plan on using me for more tests, I'll kill them all.' His good eye narrowed as he focused on Kurcher. 'Then I'll kill you.'

'Fair enough.' Kurcher's nonchalance drew surprised looks from everyone else. 'Right, Justyne, tell the *Nomad* I'll be coming over alone. Once I'm back, I'm hoping I'll have some leads to follow up. In the meantime...' He waved a hand dismissively. 'I'm tired of repeating myself. You all know the drill.'

He left the rec room with Frost, accompanying her back to the cockpit. As they entered and he closed the door, Kurcher spotted Broekow taking his position outside the cells once more. The sniper had taken it upon himself to act as guard and that meant one less thing to worry about for now.

'I don't like this,' Frost complained as she lowered herself back into her seat.

Kurcher slumped into the other chair. 'What's to like? We've got six killers on-board, we're in merc space and I've nearly been killed on two worlds in the past couple of weeks.'

'Did you ever work out who the sniper was on Summit?'

'No. I thought you might have dropped Broekow off to back me up, but you wouldn't have put that much trust in him.'

Frost didn't let on that Broekow was on her mind more often than not. 'So any other ideas?'

'Could've been one of Impramed's men. I never got the chance to ask Saib. Could've been someone who just didn't like Nova. Either way, D'Larro and I would probably be dead were it not for him.'

'Or her.' Frost adjusted the *Kaladine*'s course slightly as she realised the *Nomad* was also on the move. 'You sure that Kopetti can help?'

'Oakley was right. It is a long shot.' The smuggler would still be able to help him resupply. 'Kopetti peddles information all the time so I'd be surprised if he didn't have something for me, even if it doesn't lead to Hewn.'

'The last bit of intel he gave you was bullshit. I'm amazed you never went back to thank him for that.'

Kurcher bit at his lip as the ache in his skull became an angry throbbing. 'Just drop me off and I'll get Kopetti to dock with you once our business is complete.'

'Oakley was right about something else.'

'Oh?'

'You *do* look like shit.'

The *Nomad* was a smaller ship that resembled some bulked-up planethopper. The hull had once been blue but was now rust-coloured and pock-marked with the scars of several close shaves. It wasn't that easy to dock with either due to the occasional listing it suffered when the ragged engines spluttered every time it changed speed.

Kopetti met Kurcher straight out of the airlock as the *Kaladine* disembarked and moved away from the pack mule of a ship.

'Good to see you again,' grinned the smuggler through his dirty grey beard. 'When I heard your ship was in Callyn, I knew you'd be looking for me.'

Kurcher rubbed his temples. 'Spare me the false pleasantries. We both know you only like seeing me because I pay well.'

Kopetti's grin widened. 'Of course. So what's your poison this time?'

'Information on unusual movement in and around Callyn.' Kurcher felt like he was going to throw up. 'First though, how much Parinax do you have in stock?'

~

'So how come he's here?'

Broekow compared the medic to some excitable child, seeing his expression as he stared at Rane. 'Kurcher and I ran into him on Rikur. He gave himself up after saving us from Nova sec.'

'I heard a lot about him through news reports,' D'Larro said, his voice hushed. 'Did they ever find out why he killed all those people?'

Broekow shook his head. 'Not yet. No offense but you've probably killed a fair number yourself. Why the fascination in another killer?'

D'Larro regarded him with a look of remorse. 'I had a reason for what I did. I'm not proud of it, but it ultimately gave me the knowledge I needed.'

152

'Go on.'

'Being able to control whether someone lives or dies gives you a high that can't be matched by drugs. You must have felt it whenever you killed someone. Anyway, I used some of my terminal patients to test different theories on how best to end the life of someone who was suffering. There are more ways than just putting a bullet through their brain.'

The confusion was clear on Broekow's face. 'That doesn't make sense. Hospitals already know the most humane ways to end a life.'

'Humane.' D'Larro sniggered. 'I'm talking about working out how to control death; to understand it. It is the one great mystery that the human race has never been able to answer. What happens when you die?'

Broekow understood just why this young medic was considered dangerous. The remorse in his eyes hid something much darker. 'So you killed all those people trying to answer that question?'

D'Larro turned back to peer into the cell. 'Some. I'm fascinated with the human body and it set me thinking about how it reacted to different environments as well as understanding what happened when it was badly wounded. That's why I went to Amity during the civil war, to work on those who had been shot, burnt, stabbed or maimed in some way. To continue my research.'

'Your father was a medic too, right?'

D'Larro flinched. 'Yes.'

'Not exactly following in his footsteps, were you?'

'Was your father a sniper?' D'Larro's face had reddened.

'No, but he was a corporal in the Taurus military.' Broekow knew that he had stumbled upon a sore point. 'What about your mother?'

'Geologist. Headed up teams exploring planets in search of resources.'

'Sounds more interesting than being a medic.'

'I wouldn't know.' A distant look appeared in D'Larro's eyes. 'She left me behind.'

Broekow didn't want to push further. No point in pissing the medic off. The conversations he could have on the *Kaladine* were already limited to avoiding confrontation with Angard or trying his best to ignore Oakley's flirtatious nature. It was bad enough sharing the hold with them now. Sleep didn't come easily with those three around. No, he would keep visiting Frost when he wanted intelligent banter.

'Just don't engage with either Rane or Choice... Maric... whoever the fuck he is today.'

D'Larro smiled and nodded. 'Understood. I'd really like to study Angard more, but I feel he would squash me if I did. His biomechs are amazing though. If I could understand how they work...'

'Trust me when I tell you to steer clear of him,' Broekow warned. 'I've seen what he's capable of doing to men much bigger than you.'

D'Larro stepped back from the cell door. 'I meant what I said to Kurcher, you know. I'm a trained medic and can be of use if he lets me. How did you get him to trust you?'

'Kurcher will never trust anyone. He tolerates me because I'm handy in a firefight. It's going to take a while for me to ingratiate myself with him. Don't take it personally.'

As D'Larro nodded and walked away, Broekow heard soft footsteps behind him that brought a smile to his face.

'Good timing.'

Frost appeared alongside him. 'He gives me the creeps.'

'Don't they all?'

'Not all.' She put an unlit cigarette to her lips, decided against lighting up and returned it to her pocket. 'Need to cut down anyway.'

Broekow could see dark rings under her eyes. 'When was the last time you got some sleep?'

'Got a few hours here and there since we left Summit. I'm struggling to sleep comfortably with this lot on-board.'

'Tell me about it.'

Frost stretched. 'I'm still not sure about Kurcher's decision to let Angard out. With Oakley's brains and his brawn, they always pose a potential threat.'

'Yeah, but she's smart enough to know enlisting is the only way to be truly free. Besides, she has all the credentials to be the perfect agent.'

'Oh really?'

Broekow smirked. 'No need to get jealous.'

'In your dreams.' Frost allowed herself a smile.

'They'll all be off your ship soon enough,' Broekow told her. 'Then it'll just be the three of us, hopefully.'

Her smile vanished. 'Sieren, you have to understand something.' When she met his gaze, her voice faltered for a moment. 'There's still no guarantee you'll end up as part of our team. Kurcher is a hard man to please, as you know.'

Broekow put a hand on her shoulder. 'I do understand, but I like it here on the *Kaladine*. I feel like I have some purpose again.' His grip tightened. 'And there are other reasons to stick around of course.'

Frost noticed him moving closer and her first instinct should have been to

154

pull away while grabbing her gun. Instead, she found herself pressing up against him as they kissed. It felt too good to stop and the fact he was a crim seemed to just turn her on even more. Something at the back of her mind screamed out that she was risking everything. She didn't care. Fuck the consequences.

Taurus Galahad Assault Ship Requiem
Berg system

Somehow it seemed darker out on the distant edge of the Scutum-Centaurus Arm. Other than the Berg sun, the only other source of light glimmered dimly from the artificial lamps of the shipyard construction.

Santa Cruz had been extremely disappointed to discover how far from completion the structure was. Left to their own devices on the border of known space, the construction teams had become lazy. He had quite enjoyed delivering the speech to kick them into action, but the looks in their eyes still played on his mind. Those unaccustomed to working in deep space tended to suffer from insomnia, paranoia and even picked up a variety of psychoses. Although he had considered requesting that new teams be sent, the current workforce had assured him they would up their efforts. Besides, they needed the money.

He cast his eyes down to the planet below. What a dull world Minerva was. It had been named after the Roman goddess of wisdom and war, yet certainly didn't befit such a grand title. It was the only habitable planet though in the system and that made it the sole choice when Taurus Galahad decided on the location of their key confidential research facility.

When Minerva turned her back on the sun, the lights of the Hayes colony could be made out on the surface; pinpricks of white on a sprawling brown canvas.

Santa Cruz had not yet visited Hayes since arriving several days ago. He planned to do so soon. He yearned to see the collection of artefacts and data files again. The temptation to bring them back onto the *Requiem* for safekeeping would be great as usual; however, he knew the scientists making up the sparse population of Hayes were best left alone to continue their research. For now, at least.

The commander's gaze passed beyond Minerva for a few minutes, into the void. Beyond Berg lay the Coldrig sector, which had given up a number of its secrets already. There was so much more just waiting to be found – he was positive. Of course, some of the finds had been made in known space, including the data Cooke discovered by accident, so there was no telling where the next one would be unearthed.

Ten explorer-class ships were already in orbit of Minerva, waiting for the shipyard to be completed so they could prepare for their long expeditions into

Coldrig. Another eight were on their way to Berg. With his six-strong fleet and two guardians also in orbit, Minerva was possibly one of the best-protected worlds in Taurus Galahad space at that moment.

'Commander?'

He sighed when Connolly's voice broke the silence. 'What is it?'

'We've received a message from General Mitchell. It's a fleet-wide communication requesting assistance in the...'

'Put it through to me here,' Santa Cruz interrupted. 'I'd rather hear it from the horse's mouth.'

'Yes, sir. Patching it through.'

As the commander gazed out into the darkness, Mitchell's gruff voice echoed around him. 'This is General Mitchell. A Taurus Galahad convoy consisting of two assault ships and two transports has been attacked in the Kalbrec system by four Sapphire Nova assault vessels. Both transports have been destroyed, along with the *Madriosa*. The *Northstar* was badly damaged and left for dead. We are tracking the Nova ships near Cobb. Any assault ships able to get to Kalbrec quickly are ordered to intercept and destroy them.'

Santa Cruz smiled. Nova's retaliation had been quicker than anticipated.

'I'm awaiting your quick response,' continued Mitchell. 'The *Victory* is already in Kalbrec on an intercept course.'

Even the flagship of the Taurus fleet couldn't take down four Nova assault ships on its own, but the general wasn't stupid.

'What are your orders, sir?' asked Connolly.

'Same as before. We remain in orbit of Minerva.'

'But, sir, the general...' Connolly's voice trailed off.

'Can take care of the situation.' Santa Cruz added some anger to his tone, hoping that would end the conversation. 'We are on the other side of the galaxy. By the time we got there, the battle would be over.'

There was a moment's silence before Connolly spoke up again. 'Understood, sir.'

Santa Cruz wanted to laugh. Mitchell would be regretting sending him to Berg now. The general had clearly wanted him out of the way while the board moaned and whined about his actions. Now they would have to deal with the fallout themselves. He didn't plan on moving his fleet again for a while yet.

Turning from the view, he activated his personal console and brought up a map of the Milky Way, zooming in on Berg and the other occupied systems on that side of the galaxy. The nearest system to Berg was Ixxis, some three

157

thousand light years away. Sapphire Nova owned Ixxis, but Santa Cruz knew their presence there was weak. They had simply claimed it to get closer to Berg and the Coldrig border.

Pendium, Tassel and Wagner were all Taurus systems; Nova had managed to claim both Karstad and Ulrich. Still, these were home to relatively young colonies so any military presence would be minimal.

A smile crossed his lips when he glanced over the Pegasus system, remembering the ill-fated Sigma Royal ship of the same name.

After casting his eyes over the map, he came to the conclusion that Berg wasn't in any immediate danger from Sapphire Nova, or any other corp for that matter. He fully expected more systems nearby to be claimed over time, unless war halted progress as it so often did. He wasn't naïve enough though to just dismiss the danger Nova presented. They were aggressive and liked to hit Taurus where it hurt most. Berg would eventually be a target – no doubt they were biding their time until the right moment.

He brought up the Kalbrec system on his screen and highlighted any Taurus assault ships. It surprised him to see seven, with all but one already nearing Cobb, and a part of him was almost disappointed that Mitchell had the support he needed. It was a strange twist of fate that kept bringing Kalbrec and Cobb into the history books. Maybe the universe was trying to tell him something. Maybe Cobb was not a world to be ignored after all.

Turning his screen off, Santa Cruz pushed all thoughts of war out of his mind and began preparations to visit his priceless collection on Hayes.

Enlister-class vessel Kaladine
Callyn system

'Time to get up, Davian.'

Kurcher opened one eye and found himself lying fully-clothed on his bed, exactly where he had fallen after visiting with Kopetti. He had to admit it had been the best sleep in some time, mainly thanks to the more powerful Calmers the smuggler had sold him. Kopetti had claimed some merc outfit had tinkered with the formula in order to boost the high when taking the usual advised dosage. It certainly did the trick.

'I'm up,' he yawned.

Frost tutted. 'Yeah, but I need you clear-headed. We're nearly at that moon Kopetti told you about.'

'And?' prompted Kurcher, sitting up and opening his other eye.

'Jesus, you're hard work sometimes. That dirtball was right for once. There's a small passenger transport in orbit.'

'Good. I'll be there in a moment.'

Kurcher stood and checked that he still had his revolver at his side. He then staggered to the wash basin and splashed cold water onto his face. The Parinax had made his skin extra-sensitive and he shuddered.

As he looked at himself in the mirror, realising he needed to shave sometime soon or risk looking as scruffy as Broekow, he recalled the dream he had been enjoying before Frost had woken him. Instead of the troubled nightmares he had been experiencing recently, this time he was being straddled by some naked woman who vaguely resembled Oakley. As she had ridden him so enthusiastically, a group of people had been standing watching at the foot of the bed. Who these voyeurs were, he had no idea, but one of them was gigantic and had a single glowing red eye. Despite being watched in the throes of passion, Kurcher had felt at ease and knew that nothing could trouble him while the woman was atop him. Nothing, that was, except Frost.

By the time he reached the cockpit, he was feeling almost human again. He had even referred to D'Larro by his preferred moniker of Tranc when the medic crossed his path outside the rec room.

'Broekow's whistling,' he said as he moved up behind Frost to peer out of the screen.

She shrugged. 'So?'

'We shouldn't make him too comfy here. After all, once we find these last

159

two, he'll be leaving with the rest.'

'So smack him around a bit like you do with Rane and Choice.'

That brought a smile to his face. 'He'd probably smack back. Anyway, what've we got?'

Frost pointed at the display to her left, where the image of a ship flickered. 'It's not a corp transport. Merc-owned most likely, considering the state of it. No name on the hull or designation of any kind, so someone clearly wanted it to remain under the radar.'

Kurcher looked back up at the cockpit screen. 'And that planet?'

'Some volcanic world known locally as *Mags*. Would be a quaran in corp space, but the mercs just avoid it.' Frost went silent for a moment as she interacted with the *Kaladine*, then continued. 'The moon hasn't even got a proper name. It's just called *Mags One*. Pretty much dead.'

Kurcher stared at the pair of sorry-looking celestial bodies. 'Doubt anyone would try hiding on one of those.'

Frost looked up at him. 'Do you really think this could be Hewn?'

'Somehow I doubt that the wanted leader of Echo would corner himself in such a dangerous system.' Kurcher recalled Kopetti telling him that guardians were watching the jump points into the Echo Expanse, so the pirate wouldn't have yet returned to his small empire. 'Still, it's worth checking out.'

'Probably just some mercs trying to avoid being noticed.'

'Whoever contacted Kopetti from that ship sounded frightened and desperate. I may be walking into some ambush of course.'

Frost nodded in agreement. 'Best not go alone then.'

As the *Kaladine* settled into orbit alongside the transport, Kurcher and Broekow prepared to board it. While the enlister had considered getting someone else to accompany them, the others didn't have the same experience or background as the sniper. Angard would've likely wrecked the transport just by trying to squeeze through the doorways and Oakley wasn't the sort to get her hands dirty unnecessarily. D'Larro may have seen war; Kurcher didn't trust him. Broekow had told him about the conversation with the medic outside the cells and that made Kurcher warier.

Once the *Kaladine* had docked, Frost accompanied them to the airlock. As Kurcher stepped through into the transport, Broekow looked back.

'Keep both eyes on Choice,' he told her. 'See you soon.'

The interior of the transport was gloomy, with the power seemingly out here and there. The light from the *Kaladine*'s airlock was snuffed out as the door closed behind the two men.

160

'I know that smell,' Broekow stated in a hushed voice.

Kurcher had smelt enough dead bodies to recognise it too. He could just about make out the corridor ahead and the three doors off it. At the far end, steps ascended to the transport's cockpit. After checking that Broekow had his weapon drawn too, Kurcher moved cautiously to the first door.

Inside, he could see what used to be a storage room. It had been trashed. The lockers were all wide open; Kurcher doubted anything valuable would be left behind. Checking the corners of the room, he signalled to Broekow and they moved on.

The next was a rec room and again debris lined the floor. The smell was rife in there, but Kurcher couldn't see any bodies. When he stepped inside and began looking around, Broekow moved into the doorway behind him and watched their back. The enlister was pleased he hadn't had to tell him to. In the corner of the rec room, Kurcher found a hatch cover and one sniff told him that what was beneath wouldn't be pretty.

He moved back to Broekow and whispered to him. 'Stay here and watch that hatch. I'm just going to check out the last two rooms up here.'

'What do you reckon's down there?' asked Broekow, making sure to keep his voice low too.

Kurcher eyed it suspiciously. 'Probably an old hold converted into passenger bunks to transport people covertly. There may be someone alive – doesn't smell like it.'

The enlister left Broekow to ponder that delight and discovered that the next room had been turned into makeshift quarters, complete with an unmade bed, a personal display console and a wash basin. He couldn't guess what the room had been originally; the crudeness of the current furniture led him to believe the ship's owner had thought himself a dab hand at DIY. When he went to check the console, he saw that someone had done enough damage to make sure nobody could ever use it again.

The door to the cockpit was closed; luckily the power to it was still working. Revolver ready, he opened it and was greeted by more rancid odours. The pilot's seat was empty while the other was occupied. The lights of the cockpit display gave the corpse an even more ghastly visage and Kurcher noted how the console in front of the man was covered with blood. It was obvious to see why. The killer had come from behind, cutting the throat before he could react and the contusions on the neck gave away that the victim had been held in place as he bled out.

Kurcher cast another look around the cockpit for anything out of place, other than a stinking body. When nothing jumped out at him, he inspected

161

the dead man more closely. He'd been dead for a few days by the look and smell of him. His clothing was pretty standard merc garb, but there was nothing to hint which organisation he belonged to. Kurcher didn't much fancy rooting through the corpse's pockets, mostly due to the fact his trousers were stained with what he had let go as he died.

He turned his attention to the cockpit controls that weren't covered in blood and tried sifting through the ship files. The navigation reports had been wiped, as had any comms information. Whoever decided to kill this man had gone to great lengths covering his trail and something about the whole thing seemed familiar. Then it dawned on him and he smiled. What were the odds?

By the time he got back to Broekow, the sniper was holding a piece of metal in his free hand. When he held it up, Kurcher saw it was a broken piece of piping. Dark stains were spattered along it.

'Not the most subtle weapon,' Broekow said quietly.

Kurcher beckoned him out into the corridor. 'You read the files on everyone, right?'

Broekow nodded, then realised he was still holding the pipe and placed it carefully on the floor.

'Someone iced a merc in the cockpit,' Kurcher told him. 'Cut his throat and had the strength to hold him in place as he died. Does this scenario sound familiar to you? Who else has hijacked ships, killing the crew and then deleting all nav and comms activity to cover his tracks?'

Broekow thought for a moment. 'Fuck me. Ercko.'

'He's on this ship, likely somewhere beneath us. If it is him, I need him alive. Shoot him in the leg if you have to. Just don't kill him.'

'It still defies logic that Taurus want you to enlist this sicko.'

Kurcher could understand his views. '*This* is why. He's adept at taking down ships from the inside, plus he's a brutal bastard who tends not to leave too many people alive.'

'And he's a rapist,' added Broekow. 'How does that fit in with the corp?'

'It doesn't,' snapped Kurcher, a little too loudly for his liking.

'Can we at least get the lights on?'

'Power's been rerouted to a console on the level below. This is as good as it gets and I don't fancy using a torch to make a beacon of myself.'

Returning to the rec room, Broekow lifted the hatch as Kurcher trained his revolver on it. Below, a ladder descended into darkness and both men shared a look of apprehension. Kurcher headed down first, half expecting Ercko to pounce before he reached the bottom. As he waited for his eyes to become accustomed to the dark, he wished once more that Choice hadn't ruined his sight app. Even Kopetti couldn't fix it.

The lower level was indeed a series of tiny cubicles, each with its own bed and nothing more. Luckily none were big enough for Ercko to hide away in.

As Broekow set foot in the converted hold, he drew in a deep breath and held it for as long as he could. Kurcher had to agree that the smell was almost overpowering. It wasn't long before they located the source of that smell.

The three bodies were piled on top of each other in one of the corner cubicles, thrown there to rot in undignified positions. They were all male, dressed in similar outfits to the one in the cockpit. Their skulls had been beaten in, exposing the brain matter, and one of them had been sliced across the throat so savagely it had almost decapitated him.

Kurcher pointed out a bloody smear on the floor that ran from the hold through to a closed door at the end. Someone had either dragged themselves or been dragged while bleeding profusely and the enlister hoped it wasn't Ercko. At the same time, he also hoped it was. The galaxy would be a better place without the killer, that was for sure, but his mission was at risk if one of these dead men had managed to wound Ercko in the fight. That meant his payment would be at risk too.

Knowing that there weren't many more places Ercko could hide, the two prepared themselves for the inevitable confrontation.

~

Rane was only a third of the way through his daily exercise routine when his arm started throbbing again. That bullet he had taken while saving Kurcher and Broekow may have been removed by Frost's clumsy efforts, but it would take some time to heal properly. When he started focusing on the pain, he was reminded of the bruising on his face. If Kurcher finally came around to his thinking, it was worth a beating or two. This was too important to just let go.

Most men would have started going stir crazy locked up in the tiny cell for so many days with occasional visits from the enlister or his pilot to bring tasteless food to him. The cell was rank with the smell of stale food, shit and his unwashed body; he had learnt long ago to focus his mind and remove himself temporarily from the present.

It was Shea who had taught him how to meditate in this way and he smiled to himself when he remembered her always-smirking face. She was the only one who had treated him well during his time on Amity. Even when she vouched for him to join the misfit band of robbers plying their dubious

163

trade beneath Edison's streets, the rest of them looked at him as though he had just crawled from the sewers. Still, he learnt how to take care of himself while he was with them and gleaned some tricks that he would later develop into traits worthy of any corp agent. If Shea hadn't died during that one heist, perhaps he would have remained with them. A quarter of their group were killed that day by one Libra mech and seeing Shea gunned down so viciously was an image etched permanently into his mind.

He remembered fleeing Edison and catching a transport off Amity mere days after the botched heist, not knowing where he would go next. The following years had descended into hopping from one planet to the next, picking up new skills and information on each before moving on. It was his short visit to Sullivan's Rest though which had sent him off on a new tangent.

Killing those Sapphire Nova mercs had felt good, despite bringing back the terrible memories of what had happened on Rikur. They may not have been the men who had executed his father or raped then killed his mother, but they were still part of the same corporation. The faces of all the people he had killed since had been replaced with those of his parents' killers and occasionally those who had turned their backs on his family, condemning them. He hadn't had to imagine someone else's face when he killed Portman. The late head of Harper security had been one of the team who arrested his parents. Although that team were all gone, his work was far from over.

As Rane continued his exercises, he tried to remember whether he had felt at ease anywhere since leaving Rikur all those years ago. The only place he could come up with, bizarrely, was Cobb. It had taken him several weeks to get the colonists there to trust him enough to enlist him into the slowly building rebellion forming below Jefferson, but his engineering skills quickly got him noticed. Some of those people he could even have called friends for a time, until someone intercepted a transmission from Taurus Galahad stating that he was a wanted man. Had the message not included his mugshot, he could have carried on working under his false name. He still remembered the look on Cal Fuller's face after he had read the transmission. The fear had been clear in his eyes as he confronted Rane. Fuller was a good man and his cause was worthy. There was no way Rane was going to stick around and jeopardise everything they had been working towards.

He could tell that the *Kaladine* was in orbit of some world just by the feel of the ship. He had noticed Frost peer into his cell twice, leading him to believe that Kurcher had left her to watch over the dangerous men and woman on-board again. She was feisty enough, but wouldn't stand much of a chance should one of the crims decide to make her their next victim. Even the

164

innocent-looking D'Larro had that inner monster that would scare most normal people should it surface.

'Why do you bother?'

The voice from the intercom caught him by surprise. It crackled with static, making it hard to understand.

'I'm talking to you, Edlan Rane,' it said. 'Why do you bother waiting for something that just isn't going to happen? He will never let you out of the cell. Might as well kill yourself now and save more beatings before he inevitably shoots you.'

Rane stood up straight, stretching his spine. It had taken a moment for him to work out who the voice belonged to. 'He obviously let *you* out, Choice.'

A distorted laugh came through the intercom. 'Ah, that's where you're mistaken.'

Rane looked out into the corridor, finding it empty. 'You *are* clever after all.'

'I'm prepared to forgive you for getting me caught,' Choice told him. 'But only if you agree to help me.'

'In what way?'

'I can get out of my cell. They placed a new blocker in the system after I escaped before, but it was easy to bypass. Kurcher is off getting another psycho for his collection and his pilot has just gone to check on the others. I can open your cell too and together we can take control of the ship.'

Rane shook his head. 'Leave me out of your plans.'

'Listen, dickhead.' Choice's previous amusement was shortlived. 'Either you help me or I'll alert that pilot that you're trying to escape and she'll have no choice but to shoot you dead.'

'I doubt that somehow. She's not stupid.'

'You're just another murderer who actually wasn't even supposed to be here. You're expendable and, let's face it, better off dead. Either you help me now or I'll see to it you never leave that cell alive.'

Rane sighed. 'I know you're angry about what happened back at Harper, but you need to understand your own situation here. If you keep escaping your cell, what do you think will happen? Eventually Kurcher will either put you in cryosleep for the rest of the time or he'll get so pissed off he just blows you out the airlock.'

'I'm not sticking around to become some corp lackey like before,' growled Choice.

'Then I'm sorry you're so shortsighted.'

165

As silence returned to his cell, Rane hoped that was the end of it. When his door suddenly opened though, he knew it was a fool's hope.

'If you're so intent on playing it safe, will you dare try to stop me.' Choice's challenge was whispered, making it barely audible through the intercom.

Rane stepped back and leant against the wall, crossing his arms. What game was Choice playing? From what he knew of the man, he held grudges and this was certainly one way to get revenge. If Rane stepped out of the cell to stop him from trying to take over the ship, he would risk Kurcher's wrath and end up back at square one with the enlister. If he remained where he was, the crazy criminal could take control of the ship and that was an equally unpleasant thought.

When Choice passed by his door, giving him nothing but a cursory glance, Rane knew he had to make his mind up quickly. Stepping out into the corridor, he called to the escapee.

'Wait! I need you to listen very carefully to me.'

Choice came to an abrupt halt. He kept his back to him. 'So there is some courage left in Edlan Rane after all.'

'I admit that I underestimated you. Your ability to create apps from whatever tech you can get your hands on is quite frankly genius. Just don't waste your talent. You proved your worth when helping to capture Angard, but continuing to fight back against Kurcher and Taurus will only end in your elimination.' Rane saw Choice twitch slightly. 'Angard has accepted what is to come and it is time you did too.'

'That biomech freak takes his orders from Oakley,' Choice said, chuckling. 'I don't take orders from anyone.'

'Just remember that God loves you.'

At that, Choice turned slowly to face him. 'What did you say?'

'I said that God loves you,' replied Rane. 'Although redemption will be hard to find if you carry on like this.'

'Why are you bringing God into this?' Choice seemed shaken. 'What has he ever done for me?'

'It's Maric he has helped. Unfortunately, your actions tend to hurt Maric as they push him further from God. How can he redeem himself when you...'

Choice stabbed a finger at him. 'Don't talk to me about him. He's weak. If anything, his actions hurt *me*. Now shut your fucking mouth.'

Rane pushed on despite the warning. 'If you continue, God will turn his back on Maric and leave him out in the cold.'

Choice turned away again. 'I don't care. *I* don't believe in God.'

166

'Then Maric will be truly lost,' Rane stated sadly. 'Unless he takes control.'

Choice laughed. 'You cunning motherfucker. I see...'

Rane ignored him. 'Maric, this is your soul he is toying with. Do you wish to be excommunicated from God altogether? Take control of your body or there is no turning back.'

'You fucking son of a whore,' screamed Choice, spinning on his heel and spitting as he cursed. 'This is not... this is not...'

Rane saw Choice's rage disintegrate, leaving only Maric's calm visage. A final twitch showed that Choice was still fighting to be heard. The preacher looked up with sad eyes and shook his head.

'I cannot allow him to destroy me.' Maric blinked. 'Thank you, Edlan.'

Rane nodded to him then returned to his cell, where he sat down on the edge of his bed and allowed himself a satisfied smile. A moment later, Maric's dishevelled figure shuffled back along the corridor to his own cell and the preacher's door could be heard closing.

'Care to explain?'

Rane looked up to see Frost standing in the doorway, pistol in hand. 'How much did you see?'

'Most of it,' the pilot said. 'Heard all of it though. I was just about to get Angard to grab you both.'

'That would have been the best course of action if my plan hadn't worked. I gambled on bringing Maric to the surface and hoped he would subdue Choice. As long as we don't antagonise Choice again, I would hope Maric can now stay in control.'

Frost frowned. 'I'd feel better if we knew that for certain, rather than relying on hope.'

'You and I both.' He laid back on his bed. 'I told Kurcher I'm here to help, not hinder.'

'We'll see.' Frost took a step back and closed the door.

Rane knew he had to continue relying on hope for the time being. He *hoped* Frost would tell Kurcher what had happened. He *hoped* she didn't leave out the part where he willingly returned to his cell after defusing the time bomb that was Choice. Finally, he *hoped* Kurcher was clever enough to realise just what would happen should he deliver that data implant to Taurus Galahad.

~

The engines hummed as they held the transport steady in orbit of Mags

167

One.

The chamber was just as dim as the rest of the ship, but lights on the heavy machinery created glowing slats on the walls. To Kurcher and Broekow's chagrin, those slats in turn threw moving shadows around the engine room.

The blood trail disappeared beyond a thick support pillar ahead of them. While not as potent in there, the scent of death still hung in the air. As they squeezed between the two engines, they were met with another grisly sight; this one came as something of a shock.

The dead woman was lying several feet ahead in a pool of congealed blood, some of which had seeped through a grating in the floor. Her eyes were still wide open, as was her mouth, and bruising around her throat showed signs of strangulation. Her dark hair was also matted with blood from a head wound and a deep cut could be seen on her naked thigh.

'Jesus,' muttered Broekow, a look of pure disgust on his face. 'He's a fucking animal.'

Kurcher looked away from the body. 'Wait here. I'll go on ahead and draw him out.'

'Shouldn't we cover her up?'

'No point. Let's just get this done.'

Kurcher stepped around the corpse and crept towards the far end of the engine room, leaving Broekow to cover him. The sniper's eyes flicked back to the woman for a moment and he wondered how Kurcher could even entertain the idea of having someone like Ercko on-board the *Kaladine*. The murderer may have been adept at seizing control of a transport with swift brutality, but he was also an evil bastard. Broekow would ensure Frost stayed clear of Ercko.

As he looked back up, there was a sudden movement in his peripheral vision and a dark shape descended from above, knocking him against the metal pillar. Foul breath struck him as Bennet Ercko leered into view. As Broekow tried to lift his pistol, a blade flashed and sliced across his forearm, ripping through his sleeve and into flesh. Broekow grunted in pain and planned to bring his other hand round to punch his attacker in the side of the head, but Ercko was quick as well as strong. The murderer ducked then delivered two punches of his own to Broekow's abdomen before swatting the gun from his hand. Grasping the winded sniper round the throat with one arm, he placed the point of his knife against Broekow's neck and turned as Kurcher approached.

'I'd stay where you are unless you want your friend skewered.' Ercko's

168

strained voice passed dry, cracked lips and a black unkempt beard.

Kurcher's revolver remained aimed at the crim. 'We've been looking for you. Quite the slice of luck we should find you here.'

Ercko's eyes narrowed. 'Fuck you talking about?'

'I take it you hid here because you stole this transport and some merc organisation are after you. Callyn's probably not the smartest place to hide though.'

Ercko looked Kurcher up and down. 'You look like a merc, as does this one.'

'Yeah, I get that a lot. Some time ago, you were picked up by an enlister on Valandra and held with six other crims.' Kurcher nodded at Broekow. 'He is one of those six. After the enlister let you all go on Sullivan's Rest, I was assigned to find you and offer you a pardon, as long as you joined the merc ranks of Taurus Galahad.'

'Bullshit.'

Kurcher sighed. 'They all said that, but now Broekow here is working with me and the others have agreed to the offer too. It's either that or Taurus will keep hunting you down.'

'It's true,' Broekow said. 'You're a useful asset for them to have.'

'Shut up.' Ercko jabbed the knife against the sniper's skin, drawing blood. 'I've got a counter offer for you. Let me take your ship and I'll leave you alive. You can stay here. The transport has got enough power to remain in orbit, but that's about it.'

'Never going to happen,' Kurcher stated bluntly. 'You get this one opportunity.'

Ercko gave a weak grin, exposing discoloured teeth. 'Nice try. We both know Taurus wouldn't enlist me. I'm much too dangerous. So I guess I might as well just kill you both and be on my way.'

'They certainly didn't lie when they said you were an arrogant son-of-a-bitch.' Kurcher didn't want to waste any more time. 'I've been dealing with shit stains like you my entire life. Cowards who have to force themselves on women just to get their sexual kicks and who don't have the balls to take someone on face-to-face.'

Ercko pointed the knife at him. 'Put that gun down and I'll show you my balls. I'll ram them down your fucking throat.'

Kurcher drew in a deep breath and held it. 'Lean to your left.'

'What?' Creases furrowed Ercko's brow but he realised too late that the enlister wasn't talking to him.

As Broekow flicked his head to the left, Kurcher fired a single shot that struck Ercko just below the index finger gripping the hilt of the knife. The bullet blew both his index and middle finger clean off, sending the knife flying and blood spattering into the killer's face.

As Ercko screamed in agony, Broekow wrenched himself clear and picked up his pistol.

Kurcher watched as Ercko clutched at his missing fingers. He knew that had been a rash move – he didn't like being backed into a corner.

'Get him back to the *Kaladine*,' he ordered Broekow, ignoring the fact the sniper himself was bleeding.

As Broekow shoved the swearing killer away back towards the hold, Kurcher located the two fingers and pocketed them. Not his usual practice, something told him to make sure he returned every limb and digit of the seven crims to Taurus just in case.

They found Frost waiting for them at the *Kaladine*'s airlock and, despite his injury, Ercko eyed her hungrily. Broekow led him to the only vacant cell and roughly threw him inside as the other crims gathered to see the latest arrival.

Seeing that both men were injured, D'Larro offered his services once more stating that the wounds needed proper treatment. To everyone's surprise, Kurcher agreed this time, assigning Frost to monitor the equipment he was able to use.

'It's time you showed your worth,' Kurcher told the medic. 'Don't fuck it up.'

A short time later, D'Larro had cauterised Ercko's wound as Broekow watched over them. When Ercko was told there was no way his fingers could be re-attached, he had threatened D'Larro and told him to try. Broekow had ended the exchange by waving his pistol in Ercko's face, allowing painkillers to be administered before he was bandaged up.

With Ercko seen to and left seething in the cell, D'Larro had then stitched up the cut to Broekow's arm. Frost had stood watch over the medic as he did so. Satisfied he had done a good job, she asked Broekow to continue his guard duties outside the cells. It was only as they walked along the corridor together that the pilot and the sniper shared another lustful kiss before she pushed away playfully and headed to the cockpit.

'All done?' asked Kurcher as she entered.

'Yeah. D'Larro actually did a pretty good job. Never know what he might have done if someone wasn't standing over him though.'

'He's weak. He wouldn't do anything to jeopardise his enlisting now. Unlike some of the others, he seems to know when to stop killing.'

'What were the odds of you going over there to find Hewn and instead coming across that monster?' she asked, waving a hand at the stricken transport.

'Thank god for Kopetti, I guess.'

'Speaking of God, there's something you need to know.'

He glowered at her. 'Something to do with Maric then?'

'Choice.' She sat opposite him. 'He escaped again, but it was Rane who dealt with him.'

Kurcher was not sure he wanted to hear this. 'Go on.'

'Choice opened Rane's cell too and tried to get him to help take the ship. Rane refused and instead talked Maric to the surface. Both of them returned to their cells without my intervention.' She glanced at the enlister, seeing him rubbing at his temples. 'Rane didn't know I was watching.'

'So what, I should just believe him now?' he asked with more than a hint of impatience.

Frost shrugged and reached for a cigarette. 'Just telling you what happened. No need to be a prick about it.'

'Has Choice returned since?'

'No.' She lit the cigarette and took a long drag. 'Maric claims he is now in full control indefinitely.'

Kurcher needed another hit. The new drug Kopetti had sold him was more potent and the come-down was worse. It hadn't even been that long since his last one.

'I'll bear it in mind. We've just got Hewn to locate now, then we can offload this lot and get back to some regular assignments.' He looked out at the transport. 'That thing's dead, just like the crew. Do everyone a favour and destroy it before we leave.'

Taurus Galahad Assault Ship Requiem
Berg system

'I said harder.'

The leather strap slapped against his back again, this time leaving an angry welt. Santa Cruz grunted in both pleasure and pain. The next lash drew blood and he heard the woman straddling him gasp.

'Keep going,' he told her. 'I'll tell you when to stop.'

As she continued reluctantly, he could feel a trickle of blood running down his side to the bedsheet below. It reminded him of simpler times back on Earth when he could pick some random whore to work him until all of the stress and aggression had been released. They were always keen to beat the shit out of him as he paid well. Out there though in the cold depths of space, he had a limited choice. He couldn't approach any of the crew; the only other women were down at the Hayes colony and they were all Taurus scientists or their daughters. The one he had chosen was an administration officer who had caught his eye. She would do as he instructed because she would be too afraid to refuse.

'Enough.' The last lash had bitten too deep and would add to the other scars crisscrossing his back.

As she moved slightly to allow him to roll over, he was pleasantly surprised that she had succeeded in turning him on. It had been several months since the last woman had tried to convert his pain into arousal. She had failed miserably and he had ordered her away angrily. As most who had seen this intimate side of the commander, she soon vanished. Despite curiosity sometimes getting the better of him, he never asked what happened to those women.

He would need to be careful with this Hayes officer though. She had a very important job to do down on Minerva, documenting and storing the research, so her disappearance would certainly raise questions. He would hate to have to get rid of an entire research team again, especially now.

'Sorry if I hurt you, commander.' Her cheeks reddened as she dropped the strap.

'It was fine. Now take off your clothes.'

She hesitated, but then slowly began undressing. Santa Cruz watched her intently, studying her curves. He noticed a small scar on her thigh and likened it to a scratch one might get when caught on brambles.

172

The human body told a story and he had found from quite an early age that he could read a person's history just from paying close attention to the flesh. It was a trait that ultimately led him to become an interrogator for Taurus and that in turn fed his interest in anatomy and psyche. One thing he would never admit to was how aroused he became as he interrogated his subjects. The administering of pain and the subsequent reaction of the body had the same effect as being on the receiving end, as this woman stripping before him would discover.

When she was completely naked, she reached boldly for his manhood. He caught her by the wrist. 'Not yet. Turn around and...'

A message alert flashed at the top of his vision. He opened it as the woman turned her backside towards him. After quickly reading the abrupt note, he smiled.

'What would you like me to do, commander?' she asked him coyly.

'Get on all fours.'

As she did so, he slipped from the bed and retrieved the strap, snapping it tight between his hands. He felt elated. The message from the *Kaladine* had been good news and he hoped the next time he heard from Kurcher and his pilot would be to tell him they had completed their assignment. The fact that Winter had located Hewn and was relaying the co-ordinates to the *Kaladine* gave him even greater pleasure. It was going to be tough getting to the pirate but, between them, Kurcher and Winter would deliver.

He loomed over the waiting woman, hardly able to contain his lust much longer. He brought the strap down hard against her buttocks, getting the desired cry of pain. As he began relentlessly lashing her, the cries turned into pleads for him to stop. That just spurred him on. He would not stop until blood was drawn.

Enlister-class vessel *Kaladine*
Callyn system

'Are you sure about this?'

Kurcher flashed Frost a pained look. 'Not at all, but the last thing I want to do is spend our hard-earned wages hiring some merc goons.'

'I would've thought the last thing you wanted was to go down into a hostile situation on your own,' she remarked.

'Wouldn't be the first time and won't be the last,' he told her. 'Any luck finding out who the intel came from?'

'No. The coding looked like Taurus so I'm guessing one of Santa Cruz's spies but there was no profile as to the sender. Another guardian angel, like the one on Summit maybe.'

They arrived at the cells and cast very quick glances at Rane and Ercko. While Rane remained quiet, acknowledging them with a simple nod, Ercko was still fuming from the loss of his fingers.

'You and your whore can fuck off,' he growled, spitting at the small view port in the door.

Kurcher watched the spittle run down the glass. 'At least you only have one middle finger to give us.'

Ercko's face contorted in rage. 'I'm going to kill you slowly, enlister. First though, I'm going to have me a piece of your girlfriend. You can watch me slit her throat once I'm done.'

Kurcher and Frost moved to the final cell, where Maric was kneeling on the floor praying. As the door opened, the preacher looked up with exhausted eyes.

'How do I know Maric is in control and not Choice?' Kurcher asked him. 'He's fooled me before and I won't have him do it again.'

Maric rose shakily. 'As I said before, all I can give you is my vow. Rane's words gave me back my own body and put Choice to sleep.'

Kurcher stepped into the cell. 'Your vow is not enough.' He struck Maric hard across the face, which staggered the preacher.

'I understand your need to test me.' Maric rubbed his cheek. 'I am in control.'

Kurcher grabbed him by the collar and slammed him against the wall. 'Why should I believe you?'

Maric remained calm. 'If you still doubt me, carry on beating me until

174

you realise I'm telling the truth. I won't fight back.'

Kurcher looked into his eyes and saw only the preacher staring back, but he had to be sure. 'Choice may have managed to bypass our app suppressor somehow, but his tech is still flawed. He thinks his apps are hot shit. No, they are weak versions of the real thing. This is Maric's body, not his. He was created when Maric underwent the brainwashing dished out by the Revenants; an alter ego who contained all of Maric's hostility. Choice is nothing.'

Behind them, Frost shuffled nervously and looked along the corridor.

'I agree,' said Maric, holding Kurcher's gaze. 'I have long believed myself to be possessed by a demonic spirit, sent perhaps by the devil himself. I wonder though whether God placed him in me as a test, to prove my worth and loyalty.'

Kurcher let him go. 'Okay. You're free to join the others in the rec room.'

Maric blinked and glanced at Frost standing in the doorway. 'I don't understand.'

'I'm satisfied that Choice has been subdued for now,' Kurcher told him, stepping back out of the cell. 'But you'll be closely watched. The first sign that psycho is reappearing, I won't hesitate throwing you back in here. Any attempt to take control of the ship again and I will put a bullet through your head. Understand now?'

'I do.' Maric looked apprehensive. 'Would it not be safer to keep me in here? Why have me among the others?'

'Keeping a schizophrenic locked up alone in a cell is not a good idea. We have one person left to find and then you'll be taken to Taurus Galahad for debrief. I'm sure they would rather you willingly went over to them.' Kurcher wrinkled his nose. 'Plus you're stinking the fucking cell out and that isn't hygienic for anyone.'

'Don't ask me to clean it,' piped up Frost. 'I reckon we need a new ship after having this lot on-board.'

The three headed to the rec room, finding the others already waiting for them. Their eyes followed Maric as the preacher shuffled through the room and took a seat.

'You sure it's wise letting him out?' asked Broekow.

Kurcher was getting tired of these crims questioning his decisions. 'I have a feeling Maric won't be causing us any problems.'

'Famous last words,' muttered Oakley, leaning against Angard's broad arm.

Kurcher flinched when he saw there wasn't anywhere for him to sit. It was only his ship after all. 'It was dumb fucking luck that we found Ercko. That just leaves Hewn and it looks like we have a tip-off as to his location. We're on our way to the Iridia system, to a quaran world called Tempest.'

'That's Libra Centauri space,' noted Broekow.

'The lead we received states that Tempest is not actually quarantined and that Libra lied on their exploration reports. There have been rumours for a while now about Echo working with Libra and it looks like that may be the case. Apparently, Hewn is hidden away inside a facility on the surface.'

Angard took sudden interest. 'What kind of facility?'

'Drug production.'

It was D'Larro's turn to ask a question. 'I take it not the legal kind?'

'Doubtful.' Kurcher looked around at them. 'Once I have Hewn back here, we'll be meeting up with the *Requiem* so you can all be debriefed and I'll finally have my ship back.'

'The intel on Hewn also mentioned that a guardian is in orbit of Tempest,' Frost said from the doorway. 'Problem we have is the conflector is fried. I'd rather not get ripped off by some merc outfit, so any of you know your way around tech like that?'

Oakley and Angard shook their heads, which wasn't surprising.

'I can take a look,' Broekow offered. 'But I'm not really familiar with it.'

'Great fucking help,' snapped Frost, drawing a wry smile from the sniper.

'Rane would be able to help.' Maric's voice was hoarse and almost inaudible. 'He was an engineer I believe at one time.'

Broekow nodded. 'That's true. A very talented one apparently.'

Kurcher looked back at Frost. 'Surely there's another way?'

She shrugged. 'It's got to be worth a try. I'd feel safer if you were there with us.'

The enlister looked up at the ceiling. 'Fine. I'll talk to Rane, but we'll need an alternative option if he can't fix it.'

'What about other ships?' asked Oakley. 'Surely Libra would have more than just one guardian. Your conflector may slip us past their scanners, but we won't be invisible.'

'Let me worry about that,' Frost told her sharply.

'Getting into that facility will be tough too.' Broekow tapped at his lower lip with one finger. 'Security is bound to be tight. Could be both corp guards and pirates down there.'

'Enough.' Kurcher stalked to the door. 'I don't even know why I told you all what's happening. Your job is to sit here and wait. End of story.'

Broekow pushed his luck. 'You'll need help. I can...'

Kurcher didn't want to hear it. 'You can help by watching him.' He jabbed a finger at Maric then left the rec room and strode back to Rane's cell.

'Conflector technology,' he barked as he entered. 'How familiar are you with it?'

Rane thought for a moment. 'Reasonably. What's going on?'

Kurcher pulled his revolver out. 'I'm going after Jaffren Hewn. We need to mask our approach. You'll work with Frost to fix the conflector before we make the jump to Iridia. My gun will stay glued to the back of your head while you do.'

'No need. What happens after that? Am I to return to my cell?'

Kurcher moved closer. 'I heard what happened with Choice. For all I know, the two of you are plotting something together. Still, it seems that your actions have subdued him for now – that doesn't mean I trust you or that I would let you roam the ship.'

Rane smiled. 'I can feel a *but* coming.'

Kurcher had never wanted to beat the shit out of someone more. 'I looked into your claims about the Taurus people who went missing. Those who apparently were in some way linked to this data implant. While there were no mentions of anyone having gone missing, I did find discrepancies among the numbers and information relating to certain teams.'

'Like a scientist being assigned somewhere, but not being listed among the colony personnel or conflicting numbers in a specific research team?'

'That kind of thing. Doesn't mean Taurus made them disappear though. It could just be a mistake.'

Rane shook his head. 'You're a clever man, Davian. One or two could be classed as an error in the system. I'm guessing you found a lot more than that. I'm also guessing you tracked the route taken by certain exploration ships and came across some dead ends when it came to their final destination.'

'It's all speculation.'

'And yet you spent time investigating. You can see that something is amiss.'

Kurcher lifted the revolver. 'Yeah, you're still alive.'

The enlister ushered Rane out of the cell, meeting up with Frost at the broken conflector. As they began working, Kurcher watched him intently. The serial killer was certainly focused on the task at hand, explaining to Frost how they might be able to repair the tech, and Kurcher began wondering whether his use of Parinax had weakened his resolve. He would never have permitted someone with Rane's history to work on his precious *Kaladine*. As much as he wished it was the drugs, Kurcher knew that the doubts Rane had implanted in his mind regarding Taurus were to blame.

Before the *Kaladine* reached the jump point, the conflector was working once more. Rane told them it was only good for one more use though. Not even the most talented engineer would be able to repair it after their visit to Tempest. That was good enough for Kurcher.

To Rane's surprise, the enlister marched him to the rec room after the repair job.

'So I won't be going back in the cell?' he asked, stopping just before they entered.

Kurcher weighed the man up for a moment. 'No. I need you for another task.'

Rane smiled. 'Oh?'

'You're going to help me get to Hewn.'

Summit
Benedict system

Trin Espina stepped back to take in her handiwork and gave a satisfactory nod.

'You see, sergeant, I like to do things the old-fashioned way,' she told her captive. 'The other corps like to use apps to extract information. I always found the pain from a good beating gets results quicker. Only problem is it's made an awful mess of your lovely white uniform.'

Saib looked up at her with disdain. 'Impramed will not suffer Sapphire Nova thugs interrogating one of their officers. You were arrogant to come here and throw your weight around.'

Espina looked hurt. 'Let's not get personal. Besides, you're not the only officer being questioned about this matter.' She shrugged and began pacing in front of the bound sergeant. 'I'm here because fourteen of my men died in your *peaceful* city. I want to know who killed them and where the murderers went.'

'Your men opened fire on us,' Saib stated angrily. 'I'd say you know exactly who killed them.'

'See, that's where you're wrong.' Espina leant in close to his face. 'I know Davian Kurcher was here and that he fled Tidewell, but I want to know who the sniper was. I also want to know who Kurcher came here for.'

Saib held her gaze. 'I don't know who the sniper was. I'm thankful he or she was there to help us. If you want information, why don't you ask the enlister himself? I'm not about to help some Nova bitch who thinks she can just walk in here and...'

Espina struck the back of her hand across his face. 'One of you will help, sergeant, or my assault ship will blow your precious city to shit. Why do you think your officers aren't barging in here to rescue you? My ship will fire on anyone who tries to fight us, as your patrols found.'

'You would risk open war?'

Her lips curled into a sinister smile. 'Against Impramed, yes. Your corp is run by a bunch of doctors and surgeons who shy away from conflict every chance they get. Sapphire Nova don't work in the same way. Our people have been murdered and we *will* have justice. Now, who did Kurcher come here for?'

Saib glanced at the three Nova men near the door. 'If I tell you, you'll

179

leave Summit?'

Espina placed a hand over her heart. 'You have my word as an officer.'

The sergeant licked blood from his lip as he considered his situation. 'Some crim named Regan D'Larro. He used to be a Taurus medic.'

'So he came here to execute him?'

'No. D'Larro left on Kurcher's ship.'

Espina turned away and slowly walked towards the door. 'He was enlisting him then. Interesting. Where were they heading?'

'That I truly don't know,' admitted Saib. 'In the heat of the firefight, his ship left Summit.'

'Thank you, sergeant. One day, Sapphire Nova will take over your little corporation and we will remember the help you gave us here on beautiful Summit.'

'Nova are no longer welcome here. You have what you want, so get off our world.'

Espina gave the same faux hurt expression. 'And here we were, starting to get along.' She strode back to stand before Saib. 'As I mentioned, we don't work in the same way as the other corps, sergeant. We learnt not to leave loose ends a long time ago.'

Before he could utter another word, Espina pulled the pistol from beneath her jacket and fired a single shot through his brain.

As she made her way back to her ship, enjoying the fearful stares from the Tidewell citizens, the commander hoped she would have news from one of her scouts. Any sign of the enlister's unique ship would be welcome. After all, she couldn't afford to return to Straunia empty-handed.

She had never seen the Nova board so furious and the concern was clear to see, etched deeply into their faces. It was no wonder though. The murders at Harper were bad enough; the death of Cairns had been a massive shock to all. She couldn't believe Taurus Galahad would be so rash. When news reached her that the team she sent after Kurcher had all been killed on Summit, she knew this wasn't just down to the enlister. Now she found herself frequently wondering what task Taurus Galahad had assigned him. The Davian Kurcher she remembered had been ruthless and rough, but there was no way he would have been stupid enough to kill high-ranking Nova officers.

Espina never thought she would find herself hunting Kurcher down. The Nova board must have known about the history they shared, so she had been surprised to receive the assignment. Perhaps they were testing her loyalty. Certain actions during her time as a Nova enlister had raised more than a few

180

eyebrows and no doubt her profile report had been studied over and over.

Could she kill Davian Kurcher? She would only know the answer when the two were face-to-face once again.

Enlister-class vessel *Kaladine*
Iridia system

'This really isn't necessary, Davian.'

Kurcher finished putting on the protective suit before acknowledging Rane's comment. 'It's necessary to me. If you stray from the plan, that explosive will go off. If you try to remove it, same outcome. I'll switch it on when we get onto the surface.'

Rane looked down at the small metal cylinder dangling round his neck. 'You could just blow me up as soon as Hewn was apprehended.'

'Yeah, I could,' grinned Kurcher. He could've given Rane his word that he would deactivate it once the mission was over, but he was getting sick of lying. Two men would go into the facility and two would come out. 'You can take your weapons with you.'

'Listen, Davian, there's something you need to consider.' Rane pointed at the enlister's revolver. 'This place isn't going to be easy to breach. You need more than just two men.'

'No fucking way.'

'You need me to cause a distraction. Let me take Ercko.' As Kurcher laughed, Rane pushed his point. 'Of all the crims, he is the best suited to cause havoc down there. Let me persuade him and then you can fit him with a dud explosive device, if it makes you feel better.'

'Again, no fucking way.' Kurcher checked his revolver clip. 'You distract whoever is protecting the place and I get to Hewn. That's it. Nice and simple.'

'Simple? You need someone to help you too. Take Broekow and Angard.'

'Why the hell would I jeopardise everything on your say-so?'

'Because these crims need to feel useful. You're telling them they are being enlisted, but their doubts are growing. Angard is already on edge and doesn't trust you. If you allow him to accompany us, it may ease his concerns.'

'Oakley keeps him in check. Besides, he's not exactly one to stay under the radar. You'll be telling me next to take Maric and D'Larro too. Keep your thoughts to yourself.'

Kurcher cursed himself silently. He never engaged with dead men. The familiar itch was starting at the back of his brain again.

'Just consider the benefits.' Rane slid his sword into its sheath beneath his

182

jacket. 'They will be wondering why you're not using their *talents* to get the job done on Tempest. It's very obvious that you're trying to keep them safe.'

'Jesus, do you ever shut up?' yelled Kurcher. 'My job is to bring them all back alive. If I take them down to Tempest, there's a chance they won't survive. Not only would I not get paid but Taurus would probably throw me in prison.'

'If just you and I go down there, I doubt *we'll* survive. This isn't going to be some tiny structure manned by a skeleton crew, Davian. If Ercko and I get inside and cause the distraction, it will make the job easier for Broekow, Angard and you to get past any guards and find Hewn.'

Kurcher lifted his revolver, as if preparing to strike the killer as he had done before, when Broekow and Maric appeared in the doorway. The enlister glared angrily at them.

'What the fuck are you doing in here? Off limits, remember?' He hoped they had not listened in to his increasingly heated conversation with Rane.

'He wanted to say something to you,' stated Broekow, gesturing to the preacher.

Maric shuffled forward, nervously glancing at Rane who gave him a warm smile in return. 'I would like to go back in a cell while you try to reach Jaffren Hewn.'

Kurcher had no patience left. 'Fine. Easier on all of us.'

Maric frowned. 'You don't want to know why?'

'Not really. Could be to show you're in control of your own body still or it could be that you think Choice will make an appearance as soon as I'm off the ship. I don't care. I've got bigger things to worry about.'

'Plus it frees me up to come with you,' pointed out Broekow.

Kurcher gave the sniper a suspicious look. 'Alright.' The itch was getting intense. 'Put Maric in the cell and then keep a close eye on Rane while I'm prepping.'

Moments later, he found himself standing in the rec room, telling Angard he would also be accompanying them down onto Tempest. Something was telling his Parinax-starved brain that Rane was actually speaking sense, but Kurcher couldn't shake the feeling he was stuck between a rock and a hard place. He needed to just get the job done and, despite the clear risk to those who would be going with him, their presence would hopefully make the task easier.

Angard voiced concern, needing to understand what his role would be. It was quite simple though. He would be there to make any guards think twice about taking them on and would give them a huge advantage if it came down to hand-to-hand. Angard also might be able to get them past any unforeseen obstacles, even doors, should the need arise. Even Oakley understood that Angard needed reassurance Taurus wanted him in their ranks. As Kurcher left the room, she began working with her protector to get him as focused as possible on the imminent task.

D'Larro caught Kurcher up as he headed for the cockpit. 'Can I have a word?'

'You're not going with us too.'

'I know that,' said the medic. 'And you don't need to worry about leaving the rest of us here with Frost.'

'I wasn't worried. She'll blow your head off if you give her any grief.'

'Understood.' D'Larro looked around nervously. 'I just wanted to know how long you've been addicted to Parinax?'

In one fluid motion, Kurcher spun, grabbed D'Larro and slammed him against the wall. 'Keep your fucking questions to yourself in the future,' he snarled.

Despite being pinned and at the enlister's mercy, D'Larro managed to find the courage to blurt out a response. 'I just thought I might be able to help, that's all.'

'I'm not addicted to Parinax. I use it in my boost app and that's it, understand?'

'Your pupils are dilated, you're sweating profusely and you're definitely losing your cool much quicker. If your boost is causing these symptoms then it's defective.'

Kurcher leaned into the medic, purposefully putting weight on the younger man's neck. 'Keep your nose out of my business or Taurus will be one crim short.'

With that, he stormed away muttering beneath his breath. His next hit couldn't come soon enough.

The guardian orbiting Tempest was indeed a Libra Centauri ship. It was circling the dark side of the planet as the *Kaladine* approached and the enlister vessel quickly descended into the upper atmosphere, the conflector apparently doing its job and holding fast.

Immediately, the strong winds of the alleged quaran world struck. Frost, securely buckled into her seat, fought the gales and managed to get the *Kaladine* through the dark grey cloud cover. The wind factor was still great as the ship hurtled across the Tempest sky, making for the location of the facility. Frost could hold them steady easily enough, allowing her to take in the world that had been reported as off-limits.

184

The surface was covered with foliage that seemed almost jungle-like. Bodies of water could be seen among the greenery. White avians flew just above the tops of the trees, they too battling the wind. Evolution on Tempest had seen fit to give the creatures such aerodynamic bodies that they used the gales to their advantage, twisting and soaring with each new gust.

As Frost looked further afield, she could see great splits in the ground in all directions; a clear sign of the planet's unstable tectonics. As rain began pelting the *Kaladine* and flashes of lightning shot across the horizon, she realised the name of the world was apt after all.

The speed of the *Kaladine* saw them reach the once-distant thunderstorm quickly. The sheer scale of the storm was terrifying to behold and Frost silently thanked the engineers for building such a sturdy ship as Tempest tried its best to wrench them apart.

By the time they were nearing the location of the facility, they had caught up with the night and Tempest's only moon intermittently peered down from between the angry clouds.

'Time to go to work,' said the pilot into her comms app. 'Good luck.'

Kurcher's voice came back quickly. 'Keep sharp, Justyne.'

She unbuckled herself from the seat and checked the system alerts one by one. The lifeboat was powering up and would detach from the *Kaladine* shortly. Of the five men heading down to the surface, Frost hoped to see two again. Even though she couldn't admit it, Broekow had become more important to her than expected. The intimate moments they had managed to steal when nobody else was looking had left her lusting for more. She tried not to think of what would eventually happen to him. It left her feeling guilty and sick to her stomach.

As her app told her the lifeboat was away, she imagined the five of them squeezed together inside. Kurcher would detest being that close to all of them. She was still confused as to why he had let Rane persuade him into taking both Angard and Ercko. The former could give them an advantage, but Ercko? What use could a sadistic rapist be on a mission like this? He didn't even have all of his fingers.

An alarm flashed in her vision, making her jump slightly. An unknown ship was approaching their position.

'Shit.' Frost lit a cigarette. 'Time to go to work.'

185

Tempest
Iridia system

The alarm was starting to give him a headache.

'Can someone turn that damned thing off?' Hewn asked the nearest Libra Centauri guard, who merely looked at him blankly.

He knew why the alarm had sounded, but the way the siren echoed off the walls drove him crazy. Even the workers surrounding the great vat before him were flinching at the noise, and they were wearing protective suits.

Five long minutes later, the alarm fell silent and Hewn breathed a sigh of relief. His ears were still ringing though when he spotted Chaplin and Hengeveld heading his way. As they approached, he could tell by their body language that they were both on edge. Then again, they had been like that since he had arrived on Tempest. After all, he was the one who had opened the facility along with his Libra contacts. If they had to impress anyone, it was him.

'We've got one of our ships in pursuit,' Chaplin announced, jumping in before his colleague. 'They think it's a corp vessel but can't get close enough to tag it.'

'We should send a couple of my patrol ships up to help see it off,' suggested Hengeveld loudly. 'With all due respect, I doubt *Frankenstein* will be able to keep up with it.'

Hewn had heard the Libra officer refer to their bastardised assault ship in that way before and he didn't like it. The *Newman's Mirror* was a Sigma Royal ship his organisation had captured years ago, named after the man who had overseen its alterations. Lighter than a normal assault ship, it had been designed for one sole purpose: to protect the Tempest facility.

'Send up your ships.' He thought for a moment. 'If they get a chance to destroy this visitor, do it. We can't have other corps sniffing around.'

'Do you think they might be looking for you, sir?'

Hewn gave Chaplin a shrug. 'Who knows? Who cares? Just get rid of them.'

He accompanied the two men to the comms room and listened to them giving orders to their respective pilots. As they did so, it gave him time to study the camera feeds from around the facility.

'Someone needs to fix that,' he told them, pointing at a flickering feed that was looking down at one of the production vats.

186

Chaplin was quick to respond as always. 'I'll get someone onto it now.'

'The rising heat sometimes affects them,' Hengeveld pointed out. 'All the cameras are pretty dated now. We could do with some newer ones.'

Hewn watched them with a smile on his face as they entered into an argument about the tech dotted around the facility. Although they often held heated debates on various topics, he was satisfied he had chosen the right men to run the operation.

Jos Chaplin was not a typical pirate. Despite looking like a banker, straight-backed and peering over his spectacles, he was excellent at man-management. All of the facility workers, including the Libra mercs, seemed to respect him and he kept the production line working smoothly. In fact, the output of the facility was greater than Hewn had expected, meaning more of their unique product was being shipped out into the galaxy and leading to more revenue coming in for Echo and Libra alike.

Lars Hengeveld on the other hand was a merc through-and-through. From true Scandinavian descent with his blonde hair and blue eyes, the officer was the complete opposite of Chaplin. He was there to make sure the workforce didn't step out of line and to protect the facility. The man had a very obvious ruthless streak, but he knew not to let ego get in the way of his work. The Libra mercs under his command were loyal and watchful. It was Hengeveld who had insisted they have a couple of mechs on-site too to boost protection. To Hewn's surprise, the Libra board had agreed.

'We've got another storm on its way in an hour or so,' Chaplin stated. 'Best keep the shutters down for now.'

'Fucking storms,' cursed Hengeveld. 'We nearly lost a supply ship to the last one. Libra pilots are getting scared to come here.'

Hewn scratched at the join where his elbow and the bionic limb had been fused together. 'So we'll get Echo pilots to do the supply runs. I'm sure a simple storm wouldn't scare them off.'

Hengeveld laughed. 'Simple storm? They're getting worse, Jaffren, and you know that. The last thing we want is to lose a shipment of Eidolon to this weather. Imagine the cost.'

'I'm quite aware of the cost, but you two aren't stupid. I trust you to gauge the severity of these storms before a shipment is due out. Now, just focus on getting rid of these unwanted visitors, yes?'

Both men nodded and turned back to the comms console. Hewn linked his own comms app to the console and listened in to the reports from their pilots. When he heard a message from the *Newman's Mirror* saying they had lost their target, he swore.

'Is the guardian aware they let someone slip past?' he asked.

'Yes, sir.' Chaplin was gazing pensively at the screen before him. 'Bloody conflector tech. Whoever is piloting that visiting ship is good, I'll give them that.'

Hengeveld was already issuing orders to his patrol ships to scan the immediate area.

'Tell them to check the mountains too,' Hewn told him. 'Good place to hide.'

All three men noticed when a camera feed for one of the maintenance and venting tunnels suddenly went dark. A moment later, the facility ops system relayed an alert that the production vat directly above that tunnel was grinding to a halt due to a venting malfunction.

Hengeveld checked that the other vents were working. 'We haven't had a fucking malfunction for months. Why now?'

'Hopefully not another one of those bloody rodents,' muttered Chaplin. 'They don't get in the tunnels often, but they're a ballache when they do. The bigger ones could easily get minced in the rotors down there and that might cause it to shut down.'

Hewn tapped the blank camera screen with one metal finger. 'And this? I doubt they chewed through the wiring at exactly the same time as getting caught in the rotor.'

Hengeveld stayed silent, leaving Chaplin to offer a possible reason. 'Maybe it was a heat backlash that knocked it out.'

'Maybe.' Hewn wasn't convinced. 'Maybe not.'

Hengeveld headed for the door. 'I'll take a couple of men down for a look.'

Hewn decided to join him and called to Chaplin as they vanished back out into the plant. 'Keep your eyes peeled, Jos.'

Hengeveld was quick to enlist the help of four Libra men as they passed through the main production concourse. Two were guards; the other two were engineers who had just happened to emerge from a maintenance hatch nearby. Most of the engineering teams were employed by Libra Centauri, leaving Hewn's pirates to work solely on the drug line.

Their destination was one of the larger vats at the southern end of the facility. It was one of three housed in a vast chamber and the concoction of chemicals roiling within made the air toxic. The six men entered wearing protective masks connected to oxygen reserves. Workers around the malfunctioning vat tried to look busy as they recognised Hewn and Hengeveld.

188

As they descended a ladder to the maintenance tunnel beneath the vats, Hewn's mind was starting to work overtime. 'Remind me where the vent openings are outside.'

'The other end of this particular one comes out on a cliff face covered with moss and shit,' Hengeveld told him. 'Why?'

Hewn squinted into the dimness of the tunnel. 'Just wondering how easy it would be for one of those little critters to get into the opening. Local insects I can understand, but I don't remember there being any of those big enough to block a vent.'

They found the camera easily enough and, as the maintenance workers clambered up to take a look, Hewn listened to the sound of his facility echoing around him. The steady rhythmic thrum of the machinery made the grating beneath his feet vibrate and various liquids sloshed along the pipes around them. He found it quite a relaxing sound, unlike the screech of the alarm.

'Looks like the cam took a whack from something,' cried one of the workers. 'Cracked on the side and damage to the wiring.'

Hewn shared a concerned glance with Hengeveld. 'Someone hit it?'

The worker shrugged. 'Seems the most likely thing.'

As Hewn stepped forward to peer up at the broken camera, Chaplin's voice crackled through his comms app. 'We have another problem, sir.'

'Lars, I'm going back up,' he said, heading for the ladder. 'I want that vent checked for any signs of tampering, then get some teams working on it immediately.'

'You think we've got a saboteur in our midst?' asked Hengeveld, an almost amused look on his face.

'That or someone trying to get in.'

Hewn had just clambered back up the ladder when another alert flashed in his vision, signalling another of the vents below was grinding to a halt. After ordering Hengeveld to investigate this new malfunction too, he left the vat chamber, throwing the oxygen mask angrily across the concourse. Echo and Libra employees alike watched as he stormed past, checking the ammo in his assault rifle.

'Sir, one of our sentry guns outside just blew the shit out of something. Didn't see what it was. Now a second vent has just powered down so...'

'We have company, Jos,' Hewn growled. 'I don't think it was any rodent getting into the vents.'

Chaplin sounded shocked. 'It's nigh impossible for someone to sneak in.'

'All it takes is intelligence, guile and luck. Or someone to sell us out.'

189

'What do you want to do?'

'Let's see what Hengeveld turns up. Have the guards and mechs on full alert.' Hewn switched comms channel. 'Lars, what've you got for me?'

There was a long silence before Hengeveld's voice came back. 'Just trying to get the cam working again.'

Hewn frowned. 'I told you to check the vents. I reckon someone is definitely trying to get inside the facility.'

Again, there was a significant pause. 'Yeah, I... I checked the vent and there was a load of shit caught up in the rotors. Should get it working again shortly.'

There was something in Hengeveld's tone he didn't like. 'Get yourself back up here then.'

'Understood.'

'Jos, stay there and monitor the cams and comms. Keep your weapon close.'

With that, Hewn found the nearest group of guards and waved them over. One of the mechs loomed ominously behind them and he saw the so-called head swivel to face him. The visual sensors were glowing a light blue, making it look as though it had three large eyes.

'Stay close to me,' Hewn told the guards, as he marched away back towards the vat chamber.

The mech's loud footsteps followed them and Hewn was reminded of the time he was being pursued by one of the Sigma Royal constructs. That one had been smaller and more humanoid in shape, but was faster than he had anticipated. Losing his left hand and forearm to that mech had made him suspicious of all AI. Although the next pursuit mech he encountered had been easier to fend off thanks to his artificial arm, the mere presence of one still made him uneasy.

'Lars?' No response this time. 'Lars, are you there?'

A shot rang out from somewhere inside the vat chamber, followed by a number of panicked shouts. As they approached the doors, there was a bizarre noise from beyond, like a metallic groan, before a shuddering explosion rocked the entire facility.

Hewn stumbled and fell, as did everybody nearby. Beyond the door, the shouts turned to pained cries as a cascade of smaller blasts began. Hewn knew what that meant. Some of the chemicals they were using were highly flammable. Someone had started a deadly chain reaction.

Chaplin's voice came screaming across his comms. 'Jesus, they're guards. They're guards.'

190

Hewn pushed himself up from the floor. 'Calm the fuck down and make sense, Jos.'

'Hengeveld's guards. They came up from the maintenance hatch, made their way to the vat controls and blew them apart.' Chaplin muttered something Hewn couldn't make out before continuing. 'They threw burning debris into the vat... it's gone.'

'Where are they now?'

'Don't know, but workers are piling out of the emergency doors on the upper levels. I've sent men there to find them.'

As Hewn began relaying the information to the guards around him, there was another explosion. This time, the door leading to the vat chamber was blown into the concourse and smoke billowed from the small cleansing airlock that linked the two parts of the facility.

'Masks,' yelled Hewn. 'Get some masks on.'

They barely managed to get to the oxygen reserves before the air in the concourse became noxious. Hewn had to give credit to the maintenance teams as they appeared quickly to combat the toxic fumes.

As he looked around at the carnage, he wondered what had befallen Hengeveld. The Libra officer was resilient; he doubted even he could survive such a blast.

'We're going to find the bastards who did this,' he told the guards. 'Before they can do any more damage.'

The cost of replacing the vat and all adjacent systems would be high, not to mention having to order more chems for the process. Eidolon was not cheap to make. Replacing *people* was just a pain in the ass.

Gunfire echoed through the concourse. Hewn wondered whether one of the corps had sent in specialists to put his facility out of business. No matter who was behind the attack, all hell was breaking loose and they had to put a stop to it.

'Sounds like our saboteurs are under fire on the upper levels.' He looked at the nearest guard. 'Take three others, get up there and help eliminate them. The rest of you come with me.'

'What about the mech, sir?' asked the man he had addressed, patting one of the construct's legs.

Hewn stifled a shudder when the cold blue sensors swivelled to look at him. 'Take it with you.'

As he strode back towards the northern end of the facility with the other three guards in tow, bad memories began flooding his mind. The ploy being used by these trespassers was one he had first witnessed when he was still a part of the pirate convoy back in 2596. At twenty-one years of age, he had been inexperienced then but thought he knew everything. The rival faction had distracted the crew, himself included, by creating malfunctions around their ship after stowing away on board. Three men then opened fire, drawing the crew to their position, allowing the rest of the sneaky bastards to take control of the ship. Eventually he had grown wise to this tactic, yet he had to admit that he had not expected someone to try it on Tempest.

An alert flashed at the edge of his vision again. 'Jos, you there?'

There was a moment of silence before the response came back. 'I am, Jaffren.'

Hewn hesitated. Chaplin never called him that. 'Did you authorise the north doors to be opened? Cancel the command and keep them closed.'

'Jaffren, I...' Chaplin's voice faded into static for a moment then suddenly roared back across the comms app. 'Don't come back here, it's...'

The link cut off with a loud buzz and Hewn looked back at the expectant guards. 'Order the second mech to the northern doors now. Have it kill anything that enters.'

When he entered the comms room, the only light was flickering from the monitors. Chaplin was sitting on a chair facing the door. Even in the limited illumination, the bruise over his right eye stood out.

'You okay, Jos?'

Chaplin gave a slight nod. The vocal response came from the shadows behind the chair.

'He'll be fine as long as you play ball. Close the door and tell your men to stay outside.'

Hewn raised his rifle. 'I'd rather we just gunned you down before dealing with your friends.'

There was a loud sigh from the gloom. 'You haven't seen what's coming through the front door yet. Listen, you come with us now and there won't be any more blood spilled.'

Hewn narrowed his eyes, trying to make out the man behind Chaplin. 'You're not here for the facility.'

'Very astute. The next guard who tries edging forward gets a bullet through his skull.'

A man's scream echoed into the room from somewhere in the concourse.

Realisation suddenly struck Hewn. 'If you're here for me, that means you must be either a corp assassin or an enlister. No merc or pirate organisation would go to the lengths you have just to find me.'

'Can't say there's much difference between assassin and enlister. Now close the fucking door.'

Hewn glanced at Chaplin, whose expression seemed to be a blend of fear and shame, and found himself wishing that it was Hengeveld sat in the chair instead. 'Have it your way.'

He waved the guards away. As the door slammed shut behind them, the pirate took a step closer to Chaplin.

An unshaven and tired-looking face moved into the light, an old-fashioned revolver gripped tightly in one hand. 'Now put your rifle down along with any other weapons.'

Hewn found the man familiar. 'Tell me who you are first.'

The barrel of a gun nudged the back of his head. 'You heard him, get rid of your weapons.'

He silently cursed himself for not realising there was a second assailant in the room. This new voice was familiar though too.

'Which corp do you work for?' Hewn asked as he threw his rifle down and began pulling the pistol from his belt.

'You need to pay very close attention to what I'm about to say,' began the man behind Chaplin, ignoring the question. 'Taurus Galahad have realised the great potential in working with Echo and so sent me to enlist you. Your past crimes against the corp will be forgotten if you work with them and all of your facilities like this one will be allowed to continue production. If you refuse, I kill you right now and Taurus will hunt down every man, woman and child who is part of your organisation. That includes your two sons.'

Hewn cast a look to the monitors. One of the screens was filled with flame; another showed bodies strewn across an upper walkway.

'You could've just sent me a message. These people didn't have to die at the hands of your goons.'

The enlister laughed; his eyes remained cold. 'Yeah, because the leader of Echo would've come along willingly if I'd asked nicely. Your answer, Hewn.'

'This is bullshit, but you haven't left me much choice. Call your men off and you have a deal, Kurcher.'

'Ah, you've finally worked out who I am. You'll be seeing a few more familiar faces when we get to my ship. Now, I need your ships to stand down too – and the guardian in orbit.'

Hewn heard the enlister's cohort moving to the door. 'Jos here can order our ships not to attack yours. I don't have much sway with the commander of the guardian. Lars could've helped with that, but he was likely killed by your men.'

'They're not my fucking men,' snapped Kurcher, the side of his face twitching. 'They're a necessary evil. Anyway, *you're* the one running this place. Tell your Libra friends you're leaving Tempest.'

Hewn studied Kurcher for a moment. Despite having never met, he had heard the stories about how ruthless the man was and Kurcher's face had been circulated around Echo so they knew to steer clear. Something was off about him though and Hewn was sure he noticed a slight tremor in the enlister's right hand. The eyes gave it away though. He had been around drugs long enough to recognise an addict when he saw one. Any other time, Hewn would have found a way to escape before they got anywhere near the main door to the facility but, if Kurcher hadn't already blown his head off, perhaps there was some truth in what he was saying. Taurus wouldn't be looking for an equal partnership, he was certain; striking some form of alliance with the largest corp would certainly keep others off his back. Although Libra wouldn't like it, perhaps they too would see the benefit.

'Jos, relay the orders to our vessels. Tell them to let the enlister's ship land and then leave the planet. Then send a message to the guardian telling them Lars Hengeveld is heading off-world on a personal matter and to let the same ship past.'

'No need for my ship to land,' Kurcher pointed out. 'We came down in the lifeboat.'

Hewn gave a curt nod before issuing a final order to Chaplin. 'Tell both Echo and Libra personnel to cease fire too. They are to let Kurcher's *necessary evils* leave with us.'

For a split second, Kurcher looked as though he was going to add something more. He opted to keep his mouth shut. Instead, as Chaplin swivelled to face the monitors, the enlister waved his revolver at the door.

When Hewn turned, he was genuinely surprised. 'This is quite the coincidence. I see Kurcher's been a busy boy.'

'You have no idea,' replied Broekow, beckoning him forward.

By the time the three men stepped out onto the concourse, silence had fallen. Guards and workers stood and watched as Broekow led Hewn away towards the north door, with Kurcher walking calmly behind the pirate. All wore confused expressions, especially when they saw Hewn simply smile and nod at them.

'You realise I could just give the order and you'd be gunned down instantly.' He made sure his voice didn't carry.

'So do it,' countered Kurcher. 'You wouldn't live to see Echo's obliteration.'

Hewn had no intention of giving said order. He didn't want his last

194

thought to be of his two boys being executed. Even though they were hidden somewhere in the Echo Expanse, that didn't make them safe.

A thunderous howl echoed from ahead and Hewn instinctively grabbed for the pistol he no longer had. Standing before the open door to the facility was the biomech-infused giant he had hoped never to meet again. He had witnessed Angard's descent into insanity on-board Cooke's ship and remembered wondering how long it would be before the poor soul tore a hole in the hull and killed them all. Biomech technology may have saved Hewn's life; it had turned Angard into a monster.

'I'm starting to realise which familiar faces you were referring to,' he said to Kurcher.

The enlister didn't respond. He was paying close attention to those watching them walk the pirate out of the facility.

When Angard stepped towards them with a broad grin splitting his ugly face, Hewn saw the remains of a mech smouldering behind the crim. The howl they had heard Angard emit turned out to be his version of laughter.

'Having fun, big guy?' Broekow asked, nodding at the heap of metal.

'I feel alive.' The one clear eye regarded Hewn. 'Sorry about your mech.'

The pirate shrugged. 'Don't apologise to me. It belonged to Libra Centauri.'

'You're wounded,' Broekow said to Angard, pointing at a trickle of blood running from one thick arm.

'Just a scratch from the mech. Luckily for me, nobody here can shoot worth a damn.'

Hewn wondered how his guards could miss a target that size or whether it would have even made any difference if they *had* shot him. Even with the drug-fuelled strength pumping through Angard's body, Hewn was stunned at how the man had only come away with a small cut after battling a mech close-up.

The wind outside the facility was picking up as the storm approached and a strong gust hit them head-on. When Hewn turned to take one last look around, he realised two other men had joined them, both dressed in damaged guard uniforms. One was carrying a slim-bladed sword and wearing a satisfied smile. The other had someone else's blood sprayed across his thick beard and wasn't hiding his obvious hatred of Kurcher. It took a moment for Hewn to recognise Ercko though.

'You let this psycho loose in my facility?' he asked the enlister incredulously.

'I let two psychos loose,' was the muttered reply.

Hewn had no idea how Kurcher had managed to get this collection of killers together, but for now he had to protect his assets. He was certain that Chaplin was already preparing a message to send into the Echo Expanse letting them know what had happened and he just hoped that the head of operations wasn't also relaying the information to Libra.

'Did you kill Lars?' Hewn aimed his question at Ercko.

It was the sword wielder who answered. 'Left him unconscious down in the maintenance tunnel along with his men. Edlan Rane by the way.'

Hewn had heard the name countless times before and knew he was most likely lying. For all he knew, it was Hengeveld's blood all over Ercko. Besides, even if they hadn't killed him, the Libra officer would probably have died in the explosions.

'I don't think he believes you, Rane,' remarked Ercko. 'Can't say I blame him. After all, we are just a couple of psychos.'

As the group headed out of the facility into the blustery forest, Hewn wondered whether he should have just let Kurcher shoot him after all.

~

Winter checked the guardian's position again. His targeting system was locked on just in case, but he liked to trust his eyes rather than the computer.

The planet below was almost mesmerising to watch as the lightning flashes danced across the atmosphere. It was certainly living up to the name Libra Centauri had given it. He had to admit to being impressed how Echo and Libra had managed to build their facility among such ferocious weather conditions.

Having visited so many worlds, the quarans always held his fascination. They were often beautiful to behold from orbit and deadly up close and he likened them to the sirens of Greek mythology. It was no wonder mercs and pirates risked their lives to set up bases on such worlds.

Other planets held a very different kind of beauty. Cenia sprang instantly to his mind. Also known as *Alscion's Snowball*, the frozen world turned out to be a unique source of materials for Sigma Royal once they mined beneath the ice. During his last visit to Cenia, he had spent some time at Briggs, the largest mining colony, and had been genuinely surprised at how the people there had taken to such a cold home. Children played out in the vast plains of snow around the colony and explorers mounted expeditions across the surface that would sometimes last for months. It was an unforgiving world at times; however, one could get lost for hours just staring at the glistening snow.

Valandra was another planet he enjoyed visiting. The blue of the oceans often took his breath away as he approached, before the green dots of land began appearing. He imagined that Earth would look like Valandra one day.

The thought of his home brought him sharply back to reality. Revenants would end up burning the Earth if they had their way and he longed to get back there so he could continue cleansing the surface of their presence.

A ship was coming up from Tempest and he scanned it, smiling as the *Kaladine* was displayed on his screen. Hopefully Jaffren Hewn was on board. It wouldn't be long before Kurcher delivered the crims to Santa Cruz, then Winter could forget about all of them and get back to Earth.

He watched the guardian carefully, looking for any slight shift in direction to intercept the *Kaladine*. The Libra vessel remained where it was. Perhaps Kurcher had avoided conflict this time, but something told him that things had not been so quiet down in the facility. As the *Kaladine* moved boldly past the guardian and away, Winter laid in a course to follow.

Sapphire Nova Assault-class vessel Huntress
Callyn system

Espina sat in silent contemplation, her quarters shrouded in darkness. Her gaze was locked onto the planet they now sat in orbit of. Occasional specks of light would glint somewhere outside her ship as part of the debris reflected the distant Callyn sun.

'What were you doing out here, Davian?' she thought out loud.

To begin with, she had grown anxious when they detected the debris, believing it might have been the *Kaladine*. Scans had come back claiming it to be some unknown transport. Her pursuit of Kurcher was starting to raise more and more questions every time she visited a location. Why had Kopetti sent him to this shitty planet and who had been on that transport? More importantly, where the fuck was Kurcher now? If only Kopetti hadn't died before filling in the blanks.

She had learnt one surprising piece of information from the trader though. When she had known Kurcher, the enlister would sometimes partake of one drug or another. She never believed he would become an addict. Kopetti's stronger Parinax was designed to increase the dependency as well as the high, making it dangerous indeed.

She turned her mind back to Kurcher's recent destinations. He was clearly on an enlisting run; the fact he would have come to Mags and destroyed some random transport didn't make sense, unless the ship fired on him and he was simply retaliating. She wished she could read him like she used to be able to.

Sapphire Nova had known about Davian Kurcher for a long time, making it their business to keep an eye on who might be snooping around their systems. Enlisters for every corp often ventured boldly into space belonging to a competitor, but most of the time wouldn't cause any major problems. She herself had run-ins with Sigma Royal and Libra Centauri during her time as an enlister. She understood how things worked. Kurcher though had a different way of doing things and had made a name for himself by blasting straight through obstacles instead of taking the more diplomatic approach. She wasn't particularly surprised when she heard what had happened on Rikur. Still, she knew Kurcher didn't kill Portman. That wasn't his style.

Her comms app clicked into life, followed by a gruff male voice. 'Commander, we have that data you were after.'

'Send it through to my quarters.'

By the time she stepped from the seat at the window to her console, the information was already beginning to scroll. She took her time studying the jump point activation numbers and found herself wishing that Nova could track traffic across more systems. She didn't really know what she was looking for until it leapt out at her from the screen.

She selected her navigation officer's comms. 'This is Commander Espina. Get us to the Iridia system.'

'That's Libra space, commander.'

'Problem?' Her tone implied it wouldn't be.

As the *Huntress* left orbit, Espina settled back down at her window seat and ran a hand through her short black hair. Once this matter had been dealt with, she would have to bring a fleet back to Callyn and clean it up. It had been a merc-run system for too long.

Enlister-class vessel Kaladine
Iridia system

'It doesn't make sense.' When Frost breathed out, a cloud of smoke hid her face for a moment. 'Leaving Rane alive is fucking crazy. Why didn't you just activate that explosive and do everyone a favour?'

Kurcher waved the drifting smoke away. 'He's proving useful for now, especially keeping Ercko in check.'

'Doesn't it worry you having those two working together?'

'Of course it fucking does,' he snapped. 'I'm not stupid. Whatever he said to Ercko clearly worked though and my use of them as a distraction was justified.'

'Don't you think Hewn surrendered way too easily?'

Kurcher gave an amused snort. 'We've got all seven on board and soon we can hand them to Santa Cruz then be on our way. I don't care if Hewn has some grand plan. Taurus can deal with that now. You should be fucking happy for once.'

Frost looked like she wanted to stab the cigarette into his eye. 'I think the Parinax is causing you to lose grip on reality. Right now, we should have Rane, Ercko and Maric all locked up in the cells while keeping a close eye on the others.'

Kurcher didn't appreciate the drug comment. His head was beginning to pound and his concentration was waning. 'Just focus on your own job.'

Frost took a moment to glance at the images at the top of her vision. 'It feels like the calm before the storm. Rane and Ercko seem to be forming some sort of bond, Oakley and Angard are already a dangerous double act, plus I wouldn't trust Maric, Hewn or D'Larro as far as I could throw them.'

'What about Broekow? You didn't mention him. Don't forget he's part of this too.'

She stubbed the cigarette out. 'Like I'd forget.'

The headache was becoming a problem. 'I'm going to contact Santa Cruz. Should have done it before now really but...'

'But you've been on a high since Tempest and only now is your brain reminding you.'

That was a step too far. 'Need I remind you that you're only here to pilot *my* ship, not to bitch about the choices I make as an enlister? I can easily replace you and find someone who doesn't question my every fucking move.'

Frost didn't even turn to look at him. 'Funny. I seem to remember you saying before how you like having me here to play devil's advocate and that it keeps you sharp. I think you need to look at yourself, Davian, once this mission is complete and take time to sort your head out. The drugs are rotting your brain and making you lose your edge.'

Kurcher stormed to the cockpit door. 'This mission is on track. We've had some tough moments but come through unscathed thanks to *my* plans. Don't think you can lecture me, Justyne. You're expendable, just like everyone else.'

'That sounds like a threat.'

'Keep pushing and I'll turf you out when we rendezvous with the *Requiem*.' He slammed his palm against the wall as the door opened. 'There are too many voices on my damned ship.'

He left the cockpit before she could say anything more and made his way down past the empty cells. They still stank of those who had occupied them for so long.

Broekow was stood in the rec room doorway. 'Everything okay?'

'It will be.' Kurcher had no interest in making small talk.

He breathed a sigh of relief as he stumbled into his quarters. All he wanted to do was fall onto his bed, take a Calmer and drift off. That had to wait for the moment.

It took longer than expected for his comms link to be established with the *Requiem* and Kurcher grimaced when he heard Santa Cruz's jarring voice.

'The fact you're contacting me hopefully means you have found them all.'

'Correct. Give me your co-ordinates and we'll bring them to you.'

'We're in orbit of Minerva. Berg system.'

'That's out on the edge of the fucking galaxy.' Kurcher preferred to stay near the more heavily-populated systems. 'We're in Iridia. Can't we meet somewhere in the middle?'

'No, we can't. I need to be here and you will bring those crims to Berg immediately, understood?'

Kurcher rubbed at his eyes and took a deep breath to calm himself. 'Understood. We're on our way.'

He severed the link and opened another to Frost. 'Get us to Berg as quick as you can.'

'That means making a couple of jumps.' Her tone was sharp.

'Then do it. It's what I pay you for.'

He couldn't wait any longer. After a lengthy search through the empty containers strewn around his quarters, he located a full dose of Parinax and

201

drained it quickly before crawling onto his bed. He knew he was getting through everything Kopetti gave him too quickly; it was the only way he could keep his demons at bay. Once they had delivered their cargo to the *Requiem* and received the rest of their payment, he would contact the old trader again and arrange for another batch.

The Parinax kicked in and he immediately fell asleep, disappearing into dreams of isolation and silence.

~

Broekow desperately wanted to go to the cockpit. He tried pushing thoughts of Frost out of his head. If she and Kurcher had just had an argument, she would likely want to be alone anyway.

He watched the crims closely as they sat in conversation. He really couldn't afford to take his eyes off any of them. One lapse in concentration would undo all of Kurcher's work.

'We were all being held together before on Cooke's ship.' Hewn was in the middle of another rant about their situation. 'I can't believe that we've all been rounded up so easily again. We've been herded like cattle and you know what happens to them when they reach their destination.'

'Give it a rest,' yelled Angard, his voice making the room vibrate. 'If we're cattle, so are you.'

Hewn shook his head and waved a metal finger at Oakley. 'What about you? You're one of the more intelligent people in this room. Do you really think Kurcher was sent to enlist us?'

She glanced around at the others as their eyes turned on her. 'I didn't at first. He persuaded me to come along by holding intel that would threaten my family if it got out. He was rude, ruthless and determined. Seeing what has happened since though has changed my mind. I'm still wary of Kurcher and Taurus though of course.'

'He had every chance to execute me,' added D'Larro. 'He saved my life on Summit and that was enough to make me listen to him.'

'Why would Taurus want to enlist a murdering medic into their ranks?' Hewn asked. 'I can see the benefit of Angard's muscle or my connections, but why you?'

D'Larro shrugged. 'I have my uses.'

'We all need to believe in the redemption being offered to us.' It was the first time Maric had spoken in some time. 'Everyone here is a sinner and must atone for their crimes. It is the Lord's wish that we make amends.'

Hewn found that amusing. 'Nobody asked you, preacher. I'm sure your

202

alter ego would disagree anyway.'

Maric looked up at him with sorrowful eyes. 'Jaffren Hewn has made a name for himself by killing, stealing and lying. Echo are nothing but pirates and smugglers, intent on using others just to get ahead. You are wanted by all of the corporations, as well as being a target for Fortitude, the Knights Templar and Jericho's Bold.'

'Don't forget Schaeffer's Nine.'

'Your crimes are the most numerous here, Jaffren. You have much to do before your day of judgement arrives.'

Ercko let out a loud snort. 'You're all a bunch of whining pussies. Last time we were together, we were all locked up in individual cells. Now here we are, all gathered in an enlister's rec room playing nice. We may be the scum of the fucking galaxy, but we all have our uses.'

'Cooke had a ship with numerous cells,' Hewn stated. 'Kurcher has three. It's just a new ploy to ship us all back to Taurus for trial and execution.'

Ercko held up his three-fingered hand. 'I ain't forgotten what that fucker did to me, Hewn, but he would've aimed for my head if I was for the chop.'

Rane chose that moment to add to the conversation. 'Bennet's right. Davian chose to use our talents to get into your facility, Jaffren. He was nervous about doing so but realised it would show Taurus further what this bunch of crims were capable of when they set their mind to it. Their worth was shown by working together to get to you.'

'All you did was piss off Libra Centauri by setting the drug production back,' shrugged the pirate.

'The galaxy would be better off being rid of any drugs,' Rane countered, glancing at Ercko. 'We should've levelled the place.'

Hewn laughed. 'You weren't among us on Cooke's ship. I still don't understand why Kurcher lets you walk around here like you're part of the crew.'

'He doesn't.' Rane nodded at Broekow. 'Sieren there is more a part of this crew than any of us. That's why he's allowed to carry a weapon on the *Kaladine* and we aren't. I would suspect that Davian has told him to blow me away should I set one foot out of line. Is that correct?'

Broekow nodded. 'Not just you.'

At that, Hewn turned to regard the sniper. 'Once a corporation man...'

'Keep talking and I'll introduce you to one of the cells,' growled Broekow. 'Take this for what it is. Kurcher had a chance to kill all of you but didn't. Of course he doesn't want you on his ship. Between you, you've killed hundreds of people but you also have your own unique talents and Taurus are ruthless enough to recognise that. By all means, turn them down, Hewn, and see where you end up.'

Ercko chuckled behind his beard. 'Lapdog.'

Broekow chose to ignore that. 'The only person here with a question mark over their head is Rane and he knows that, but the fact he saved Kurcher and I on Rikur then helped infiltrate your drug plant makes him another valuable asset for the corp.'

'Thank you, Sieren.' Rane was beaming.

'Or they might just shoot him in the head the moment he leaves the *Kaladine*,' said Hewn. He watched the smile fade from Rane's lips. 'I've heard enough. I'm getting some rest. If any of you come near me, I'll snap your fucking neck.'

Broekow stepped aside to let him pass. Hewn's mechanical arm would certainly have been strong enough to break bones and he wondered whether Kurcher had even considered how dangerous the limb could be.

'He's got a lot more to lose than the rest of us,' Rane pointed out. 'He has spent years getting Echo to where it is today. Now Taurus are likely to muscle in on his work.'

'He'll disappear back to the Expanse first chance he gets.' Broekow scratched at his beard. 'He won't let himself become a corp lackey, even if they keep their word.'

'Promises are made to be broken,' grunted Ercko.

Broekow noticed the looks being exchanged between the two men who had caused the distraction down on Tempest. Had Rane and Ercko not infiltrated the ventilation system and drawn attention to the southern end of the facility, he and Kurcher would have struggled to get in unnoticed. It was a struggle enough to squeeze through the dangerous vent ports. Still, there seemed to be something going on and Broekow would keep an eye on them. The last thing they needed was an alliance between those two. Maybe Kurcher had made a mistake allowing Rane to persuade Ercko to help.

'How's the arm?' D'Larro asked Angard as the room went quiet.

'Fine. Not going to fall off any time soon.'

The medic laughed as he moved to stand beside Oakley. 'I just wish you'd let me take a look. It could get infected. Also, I'd like to review your drug supply. I think we could find a way to...'

'No.' Angard's face twitched.

'But if I could just take a look.'

'He said no, Tranc,' snapped Oakley, making D'Larro's nickname sound more like an insult. 'You need to learn when to leave people be.'

204

'Sorry.' The medic stepped away again. 'Just wanted to feel useful.'

'Why don't you look at my burns then?' suggested Ercko. 'Fucking fires licked up my arm and part of my thigh before I put them out.'

D'Larro looked uncertain. 'You told me to go fuck myself when I offered to take a look before.'

'I was hurting. Come see how bad they are.' As D'Larro cautiously approached him, Ercko sat back and opened his legs. 'It was my inner thigh by the way.'

'Bennet, leave him be,' warned Rane.

'Just having some fun. I like the innocent-looking ones.' Ercko let out a wheezing laugh, winking first at D'Larro and then at Oakley.

'Try anything with me, asshole, and I'll cut your heart out,' growled the medic, surprising everyone.

'Well said.' Oakley was wearing one of her more wicked smiles now. 'Same here, except I'll cut your dick off and shove it down your throat. Or just get Angard to wrench it off instead.'

'I'd much rather you tried wrenching it off with your petite little hands,' leered Ercko.

Maric stood suddenly and marched towards the door. 'I won't sit in here and listen to this filth. I wonder whether there is any redemption for some.'

Broekow blocked his way. 'Where do you think you're going?'

The preacher sighed. 'To a cell, where I can be alone with my thoughts.'

Broekow thought that an amusing thing for a schizophrenic to say. He held his tongue. He still didn't trust that Choice had been fully subdued as Maric claimed, but it had been a long time since the psycho had reared his head.

'I'll see you to the cell.'

'Not necessary.'

'Afraid it is.' Broekow glanced back into the rec room. 'Knock off the arguing and behave like normal human beings just for a while, yeah?'

He accompanied Maric along the corridor and shook his head as the preacher entered one of the cells, sat down on the bed and pulled out his battered book.

'What is it you read in that?' he asked, genuinely curious.

Maric gave him a knowing look. 'It belonged to a young man who believed everyone back on Earth was good but who was blind to the evil lurking in the shadows. He began a journal, documenting a visit to his mother in an attempt to save her from such evils. She was already lost though and that journal became his only light in a world of darkness.'

'You mean the Revenants?'

'Call them what you will. Those lost souls had already taken my mother's mind by the time Taurus Galahad soldiers put a bullet through it.' Maric looked down at the book and stroked the cover with affection. 'Without this, no piece of Maric Jaroslav would have survived.'

Broekow frowned. 'But much of the writing inside was made by Choice, not you.'

'Was it?' Maric leant back against the wall and began flicking through the pages. 'If it makes you feel better, you can lock me in.'

It did make Broekow feel better and he pondered Maric's words as he headed up the corridor. When he found himself at the cockpit door, he drew in a deep breath and looked over his shoulder before entering. The smoke inside stung his eyes.

'What?' Frost was definitely not in the mood for company.

'Just checking on you.' He moved round to the co-pilot seat so he could see her properly, his eyes drinking in her lithe body before reaching her face. 'I heard you and Kurcher having a set to.'

She stayed silent, staring out of the main screen, so he lowered himself into the seat and crossed his arms.

'Where're we heading?'

'Berg.'

Broekow dared another look at the fuming pilot. 'That's a long way out.'

'Tell me something I don't know.'

'Okay. I reckon Ercko is going to lose his dick before we reach our destination.'

'I said tell me something I *don't* know.'

'Okay. Maric is reading his crazy book in a cell because the others were being too lewd for him.'

At this, Frost turned her head slowly and met his gaze. Her icy demeanor cracked and she chuckled softly. 'He doesn't know the meaning of lewd. If Choice was around, he would have joined in, no doubt.'

'True.' He saw something stirring behind her eyes. 'Is there anything I can do to help? Talk to Kurcher or something?'

She sat watching him for a moment, then stood and walked to the door. 'There is something which would really help.' The lock clicked into place.

A moment later, she had lowered herself onto his lap and began grabbing at his belt as she kissed him. She bit his lip, the taste of blood firing his lust. It was too long since he had been with a woman; she was the only one on his mind since they first met back at Sullivan's Rest.

Their responsibilities were forgotten as they finally gave in to temptation.

Cobb
Kalbrec system

This was it. This was the fleet that would strike fear into the hearts of the corp supply depots.

'Jesus.' Fuller shut his eyes tight, rubbed at them and then looked back at the ships, hoping by some miracle they wouldn't still resemble a load of rickety rust buckets.

The staff of one small depot might go pale seeing the Cobb Resistance landing outside; a guardian would likely obliterate them before they could even get into orbit. The weapons welded to the hulls would be as effective as a mosquito bite on a cow, not that they had such creatures on the dying world.

Fuller shook the pessimism away. Numbers would count for something surely if his fleet came upon a corp ship; they just had to ensure they avoided that scenario. These vessels had been calibrated and customised to sneak in, raid the depot and get out before any guardian or assault ship turned up. He hoped the merc-built conflectors would be reliable.

'The general checking his fleet before the eve of battle?'

Fuller gave an amused snort. 'Hardly a general. Hardly a fleet. Hopefully no battle.'

Marie moved up alongside him. 'They're all looking to you, Cal. You're the man with the plan.'

'Just a test run. We're not going to get into any scrapes and I doubt there'll be much to salvage. The main aim is just to try out the fleet and see whether we can persuade anyone else to join us.'

'Anyone left alive on the surface is likely to be a bit protective over their supplies. If they have weapons, they're more likely to fire on you before you can say hello.' She pursed her lips as her imagination ran wild. 'For all we know, some colonists might have disappeared off to the far side of the planet.'

'Doubtful. Taurus set us all up on this continent for a reason. It had water and vegetation. The land masses on the other side of Cobb were dry and difficult to colonise.'

'Just as this one is now.' Marie turned to face him. 'Let's just take the fleet and get everyone away from Cobb.'

'And go where?' he asked, raising an eyebrow. 'We can't go to Sol or any

208

other Taurus system. They'd wipe us out to make sure we couldn't cause any trouble.'

She thought for a moment. 'Find a planet in Impramed space. You said they needed all the allies they can get.'

Fuller noticed how nervous she was. 'You've changed your tune. You were all up for striking out at the corp depots and using Cobb as our base. What's different?'

'Sometimes the unforeseen happens and it changes your view.' Her shoulders sagged as she saw the concern on his face. 'I'm pregnant.'

His jaw dropped open. 'You sure?'

'Yep. Very.'

'I... uh... I don't...'

Marie smiled and laid a hand on his forearm. 'I didn't mean for it to happen. Not great timing, I know.'

'That's an understatement.' Fuller wanted to be angry at her but wasn't. 'You're staying here then. I can't risk taking you with the fleet.'

'I can come with you on this test run, surely?'

'No way. You'll stay here and run this place in my absence. You basically run it anyway.'

She frowned and turned back to gaze at the ships. 'What about finding somewhere in Impramed space for us all?'

'They're too scared to help us,' he stated with a hint of sarcasm. 'They think they would suffer Taurus Galahad's wrath and unfortunately I believe they're right. We have to stick to the original plan and try to rebuild here.'

'Okay.' Her head bowed slightly. 'Don't give Dale a hard time for this.'

Fuller rolled his eyes. 'Cretin is the father? For fuck's sake, Marie. The guy's a joke.'

That stoked the fire. 'Don't call him that. He works hard down here and tries his best. Just because you don't like him, it doesn't mean he's a bad person.'

Fuller held his tongue this time and gave a frustrated sigh instead. Dale Rettin was an engineer who had made claims he could repair or build anything when he joined them. Turned out he liked to exaggerate and his boasts had nearly cost lives when machinery he had *fixed* exploded. Cretin was a much more apt name for him.

'I'm just looking out for you,' he told her, after a moment of awkward silence.

Her face softened. 'I know. To be honest, I'm looking out for you too most of the time. Promise me you'll be careful when you take the fleet out tomorrow. No heroics.'

Fuller grabbed her hand. 'No heroics. Just recon. I need you to keep an eye out for any corp ships in the vicinity while we're out. It'd be embarrassing to get caught while out on our first run.'

'Understood. Conflectors will hide you anyway.'

'Maybe.' He shrugged. 'Maybe not. Not sure I trust any merc tech... or any mercs for that matter.'

'It'll all be fine.' Marie gave him a playful punch on the arm. 'With you leading the fleet, we'll be stocking up on supplies and increasing our numbers before the month is out.'

As she began talking about other matters, Fuller's mind was elsewhere. He was feeling a cold dread seeping through his body. If the fleet failed in their mission, the Cobb Resistance would die out as quickly as it began and the members left behind in the bunker beneath Jefferson would perish. The thought of Marie lying dead, buried for eternity under the surface of a dead world, turned his stomach. Their survival was his responsibility and he knew that one bad decision would cost them all. He had to choose the right supply depots to hit at the right time.

He suddenly felt claustrophobic, despite the chamber they were in being vast. 'Listen, I'm going up to the surface for a while.'

Marie tilted her head to one side and gave him a suspicious look. 'You okay? Want me to come?'

'I'm good. You go get some rest. I need you bright for tomorrow.'

'Fine.' She hugged him and kissed his cheek. 'Don't stay out too late.'

Minutes later, Fuller found himself heading up the stairwell that led to one of the surface maintenance hatches. When the metal door opened with a monstrous mechanical growl, he shivered. None of them liked to return to the surface anymore. At night, though, there was a strange calm that descended on Cobb.

Jefferson's derelict buildings towered over him as he emerged from the bunker, their dark windows like hollow eyes watching his every move. Before the war, the colony had been growing quickly, but survivors had been scavenging materials since Taurus left them for dead. A few structures had been partially dismantled and resembled the carcasses of some type of large mech. He felt a pang of guilt at the fact his people had taken most of the surrounding metalwork. The corpse of Jefferson was proving useful though.

The sky was dark and the lack of stars told him the cloud cover was thick that night. It was a rare sight when the distant suns appeared. To the north, the underside of the clouds was tinged orange; illumination from one of the remaining surface settlements. How many were left there, he couldn't say. He used to visit survivor camps, trying to persuade more to join the Resistance. Sometimes it worked and he would return with the dirty, hungry stragglers stumbling along behind him. The last time had been a nightmare. The survivors were almost feral, protecting their meagre supplies with a surprising level of aggression. He had lost two men that day, one shot down in cold blood by an old man with a waist-length beard and the other stabbed to death by a woman wielding a rusty knife. They hadn't been out on a recruitment mission since.

A breeze blew across the dusty street. The air was cold and Fuller wanted to breathe it in deep. To do so meant suffering the smell. Even after all this time, the oxygen seemed tainted. It was as if Cobb itself was carrying the scent of death.

He remained on the surface for an hour, alone with his own thoughts of what might have been had the war not erupted and had Taurus not made the decision to make an example of Cobb, to show their other colonies what would happen if they rebelled against the corp. When he returned below, his doubts had subsided. The Resistance would succeed and Taurus Galahad would pay.

Enlister-class vessel Kaladine
Iridia system

'This is insanity, Davian.' Rane couldn't believe what he was hearing. 'You'll condemn everyone on this ship.'

Kurcher's hand rested on his holstered revolver. 'You tried to get into my head. For a time, I admit it was working. I truly started believing you'd been intercepting Taurus comms and even began buying into your conspiracy theories. The truth is you're a lying, manipulative serial killer who uses everyone he comes into contact with and I'm done with you. As much as I would love to execute you myself, I'm going to let the corp deal with you as they see fit.'

'So the great enlister, Davian Kurcher, lets me live? There's still a part of you that knows I'm right about this.'

'Get out of my quarters,' Kurcher snarled. 'I agreed to hear you out and now we're done.'

Rane looked around the untidy mess where Kurcher had been hibernating for most of their journey from Tempest to the jump point. The sickly sweet Parinax scent was still in the air.

'They'll make you and Frost disappear too,' he said, reminding Kurcher for the fifth time since he had stepped into the dim quarters. 'Probably before they've even found out who has the data implant.'

'Bullshit.'

'Hewn has clocked onto the fact Taurus will kill us all once we reach the *Requiem*. He knows how the corps work. He left Tempest because he wanted his operation to continue producing that poison and to protect Echo, but he's realised what is really waiting for us.'

'So what?' Warning signs of Kurcher's temper were beginning to show. 'How much clearer can I be? I want all of you off my ship. I don't care if they torture you slowly or kill you outright. That's up to them.'

Rane wrinkled his nose in disgust. 'Just as long as they pay you, right? So you can go buy more Parinax and spend the rest of your life as an addict. That shit has melted your brain, Davian. Back on Rikur, at least you had control of your faculties. Now you're just thinking about your next hit.'

'Fuck you. I won't be lectured to by a crim. Get out.'

Rane stood his ground. 'I'm asking you one last time, Davian. Please don't rendezvous with the *Requiem*. Let's find out what this data is that the corp is

212

so desperate to get their hands on and make a sensible decision as to what to do next.'

Kurcher made to pull his revolver. 'No. You've had your chance.'

'So have you,' sighed Rane.

As Kurcher raised his revolver, Rane darted forward and swatted it aside. Once, the Parinax would have quickened the enlister's reactions, but he felt ludicrously slow as the killer avoided his clumsy lunge. Kurcher was more surprised when Rane's elbow smashed into his face, sending him reeling backwards. As his vision swam, he found his legs taken out from beneath him and the side of his skull struck something as he fell.

Despite not being knocked unconscious, Kurcher found he couldn't move for a few minutes. His head was throbbing, this time from the fall rather than the drug withdrawal. He had blood in his mouth. When he was finally able to sit up, Rane had gone. To Kurcher's relief, his revolver was still lying on the floor.

'Justyne?' he croaked as his comms app came online.

'I'm here.'

'Rane attacked me.' He grabbed the nearest surface to pull himself to his feet. 'Where is he?'

He heard Frost's sharp intake of breath before she answered. 'He's in the rec room with the others.'

'Shit. Seal yourself in the cockpit. This could get messy.'

'What's happening? Why did he attack you?'

Kurcher scooped up the revolver and headed out of his quarters. 'I think he's about to screw us over. Is Broekow with them?'

'Yeah. What're you going to do?'

'Guess I'm going to have to defuse the situation.' He could hear raised voices from the rec room. 'Then I'm going to blow Rane's fucking head off.'

He knew what had happened as soon as he walked in. Silence had fallen and the crims were staring at Rane. Angard, Hewn and Ercko looked ready to explode, while D'Larro, Oakley and Broekow just looked confused. Maric was the only one seated and his expression was typically blank.

'I fucking knew it.' Hewn turned on Kurcher. 'You lying bastard.'

'Is this true?' asked Oakley.

'I can't believe it,' D'Larro muttered, shaking his head.

Kurcher took a deep breath before he addressed the room. 'Look, I don't know what Rane has been telling you, but he just did *this*.' He pointed at his bloodied nose and mouth before continuing. 'Are you really going to believe a piece of shit like him?'

213

Hewn took a step towards the enlister, making Kurcher's trigger finger twitch. 'What is it exactly we aren't supposed to believe? That some corp bootlicker like you wouldn't come up with a whole set of lies in order to get us here? Or maybe that Taurus plan on making us disappear once you make your delivery?'

Kurcher glanced at Rane, who held his hands up and smiled apologetically.

'Sorry, Davian, but you left me no choice.'

'My orders were to enlist you,' said Kurcher, trying to keep his cool. 'Why would I put my neck on the line getting to each of you otherwise? If the corp wanted you dead, I would've just killed you and left.'

'That's true,' admitted D'Larro. 'As I've said before, he protected me from harm back on Summit.'

'It's called protecting your assets,' Rane told the medic. 'If whoever is carrying the data was killed, chances are the data would be corrupted. I decided to help Davian because I believed I could persuade him to do the right thing and to find out why Taurus were so keen to get hold of the data. Unfortunately, the Parinax surging through his brain has made him lose sight of the bigger picture.'

'Shut your fucking mouth,' warned Kurcher.

'Ask Tranc,' continued Rane, ignoring the enlister. 'He knows an addict when he sees one.'

D'Larro looked across at Rane, then Kurcher, before simply nodding.

'Holy shit.' Ercko seemed genuinely amused by this revelation. 'So we've been herded together by a junkie? That's fucking priceless.'

Kurcher's temper finally got the better of him as he aimed his revolver at Rane. 'Enough talk. I've got a job to do and I'm taking you all to the *Requiem*. This psycho wasn't even meant to be here and now you all suddenly believe his lies. You're all letting him manipulate you.'

Hewn's metal fingers flexed. 'I reckon it's you doing the manipulating.'

'For fuck's sake! I took Angard, Broekow and Ercko down to Tempest with me,' cried Kurcher. 'Why would I do that if not to prove their worth to Taurus?'

'Because I told you to.' Rane paused for effect. 'I explained that you needed to keep up the façade by using their skills to get to Hewn. Get them working together and it will raise morale. I hoped you would then make the right choice once they were all accounted for.'

Kurcher wanted to squeeze the trigger and watch Rane's brain explode out the back of his skull. It suddenly struck him that he had allowed himself to be manipulated. Had Rane planned all along to turn the crims against him, biding his time until they were all together? The serial killer had already ingratiated himself with the likes of Ercko, D'Larro and Maric. Even Hewn was siding with him.

Rane carried on with his explanation. 'Davian was protecting the data as best he could without knowing which one of you has the implant because Taurus ordered him to. I had to persuade him to start making you feel like the corp wanted to enlist you. You all had your doubts, but the events on Tempest smoothed that over.'

Revolver still pointed at Rane, Kurcher looked over at Broekow. 'You going to say anything? Didn't I tell you there was a chance you would be able to join Frost and I?'

It was clear the sniper was rattled by what he had heard. 'You did, but I've heard things since being on the *Kaladine* and I've never trusted Taurus since they turned on me.'

'The truth must come out.' Maric was looking down at the floor, his eyes distant. 'It is not just those branded as criminals here who must seek redemption. Confess your own sins, enlister.'

Kurcher shook his head as he looked from one face to the next. 'You're all fucking mad. Sieren, help me get them in line.'

Broekow placed a hand on his pistol. 'As much as I hate to agree with Maric, maybe he's right. I knew you were addicted to Parinax and I've seen the way it's been affecting you recently, but that's not what concerns me. I also know Frost has been hiding something; seen the guilt in her eyes. Is Rane's data implant theory true?'

'We're going round in circles,' yelled Hewn. 'I'm not about to be led to my death.'

Kurcher swung his revolver towards the pirate. 'All of you stand down or I'll incapacitate you for the rest of the journey.'

'Wait.' Oakley pushed past Hewn with Angard towering behind her. 'We're forgetting one other person on this ship. If Kurcher won't admit what's really going on, why don't we ask Frost?'

'Stay the fuck away from her,' snapped Kurcher, taking a step back towards the corridor.

'She'll be locked away in the cockpit,' Rane remarked. 'Besides, you don't want to hurt the only person who can pilot this ship.'

'I'm a trained pilot,' Hewn told him.

'Plus you had your own ship, Rane,' Oakley pointed out. 'I say we interrogate Frost.'

215

Angard cracked his knuckles. 'I can get us through the cockpit door.' His suspicious gaze fell on Kurcher. 'You know I'm not fond of you, enlister, but I was ready to believe you. If you've been lying to us this whole time, I'll enjoy removing your limbs.'

Suddenly Broekow's pistol was in his hand. 'Nobody touches Frost.'

'Except you, right?' sniggered Ercko. 'Your girlfriend knows what's waiting for us and I for one am happy volunteering to make her squeal.'

'You lay one finger on her, you sick fuck, and I'll kill you.'

That made Ercko laugh more. 'Seems she screwed you in more ways than one, eh?'

As the crims began arguing and shouting their own opinions, Kurcher could feel the sweat beginning to run down his brow. The mission was fucked, all because of the one man he should have executed long ago. Rane was simply stood in silence listening to the cacophony around him.

Kurcher had relied on his instincts all of his life to survive. Now was no different. He just hoped Santa Cruz would understand if one or two of the crims were killed in the process. As he returned his aim to Rane, intent on removing the antagonist from the dire situation, a hand grabbed his arm and pushed it back down.

'It's true.' The room fell silent as Frost stepped alongside Kurcher, pistol in hand. 'One of you is carrying a data implant that Commander Jorelian Santa Cruz of Taurus Galahad wants and his intention was to find it then dispose of you all.'

There were some stunned expressions, including Kurcher's. The enlister snapped out of it quickly. 'What the fuck are you doing?'

Frost gave him a look he had seen many times before. 'Saving your life. And mine.' She stepped fully into the room, avoiding Broekow's gaze but noticing Rane give her a nod of approval. 'I'm not telling you all this so we can become friends. In fact, if any of you psychos try to hurt Kurcher or me, we won't hesitate in putting you down. I don't really care whether the data carrier dies or not, apart from the fact it stops me getting paid.'

'So why come clean?' Hewn asked her.

Frost swept her free hand out in an arc. 'Look around. This situation is fucked. We could insist on sticking with the original plan, but my guess is that some of you would try taking us out and we might gun down Hewn and Ercko but Angard would probably go into one of his tantrums and destroy the whole ship. This doesn't end well for any of us, the way I see it.'

'What's your solution then?' Broekow watched her carefully, the trust that had once been in his eyes having dissipated.

216

She pushed her emotions away, addressing the matter at hand. 'We work together to find out who has the data and try to extract it. Once that is done, we go our separate ways. Kurcher and I take the data to Santa Cruz. I doubt he'd care much about where you all were as long as we had what he wanted.'

'He'd kill you both,' Rane said. 'No, we need to find out what this data actually is before handing it over to a power-hungry madman like him.'

Kurcher stepped in, having lowered his revolver. 'So instead we should hand it over to a madman like you?'

'At least Rane won't bring down the wrath of the Taurus military on us,' muttered Hewn.

Frost held her hand up. 'You can argue all you like later. We're against the clock here. Santa Cruz is expecting us in the Berg system so we need to work out how to find the data quickly.'

Ercko made to step towards her but found Broekow in his way. 'So are you in charge now then, beautiful? We can't exactly trust you now, can we?'

Broekow's action didn't go unnoticed by Frost. 'I doubt any of us trust the rest right now. The fact is we have to work together on this. The alternative is I just overload the engines right now and scatter us across the system.'

'You've been found out,' grinned Ercko. 'So you'll say anything right now to stop us cutting your throats.'

'Shut up, Bennet.' Rane stepped next to Frost, who instinctively moved back. 'She's right. In order for all of you to get on with your lives, we need to find the data. Don't forget that Frost is tied into the *Kaladine* systems so could destroy the ship any time she wanted.'

'And nobody is getting their weapons back,' added Kurcher. 'Let's just get on with this.'

There were several hate-filled glances. Hewn shook his head to show his disapproval, but even he couldn't argue with the logic.

'You get a stay of execution, enlister,' rumbled Angard.

'As do you,' Kurcher countered.

Frost waited until the atmosphere in the room seemed to settle somewhat before speaking again. 'First things first. How do we find out who has the data?'

'There is one person who might be able to help,' stated Broekow, his gaze lingering on the pilot. 'But we'd need to wake him up and that's risky.'

Maric had been lost in his own thoughts when he found that everyone was staring at him suddenly. 'I'm afraid that is out of the question. Rane found a way to subdue him and I will not have him back in control.'

'But Choice is bloody clever when it comes to apps and similar tech,'

Oakley said, stating the obvious. 'Surely he could concoct something.'

'He is asleep indefinitely.' Maric's tone was as sharp as they had ever heard it. 'You would need to find a different solution to your problem.'

Kurcher decided he needed to take the front foot again rather than fade into the background. He and Frost still had all the power while the crims were on their ship. 'The preacher's right. I for one don't want that weasly prick awake again. He's the most untrustworthy one among you and that's saying something.'

'There must be a way to scan for the implant,' D'Larro thought out loud. 'Do you have a scanner on the *Kaladine*?'

'The implant can't be picked up by standard tech,' replied Kurcher, remembering the report first downloaded to him by Santa Cruz. 'It's got a clever firewall protecting it.'

'All firewalls can be broken down,' commented Maric. 'You just need the right technology to do so.'

Rane eyed him warily. 'I'm hoping that's your old knowledge speaking and not Choice.'

Maric looked shocked as he peered up through his growing fringe. 'I was not always a preacher, as you well know.'

'Sullivan's Rest,' blurted out D'Larro. 'With all the mercs and pirates there, someone is bound to have a scanner that could break down the firewall and locate the implant. Using their medical equipment, I could then extract it.'

Kurcher gave Frost a troubled glance. He remembered what Coyle had said when they last spoke and he didn't want to be thrown in a cell as soon as he stepped off the ship. Then again, he also remembered what the merc had shouted after him. *Something always brings you back, Davian.*

'Don't you have tech we can use?' he asked Hewn.

The pirate shrugged. 'Perhaps, but Frost said time is of the essence and we would have to get to the Echo Expanse before then searching for a suitable scanner. Sullivan's Rest is closer. Just don't expect me to go wandering round the station. I'd rather not get knifed in the back by a member of Jericho's Bold.'

Kurcher thought for a moment. 'Fine. Justyne, head for Sullivan's Rest. I need to think of a way to get Coyle to let me back in.'

'Some of us can be quite persuasive, don't forget,' Oakley reminded him.

Angard was quick to voice his disapproval. 'I'd rather he didn't pimp you out, Tara.'

As Frost headed for the door, she glanced back at Broekow. The sniper

218

looked away quickly and moved to sit opposite Maric. She really needed a cigarette, but had one last question for the room.

'Did Cooke come into contact with any of you prior to his letting you go?'

The crims exchanged looks for a moment.

'He got close enough to pretty much all of us,' D'Larro said. 'I recall him pushing me out of my cell. I also saw him do the same to Broekow, Ercko and Maric.'

'He grabbed me by the wrist at one point,' Oakley stated, holding her left arm up.

Angard snorted. 'He wouldn't dare touch me, but I doubt I'd feel it if he shot something small like an implant into me. I'm numb to things like that.'

'So it could be absolutely any of you.' Frost gave Kurcher a look of despair. 'Great.'

Kurcher was reluctant to holster his revolver, although Frost had seemingly defused the situation well enough for now. He needed to show willing. He cast his eyes around each of the crims, watching as they sat in quiet contemplation. Even Hewn with his distrustful glare was now leaning against a wall and staring down at the floor.

'I am sorry about hitting you, Davian.'

Kurcher bit his lip at the sound of Rane's voice. When he turned to look into the killer's face, he couldn't help himself. His fist connected with Rane's jaw and lifted him off the floor. A second punch landed hard against the side of his face, sending him sprawling.

'Guess I deserved that,' groaned Rane, rolling onto his back.

Kurcher stood over him. 'Once all of this shit is out of the way, you and I have some unfinished business.'

Taurus Galahad Assault Ship *Requiem*
Berg system

Santa Cruz sat in silence, listening to the conversation between the officers around his table. He was taking the time to study each of them, watching their mannerisms and seeing how they interacted with their counterparts. He had selected them to be a part of his fleet for several reasons. They had all worked together before and were respected by those working under them, plus they were five of the most ruthless Taurus Galahad had to offer. The most important factor though was that they had the same beliefs as he did. They would do what was best for the corporation, especially when it meant the end of the competition.

Leading the conversation was the only woman at the table. He had known Neri Ishlan for many years and had come through part of the early training process with her. Her rise to power had seen her take command of the *Ravenedge*, which suited her well. The assault ship was dark and sleek, cutting an ominous silhouette against the void. She had fallen in line behind Santa Cruz without question.

The four men trying their best to keep up with her banter were slowly getting drunk. He would allow it that evening. They deserved some calm before the coming storm.

Although O'Brien was loud and could be obnoxious, the crew of the *Mantheus* loved him. It was often said they would follow him into the fires of hell and Santa Cruz imagined they might have to one day.

Fernandes seemed to have a laid-back attitude much of the time and often spoke to Santa Cruz as though they were kin, just because both had Latin American blood. It was an annoying trait that could be overlooked as Fernandes was fiercely loyal to the cause. He was also the only one at the table who had named his ship at its conception. *Tucana* was apparently where he had been born.

The final two officers were almost like brothers, having come up through the ranks together. Byrne was a scowling hulk of a man with a deep scar across his throat; a reminder of a time he got too close to one of Jericho's Bold. Thomadakis was also well-built, but his skin was darker and untouched. There was one other major difference between them: the crew of the *Exodus* were afraid of Byrne whereas Thomadakis commanded respect on the *Arcturus* through being charismatic.

'A poor choice of words,' smirked Ishlan, wagging a finger at O'Brien. 'I'll work alongside you, but I won't get into bed with you.'

The commander of the *Mantheus* looked wounded. 'One day, Neri. One day.'

As the five drank back the last of the whisky Akeman had given Santa Cruz, they all glanced to the head of the table.

'Do you not feel like celebrating, sir?' asked Byrne. 'Taurus can't see us this far out.'

Santa Cruz gave a half-smile. He liked them calling him *sir*. His role in the corp dictated that his rank was higher, but it still made him feel powerful.

'They can see us wherever we are,' he replied. 'And no, I don't believe in celebrating until I have reason to do so.'

'There are plenty of reasons,' cried O'Brien, brash as usual. 'We have the most systems, the most worlds and the most ships. The other corps are dying out slowly. Taurus will take full control of the galaxy in time.'

Santa Cruz regarded them for a moment with unimpressed eyes. 'When exactly? Ten years? Ten thousand years? The likes of Nova, Sigma and Libra won't just lay down and die. Neither will Fortitude or the Knights Templar. Jericho's Bold, Schaeffer's Nine, Echo. None of these organisations will accept us running the galaxy. Besides, more factions appear every month.'

'Insignificant ones,' Fernandes pointed out. 'There will always be mercs, pirates and smugglers out there, no matter what.'

'Unless they wipe themselves out,' grinned Byrne. 'Could happen.'

Santa Cruz sat back and turned to watch Minerva. He could see one of the guardians and an explorer-class which had apparently docked with the defense vessel. He imagined that anyone approaching the planet would wonder why so many ships were in orbit. Even Earth wouldn't have that many.

'There are six of us,' he said eventually, looking back at the officers. 'As I said before, we are a fleet that officially doesn't exist due to the confidential assets we are protecting. I aim to speak to the commanding officers of the explorers and the guardians soon, to make sure they understand the importance of what is happening here.'

'Are you aiming to increase the size of this fleet, sir?' Ishlan asked him, already guessing what he was about to say.

'I am. We may need to leave Berg on a whim at any time. I would like to enlist other ships before that happens. Thoughts?'

Ishlan was quickest to respond. 'There may be some in Wagner soon. Patrol routes of the outer systems always go through there, refuelling at

Karina.'

That was why he liked her. Her mind was so sharp, even when under alcohol's influence. 'Good idea. We'll check which ships are due there and I may send one of you on a recruitment mission.'

'I'll go, sir,' volunteered Thomadakis. 'I know a few people on Karina. Might be they have some ships on the surface under construction or being repaired.'

'Would any of these people happen to be female?' Byrne gave his friend a wink.

'Any other thoughts?' asked Santa Cruz, severing the banter between the two before it could begin in earnest. 'We would need loyal men or women who will accept my orders without crying to General Mitchell or the Taurus board.'

'It would help if we knew where the fleet might suddenly have to jump to,' O'Brien remarked, looking into his empty glass. 'Is there nothing you can tell us?'

'I'm afraid not. I don't know myself yet. All I can say is that we won't be sat at Berg too much longer.' A message alert appeared in his vision. When he saw Winter's unique code, it suddenly made him anxious. 'One moment.'

As the officers talked among themselves in hushed tones, Santa Cruz read the brief report. He didn't like what he saw. For the second time, the data was tantalisingly close and yet he felt as though it was suddenly slipping away again.

He sat back and read Winter's message again. It might be that Kurcher was heading to the Vega system for a valid reason. The *Kaladine* might have needed refuelling or repairing before making the journey out to Berg. Perhaps the enlister's pilot was going to take a more unorthodox route so as to avoid the other corps, especially if Sapphire Nova were on the prowl for revenge after the problems on Rikur.

All he could do was wait to hear from Winter. He just hoped he wouldn't have to give the order to eliminate another enlister.

Enlister-class vessel Kaladine
Vega system

He missed Valandra. The vast oceans, the verdant land with so many places to hide and the women. He missed the Valandran women most of all.

Ercko paced the corridor, casting the occasional look towards the cockpit at one end and the stairs down to the hold at the other. He couldn't sleep like the others. His mind was too active. One moment he was thinking about the layout of the ship, pondering how he might be able to gain entry to the lifeboat without the alarm going off; the next he was imagining how he would kill everyone on board.

With most of the crims down in the hold trying to get some sleep before they reached Sullivan's Rest, he felt like he had the ship to himself. Kurcher and Frost were in their respective quarters too, but no doubt the clever pilot was linked in to the *Kaladine* systems to keep an eye on everything.

The cell doors were all closed. As he wandered past, he saw Maric sitting on one of the beds flicking through his tattered tome. The preacher never seemed to sleep and yet always looked on the brink of exhaustion. Ercko smiled at how easy it would be to snap the man's thin neck.

He paced back the other way, passing the rec room, quarters and storage before coming to a halt at the top of the stairs. To his left and right, the corridor continued round to the engine chambers and he could feel the steady thrum of power beneath his feet. Perhaps he could sabotage the engines, just as he had done on a number of other ships.

Being cooped up on the *Kaladine* was worse than being locked up in Rockland. At least inside the prison, he had more space to move around in. Despite the heinous crimes committed by those incarcerated there, Rockland's security had no need to restrict their movements. Even if they had tried to take control of one of the sec ships, the automated turrets would have ripped them apart. In the ten years he spent there, he only ever saw three prisoners killed by the sentries. That was enough to deter him.

He also remembered the frequent trips down to Aridis for work detail in the mines, where he and his fellow inmates would spend a month at a time on the surface drilling and moving minerals. Those had been like field trips for him.

As he turned to gaze along the entire length of the corridor, he realised the *Kaladine* was not dissimilar to the security transport he had overthrown. He had waited a decade for the right moment and hadn't hesitated in slaughtering the guards he encountered. Just a lucky break when the engines broke down. At the time, he had found it amusing having heard some of the sec team on Rockland just a week before complaining that Taurus Galahad weren't maintaining their ships properly. It wasn't quite so funny when he had to get the transport working again; thankfully some of the other escapees knew their way around an engine.

As he walked past Frost's quarters, he heard muffled voices from within. It seemed Broekow had stolen into the pilot's room for a late-night chat. He put his ear as close to the door as he dared, trying to make out what was being said.

'You've disobeyed a corporation order.' Broekow's tone was sharp. 'I know you were helping Kurcher, but admitting the truth has really complicated things.'

'Would you rather I'd stayed quiet?' snapped Frost, clearly trying to keep her voice low and failing. 'You would have torn him apart.'

'Did you really do it for Kurcher?'

'Don't flatter yourself.'

'Taurus isn't going to like this. If that data is so important, they won't want us getting our hands on it. If what Rane says is true, as soon as we extract the implant all of us are as good as dead.'

Frost sighed loudly. 'I did what I thought was right in the circumstances. If Rane hadn't have opened his mouth, none of you would be any the wiser.'

'So I'm one of *them* again now, am I?'

'You always were. I just lost sight of that. To be honest, I'm still waiting for you to put a bullet in my head for keeping the truth from you for so long.'

'You know I'm not like that.' Broekow sounded genuinely hurt. 'If Hewn or Ercko had been holding a pistol when we found out, I doubt many of us would be alive now.'

Ercko grinned. He liked hearing his name in other people's conversations, even if not in the best context.

'I think you should go,' said Frost after a long silence. 'I have to get back to work and you're not...' Her sentence ended abruptly.

Ercko had an image in his head of Broekow strangling the pilot. 'Throttle the lying bitch,' he muttered beneath his breath.

'Stop, Sieren.' Frost's voice was shaky and uncertain. 'You're a criminal who needs to remember his place and I'm...' Again, she cut off suddenly.

The noises Ercko then heard from behind the door made him want to laugh. Broekow was no murderer in his eyes. Despite knowing Frost was

224

taking him to be executed, the sniper seemed oddly forgiving. Either that or he wanted one last fuck before the shit really hit the fan. He didn't need to listen to them going at it. It reminded him too much of all the women he had loved and killed.

He headed into the rec room and waited. Half an hour later, he saw Frost walk past the door. She glanced at him and looked away again quickly. That was his cue to follow.

'That didn't take long,' he said, taking a look behind to make sure Broekow wasn't in sight. 'Sounds to me like you need a real man.'

Frost spun to face him, pistol already in hand. 'Fuck off, Ercko. I'm not in the mood.'

'You were in the mood thirty minutes ago.' He placed his hands on his hips and pushed his groin forward. 'Try me for size. You won't be disappointed.'

She looked thoroughly sickened by the notion. 'I suggest you turn around and disappear before I shoot it off. May take me a few goes. Small targets are harder to hit.'

Ercko looked her up and down. She wasn't his usual type, but her feisty nature still managed to arouse him. 'I just thought you seem to like crims on death row. Besides, you can't shoot me. I may be the one with the data.'

'At this point, I'd take my chances.'

'That'd piss Kurcher and Taurus off even more. Don't want to upset them now, do we? So, you see, you can't blow my dick off but you *can* blow it.'

Frost stepped closer to him and he breathed in her scent, not even minding that he could still smell Broekow on her. Then she drove her knee hard into his balls.

'Stay the fuck away from me,' she snarled, as he doubled up and crumpled to the floor.

By the time he had managed to get his breath back, she had vanished into the cockpit. Her time would come and he would enjoy keeping her alive longer than his other victims. Frost seemed like she would be able to take a fair amount of pain before begging for death.

As he stumbled for the hold, one hand clasping his bruised groin, he pulled the tiny vial from a hidden pocket of his jacket and peered at the clear liquid inside. Four doses of Eidolon. One drop to cause ghost-like hallucinations, two to give a high that feels like an out-of-body experience, three to fall into a heavy sleep with unusually vivid dreams. A fourth drop could potentially induce a coma or even kill. He had to hand it to Hewn: the pirate's organisation made some potent shit.

225

The walls of the hold were all but hidden in darkness. Ercko could see the massive bulk of Angard on a bedroll that he was too large to fit in. Each breath from the giant rattled from him like steam through a pipe. Ercko still couldn't get used to sleeping with that noise going on. Hewn and D'Larro were asleep further into the long chamber, with Rane's back just visible as he lay facing the wall.

With Maric upstairs in the cell and Broekow probably sleeping off his encounter with Frost in her quarters, Ercko crept through the hold towards the only crim he hadn't seen. Oakley was fast asleep on top of her bedroll and had been hidden from view by Angard's torso. Ercko stood looking down at her for a moment. She was as beautiful asleep as she was awake and he couldn't help but imagine how peaceful she would look if she were dead. Her slow breathing caused her breasts to rise and fall. He almost found the motion mesmerising.

He took another wary look around the hold and then leant over Angard to double-check he was out for the count. It was disconcerting that the brute's dead eye didn't close when he was asleep.

Ercko quietly opened the Eidolon vial and crouched down next to Oakley. The ache in his groin was joined by a sudden yearning as he thought of what would happen next. As Oakley's lips parted slightly, he dripped three doses into her waiting mouth. He really didn't need her waking up though, so gave her the dangerous fourth and final dose. After he had returned the empty vial to his pocket, he waited for a few minutes until he saw her eyes suddenly flick open then roll back in her head.

With practised speed and silence, Ercko lifted Oakley easily from her bedroll and carried her to a dark corner of the hold away from the sleeping crims. Without hesitation, he began hungrily pulling at her trousers and kissed one of her covered breasts. Her body briefly shook and she made a gargling noise as saliva ran from her mouth. If she overdosed, he didn't care. He would enjoy this.

He fumbled at his belt as he drank in her pristine skin. Then something made him hesitate. The hold was completely silent. No steam pipe. As he looked up, a huge silhouette blotted out the light from the stairs and the next moment he was being lifted into the air by one enormous hand.

'Wait a minute,' he yelled, looking into Angard's good eye.

'Fucking rapist scum.'

With one flick of his wrist, Angard launched Ercko across the hold, sending him crashing hard into the wall. Winded, Ercko looked back to see Oakley's loyal beast scoop her up and bring her back into the half-light.

226

'Tranc.' Angard's call had the medic rushing to help immediately, rubbing sleep from his eyes. 'He's given her something.'

D'Larro examined her face quickly. 'What was it?'

'Eidolon.' Rane stepped from the shadows. 'Must've got it from Jaffren's facility.'

Ercko found his voice. 'You lying fucking bastard.'

Hewn was awake too. 'How much did you give her, you piece of shit?'

Ercko didn't answer and instead charged at Rane. 'You promised me I...'

He was cut short as Angard's fist struck him in the side of the head, sending him sprawling back to the floor. His vision was swimming, his ears ringing. It was as if he had been hit by an actual steam pipe. D'Larro said something. His voice was muffled and distant.

As Ercko rolled to his back, Rane appeared above him and leant down to whisper in his ear. 'I apologise, Bennet. I had to coax you into helping on Tempest somehow and Tara is such a sweet temptation.'

Before he could utter a reply of any kind, Ercko was once again lifted into the air. This time Angard was really mad. One headbutt shattered his nose and twice a giant fist slammed into his stomach, feeling as though it would punch straight through him. Angard let out a visceral roar and snapped Ercko's left arm like a twig before throwing him against the wall again.

As he lost consciousness, the last thing Ercko heard was Kurcher's distant voice demanding to know what was going on. The last thing he saw was Rane's smiling face.

Earth
Sol system

Rees cursed as he switched the monitor off.

He didn't need to see yet another missile destroying even more of Earth's history. The only good thing about it was so many Revenants would die. Still, he had to question the overall effectiveness. The Revenants were like a plague of rats; kill a thousand and another two thousand would replace them.

As he gazed out of his panoramic window overlooking the Taurus Galahad headquarters' main building, he struggled to imagine what Earth would be like if the war against the Revenants lasted for another thirty years. In the three decades since the Holy Revolt, the religious fanatics had covered a troubling proportion of the planet. He could only imagine what it was like for those normal people left in ravaged countries like England, Spain and Russia. They would be living in fear most days, hoping that the wretches didn't find them.

He turned his attention on the reports that had been streaming in from his agents based in different corners of the galaxy. The Revenants were the least of the corporation's problems, it seemed.

Sapphire Nova were out of control, rampaging across numerous systems in some sort of bloodlust; revenge for the events that played out on Rikur during Kurcher's visit. Nova weren't just attacking Taurus ships though, they were taking on anyone who stood in their way. One intercepted Impramed report told of a number of deaths on Summit and blamed Nova. There had also been minor skirmishes with Sigma Royal.

The battle between Mitchell's fleet and a number of Nova vessels in the Kalbrec system still bothered him too. Nova were simply there to fight and the general had been forced to oblige. Two of the enemy ships were destroyed while the remaining pair fled the system. Mitchell wasn't really prepared for the ferocity of the battle and was lucky to survive.

There were many things that were playing on his mind. Cooke's betrayal and death still didn't sit right with him while Kurcher's current mission was unorthodox to say the least. He liked to know everything about his enlisters' movements and hated being kept in the dark. Santa Cruz was to blame for this, but Mitchell had sent the scheming bastard all the way out to Berg.

The rest of his enlisters were all busy on missions he had given them. Just that morning, he had received an update from three of them. One had just captured a talented hacker on Carson Freight Station and was working to enlist him. Another had caught up with a pair of escaped military prisoners on Galt and had to execute both. The third was after a Knights Templar messenger who killed a Taurus officer during a drunken bar fight.

Davian Kurcher was very different to any other enlister. He was more of an executioner really, but Rees had always given him the tough assignments; those he knew required the heavy touch. He had also sent Kurcher after Edlan Rane and, much to his chagrin, Santa Cruz had reassigned the enlister, meaning Rees had to send someone else to track down the killer. That assignment had gone cold now. Rane was probably hiding on some unoccupied world in a backwater system.

Just to add to their concerns, Libra Centauri were still being very secretive. They crept around the outer systems; nobody really knew what they were up to. There had been no reaction to their ship being destroyed in Tacit, which worried Rees even more. What exactly were they planning, if anything? Then again, Sigma hadn't retaliated either so perhaps they were just biding their time, hoping to find a weakness in the Taurus armour.

He tried shaking the negative thoughts from his mind and took a seat behind his desk. It was time to focus on how best to secure the corporation's future.

He had read through the proposal from Lenaghan several times before, but was always pulled away on something urgent before he could reply. Reading it again, Rees absorbed all of the facts and figures before patching his personal comms though to his plump associate. He chose audio only; no need to stare at that ugly face.

'Been waiting to hear from you, Solomon.' Lenaghan sounded flustered as always.

'Can you talk?' Rees asked him. 'I have some views on your proposal I'd like to discuss.'

Lenaghan sighed. 'As expected. Go on.'

'Is your reason behind wanting to move Taurus headquarters truly because of the Revenant threat?'

'Of course it is. Eventually those freaks are going to break through.'

'So why not propose we move to Mars? Surely we should stay in Sol.'

'Mars doesn't have the resources, Solomon, you know that. What other planet could we move to in Sol exactly?' Lenaghan snorted. 'No, we need to look at a system like Lincoln. Galt would be an excellent world to run Taurus from. Best protection in the galaxy and we would have Shard close by too.'

'So nothing to do with having the Knights Templar nearby?'

'Of course not.'

Rees knew that would put Lenaghan on the defensive. The judicial officer had known about his colleague's frequent trips to Temple for some time. Lenaghan was a gambler and enjoyed trips to the arena too. No doubt he also went there seeking female company, away from the ever-watchful eyes back on Earth.

'Don't you think we need to focus our attentions on pushing back the Revenant tide?'

'We can do that and still be sat safely on another world light years away,' replied Lenaghan. 'Unless you're planning on eradicating them yourself.'

'You're also thinking we need protection from Nova attacks,' Rees said. 'Why don't you go and establish a base on Galt with some of the other board members, leaving the rest of us here? That way, we have the opportunity to move between the headquarters at will. If Nova tried anything in Sol, we could simply leave Earth and head to join you on Galt.'

Lenaghan was silent for a moment before responding. 'Not a bad notion, but I can't help thinking you just want to get rid of me.'

Rees smiled. That was exactly what he wanted. 'Consider that my official feedback on your proposal, Fraser. If the rest of the board agree to creating a second headquarters on Galt, I am happy to proceed.'

'Let's all convene tomorrow morning then to put this to the vote.'

'As you wish.' Rees terminated the link.

Lenaghan's plan did have merits, though there were definitely selfish reasons for him moving to the Lincoln system. With threats seemingly appearing from all directions, Rees agreed that Taurus had to take some drastic measures to protect itself. These were uncertain times after all. The only certainty was that war was coming.

Enlister-class vessel Kaladine
Vega system

'Is he awake yet?'

D'Larro looked up as Kurcher entered the cell. 'No, and I doubt he will be any time soon. I'm surprised he's still alive after that beating.'

Kurcher shoved the medic aside so he could see Ercko's swollen face. 'Having seen what Angard did to Oakley's guards back on Cradle, I'm surprised he's even in one piece.'

'One broken piece,' added D'Larro. 'We need better medical equipment than what you have on board if he is going to survive. That punctured lung isn't going to get any better here, that's for sure.'

Kurcher leant down to get a better look at Ercko's wounds. They had laid the unconscious man on one of the cell beds and removed his blood-stained shirt so D'Larro could tend to as many of the injuries as possible. Ercko's skin was bruised and torn, making it look as though he had been in a fight with some wild beast. If he had been awake, Kurcher would have explained just how lucky he was to get away with a broken arm, shattered ankle, a couple of snapped ribs and a concussion. Angard had also knocked some teeth out. Ercko seemed to be used to losing those.

'We'll find what we need at Sullivan's Rest,' he told D'Larro. 'Probably for the best he's going to be out of it for some time. I still can't believe the idiot tried to rape Oakley.'

'What did you expect?' D'Larro asked. 'Unlike most of the rest of us, Ercko can't play nice. It's not in his nature.'

'What's the update on Oakley anyway?'

'He gave her a potentially lethal dose of Eidolon. We managed to get to her in time, thanks to Angard and Rane. Once she threw up, her life was no longer at risk. If we'd waited much longer, she could have died. It was a close one.'

'Fucking Eidolon.' Kurcher grimaced as he turned away from Ercko and headed for the door. 'I knew taking him down to Tempest was a bad idea. I blame Rane.'

'I wouldn't.' D'Larro shrugged when the enlister scowled at him. 'Rane woke Angard when he saw what was happening. He saved Oakley's life really.'

That didn't sit well with Kurcher at all. How many of them was Rane manipulating?

'Good job I don't take advice from murdering psychos like you then.' Kurcher nodded at Ercko. 'He stable?'

D'Larro looked positively pissed off. 'For now. You took advice from Rane, didn't you?'

That was too bold of the medic. Kurcher grabbed him and flung him from the cell before locking the door. He jabbed a finger at D'Larro.

'Next time, try thinking before you speak or I'll cut out your tongue. Now, keep an eye on Ercko and make sure Oakley is okay too. Can't have her suddenly dropping dead. If she does, you know exactly who'll get the blame and you've seen what Angard is capable of.'

When they entered the rec room, Oakley was still shuddering beneath a blanket. Angard's powerful arm had pulled her close. He was gently stroking her hair. It was clear to Kurcher that not only was she suffering the effects of the drug; the attack had also brought unwanted memories to the surface.

As D'Larro began persuading Angard to let him examine her again, Kurcher approached Rane, who was in conversation with Hewn.

'You didn't see Ercko taking the Eidolon?' he asked, butting straight in.

Rane still had a dark bruise of his own where Kurcher had hit him. 'Despite his foul mouth and general poor hygiene, the man is cunning. I was busy trying not to get shot.'

'She's lucky he hadn't got his filthy hands on a larger vial,' Hewn told them.

'The last man who tried that on with Tara ended up dead,' Rane remarked. 'And it wasn't Angard who killed him.'

'Ercko's locked up.' Kurcher saw Oakley's tearful eyes flick in his direction. 'And I doubt he could walk even if he was awake.'

'How long til we reach Sullivan's Rest?' Hewn asked him.

'Day or so.' Kurcher looked around at the crims and shook his head. 'Christ, I can't wait to be shot of you.'

With that, he left the rec room and went to find Frost. Maric was still reading in the cell that had become his own personal quarters and the preacher gave Kurcher a cursory nod as he passed.

When he entered the cockpit, Broekow was leant against the wall just inside. The enlister pushed past him and gave Frost a disapproving look.

'Go keep an eye on them,' he ordered the sniper. 'Things are tense back there.'

Broekow smirked. 'Now I know you really are just full of bullshit, I'm reluctant to jump to attention when you snap your fingers. I was never going to be a part of your team, so go watch them yourself.'

'Look, you're the only one I could rely on. Yeah, I lied to you, but I was also fucking glad you were there when we went after the others. I would have requested your transfer to the *Kaladine* once they had found the data.'

'How can I believe that?' laughed Broekow. 'Maybe it's the Parinax talking. You're a liar, just like the rest of Taurus Galahad. I actually thought I had found somewhere I fit in finally.'

Frost blew a cloud of smoke into the air. 'You do fit in. Davian will enlist you once this whole mess is sorted out, I swear. Now, if you two could stop whining and let me concentrate, that'd be great.'

When Broekow looked down at the pilot, Kurcher noticed how his eyes softened and a wry smile played across his lips.

'You're lucky to have her,' the sniper told him. 'She's the voice of reason on this ship and you'd be fucked without her.'

When Broekow stepped out, Kurcher ran two hands through his hair and let out an exasperated groan. 'This whole thing is driving me crazy. First Rane unravels everything we have been working towards, leading to all of them wanting to kill me, then Ercko tries raping Oakley. Why the fuck did I agree to this job?'

'Money. It was too much to pass up and you know that. Besides, I reckon they all wanted to kill you long before Rane blew our lies wide open.'

'Actually, you were the one who admitted everything,' he reminded her. 'Rane just manipulated us like he does everyone he comes into contact with.'

'I never did get any thanks for saving your skin.'

Kurcher shrugged. 'They may still decide to kill us yet and jettison our bodies. The *Kaladine* may become a ship run by a group of misfit crims.'

'I'd destroy her before I let that happen.'

Kurcher leant on the back of the seat. 'I can't help but wonder whether we're going down the same road as Cooke did.'

'Yeah, and look what happened to him.' Frost shrugged. 'We can't deviate now. If we opted to head for Berg, we'd be dead long before we got there. As much as I hate Sullivan's Rest, I reckon it may actually be our best option.'

'I can't shake the feeling that we may be signing our own death warrant. Taurus eliminated Cooke and his team because he went off-mission. I'm not interested in playing this data off against all of the corps like he supposedly did, but we are still defying a direct order.'

'Why not contact Santa Cruz then and tell him what the situation is?'

'Because I know what he will say.' Kurcher imagined the look on the commander's sour face. 'He wouldn't agree with the plan and it may just put a bounty on our heads. If we can get to the station and find the implant quick enough, we can still be on our way to Berg and deliver it as promised.'

'And the crims?'

'It'd be in our best interest if they never left Sullivan's Rest,' he said, wondering how best to make that happen. 'Rane is the only one who will remain with us. I have my own plans for him.'

Frost turned suddenly to face him, cigarette hanging from her lip. 'But you just told Broekow you'd vouch for him.'

Kurcher met her glare. 'No, you told him I'd enlist him. I said I *would* have. We need to tie up all loose ends, Justyne.'

'You're not killing him,' she told him defiantly. 'You said it yourself that he's been useful. I thought...'

'No debate,' he said, cutting her off. He had to start stamping his authority again. 'After we've found the data, you and I will go back to how we were before all this shit happened. If it makes you feel any better, I won't kill them. I'll arrange something with Fortitude so they can deal with it in their own way.'

Frost seemed at a loss for words and looked back at her console. As he decided to leave the suddenly-uncomfortable cockpit though, he heard her mutter.

'I'd almost forgotten how cold you were.'

Her words lingered in his head as he began a check of the ship, moving from room to room to ensure everything was working as it should. He had spent too long hiding away in his quarters lately, leaving the crims to wander freely. The old Kurcher wouldn't have put up with Broekow having access to the cockpit or letting someone like Rane loose on the *Kaladine* in any way.

Perhaps it was the Parinax boost he was riding on. He felt energised. The past few days had been trying to say the least, testing both his patience and his willpower. Now the end of the mission was in sight. Rane had simply caused a minor delay and diversion.

He had often thought about the disappearances Rane urged him to look into. To begin with, there were definite similarities with what the men and women who vanished were working on and that had fuelled his imagination. With Rane whispering conspiracy notions into his ear whenever he could, Kurcher had seen patterns where perhaps there were none. Once the serial killer divulged the truth of the mission to the others though, it was suddenly clear what had been happening. Rane's manipulation had nearly succeeded; instead it had opened Kurcher's eyes to the fact he couldn't trust a word any of the crims said. He was more pissed off now that he had allowed himself to be taken in by the bullshit.

He passed the cells and took a look at Ercko. Seeing the pulverised crim still lying unconscious, he carried on with his checks. The dour faces in the rec room did nothing to sap his renewed energy and he headed into the storage room to make sure everything was accounted for.

Items in storage reminded him of people they had crossed paths with during the mission to find the seven. The razepistol he had taken from Beck before killing him with it; the holster he had pulled from the Sigma Royal enlister's colleague; Rane's sword; the uniform he had used as a disguise to get into Oakley's estate. Even Ercko's severed fingers were there, reminding him of the gruesome discovery over on the transport.

After storage, Kurcher made his way down to the hold and was unimpressed by the smell that greeted him. He was pretty sure it was the combined odour of Angard and Ercko, who seemed to be the only two not bothered about personal hygiene. He had seen Oakley once dabbing at Angard's neck and shoulder with a wet cloth, but doubted anyone would want to get close enough to Ercko to do the same. He made a mental note to have the *Kaladine* fumigated once they had gone.

His final destination was the engine chambers. They sounded as though they could do with a tune-up. It was no wonder considering how strained they had been recently. Frequent system-hopping and fighting against varying degrees of gravity would take their toll eventually. He wasn't too concerned though as Frost would already be aware of how they were performing. Her pilot app warned her of maintenance requirements well in advance.

As he headed back up to the main corridor, Kurcher decided he would perform some diagnostic checks on the lifeboat systems. The small emergency vessel really had to battle the winds on Tempest before it landed so heavily. He hoped that hadn't caused any damage.

He descended to the lifeboat's airlock and keyed in the access code. For a moment, the door hesitated as the security panel made an odd bleeping noise. Then the airlock opened and he stepped inside. He would have to mention the issue to Frost so she could take a look at the back end of the security system.

The diagnostic procedure took just under an hour, coming back with no major problems. As he stood from the pilot seat, he noticed a leaf on the floor which must have blown in from Tempest. The green and red looked bizarre against the dark metal of the grating, the colours enhanced by the Parinax. It was a rare moment he appreciated something so mundane.

When he returned to the *Kaladine*, a quiet had settled over the ship and he knew the crims would be contemplating what would happen when they reached Sullivan's Rest. That reminded him he had to contact Coyle and try to reason with the bastard well before they got anywhere near the station.

He walked past the cells and came to a sudden halt. He wasn't going to look in on Ercko, but something told him to keep an eye on the killer as often as possible. He stepped back and looked through the glass.

'Fuck.'

He slammed his palm against the door lock and slipped inside. He knew there was nothing he could do as soon as he saw Ercko up close.

Fresh wounds glistened in the cell's dim light. There were deep cuts to his wrists, his face and one fatal slice across the throat. Blood had seeped into the bed and had formed a pool on the floor. A splash of red had sprayed onto the pale wall too, released as the throat was cut. One eye had been gouged out, leaving only a raw void, but the other was still closed as though Ercko was sleeping.

Kurcher was at a loss for words. He had checked on Ercko barely a couple of hours before and the man was alive then. His shock turned to anger. Which one of the crims would dare to murder Ercko, knowing there was no way to escape? Who had the motive to do such a thing?

He leant down to examine the wounds more closely. It was similar to Rane's handiwork, that was for sure. Clean cuts designed to make the victim suffer and one final stroke to end their life. If Ercko had still been unconscious though, what was the point of delivering pain before death? Plus, the eye injury was not as surgical as Rane's previous work.

As he studied the dead killer's bloodied face and then the open wound across the throat, Kurcher noticed something out of the corner of his eye. Ercko's trousers were soaked in blood. The belt and fasteners had all been cut. Not many things made him nauseous; finding the killer's penis had been severed made bile rise in his throat. Perhaps this was a certain blonde taking revenge. Perhaps she worked with Rane and some of the others to get rid of Ercko once and for all.

Kurcher recoiled from the corpse and opened his comms link. 'Justyne, I need you in Ercko's cell now.'

Frost's reply didn't come back as quickly as usual. 'Problem?'

'Could say that. Someone iced him.'

'Are you fucking kidding me?'

Kurcher's temper was threatening to boil over. The Parinax kept it simmering. 'You didn't get any alerts?'

'I... uh...' Frost was clearly rattled. 'I was busy. Didn't think I needed to

236

keep a vigil.'

Kurcher knew exactly what *busy* meant. 'Just get your ass here. Alone.'

He needed to locate whatever weapon was used to end Ercko's pitiful existence. None of the crims apart from Broekow was allowed to carry weapons on board. How one of them got their hands on a blade perplexed him. He checked the soiled bed clothes and turned up nothing. He didn't really expect to find anything as the killer probably took it for protection or to try hiding elsewhere. He was quite surprised then when he found the murder weapon lying under the bed. Confusion intensified when he saw it was his own knife.

'This is fucking insane,' he told himself as he reached down and found only an empty sheath at his hip.

'That what I think it is?' asked Frost, stepping into the cell.

'One of them lifted it from me.' Kurcher thought back to who he had come into contact with. He had been near to all of them at one time or another and hadn't thought to check the knife was where it usually was. In fact, he hadn't checked since his recent tussle with Rane.

Frost cast an eye over Ercko and wrinkled her nose in disgust. 'I can't say I'll mourn this bastard, but it's another spanner in the works.'

Kurcher tightened his grip on the knife. 'Cut the engines and hold position. We're going to find who did this.' He turned to face her. 'Where were you?'

'Like I said, I was busy. You think I'd do this?'

'Of course not, but you need to stay sharp.'

She bit back her instinctive reaction. 'We can find out who did this easily enough.'

'This is fucking insane,' he repeated. 'It could've been any of them or *all* of them.'

Frost's eyes moved quickly as she accessed the systems through her app. She cursed before focusing back on Kurcher. 'The *Kaladine* isn't showing any alerts on this cell door at all, not even when you've gone in and out. Must be a glitch.'

'Can you sort it?'

'I need the cockpit console.'

'Meet me in the rec room when you're done.'

Once Frost had gone, Kurcher examined Ercko one more time in an attempt to gauge who had killed the crim. At first glance, the wounds matched those inflicted by Rane on his victims. Something was amiss about the savage way the eye had been gouged. Ercko's manhood being severed pointed at Oakley. She had threatened to do so on several occasions and the

237

attempted rape may have pushed her over the edge. Then again, D'Larro had form for killing patients. Perhaps he had killed Ercko and tried to frame someone else.

Kurcher sighed as he looked at the dead man's face. Had Ercko woken up and been silenced quickly or had he been sliced up while still unconscious? Someone would pay for adding yet another obstacle to the fucked-up mission.

When he entered the rec room to confront the crims, Kurcher had the bloody knife in one hand and his revolver in the other.

~

'What're you up to?'

Winter had realised some time ago that the *Kaladine* was heading for Sullivan's Rest and déjà vu had kicked in, reminding him of his pursuit of Cooke. He sincerely hoped history wasn't about to repeat itself. Now that the enlister's ship had come to an abrupt halt, Winter knew something was wrong.

He had been monitoring from a fair distance behind them, shrouded by the unique conflector fitted onto his stalker. They hadn't encountered another ship and he didn't detect any comms signal from the *Kaladine*. They had clearly stopped due to something happening internally and that concerned him.

There was a part of him that wanted to simply disable the ship and take control of the situation himself, but that would be overstepping the mark. Until Santa Cruz gave him the nod, he had to skulk in the shadows. If the commander had sent him instead of Kurcher, the mission would have been finished by now. The enlister was proving to be as unpredictable as Cooke was, if not more.

Having read up on Davian Kurcher, Winter found few similarities between the two enlisters apart from their profession. Jed Cooke was a family man who made sure his wages went straight to his wife and daughter. He had a team who did most of the dirty work. Even so, they respected him. Cooke was intelligent, confident and cunning, devising impressive strategies for capturing their targets.

Kurcher on the other hand was a ruthless individual who seemed to only look after number one. His methods were direct, risky and violent. His military background was not to be scoffed at and his time on Cobb particularly couldn't be ignored. He was a dangerous man who liked killing. In fact, Kurcher had more in common with the crims he hunted down than

238

with the other enlisters.

He needed to speak directly with Santa Cruz this time. The link to the *Requiem* took longer than he would have liked. Comms to the outer systems sometimes faltered, so he patiently waited until the commander's visage appeared on the screen.

'I'm guessing I won't like what you have to tell me.' Santa Cruz's lips froze for a second as he spoke, showing Winter just how unstable the link was.

'Kurcher has come to a halt just a couple of hours out from Sullivan's Rest. No comms being emitted and I haven't found any other ships approaching, so he isn't meeting someone.'

Santa Cruz thought for a moment. 'Just keep an eye on them for now. Be ready. Your talents may be required.'

'Sure you don't want me to give Kurcher a nudge?'

'Not yet. I may contact him shortly to check on their status. If I find anything amiss, I'll let you know.'

Winter nodded. 'And if you need me to get onto the *Kaladine*, what are my orders?'

'Kurcher and his pilot would be your primary targets. The crims I would need alive.'

'Understood.'

Santa Cruz closed the link. Winter opened his confidential data files. After finding schematics for the *Kaladine*, he began looking for the best place to infiltrate the vessel.

~

Kurcher studied the seven bewildered faces again, looking for any telltale sign one of them was lying. All had denied killing Ercko. He hadn't expected a confession. Still, he couldn't hide his frustration.

'I wish I could've executed every last one of you,' he growled, waving his revolver at them. 'Then I could've avoided this shit.'

'I didn't kill him,' stated Hewn for the third time. 'But you can't seriously tell me you're surprised this happened. Ercko was a sick bastard who liked making enemies and everyone here is a killer.'

'I'm not,' snapped Frost from the doorway.

Hewn snorted at her. 'I'm sure even you have killed people when protecting Kurcher or your ship.'

'Can't you just check the *Kaladine* systems to find out more?' Rane asked.

'Not right now,' Kurcher replied. 'There's a coincidental glitch.'

239

Rane frowned and placed a finger to his lips as he pondered this. Beside him, D'Larro held out his hands towards Kurcher.

'Surely if someone had cut Ercko up like you say, they would have his blood on them. Let me see the body and perform an autopsy. We might find some clues.'

'You patched him up after Angard beat seven shades of shit out of him,' Kurcher told the medic. 'There was plenty of blood then and you managed to wash your hands clean. It might be worth checking clothing though. As for clues, I've already told you how he was killed. I'm not ruling any of you out.'

Angard rose from his seat. 'If I'd killed that rapist, there wouldn't be much left of him. I'm not really into poking someone with a knife or making delicate little cuts. Given the chance, I would've ripped his head off.'

Kurcher regarded him coldly. 'True, but Oakley is into that sort of thing and you go wherever she goes.'

Angard clenched his teeth. 'Tara is in no fit state to even attempt it.'

Oakley grasped his arm and her expression made him sit back down. 'I can talk for myself, Horsten.' Her troubled blue eyes turned to Kurcher. 'I admit that I wanted Ercko dead, long before he tried to rape me, but I'm not stupid enough to murder him while we're all stuck on this ship. If I had killed him, I certainly wouldn't have tried to frame someone else.'

'You threatened to cut his dick off,' Frost reminded her.

'So did you as I recall,' noted Oakley, shooting the pilot a venomous look. 'You're not all sweetness and light.'

Kurcher lifted his knife so they could all see it. 'What about this then? Someone stole my knife right from my belt and that needed a light touch. Unfortunately, I've gotten too close to all of you at one time or another. I'm starting to see a joint effort here. Maybe you all worked together to get rid of him.'

'Bennet Ercko was an evil man.' Maric stepped forward. 'Despite his inability to redeem himself in God's eyes, it was still a despicable act to murder him. We are all sinners – one of you is now tainted by this act. Confess and the Lord will listen.'

'Whatever.' Broekow caught Frost's eye. 'So what happens next?'

'All of you down into the hold,' Kurcher ordered, waving the revolver again. 'Except D'Larro.'

The medic looked ashen. 'Why me?'

Kurcher ignored his question. As the others began filing out, he grabbed Broekow by the arm. 'Watch them closely,' he whispered. 'They don't leave the hold.'

240

'I get to keep my pistol then?'

Kurcher nodded. 'I know where you were when Ercko was murdered.'

Broekow looked into the enlister's eyes for a moment then left the rec room.

'I would like to request I go back in the cell.' Maric was standing in the corridor, holding his bizarre book. 'By all means, lock me in. I would just prefer to be alone so I can pray.'

Kurcher looked the preacher up and down. 'Looks like you could do with getting some sleep.'

Maric gave a rare smile that brightened his face somewhat. 'I would sleep better in the cell too. Lying alongside the others doesn't make for a comfortable rest.'

'Fine.' Kurcher saw Frost lurking nearby. 'Justyne, lock him up then go see whether you can get to the bottom of that system glitch.'

She beckoned to Maric, who shuffled his way along the corridor. 'What're you going to do?'

Kurcher looked back at D'Larro, who was wringing his hands nervously. 'We'll be in Ercko's cell.'

When the two were standing over the dead man with the cell door closed, Kurcher handed the medic his scalpel and several bandages.

'We'll need him on the floor,' D'Larro stated.

'Blood's already soaked through the bed.'

'I need him on a harder surface. Also, have you got sutures so I can stitch the wounds together once we've finished?'

Kurcher kept an eye on the scalpel. 'Don't worry about that. The drainage system in here will take care of the blood. There's no need to sew him up again.'

D'Larro shrugged. 'Okay. So what are we looking for?'

'Clues. Check all of his wounds and tell me what you make of them.'

'You trust me enough to do an autopsy then,' said the medic as he cast his eyes over Ercko's body.

'Can't really call this an autopsy. I know you always carried out your *work* when the chances of being caught were minimal and I know you're clever. I doubt you'd risk killing Ercko.'

As the two lifted the heavy corpse from the bed onto the floor, D'Larro shook his head. 'It was never a bloodlust like some of the others on this ship. I killed terminal patients who were never going to survive and the information gleaned from them was vital in my understanding of the human body. Pain, suffering, death. There are ways to control them all.'

241

'I don't give a shit.' Kurcher stepped back from the body, pulling his revolver once more for effect. 'Get on with it.'

He stood watching as D'Larro opened Ercko's shirt and removed the soiled trousers, exposing the butchered member.

'Not a particularly clean cut,' the medic remarked. 'It was hacked at, basically. My guess is this wouldn't have been Oakley. She would have taken her time and enjoyed it. This looks rushed.'

'What about the other wounds?'

D'Larro moved up Ercko's body slowly. 'Series of old scars on his stomach and chest. I'd say he had been stabbed several times before years back, but no fresh wounds. The wrists are interesting though. Purposeful cuts to sever the artery but not done in the most effective way. The blade cut across rather than along the wrists. I'm not sure why they would cut his wrists *and* his throat.'

'Even I can tell the throat wound wasn't designed to just bleed him out. It's vicious.'

D'Larro nodded as he prodded the sliced skin with his scalpel. 'The blade was pushed deep into his neck then pulled across swiftly. It was torn open rather than sliced.' The medic glanced back at the wrists. 'In my opinion, he was still unconscious when this was all done.'

'Why do you say that?'

'Cutting the wrists of someone like Ercko would have been difficult if he were awake. Plus, look at the blood spatter on the wall. It shows that he was still lying down when they tore his throat open. I reckon the penis was removed once he was dead.'

Kurcher knew the crims were cold; to murder the man while he was out for the count was downright sadistic. 'What about the eye?'

'Again, it wasn't done cleanly. Look.' D'Larro used the tip of the scalpel as a pointer. 'The eyeball is lacerated and punctured, but the optic nerve has been shredded where it was cut. It was done by someone clearly in a hurry. If I had to guess, I would say this was also done after he had died.'

'So whoever did this cut Ercko's throat first then set to work gouging his eye out, slitting his wrists and cutting off his dick?'

'I reckon so. It was someone who felt they had very little time to do all this, but still made sure that others would be suspected.' D'Larro's brow furrowed. 'Why do that though when surely they knew you would investigate before we got to Sullivan's Rest?'

Kurcher was wondering the same thing. 'Is there anything else you can tell me?'

242

'Help me roll him over.'

The body seemed heavier than before and Ercko's face hit the floor with a fleshy slap. Another wound was revealed and D'Larro set to work examining it.

Kurcher felt an anxious twist in his stomach. 'Thoughts?'

The medic used his scalpel to pull the wound open. 'The cut was made just below his right scapula. There was an initial incision, then it looks like a second was made to go deeper. There's a tiny hole here too about an inch and a half down. Looks like he was pricked with a needle. I can only think of one reason that's there.'

Kurcher cursed. 'The data implant.'

~

Frost's eyes were starting to hurt. Unlike Kurcher, she couldn't just give her body a boost on command. Both fatigue and eye strain were making her task difficult, so she reached for the only thing that could help. After lighting the cigarette, she downed the last dregs of coffee and waited for a few seconds before returning to the scrolling system files.

The so-called glitch in the system was getting on her nerves and those were already shredded to hell thanks to Ercko's murder. Her first thought was that there was a malfunction with the wiring around the cell door. There were no error codes logged. According to the *Kaladine*, nobody had been in or out of Ercko's cell. She had then checked the other cells and those were also showing the same problem.

Her next thought was that somehow a virus had been downloaded to them, perhaps by one of the ships that had pursued them to begin with on Tempest. It wouldn't be the first time someone had used viral means to gain access to an enemy ship. Some pirates were very fond of crashing entire systems just to board a target vessel. Maybe Hewn and his organisation had opted to try those methods.

She wondered how far the false reading glitch had spread and checked other doors around the ship. Logs were in place for the rec room, storage, their quarters and the cockpit. The airlock logs were also in place. When she opened the files for the lifeboat systems though, she found no trace of the airlock logs from when Kurcher had taken it down to Tempest.

Leaning forward with the cigarette hanging from her lips, she tapped in a request for a diagnostic report from the lifeboat and waited. Most of the systems in the smaller emergency vessel had their own server and could link easily enough with the *Kaladine*.

A message flashed in her vision, highlighted red with urgency. When she read it, her eyes widened and the cigarette slipped from her mouth, bouncing off her leg onto the floor. Someone was downloading jump point data that was usually locked up safely in the *Kaladine*'s protected navigation systems. Codes to activate jumps to Almaz, Callyn, Genesys and Oralia all flashed past.

She accessed her app commands and put a trace on where the download was originating. A moment later, a burst of static exploded across her vision and she cried out as pain rifled through her skull; a shock direct from her app implant. When she opened her eyes, everything except her app message was blurred and that only showed an error code. She had heard of firewall tech being sold on the black market that was designed to create a block and hit anyone trying to access the respective system with a surge of electricity. How did such a thing get into the *Kaladine*?

As her vision cleared and she rebooted the app, she used the cockpit monitor to try pinpointing the download source. It returned an error message. At the same time, the diagnostic report from the lifeboat also failed.

Frost scooped her cigarette off the floor and put it back in her mouth. 'Someone thinks they're clever.'

Then it all made sense. She quickly accessed the back-up server on the lifeboat, linked to the primary systems and checked the status files. The jump point codes were being downloaded directly to the emergency vessel's navigation files.

'Davian, need you to meet me in the lifeboat right now,' she said, leaping out of her seat and grabbing her pistol.

By the time she descended to the airlock, Kurcher was already following her down. When she typed in the access code, the system refused to open the door.

'I can get it open.' Thankful her app was working again, she accessed the *Kaladine* and went through to the lifeboat's back-up server once more. 'I figured out who did it, by the way.'

'So did I,' growled Kurcher, gripping his revolver with both hands.

Via the back-up, Frost managed to gain control of the airlock and it slid open. Kurcher leapt into the lifeboat before she could move and took aim at the lone figure standing at the controls.

Choice turned to face them. 'Stay back, both of you.' He grinned at Frost. 'You're smarter than I thought. Fucking back-ups are a thorn in my side, just like you. Didn't think you'd have one in here.'

'Maybe you should've checked,' Frost told him, raising her pistol. 'This is

244

my ship and I made sure nobody could ever take her from me.'

'Give me the data implant,' Kurcher ordered, edging closer. 'I don't know how you worked out Ercko had it, but you'll hand it over right now.'

Choice was genuinely amused. 'All I want is to take this lifeboat and disappear. If you try to stop me, I'll send the engines into overload and blow the *Kaladine* apart.'

Frost shook her head. 'A bluff.'

'Try me and find out. I managed to open the cell and the airlock, wipe your door logs plus I placed that nice little blocker in the system just in case you tried to snoop. How's your head? Still hurting?'

'Fuck you.'

Choice laughed. 'I even managed to design a way to locate that data implant you're so keen to get hold of. Took me a while to tune the tech to the right frequency to bypass the firewall, but the time you gave me on my own in the cell to work on it was appreciated. Couldn't believe my luck when it was in that piece of shit, especially when you'd just locked him up. Just a pity he didn't suffer as I cut the prick up, which I suppose has two meanings in this case.'

Kurcher took another step. 'Enough. Hand it over or I'll just take it from your corpse.'

'Are you annoyed?' Choice asked him, ignoring the demand. 'Angry that you didn't realise I had been impersonating that feeble-minded preacher? Or is it more the fact that I made you think one of the others killed Ercko? Either way, I made you look pretty stupid.'

'Actually, if you think about it, you did me a favour.' Kurcher smiled when he saw a flash of confusion on Choice's face. 'By extracting the data implant and getting yourself caught before you could flee like the coward you are, you've made my job much easier. Now I don't need to take all of you to Taurus. I can dispose of you like I always wanted to. Besides, you saved me having to waste a bullet executing Ercko.'

Choice twitched. 'I know you, Kurcher. You're seething inside, I can see it. I also know you're just trying to provoke me. Rane helped Maric back to the surface for a time but you can't. Both the preacher and I hate you for what you've put us through since Rikur.'

'I'd be willing to bet you hate Rane more,' Kurcher said, shrugging. 'It was he who helped us catch you and it was he who subdued you by appealing to Maric.'

'I've had enough of this shit.' Spittle flew from Choice's lips as it so often did when his temper erupted. 'You let me leave right now in this lifeboat and

245

I won't blow the engines.'

Kurcher glanced at Frost before answering. 'No deal. My counter offer is hand over the data implant and I won't kill you.'

Choice twitched again. 'I accessed the data. Got to see what's so fucking important. If I destroy the implant, you'll have to keep me alive.'

'How did you access the data?' Frost asked. 'With the lifeboat systems?'

'It's a basic implant,' Choice said with contempt. 'I could use any system to see what's on it.'

Kurcher and Frost exchanged another knowing look before the pilot continued. 'No, you couldn't use the lifeboat to access it. Something unusual like that would need specialist tech to open it up. You're lying again.'

Choice clenched his fists. 'You stupid bitch. The tech around the data was built by Taurus, but the firewall filter was probably bought from mercs by Cooke. Once I got around the latter, it was simple.'

'I saw where you cut the implant out of Ercko,' Kurcher told him. 'It was too small to be able to insert into a port. Frost's right, you're talking shit again.'

'I'm the fucking genius here,' yelled Choice. 'You're the one who gave me what I needed to build the app to subdue Angard. All I had to do was use the parts left over to create a crude adapter for the implant.'

The conversation had been going on too long for Kurcher's liking. 'I don't believe it. There's no way you could've built something like that with the components we gave you.'

'Open your fucking eyes, you dumb shit. It's connected right now.'

'That'll do,' grinned Kurcher, pulling the trigger.

His bullet shattered Choice's kneecap and the crim let out a wail as he crumpled to the floor. Kurcher stepped over him and peered down at the control console, relieved to see the crim's adapter lodged into one of the data ports. He was glad Choice never lied when pushed that far.

'You motherfucker,' screamed Choice. 'I want my life back.'

'It was never yours in the first place.' Kurcher swung his revolver down, catching the wounded man on the side of the head and knocking him out cold.

'You're not going to kill him?' Frost holstered her weapon.

'Not yet. We have some pressing matters to attend to. While I throw him in a cell and make sure he won't escape again, I want you to take the implant to the cockpit and access the data.'

Frost hesitated. 'Is that wise? Santa Cruz won't like us seeing what's on it.'

'I don't give a shit. I want to know what we've risked our lives for. It may help me understand why it got Cooke killed too.' He saw the look on the pilot's face. 'It's time we took control of this situation.'

When Frost was alone in the lifeboat, she quickly checked the controls and wiring surrounding the data port, hoping that Choice hadn't put some booby trap in the system. When it came back clear, she gently pulled the adapter out. A tiny blue dot highlighted where the miniscule implant had been inserted.

As she headed back into the cockpit, Kurcher's voice echoed along the corridor from the cells.

'Get Angard to put Ercko's body in the airlock so we can jettison it.'

She heard D'Larro reply. 'What happens then?'

'Just get it done.'

As Frost settled back into her seat, she wondered what Kurcher was planning to do with the other crims. The old Kurcher would have likely blown them all out of the airlock. She got the impression he wasn't about to perform a mass execution. She found it hard to know just what he was thinking. Perhaps the Parinax had addled his brain or perhaps he was actually concerned as to what Santa Cruz would do once they delivered the data.

She pushed the adapter into one of the ports on her console. A request appeared on the screen, asking whether she wanted to upload the data to a secure file in the *Kaladine*'s logs. She pondered this for a moment, then declined and was instead asked whether she wanted to access the data direct from the implant. Before she gave the command, Frost lit another cigarette for courage.

When Kurcher entered the cockpit, he found her leaning close to the screen and frowning in confusion.

'So what're we looking at?' he asked, trying to make out the data.

'I have no clue,' she admitted. 'Do these make any sense to you?'

Kurcher watched for a moment as lines of unusual symbols scrolled past. 'I can't make out anything familiar. It must be some new code.'

'Or some old code.' Frost tapped the screen. 'I don't know what Cooke originally downloaded this from and there's no date anywhere. Data files tend to have origin dates in them. This doesn't.'

'No way of finding out what it is?'

'I wouldn't know where to start.'

Kurcher was just as confused as she was. 'Is this it then? Nothing else?'

'Keep watching.'

The symbols continued scrolling for another minute before they were

247

suddenly replaced by a diagram. Numerous points appeared on the screen, each displaying four tiny symbols alongside. As more of the diagram appeared, Kurcher realised what they were looking at.

'That section looks like part of the Orion Spur.'

Frost nodded. 'I've never seen a map of the galaxy like this, but I'm pretty sure those symbols alongside the systems are co-ordinates. Or code for the co-ordinates maybe. There is more though.'

As they watched, unknown points began appearing throughout the outer sectors of the map; systems yet to be discovered in the vast wilderness that was Coldrig, Krondahar and Farrin.

'What the fuck is this?' Kurcher asked, his eyes glued to the screen. 'No corp has been out that far yet.'

'Maybe they have,' shrugged Frost. 'Maybe that's the big secret and the reason this is so important. Still, it's this last part that stumps me.'

One final point appeared and Kurcher leant closer to make sure he wasn't seeing things. 'That's outside the galaxy. Any theories what it could be?'

'Could be a rogue star. If it is, maybe Taurus have found a way to jump to systems outside of the Milky Way. They could have found new wormholes somewhere.'

Kurcher stared at the point in question, noting the symbols next to it. 'That's the only thing it could be, right?'

'I'd say so. It could be the start of a series of jumps which lead to the next galaxy, like stepping stones. That would be quite the find.'

'It's out beyond Krondahar so the nearest occupied system would be Valen. With Nova sniffing around that sector, it's no wonder Taurus want the data so bad.'

Frost rubbed at her tired eyes. 'So what's the plan?'

'I think it's time I spoke with Santa Cruz.'

~

A painful spasm rippled through Angard's left shoulder as he lifted Ercko's body and he glanced at D'Larro, who hadn't seen him flinch. Oakley was stood just outside the cell door looking the other way too, which he was thankful for. The last thing he needed was for her to worry.

As he carried the sheet-wrapped corpse to the airlock, he heard Oakley's dainty footfalls following.

'Why don't you stay with the others?' he asked, a sharpness in his voice.

'I'd rather make sure that bastard gets jettisoned,' she replied coldly.

Angard tried to ignore the pounding headache threatening to split his skull apart. 'He can't exactly hurt anyone now.'

'Good. I'm actually pissed off Choice got to him before I could. He would have been awake when I started on him.'

Angard stepped into the airlock and unceremoniously dumped Ercko onto the floor. As Oakley moved alongside him and gazed down at the bloodied sheet, he flexed the fingers of both hands. The numbness was setting in already, adding to the other early signs his drug supply was running low. The difference this time was that he didn't care.

Her small hand suddenly gripped his and he felt a pang of guilt. It was selfish leaving her to fend for herself, but he had made the decision back on Cradle that he couldn't carry on living a nightmare. Had it not been for Kurcher's bad timing, he would have most likely already been dead. Stuck on the *Kaladine* though and being shipped back to the corp had made him realise enough was enough. That's why he had approached the only other person on the ship he held slight respect for to help him end it when the time came and his supply ran out. Broekow had taken some persuading but reluctantly agreed eventually. The sniper would make it quick.

As they left the airlock, she gave his hand a squeeze. 'I know you're not usually the most talkative person, but you're being very quiet. Everything okay?'

Oakley had come to see him as a protector more than anything and he knew that their friendship was based around that key fact. Still, he enjoyed her company and liked to think that she might be saddened when he died, and not just because she would suddenly become vulnerable.

'Yeah. Just trying to get my head around everything that has happened. Feeling like a caged animal though. You know I don't like being cooped up like this.'

'Would you rather be living on your very own quaran again?'

She quite often asked him that. If he answered honestly, he would have loved to have gone back to Kalvion. His time spent there alone had been bliss. The only other lifeforms on the storm-wracked world were the indigenous species that consisted mainly of insects, the larger of which eventually became his food. He had become quite fond of the oversized grubs that were in abundance around the forested region he lived in.

He had, however, planned to die on Kalvion originally. The drugs he took from the Knights Templar after rampaging across their station had kept him going until they ran out. He still recalled getting the same headache, spasms and numbness as he sat in the cave he had made home. They were always the first symptoms; the painful stage. It was not long before the second stage set

249

in and his panicking brain fought to survive in any way possible. The following two stages he knew would be a violent rage fuelled by the dregs of the drug and then full shutdown.

It was crazy timing that the Taurus survey ship landed as the second stage began. Instinct drove him into forcing the terrified crew to take him back to Shard. Once back at the research facility, he was just about to enter the third stage and that led to the slaughter of a number of scientists before he was given a new drug supply. He hadn't cared whether the scientists were those who had performed the tests and the operations on him. They were all to blame for turning an innocent orphan into such a monster.

He realised he hadn't replied to Oakley and shrugged. 'Give me daily storms and bugs for dinner over dealing with corporations any time.'

When they entered the rec room, a conversation between Hewn, Rane and Broekow ended abruptly.

'Did you throw the preacher in the airlock too?' asked the pirate. 'I reckon the galaxy would be better off without him as well.'

'It'd be better off without all of us,' Angard said, sitting down with his back to the wall.

Oakley poured coffee for herself and her protector. 'We can't exactly blame Choice for doing what he did. He had an opportunity and he took the chance. That's more than we've done.'

'So why don't we take advantage of this situation ourselves?' Hewn slammed his metal hand down onto the table. 'With that implant found, we're surplus to requirements. We need to take the ship *now*.'

'We need to trust in Davian,' Rane stated. 'I know you think he'll just execute you, but you're wrong. He knows there is something amiss within Taurus and he's seen the files on those who have disappeared. Keeping us alive gives him an advantage at the moment. Even Choice has a part to play.'

'Yeah, he's being kept alive to overload my biomechs again if need be.' Angard really hated being switched off like some machine. 'A schizophrenic preacher doesn't have many other uses.'

'You've helped Kurcher realise how dangerous Taurus are,' Broekow said to Rane, one hand noticably near his pistol. 'It feels more like you've manipulated this situation.'

Rane scowled. 'Davian has his own stubborn mind. I merely shared my findings with him.'

'So you're just taking time away from your murder spree to help us.' Broekow laughed and shook his head. 'Now I've heard everything.'

As the debate continued, Angard placed the back of his head against the wall and enjoyed the coolness of it. The sensation made him feel slightly better. He didn't really care to listen to the arguing anymore. Most of the crims were all talk anyway.

As Oakley settled down alongside him yet again and sipped at her coffee, he could feel the guilt returning. It was something he would need to shake off before the end.

~

Kurcher felt nervous. It wasn't the thought of speaking directly with Santa Cruz that made him so, more the fact that his Parinax supply had dwindled so much that he could only afford a handful of short, sharp doses. He allowed himself one such shot before requesting the link with the commander.

As he waited, he began wondering whether he was doing the right thing yet again. Now that he and Frost had viewed the coded data on the implant, perhaps that would put their lives at risk. Then again, maybe the reason Cooke had been killed was down to the late enlister trying to blackmail Taurus Galahad. That was something Kurcher had no interest in doing, but he needed to know what was going on. Although the Parinax had dulled his anger for the moment, it was still there festering beneath. He had risked his and Frost's life many times before, but he always had control of their previous assignments. Santa Cruz had sent them on a mad dash from system to system just to find some map and that didn't add up. There must have been something else to it.

Just as he thought the comms link was about to fail, Santa Cruz appeared on his screen. Despite some minor distortion, the commander's face was as stern and emotionless as usual, although there was something unnerving in those dark eyes.

'Is there a problem, enlister?'

'You could say that.' Kurcher tried his best to hide his contempt. 'There's been an incident which led to an unforeseen development.'

The commander raised an eyebrow. 'Go on.'

'Bennet Ercko is dead.' Kurcher let that sink in before continuing. 'To cut a long story short, he was murdered by Choice... Maric's alter ego.'

'I know who he is,' snapped Santa Cruz. 'How could this happen?'

'Ercko tried to rape Oakley and was beaten unconscious by Angard. We put him in a cell but Choice hacked into the ship systems and got to him.' Kurcher leant closer to the screen. 'Ercko was carrying Cooke's data implant.'

There was a flash of concern across the commander's face. 'And?'

251

'The data is safe. Choice had created an adapter he could use to access the data. We stopped him before he could escape the *Kaladine*.'

'I'm assuming then that Choice is dead and you are due to take care of the other crims, unless you already have done.'

'Choice is alive and restrained. The others are still alive too.'

Santa Cruz glared at him, clearly trying to weigh the enlister up. 'Then your next orders are clear. Execute the rest of them and deliver the implant to me in Berg.'

'I have questions first,' Kurcher said boldly. 'Call it curiosity. I accessed the data myself to see what exactly I had risked my life for. The code I couldn't read, but the galaxy map was interesting.'

As Santa Cruz fell silent and leaned back from the screen, Kurcher wondered whether this was Cooke's mistake. Was the commander signing their death warrant as he coldly regarded the problematic enlister?

'That data was not for your eyes,' Santa Cruz told him. 'Your mission was simple. Find and retrieve.'

'Simple?' Kurcher's anger threatened to push through the Parinax. 'I was nearly killed on Rikur and Summit. I have Nova goons on my tail most likely, not to mention Echo, who are probably searching for Hewn. This mission has placed quite the bounty on my head and I want to know what's so fucking important about this data before I get a bullet through the brain.'

'Bring it to me and I will explain.'

Kurcher didn't like the calmness in Santa Cruz's voice. 'No offense, commander. I would rather you told me now. It's very easy for someone to disappear in an outer system like Berg.'

Santa Cruz leaned forward again. 'You think you'd end up like Cooke? I doubt you're stupid enough to try blackmailing the corporation who pay you so well.'

'I never said I would blackmail you. I'm asking for an explanation and also a guarantee that we won't be disposed of once you have your precious data.'

'I'm not sure why you think we're in the business of getting rid of our own people, especially talented ones like you. I need that data, enlister, and assure you that no harm will befall you or your pilot when you reach Berg. If you think me such a monster then send the data to us on your lifeboat once you reach the system. I'll pay you and you can get back to work.'

Kurcher was starting to feel uneasy. How many times had Santa Cruz promised this in the past to others? Rane's intel had unearthed the disappearances and it was something Kurcher couldn't just ignore. Still, he had to be rid of the data somehow.

'Will you tell me what the data is or not?' he asked. 'I'm closer to Sol so could always drop it at Taurus headquarters.'

That induced a slight twitch at the side of the commander's mouth. 'The data needs to be delivered directly to me. I will explain why and hopefully then you will understand how important this is.'

'I'm all ears.' Kurcher shrugged off the feeling of dread eating away at him and focused on what he was about to hear.

'When the five corps were formed following the downfall of Sapien, there was no truly bad blood between them. There were differences of opinion but nothing violent. Over the sixty years that followed, it was more about space exploration than anything else. Even Impramed realised the benefits of jumping to new systems and searching for resources, although their official mission statement was to further medical science for the entire human race.'

'This is a history lesson I've already had,' muttered Kurcher as Santa Cruz paused for breath.

'Doubtful. Hostilities between corps began in 2595, just as you turned fourteen and were taken in by Taurus Galahad following the death of your mother. It's what happened the year before that caused problems across the known galaxy.'

Kurcher didn't like being reminded of his mother and Santa Cruz knew that. He had almost forgotten that the commander was the highest-ranked interrogation officer in Taurus. He knew how to get to people.

The explanation continued. 'During the early part of 2594, a Taurus deepspace exploration team arrived at their destination in Coldrig; an unremarkable moon orbiting a gas giant. On the surface, they discovered what appeared to be wreckage from a ship of some kind. It was so old that it was impossible to move without falling apart. However, buried just below the surface was an artefact they managed to extract and return to the corp scientists.'

'Wait, back up a second. Just how old was the wreckage?'

'Let's just say that it predated the human race.'

Kurcher was sceptical. 'We've never found any evidence of intelligent alien life before, just indigenous animal species.'

'We always believed something was out there though. Finally, we had proof. The artefact turned out to be a data module and work began to try powering it up. As you can imagine, it sparked an increase in exploration vessels being sent into Coldrig. Three more artefacts were found over the following six months.'

253

'So that's why an outpost was set up so far out in Berg.'

'Correct. The best scientists in the corporation were sent out there to Minerva, to oversee the research projects. Eventually, it paid off and a breakthrough was made as the alien dialect began to make some sense. Unfortunately, someone leaked intel and the other four corps caught wind of the finds. Believing that there must have been more evidence of this alien race in the likes of Krondahar and Farrin, Nova and Libra headed off to claim systems closest to those unexplored sectors.'

'This is...' Kurcher couldn't quite find the right words. 'So you've been keeping it secret all this time. Why?'

Santa Cruz looked to his right, watching something the enlister couldn't see. 'Because more discoveries were made within colonised space, and not just by Taurus. Nova found something in the Bastion system, Libra reported a huge find in Meddian and even Sigma Royal claimed to have unearthed an artefact in Kember. We had foolishly believed this race was local to the Coldrig sector, but suddenly it showed that they were spread across the galaxy at one time. The great mystery was what exactly had happened to them and why we were just finding random data artefacts.'

'Sounds like they died out,' Kurcher remarked.

Santa Cruz returned his gaze to the screen. 'Perhaps. I was brought in by the board to oversee the research projects and to protect the data at any cost. What the teams on Minerva discovered more recently was incredible. Over the years, they had been piecing together numerous extracts of data hidden away in the alien files. They were finding star maps, jump point information, planet intel and more. They then found references to a data library that housed historical information recorded over centuries by this race. Imagine a vast hub where they would store all of their knowledge, including specifications for their technology.'

Kurcher tried to imagine such a place. He could only think of pictures he once saw of the old libraries back on Earth. 'Quite the find then if you could locate it before the other corps.'

'Exactly, and they are already aware it exists, I'm afraid. This is why the corp wars began and why hostilities are rife at the moment. We are all searching for the holy grail. I can't let one of the other corps find it first.'

Realisation struck Kurcher. 'The data Cooke found points a way to this library, right?'

'He had no idea what he had discovered,' Santa Cruz said angrily. 'All he knew was we needed it and the other corps were still looking for it. Having deciphered a portion of the alien data, we knew there was an artefact somewhere in one particular region of the Milky Way which held the co-ordinates to the library. Cooke just happened to stumble on it while collecting that sorry group of crims residing on your ship.'

'Did your scientists say anything else about the location of this place?' Kurcher was trying to work out just how much the commander already knew.

'This is not a *place*, Kurcher. The library is a machine; a structure built among the stars. All information points towards it just waiting silently in the void for someone to reactivate it. As to the location, we know it is outside the galaxy somewhere. That's quite the haystack to search.'

'No shit.' Kurcher's mouth was suddenly dry. He could still recall his studies as a boy, learning how the human race had opted to focus solely on the Milky Way following the new technological age. Data previously gathered on what was beyond the edge of the galaxy had been questioned and some of it ultimately wiped by fanatics, with those scientists labelling it as inaccurate or false. A shroud of mystery around what lay in deep space had been re-established once more. 'The map we saw showed one point out beyond the Krondahar sector. Frost thought it was likely a rogue star.'

Santa Cruz absorbed that information and began tapping a finger against his lip. 'It could be, but we won't truly know until someone gets there. Now do you see how important this data is?'

'Sure. All this time, the location of your holy grail had been just under the skin of a convicted rapist and was discovered by a schizophrenic preacher.'

'So now you know what's at stake.' Santa Cruz chose to ignore Kurcher's crass attempt at humour. 'I need it delivered to Berg immediately.'

Kurcher tilted his head as he considered his next move. 'Who else knows about all this?'

The commander's face flushed slightly. 'My research teams on Minerva and I know the whole truth. The Taurus board and certain high-ranking officers know about the finds, but are not fully aware of the library. I needed more intel on it before filing the official report.'

'What about your people who disappeared?' The question was asked before Kurcher's brain kicked into gear. 'Scientists, researchers, explorers. Most of them were part of the teams based in Berg, weren't they?'

Santa Cruz pursed his lips and sighed before shaking his head. 'What is this fascination with missing people? Explorers are lost on missions sometimes, people occasionally die accidentally or from illness.'

'I never said anything about them dying.'

The two stared at each other for several seconds, both trying to gauge just what the other was thinking. Santa Cruz eventually broke the uncomfortable silence.

'It's very obvious to me that you won't simply follow orders like other enlisters and that someone has managed to get into your head, making you paranoid. I have a proposal for you which would ultimately benefit both of us greatly.'

'Firstly, I'm not like other enlisters. You know that, Rees knows that and even that prick Mitchell knows it. Secondly, I just want to make sure that I'm not about to disappear, as others who have come close to this data tend to.'

'Fifty thousand,' said Santa Cruz, raising his voice. 'That's the offer if you do one last thing for me before you can get back to whatever you call normal.'

Kurcher couldn't hide his surprise. That much money would certainly make his life somewhat easier, although no doubt Frost would take a cut. Hell, he could even make himself disappear for a couple of months and take a huge supply of Parinax with him.

'Why so much?' he asked, suddenly wary. 'I'm guessing it's going to be something I don't want to do.'

'You have the co-ordinates of the alien data library which can help Taurus run the whole galaxy. Take the *Kaladine* to those co-ordinates, locate the library and activate it for me. As much as I wish I could be the one to first set eyes on it, I must remain in Berg for now.'

Kurcher laughed. 'No fucking way. I'm not an explorer and my ship isn't designed to travel that sort of distance through deep space.'

'If I sent a fleet of explorer-class vessels out there, it will draw attention, especially from Sapphire Nova. One enlister ship that finds it easy to slip past unnoticed would fare much better. As for the distance, you can jump to the co-ordinates.'

'How?'

'You'd need to jump from the Valen system. I can send you the decipher code for the co-ordinates on the map you have. Your pilot only need enter them as normal then perform the jump.'

'Valen is Nova space.' As if Santa Cruz needed reminding. 'That's too much of a risk.'

'You'd be in their system for mere minutes,' the commander assured him.

Kurcher thought for a moment. Another variable gnawed at him. 'Say we get all the way out there, further than any other human has ever been. That's a long way from known space. Once we find this thing... *if* we find it, how the fuck are we supposed to get back?'

Santa Cruz sighed. 'You need to listen very carefully to me, Kurcher. I'm

256

the one taking a huge risk here, sending an unorthodox, uncouth and dangerous man like you to carry out the most important task in the history of the human race. I am certain that the point displayed on the map you saw is the location of the machine. I have also spent enough time studying the data files we deciphered to understand some of the workings of this library. It's the information inside it that holds all of the mystery to us now and we need to unlock it.'

'I'm not hearing an explanation as to how we get back.'

'Once you locate the library, you need to send a specific code directly to it which will power it up. I can send you this code. Once activated, the machine will create a wormhole directly to Berg, allowing you to pass through and opening the gate for my teams to head out there to start studying it.'

'So the code you'd send me would have Berg's co-ordinates embedded into it?'

'Correct.'

'And you just want Frost and I to go out there, activate it and then come back straight away?'

'Yes.'

Kurcher tapped the arm of his chair. 'A lot could go wrong. If your code doesn't work, we can't activate whatever jump tech this thing has and we're stuck out there. It might not even be there. If this other race have died out and their own ships have already turned to dust, what's to say this library won't be dead too?'

'Because it isn't, Kurcher. I told you it was a hub. The only reason we are able to access the data files discovered in Coldrig and around known space is because they are linked to it. If it was dead, we'd have nothing.' Santa Cruz sounded almost excited. 'I'm not saying this is without risk. You would be on your own out there until the gate was opened and comms could be re-established.'

Kurcher tried to ignore the voice at the back of his mind. 'So worst case scenario is that we have to go into cryo until someone comes to get us. I don't intend being frozen for a few centuries.'

'Do this for me and you will have the full protection of Taurus Galahad should Nova or anyone else try taking you out. What else do you want?'

That question had lots of answers. He wanted the ghosts of his past to stop haunting him. He wanted to be able to sleep without the use of Parinax. He wanted to be left alone.

'A hundred thousand.' Money would help too of course. 'Up front. Plus Rees' guarantee that no harm will come to me or Frost upon our return and that we can get back to doing what we do best.'

Santa Cruz tried to hide his anger, but his eyes were aflame. 'Seventy thousand. Half now, the rest on your return. Rees has no say in matters relating to this. He is a judicial officer.'

'Which makes him the man I have to answer to,' added Kurcher. 'As well as one of the only people in the corp I actually trust... to a degree.'

'Very well. I'll get you his guarantee.'

'And one hundred thousand up front. Something like this actually should be paying a lot more, but I'm a fair man.'

Santa Cruz swallowed his rage. 'Agreed. Head to Valen and you will have the co-ordinates as well as the activation code before you get there. Do not try to access the library yourself. There will be defenses in place and we are yet to fully understand them.'

'I don't intend on spending any more time than I have to out there, commander. If you're sending me on a wild goose chase though, I won't be happy.'

Kurcher thought for a moment about what Frost was going to say. The way he saw it, either he accepted the task and they got paid a shitload of money or Santa Cruz had them killed and took the data for himself. After what happened with Cooke, he knew the commander was being watched carefully so another dead enlister would certainly jeopardise his rise in the hierarchy, if not put him on trial for his actions.

Kurcher didn't even really care a great deal about the alien discoveries. There had been countless times the human race thought they had found evidence of intelligent life among the stars, only to be disappointed. Admittedly, there was something in what Taurus had found though; enough to warrant the disappearance of people who got too close to it. Perhaps they had all wanted to share the information with others and Santa Cruz had been forced to silence them for the good of the corporation. That didn't make it right of course, but Kurcher could understand the commander's thinking.

'One more thing.'

Kurcher had almost forgotten Santa Cruz was still there as his drug-fuelled mind began to wander. 'What's that?'

'Get rid of those crims before you reach Valen. They have no use anymore.'

Kurcher looked into the officer's eyes and saw the coldness had returned. *They have no use anymore.* Just like himself and Frost once the task was complete.

'I'll keep an eye out for the money, the guarantee and those codes.'

258

Kurcher severed the comms link and ran one hand through his hair, trying to work out just how he was going to explain this one to Frost.

Taurus Galahad Assault Ship Requiem
Berg system

Santa Cruz was still seething when he contacted Winter.

The Taurus agent calmly listened as the details of the conversation with Kurcher were relayed, including the information on the historic finds.

'Remarkable.' Winter's somewhat distorted image smiled. 'Congratulations on the discovery, commander. You must be excited to get your hands on the library.'

Was there sarcasm in Winter's tone? Santa Cruz couldn't tell. 'My excitement has been replaced with anxiety thanks to Kurcher. There don't seem to be any trustworthy enlisters left in Taurus.'

'It's not a profession that sees many scrupulous individuals hired.'

'You've done an excellent job,' Santa Cruz told him. 'Unfortunately, Kurcher has forced my hand now. Having appealed to his greed, I'll make use of him one last time though. I want you to follow them and destroy the *Kaladine* once they have activated the machine. No survivors.'

Winter's icy-blue eyes could just be made out. 'I'll be able to return to Berg though, as you told Kurcher?'

'You have my word. The enlister and his pilot have always been expendable. You are definitely not. I know I can trust you.'

Winter looked away from the screen for a second. 'Consider it done, commander. The *Kaladine* is on the move again. I will report in before Valen.'

'You'll have the jump codes shortly.'

When Santa Cruz stepped away from his personal console, his head was aching. He was relying on other people too much and it was causing him great stress. He had never expected to use someone else to turn the machine on and had dreamt of the moment he came into contact with it. Kurcher had robbed him of that moment and Santa Cruz found himself wishing he could see the look on the enlister's face as Winter opened fire.

After fetching a cup of coffee to steady his nerves and battle the tiredness setting in, the commander returned to his console and accessed one of the confidential files. He looked down the list of names on his screen and found what he was looking for. Within minutes, he had forged the guarantee using Rees' unique seal of approval and silently praised himself for ensuring he had taken the time to copy the boards' personal information when he was last on

Earth. Being the highest-ranking interrogation officer had its perks.

Next, he prepared to transfer the payment to Kurcher. Despite having to take the large amount from his own funds, Santa Cruz chose to use money he had hidden away in an account held by one of his financial contacts on Carson Station. He would likely be able to reclaim it once Kurcher was dead. It made him feel somewhat better using funds that had come to him from mercenary payments and private ventures that Taurus Galahad would have frowned upon. He liked to keep his options open where possible, seeking out opportunities wherever he went.

As he prepared to send everything through, he felt slightly more at ease. One hundred thousand was a just sacrifice considering the benefits he would soon reap.

Enlister-class vessel *Kaladine*
Valen system

They watched as Ercko's body drifted off into the darkness, a twirling white figure that was quickly consumed by the void.

Frost glanced at Kurcher, noticing how distant he had been during their two-system jump to reach Valen. 'This is our last chance now, Davian. We may not come back from this next jump. Let's just send the data to Santa Cruz and get out of here.'

'Would you have me give him the money back too?' Kurcher asked, still staring out into space. 'Don't you want to see what all this is about?'

'Not if it means we're stuck out there. There's danger money and then there's this. You've agreed for us to go to a point outside the Milky Way, for fuck's sake.'

'It's about survival, Justyne. Doing this will shake off those hunting for us and secure our future.'

Frost jabbed a finger at him. 'Don't pretend you did this for anyone but yourself. Plus, why the hell are we taking *them* with us?'

Kurcher finally turned to look at her. 'If you want out, take the lifeboat. I'm sure Nova will be glad to come pick you up.'

'Fuck you.' She drew in a deep breath, realising how much she needed a cigarette. 'I still don't get why we had to jettison the body in one of their systems.'

Kurcher gave her a weak smile. 'Didn't want to dump our trash in our own backyard.'

Frost checked on the status of the Valen gate via her app. 'It's nearly time.'

'Good. Follow me.'

He led her to the rec room, peering into the only occupied cell as they passed. Whether it was Choice or Maric staring back at him, he didn't care. The restraints were still in place and that was all that mattered.

'This is going to be brief,' Kurcher announced as he entered. 'Commander Santa Cruz ordered me to execute you all. Luckily for you, I chose not to carry out that order.'

The six crims exchanged confused looks and let the enlister continue.

'You're welcome, by the way. I have reasons for keeping you all alive and I know you have doubts as to where we are about to jump to. I explained

262

what we are supposed to find out there, but didn't tell you why I agreed to do this. Accessing this data library will keep us alive, plain and simple. If I had taken us to Berg, I believe Santa Cruz would have made us all disappear. Once this task is complete and we have returned to occupied space, you are free to go your own way. I suggest you choose a good place to hide though as it is likely Taurus will eventually send someone else after you. That someone could even be me.'

'So why take us with you then let us go?' Hewn asked.

'As I said, I have my reasons. It may be that my moral compass is fucked at the moment. This whole assignment has left a bitter taste in my mouth and I want to wash the last few weeks away. I've made a living from killing people and I intend to pick up where I left off after this little venture is out of the way. I don't give people a second chance usually. Maybe you'll bear that in mind later on.'

Rane had been grinning since Kurcher mentioned Santa Cruz. 'You want us to become contacts you can call on in the future.'

'I never said that. You all have some worth, I will admit, but I won't hesitate executing you if Taurus pay me to do so again.'

'What about Choice?' Angard was rubbing his scalp as if trying to sate a constant itch.

Kurcher knew he couldn't let the unpredictable schizophrenic go again. It would be a mercy killing. He would keep him alive though until Angard left the ship, just in case the disruption app was needed again.

'Let me worry about him,' he told Angard.

'And do I get to join you when this is over?' Broekow addressed Kurcher but looked at Frost.

Kurcher shook his head. 'You'd survive longer if you went your own way, trust me.'

Sensing the conversation was drawing to a conclusion, Frost stepped in. 'We'll be jumping in twenty minutes.'

She and Kurcher made their way swiftly to the cockpit, where they both settled into their respective seats and strapped themselves in, just in case. As Frost lit a cigarette, Kurcher suddenly began laughing.

'What's so funny?' she asked, her tone betraying just how she was feeling.

'The whole thing is surreal. You and I are about to make history. We're working for an egotistical bastard who wants us dead. On top of that, there are seven people back there who *should* be dead but who get to come on this joyride with us. If these aliens were still alive and happened to be at the same co-ordinates, imagine their surprise when they realise just who the human

263

race have sent out there.'

Frost looked across at him and saw there were tears in his eyes. She had never seen that before in the whole time she had known him. Something wasn't right.

'How much Parinax are you on right now?'

'Enough to put my mind at rest and get this job done.'

'You're too fucking high, Davian. Get your head in the game.'

Kurcher snorted. He would regret taking such a big hit of Parinax once the effects wore off, but he quickly shrugged that thought away. He was sharp and that was all that mattered.

Even his decision to keep the crims alive didn't bother him. Angard was suitable protection for them and Oakley could hopefully keep him calm. Choice was there as a back-up if she couldn't pacify the giant. Broekow was good in a fight and had come to understand the way they worked. In another life, the sniper would have made a good enlister. D'Larro's medical training had proven useful, even though one of his last patients had died. For once, it wasn't the medic who had murdered him though.

Kurcher was still undecided as to what to do with Hewn. Though the pirate had links across the galaxy that would be extremely useful, no doubt a number of organisations would pay good money for the leader of Echo to be delivered to them. Hewn had a lot of enemies after all, which was the only thing they had in common.

As for Rane, Kurcher had ignored the inane grin on the killer's face. Rane would be thinking he had the enlister's complete trust. However, while he was useful in a number of ways, there was no way Kurcher was going to let him go. He had spent too long chasing Rane and trying to understand why he chose to kill certain people. There was method in the madness apparently; Rane was yet to divulge that. At the end of the day, he was just another sick individual who needed putting out of his misery.

'Davian, we're getting a message.'

Kurcher shook the thoughts from his head and noticed that the gate ahead of the *Kaladine* was beginning to shift. 'From who?'

Frost's eyes moved quickly as she scanned it. 'Anonymous. It says that two Nova assault vessels are on approach to jump to Valen.'

'Can we jump before they get here?'

'Should be able to. That gate is so slow though.'

Kurcher checked the console in front of him. 'That's Nova tech for you. I think our anonymous friend must be tied somehow to Santa Cruz. I wouldn't put it past that bastard to send his spies out to keep an eye on us.'

'It's opening,' Frost said, ordering the *Kaladine* forward. 'The ship's nav system is going crazy ever since I input our destination.'

As the wormhole yawned, Kurcher noticed that Frost was sweating. 'It'll be okay. Just stay calm.'

The pilot blew a cloud of smoke at him. 'I'd better get a big fucking cut of that payment.'

A moment later, the *Kaladine* was drawn into the wormhole. As the gravitational waves pushed them along the passage, Frost hardly looked up from her console. Kurcher found himself gripping the edge of the seat.

Standard jump time between systems was mere seconds. As they passed the minute mark, Frost wiped the perspiration from her brow.

'This doesn't feel right,' she stated, more to herself than Kurcher. 'The stability is the worst I've ever seen. The further we go, the weaker the wormhole gets.'

'Remember just how far this is taking us.' Kurcher used his best reassuring tone. 'Plus there's no gate at the other end to hold it all together.'

'A hundred and fifty thousand light years from Sol. Don't remind me.'

As they approached their second minute inside the passage, the *Kaladine* was suddenly spat back out into space and light blazed into the cockpit.

'You were right.' Kurcher shielded his eyes from the rogue star.

Frost moved the ship, turning away from the blinding orb. A more-distant blue glow came into view.

'She's a binary system,' said the pilot softly. 'Beautiful.'

'Any planets?' Kurcher wasn't there to sightsee and he was already starting to feel apprehensive. The all-too-familiar itch was starting in his brain again.

Frost ran a scan, taking a sharp intake of breath as it finished. 'None. That seems improbable. Planets have a better chance of being born in a binary system. There's a fair amount of debris orbiting the two stars as well as...'

As her voice trailed off, Kurcher glanced across and noticed lines of data scrolling down each screen at the main console. When he looked closer, he saw the same symbols found on the data implant.

'What's going on?'

'I'm not sure. We just started receiving this.' She studied the screens for a moment. 'I recognise some of the co-ordinate symbols mixed up in it. Hold on.'

The *Kaladine* accelerated, veering away so that neither star was visible from the cockpit and instead looking directly into the void.

Kurcher could see twinkling pinpricks across the vast black canvas and nothing more. He cast an unsure look towards Frost. She was lost in her screens.

'What exactly are we looking for?' he asked finally, growing impatient. 'There's nothing out here.'

When she didn't reply, he cursed and slouched back into the seat. Santa Cruz had been so certain. Had that Taurus bastard managed to get him to chase after shadows, knowing there would be no return? Surely he wouldn't have paid them so much if that was the case. Kurcher felt his stomach tighten as he realised he had stranded them in deep space.

As he gazed out into the darkness, something odd caught his eye. A cluster of stars he had noticed a moment ago vanished. Several seconds later, another cluster adjacent to the first blinked somehow out of existence. He leaned forward, watching as a number of the tiny specks were snuffed out.

It dawned on him exactly what he was seeing. 'Holy shit.'

The structure had been waiting silently in the shadows; a shy leviathan choosing the right moment to reveal itself. The blue light of the more distant star illuminated one side as it turned slowly, showing a hull made of some dark material. There were no lights across the smooth surface and no immediately obvious ports. It loomed before the tiny *Kaladine* like a titan awoken from some deep slumber.

'A library.' Frost uttered as she sat in awe. 'Fuck.'

The machine rivalled Sullivan's Rest in size. It resembled some sort of odd fishbone and was definitely not of human design. The top was a slim metallic dome with a wide shaft hanging below it. Two sharp-looking prongs stuck out from either side of the shaft, almost similar to the pylons of stations back in the known systems. The base of the shaft was cone-shaped and showed faint ridges as it turned further into the dim glow.

'Do we send the code yet?' Frost asked.

Kurcher struggled to tear his eyes from the alien machine. 'Not yet. I want to see this thing close-up before we activate it.'

'I don't want to take us too close. Santa Cruz said something about defenses, didn't he?'

'Fine. I'll leave you to decide a safe distance.' He made to leave the cockpit.

'Where're you going?'

'Didn't realise I had to tell you every time I wanted to take a piss.' He needed to top up his dose or spend their interaction with the library distracted by withdrawal, which seemed to be hitting him much quicker than normal.

'Fine. You know, whoever made that must've been fucking smart. If the

266

whole thing is one big data server, it's mind-blowing.'

Kurcher left without another word and found Oakley standing just outside the cockpit.

'I need to speak to you,' she said, keeping her voice low. 'About Horsten.'

'What about him?'

'I think his drugs are starting to run low. He's started showing minor symptoms... the calm before the storm.'

'For fuck's sake,' snapped Kurcher. 'You couldn't have said something sooner?'

Oakley remained calm as she shook her head. 'I only just noticed. I think he may have been pretending to be fine since we left Vega.'

'You *think* his drug supply is running low and you *think* he has been pretending. Why don't you just go ask him and leave me out of it? I don't know what you expect me to do about this.'

Her cool tone became sharper. 'I'm letting you know out of courtesy. This is your ship after all and we're in your charge.'

'I'll just go shoot him in the head then,' Kurcher told her. 'That'll sort it out.'

'You really are a selfish prick.'

As Oakley stormed away, his vision blurred for a split second before that itch began deep inside his skull. He quickly headed to his quarters, reaching for the Parinax stash as soon as he entered. The first few containers were empty and found themselves flung across the room. By the time he had gone through them all, he just had two small doses left.

What the hell was going on? He had more left, he was certain. The thought crossed his mind that someone had stolen them. Only Frost had access to his quarters. Then again, she often scolded him for using it, so maybe she had thrown them away. No, she wouldn't have dared.

Before he realised what he was doing, he took both remaining hits and waited as they kicked in. Looking down at the empty tubes, he swore and began searching for any more that might have been hidden from his initial scan. Despite the warmth and usual calming effect of the Parinax though, a cold dread began eating at him. He had gone through the entire supply Kopetti had sold him, even though the lying old smuggler had told him they would last a couple of months at least.

He had to get a grip and told himself to just get their task at hand finished so they could get back to occupied space. Then he could find himself a new supply before withdrawal turned him into a paranoid wreck.

En route back to the cockpit, voices called to him as he passed the rec room.

'I haven't got time,' he growled.

'Is it there?' asked Hewn.

'Yes.'

D'Larro grinned. 'What does it look like?'

Kurcher wished he had never told them about the library. In fact, he wondered whether the Parinax was giving him loose lips.

'None of your concern,' he said bluntly. 'I'm sending the code and then we're going back.'

'I believe it wise to think about this, Davian,' remarked Rane. 'Don't send the code yet. We don't know what might happen. What if Santa Cruz actually gave you a code to activate the machine's defenses?'

Hewn pointed a metal finger at the serial killer. 'You've listened to *him* enough. This isn't the time for a hesitant approach.' The pirate approached Kurcher. 'Imagine what we could achieve if you joined Echo and we use the data in that library ourselves. We should try to access it somehow and work out a way to send it a code that opens a jump into the Expanse, say to the Freeman system.'

Rane gave a derisive snort. 'We don't know the first thing about it, Jaffren. We don't know what it contains or what it might be capable of.'

'Then we find out. There must be ways to dock with it; to get inside the thing.'

'As much as I hate to agree with any of you,' began Broekow, stepping forward from the back of the room, 'Rane's right. Trying to get into that machine would be reckless and would most likely end badly for us all. Stop to think for one moment. This is an *alien* creation, meaning we don't know the first fucking thing about how it works or who built it. This isn't the time to get greedy.'

Hewn laughed. 'You don't get anywhere without a little risk.'

'Shut up, all of you.' Kurcher had no patience left. 'You don't get to make the decisions on this.'

Frost's voice came across his comms app. 'Need you back here now.'

Detecting the urgency in her tone, Kurcher left the crims to argue. As he returned to the cockpit, he noticed that the *Kaladine* was starting to circle the monstrous machine from much further out than he had anticipated.

'Problem?'

'Two Nova assault ships just arrived.'

'What? How's that possible?'

268

'Either they had the same deciphered co-ordinates we did or they somehow found a way to get through the jump point we opened. What matters is that they've seen us and are moving to intercept, hence why I'm moving us round the other side of that thing and buying us time.'

'Do you know which ships they are?'

Frost checked her data. 'The *Kaban* and the *Huntress*.'

Kurcher felt his guts twist. 'Fucking typical.' He saw Frost frown. 'The *Huntress* belongs to Trin Espina. I should've known they'd send her after me.'

'We can't fight off two of them. I doubt we'd last that long against just one.'

'It's been a few years since I last saw Trin, but I doubt she's changed that much.' Kurcher closed his eyes, trying to focus. 'She always was a good tracker. Whether or not Nova knew the library was here, I won't be able to tell until I speak with her.'

Frost gave him an incredulous stare. 'You can't reason with her. Firstly, she is a Nova officer. Secondly, she's a psycho bitch if what you told me about her is true.'

'Nova will want me alive if possible.'

'Don't count on it.' Frost checked her data again. 'Shit, the *Huntress* is faster than a normal assault ship. She's closing while the *Kaban* is lingering behind.'

A weak smile passed across Kurcher's lips. 'She never liked slow ships.'

'If they fire on us, we're screwed,' cried Frost. 'And our weapons wouldn't do much damage to them in return.'

Kurcher knew they couldn't possibly outrun the *Huntress*. Besides, where would they run to? Trin had always reacted best when someone was direct with her, even in the bedroom.

'Open a comms link to the *Huntress*.'

Frost went to query his order but thought better of it, nodding as she opened the link.

'This is Enlister Kurcher. Considering where we all are, I want to speak with Commander Espina immediately.'

Silence followed and Kurcher hoped his intel wasn't out of date. If she had been replaced as commander, he had no idea who he might end up in conversation with. That was if they didn't just blow the *Kaladine* apart as soon as they were in range.

'Never thought I'd run into you again so far from home.' Espina's voice was as lusty as ever. 'Are you alone?'

Kurcher could tell she was speaking through her personal comms. 'Yeah.'

'I've been charged with tracking you down to answer for the murders of Nova personnel on Rikur. You're already aware of that, I'm sure. In addition, you killed a number of Nova soldiers on Summit.'

'Soldiers? They were goons sent to kill *me*. Besides, I didn't kill that many of them.'

'To begin with, the Nova board wanted your head but they soon realised you were up to something, jumping from one system to the next, and decided they'd rather I took you back to Straunia.' Espina chuckled before continuing. 'Little did I know what exactly you would lead me to. Now I get to apprehend you and secure a historic find for Sapphire Nova.'

'You realise there isn't a way home,' lied Kurcher. 'Once I was finished here, I was to set a course back to the Milky Way and go into cryo for as long as it took.'

'We both know you wouldn't come out here unless there was an easy way back. You forget how well I know you, Davian.'

'I've changed since we last saw each other. No doubt you have too.'

'Not really. I'm still a bitch and I'm still prepared to do what it takes to get ahead in this fucked-up galaxy.'

'Only we aren't in our galaxy now.'

'Listen, I'm not here to play games. There's a bounty on your head and I mean to collect it. Surrender your ship and anyone else on board, including your pilot. Is she still as naïve as ever?'

Kurcher didn't look at Frost. He could imagine the expression on her face. 'Trin, consider the situation. You've brought your ship and crew, plus the *Kaban*, out here with no idea how to get back. You and I need to work together to ensure we both survive.'

'The last time we worked together, we ended up letting a crim slip away unnoticed while we were fucking. You were always a bad influence on me and I don't intend on revisiting our sordid past.'

'You left out the bit where we chased the crim down afterwards though. As I recall, you shot him in both kneecaps then watched as he tried crawling away.'

'Until you ended my fun and put a bullet in the back of his head.'

'You don't seriously believe I'll surrender, do you? You'll blow up my ship as soon as I set foot on the *Huntress*. I have a job to do and I propose you help me.'

'What job?'

Kurcher thought for a moment. He had to choose his words carefully.

'That machine out there proves the existence of another intelligent species in the universe. We need to study it and you probably have better scientific equipment than I do.'

'When did Davian Kurcher become a scientist? Come to think of it, when did he start caring about anything other than himself?' There was an edge of bitterness in Espina's tone this time.

'Trin, we can both benefit from this.'

A soft sigh came through comms. 'You left Harper in quite a state. Paranoia is rampant there now as sec forces believe you had help from the inside. Personally, I know you didn't murder Portman. Wasn't your style. Still, you managed to get yourself implicated in his death by just being in the colony at the wrong time. So, I send a squad of mercs to track you down, thinking I could be lazy and let them deal with you. You gun them all down with the help of a mysterious friend and disappear off to Callyn.'

Kurcher didn't like where this was going. 'What's your point?'

'Your supplier, Kopetti, told me as much as he knew before he died. No staying power, that old prick. It really bothered me though why you would destroy a small ship out near a dead planet like Mags, unless you were trying to cover your ass for some reason.'

That dread hit him again, this time burrowing deep into his guts. Not only did she know Kopetti had given him the Parinax, she had also severed his best supply link.

Espina continued, her voice back to a soft purr. 'Then I find you've gone to Tempest. Didn't really feel like taking on the guardian there on my own so I brought in the *Kaban* to help. Libra didn't seem to want a fight on their hands, despite the fact the guardian could probably have destroyed us both and pointed us in the direction your ship had gone as long as we left the surface alone. Interesting. The point to all this, Davian, is that you've led me on quite the chase and, now that I find you, your solution is to partner up like old times despite all the problems you've created for Nova, as though the lives you took mean nothing. They weren't crims you killed, they were officers.'

'So that's a no, is it?'

There was no immediate reply from Espina. Kurcher tapped on Frost's shoulder. When she looked up at him, he indicated that he wanted to see the Nova ships. As one of the screens flickered and brought up the image of the approaching *Huntress*, the assault vessel fired a single fusion pulse which slammed into the *Kaladine* near to the starboard engine.

Frost flinched as the ship shuddered and slowed. 'That fucking bitch.'

271

'Didn't think you were alone,' came Espina's calm voice. 'Consider that a warning, Davian. Next time, I'll order the fusion beam to cut your ship in half.'

Kurcher signalled to Frost and she severed the comms link. 'What's the damage?'

'No hull breach, but that pulse did enough to cause one of the engines to partially shut down.'

'We need both engines if we're going to get out of this. Can you repair it?'

Frost grimaced. 'Yeah, but I'll need help.'

'Do it.'

She leapt from her seat and ran to the door. 'What about you?'

'Someone has to keep Trin occupied.' When she had left the cockpit, Kurcher took a moment to gather his thoughts before reconnecting the link to Espina.

'I have a feeling we're really alone this time,' chuckled the Nova officer. 'Now you can act like your normal self.'

'If anything happens to me or this ship, Taurus will be swift and brutal in their retaliation. It won't be a war, Trin. It will be a massacre.'

'Sticks and stones,' she scoffed. 'Taurus Galahad are a bunch of dickless cowards with massive delusions of grandeur. Nova are ruthless and have the firepower to back up their actions.'

Kurcher could see that the *Huntress* was almost upon them. 'You said your orders were to take me alive for questioning. Leave my ship alone and I'll come with you.'

'This isn't a negotiation. You don't hold any cards here.'

'That's where you're wrong.' He couldn't be sure he was doing the right thing, but options were limited. 'I'm holding the key to that machine out there.'

It was a few seconds before Espina replied. 'Unlikely. Why would an enlister be trusted with something so important?'

'I'm out here, aren't I? I can unlock that thing and wake it up. Work with me on this, Trin, and we can reap huge rewards.' He hoped he wasn't taking a step too far. 'Forget Nova, forget your orders. Look at what's sitting out there. Every corp want to get their hands on it, but they're not here.'

'I'm an officer now.' There was a regretful edge to her voice. 'This sort of find will earn me a huge promotion and a shitload of money.'

'When we were together, you loved being reckless. Fuck Nova, fuck Taurus. It's just you and me again.'

She went quiet again for a moment. 'Let's talk face-to-face. I need to be able to look into your eyes to know whether you're being honest.'

'Fine, I'll bring the lifeboat over.'

'No. We'll dock with the *Kaladine* and then you can come over.'

Kurcher scratched at his temple. 'How do I know you won't just destroy my ship once I step over?'

Espina laughed loudly. 'Because you'll leave key data there to make sure that doesn't happen. You forget how well I know you.'

She had forgotten how well he knew her too. 'I'm not comfortable with...'

'As I said before, this isn't a negotiation,' snapped Espina, severing the link.

Kurcher took one last look towards the looming *Huntress*, his eyes lingering on the Nova emblem boldly displayed below the apt name. There was no way Trin would agree to working with him again, he knew. She would send more goons onto the *Kaladine* first to secure it and that meant killing anyone who fought back.

It was time for the crims to show their real worth.

~

Winter gripped the arms of his seat tightly, willing the wormhole to end. Not many situations made him sweat; heading into a jump that would take him beyond the Milky Way was one of them.

He distracted himself by checking the weapon systems for the tenth time. His stalker was ready to face off against the Nova assault ships that had pursued Kurcher, but he really wasn't sure what he would find when he emerged. Against assault vessels, he had the maneuverability and speed to keep from being lanced by a fusion beam. His hull plating, however, was minimal. One lucky strike and it would be over. Then again, he had his prototype weapon should the need arise.

It caught him by surprise when he was catapulted back into space and took him a few seconds to get his bearings. His stalker picked up the *Kaban* first. He cursed when he saw the other ships. The *Huntress* had docked with the *Kaladine*, which was bad news. He was surprised how fast the assault vessel had caught up with the enlister. His focus would be elsewhere though.

As the stalker moved silently for the *Kaban*, Winter caught sight of the machine. One side of it was reflecting a thin strip of blue light from the distant star while the other had a fading orange hue. So *this* was what that maniac Santa Cruz had been so desperate to find. Proof that some other sentient race had been out among the stars and, more importantly, that they had left behind something of great benefit to Taurus Galahad.

273

As awe-inspiring as the alien structure was, Winter had orders to follow. He soon moved into range of the *Kaban*, which seemed to have been holding back. Once he attacked, he would give away his position. Back at Rikur, when he had struck the Nova transport to help Kurcher escape, he had been able to stay hidden thanks to the number of ships nearby. There was no such cover here.

Settling back into his seat with a deep breath, he opened fire.

~

Kurcher met the Nova men at the airlock.

'What a surprise. She's not with you.'

One of the soldiers stepped forward, glaring at him through a narrow visor. '*Commander* Espina has other matters to attend to on the bridge. Come with us.'

Kurcher weighed the man up. A sergeant by his insignia, the officer seemed unimpressed with the enlister.

'What could be more important than meeting with me?'

'We're not here for small talk,' growled the sergeant.

'That's good then. I prefer to verbally spar with those of a high IQ.'

The sergeant's jaw clenched. 'Who else is on board?'

'My pilot. Don't get any ideas though. She has orders to shoot anyone other than me on sight.'

'I was told there would be others. Tell me where they are.'

Kurcher shrugged. 'Just the two of us.'

'Lying fucker.' The sergeant nodded to two of his men, who moved either side of the enlister. 'Check him for weapons, then take him to the holding cell.'

Kurcher let them search him, hating every second of it. His aching brain screamed at him to break the neck of the nearest man, but he needed to hold his resolve if he hoped to survive.

As he was led through the airlock into the *Huntress*, he heard the sergeant call out to his remaining five men to sweep the *Kaladine*. The order was to kill anyone else they encountered.

There was a soft crackle of static in his ear following by Frost's whisper. 'Heard all that. Sit tight, Davian.'

~

The *Kaban* lost another missile port to Winter's focused attack, triggering an internal explosion that nearly tore the hull asunder. Winter took some grim

274

satisfaction knowing that any Nova personnel manning the port would have been swallowed by the flames.

As he brought the stalker about, zipping beneath the assault ship as it turned to try bringing him into range of its fusion beams, he glanced at his screen to see the *Huntress* still latched onto Kurcher's vessel.

Winter found he was unable to keep his eyes from the alien machine too. There was something sinister about the way it hung quietly in the void, as though it was watching every move made by the tiny ships. At times, it would vanish in the darkness only to reappear when the binary stars reflected off the strange body.

The cockpit glowed green as a fusion beam shot across his prow and he cursed himself for getting distracted. Although it had been damaged, the *Kaban* was still a threat and he had to bank suddenly to avoid another beam.

'Release decoy buoy.'

His command was carried out instantly by the stalker. He hoped it would at least distract the assault ship for a moment to allow him to regroup. He considered activating the prototype; once fired, it needed time to recharge. He had to be in a position where the shot would cause the most damage to the Nova ship.

The fact the *Huntress* was not already bearing down on him made him nervous. If Nova massacred Kurcher and the crims, he would need to reconsider the situation. Out this far, he had no way of contacting Santa Cruz but the commander's priority was to get the machine back to Berg. Winter had the code to activate it too; was it best to get away from the *Kaban* and approach the machine himself? If Nova saw him do that, would they try to destroy it before it made the jump to Berg?

When the assault ship launched two missiles, Winter smiled. No tracking systems would be able to lock onto the stalker, but the commanding officer of the *Kaban* must have been getting flustered enough to try. Both missiles began hunting for their target. He watched as they simply disappeared into space.

It was his turn again. He aimed the nose of the stalker directly at the *Kaban*'s underbelly and located one of its fusion cannons. Three strikes from his own weapon obliterated the cannon, sending a green burst of energy spewing forth. If he had to, he would take the assault ship apart one piece at a time.

~

'Just get the job done quickly or I'll leave you here when we go to aid the
275

Kaban.'

The sergeant flinched at Espina's tone. 'Understood, commander.' As she cut off abruptly, he turned to the others. 'You heard the lady. Let's go.'

'Hardly a lady,' muttered one soldier, a cocky twentysomething who the sergeant knew had been chosen for duty on Espina's ship thanks to acing his combat training mere months back.

As the six Nova men continued deeper into the *Kaladine*, passing the empty rec room, the sergeant found himself pondering the bound wretch they had found in one of the cells. He had been caught in two minds as to whether to kill him or not, opting for the latter until they had finished their sweep. None of them had silencers; the gunshot would have echoed throughout the enlister's vessel. Then again, he could have run the prisoner through with his knife. He didn't fancy messing up his blade.

The next doorway was open and they quickly checked the room beyond, finding a number of storage units. Some were hanging open, others locked up tight. They moved on, finding two sets of quarters but nobody home. One clearly belonged to a woman, as the cocky soldier held up an item of underwear and grinned at his colleagues. The other room was unkempt, with disgarded Parinax containers strewn across the floor.

Knowing that whoever was left on the ship must be below, the sergeant waved his men on, taking two with him to the starboard engine and sending the other three to the port side, led by *Cocky*.

'Eyes open,' whispered the sergeant. 'Shoot anything that moves. Don't hit the fucking engines.'

When he set foot on the grating of the lower level, he could just make out the others descending opposite. The room was dark and the only light was emanating from a portable unit beside the starboard engine. As he turned to squint into the shadows, there was a subtle movement. A soldier behind him let out a gurgling cry. Instinctively, the sergeant threw himself forward and came up with his assault rifle aimed back at the stairs. One soldier was dead, crumpled over the bottom step with his head barely attached to his neck. As the other soldier who had been following looked for any sign of an enemy, there was a flash in the darkness and a bullet took him through the skull.

The sergeant took a blind shot at where he thought the flash came from. He heard his bullet ricochet off the wall. When he looked across to *Cocky* and the other two soldiers, his jaw dropped open. One Nova man dangled lifelessly in the hands of a gigantic figure. Another lay dead on the floor. *Cocky* backed into view clutching a bleeding hand and pulling a knife with the other.

'Come on then, fuckers,' yelled the young soldier. 'Try me one-on...'

Two bullets ended his vocal challenge. A figure stepped from the shadows, the barrel of his customised assault rifle still smoking.

The sergeant blinked as sweat ran into his eyes. He weighed up his options. Any hope of moving unseen in the dark was obliterated as a woman's voice commanded the lights back up and he found himself surrounded by an odd group of assailants.

He dropped his gun and raised his hands. Discretion was the better part of valour, after all.

'Put him in with Choice,' grinned the one who had killed *Cocky*. 'See how long he lasts.'

'We need to know where they took Davian first,' pointed out a man holding a bloodied sword.

'Fuck the enlister,' cried the first, flexing a bionic arm.

The woman who ordered the lights up came into view. 'Don't be an idiot, Hewn. Davian's the only one able to get us home again.'

Hewn chuckled. 'Typical.'

The swordsman stepped closer to the sergeant. 'Tell us where they took the enlister.'

The Nova man glanced at the bodies of those who had followed him to their deaths. 'One of the holding cells on the *Huntress*, ready for interrogation.'

'And I'm assuming she's a big ship? Lots of corridors and rooms to get lost in if you don't know the way?'

'I suppose.'

The swordsman wiped the blood off his blade on the sergeant's sleeve. 'You'd better come with us then.'

~

Kurcher didn't know quite how to feel when Espina glided into the holding cell. His first thought was that she hadn't changed one bit. Same beautiful eyes, same provocative walk, same cold expression. Then he noticed the uniform and the sun pins proudly displaying her rank. The old Trin never wanted to wear the blue and yellow of Sapphire Nova.

As she sat down across the table from him and crossed her arms, Kurcher noticed the two guards at the door shifting uncomfortably. No doubt they had witnessed what she did to prisoners before.

'There's another ship out there,' she began, showing no emotion now they were sat together in the same room. 'It came through after us and is now

277

attacking the *Kaban*. Who is it?'

Kurcher tried to ignore the irritating itch in his brain and the pain that felt like his skull was about to implode. 'No idea. Wish I knew, then I could thank them.'

She stared at him for a moment. 'That surprises me.'

'What?'

'The fact you're not lying. It also pisses me off.'

Kurcher gave her his most dashing smile. 'It's probably whoever killed your men on Summit. Taurus must've sent someone to clean up after me. You know what sort of mess I make.'

A flash of annoyance swept across her face. 'You need to tell me what you know about that machine out there.'

'Having seen you naked on more than one occasion, I'm finding it difficult to concentrate right now.'

She shot up from her seat and struck him across the face with the back of her hand. 'I'm in no mood for games.'

Kurcher rubbed his cheek. 'That brought back the memories too.'

Espina looked back at the guards. 'Leave us.' When they had eagerly departed, she walked around the table and grabbed his face with both hands. 'Is it the memory of me naked or the drugs making your concentration lapse?'

He shrugged. 'Bit of both.'

She kissed him hard then suddenly bit his lower lip, drawing blood. 'I'll admit that there are certain things I missed about you. You were always a good lay.'

Kurcher licked at the blood. 'I meant what I said before, Trin. We can both come out of this situation well, if we just work together. Forget Nova. Join me and we'll get rich off whatever the fuck that thing is out there.'

'And what is it?' she asked, still holding his face.

'An alien library.' He hadn't meant to blurt it out. 'The biggest find in human history. Play the corps off against each other and we stand to make a fortune.'

Espina's dark eyes studied him carefully. 'If only it were that easy. You started something big on Rikur and I've been charged with catching you. If I go rogue now, there's nowhere in the galaxy I'll be safe.'

'You never used to care about Nova. I'm not buying it.'

She returned to the other side of the table, standing behind the seat this time. 'Look around, Davian. I have a ship that could best any in the Taurus fleet, I have a crew under my command and I have the respect of Nova, who

I sincerely believe will win the war. Now I have this alien machine and you're locked up in a cell. If you were in my shoes, I doubt you'd be willing to strike a deal with some old flame just for money.'

Kurcher wiped his lip. 'So what now? You're not going anywhere if I don't give you the data to activate that machine. I'm willing to strike a deal here but it's for you alone, not Nova.'

Espina laughed. 'I missed your bravado too. You always thought you were right, even after I proved you weren't.'

As she began circling the table, he gave an amused snort. 'This time, I *am* right.'

A serrated knife appeared at his throat. 'Now *that* is a lie. Tell me what I need to know and I'll make sure you go back to Straunia in one piece. Every lie now though will cost you something.'

Kurcher felt the blade cutting into his skin. Something told him she meant what she said. Perhaps the old Trin wasn't in there after all. 'What do you need to know then?'

With the knife still against his throat, she draped her other arm over his shoulder. 'How do I activate that machine?'

'I thought you'd be asking what happened at Harper as a priority,' he dared to remark.

'All in good time.'

He would have to tell her something she wanted to hear and hoped she wouldn't read him like a book. 'There's a code that fires up the library, but there's no telling what might happen after that. The code is stored in the *Kaladine*'s memory.'

'Protected by some firewall, I'd wager?'

'Of course.'

Her narrow face loomed in front of his. 'You'll give me access to all files from your ship, including this code. I'll then download everything to the *Huntress* and activate the machine myself. Now, what were you going to do once it had been activated?'

He smirked. 'Tie a rope round it and drag it back.'

Espina's expression didn't change as she dragged the knife up the side of his neck and nicked his ear lobe. 'Don't test me, Davian.'

Truth be told, he hadn't meant to say that. Now he could feel the blood running down his neck. He grimaced. 'Take me to my ship and I'll show you everything.'

Her free hand grabbed his manhood and squeezed. 'Don't make me take this too. I kinda liked it.'

'I've already seen one dick sliced off recently thanks.'

'Well then, you'll...' She hesitated as someone spoke into her ear, then moved away from Kurcher and sheathed her knife. 'My men have returned from your ship. Apparently they killed a handful of crims they found hiding in your engine room.'

If that was true, had Frost been with them? Was he truly on his own now? No, he couldn't believe experienced killers would allow themselves to be cornered and slaughtered, especially after he had given the storage room code to Oakley and D'Larro.

'Good,' he said, forcing a weak smile. 'Saved me a job later on.'

'I'm on my way to the bridge now so we can deal with that other ship. Get comfy, Davian. I'll be back later to finish our chat.'

When she had left the room, his shoulders sagged. He clutched at his head. The pain was making him feel nauseous, the bile rising in his throat. His whole body was starting to tremble and itch. He needed a hit.

Minutes felt like hours as he struggled to hold himself together. The walls of the holding cell were closing in on him and he began hearing strange sounds from outside the door. If Espina came back, he wouldn't be able to focus and that knife of hers was nearly as wicked as her tongue.

When the door opened again, all he could do was lift his head from the table. Two Nova men entered and approached, the eyes behind their visors just blurred circles to him. He forced himself to sit up straight, but his dignity had left with Espina and he vomited.

'Jesus, what a mess,' came a familiar voice.

The two soldiers pulled Kurcher roughly to his feet and led him from the cell. In the corridor, the guards and a third body lay in pools of their own blood. Another Nova soldier stood over them. In his hand was a long blade glistening red.

'Fuck's sake, Rane, I thought you weren't going to kill him,' one of the other soldiers snapped.

'We couldn't have the poor sergeant raising the alarm.'

'Can you see well enough to fire a gun?'

Kurcher tried to focus on the soldier addressing him. 'I... uh... yeah.'

His own revolver was thrust into his hand.

'Those distractions aren't going to keep them at bay long,' stated Rane.

They moved as swiftly as they could through the *Huntress*. The few Nova men and women they ran into were gunned down before they could raise their own weapons. Three times, Kurcher saw Rane's sword flash and blood spray onto the walls.

His ribs were aching. When he glanced down, he saw metal fingers clutching him. Now he knew he was suffering withdrawal hallucinations. Crims would never rescue an enlister.

A figure stepped into view ahead of them. All he could make out was the blue and yellow of the uniform. His first shot missed; the second struck the figure in the shoulder and spun him around. Rane's sword skewered the reeling man before he could regroup.

Somewhere in the assault ship, there was an explosion.

'Your little devices came in handy.'

Kurcher's head cleared for a split second. 'Broekow?'

'At least you're not completely fucked then,' said the sniper.

They turned a corner into a long corridor that led to an airlock. Standing at the end, Kurcher could make out a hulking figure he just couldn't mistake. The person standing alongside Angard though was leaning against a wall, clutching a book to his chest. He couldn't tell whether he was seeing things or not.

As they started along the corridor and a fresh wave of nausea hit the enlister, a group of Nova soldiers appeared from one of the junctions ahead and opened fire. Kurcher found himself thrown to the floor as Broekow and Hewn flung themselves aside to avoid being sprayed with bullets. Both men returned fire with stolen assault rifles.

Kurcher looked around frantically, trying to locate cover. Rane was nowhere to be seen, he realised. Cursing, the enlister let off two shots at the soldiers and one fell.

'More coming,' yelled Hewn.

As four more soldiers appeared, a figure rushed from one of the junctions ahead. Rane raced across the corridor in front of the soldiers, catching them by surprise. One man's head rolled as another found his weapon knocked from his hand. Before they could react, Rane had vanished into the opposite junction.

As bullets bounced off the floor and walls around him, Kurcher knew one would have his name on it sooner or later. Hewn's luck held as a bullet ricocheted off his bionic arm and Broekow was as accurate as ever, making sure he struck a target with each burst.

To their relief, Angard was suddenly upon the soldiers. Men were flung in all directions as he ploughed into them, smashing skulls and breaking limbs with his bare hands. One soldier managed to fire a single shot that hit the giant in the thigh. Angard didn't even flinch as he lifted the terrified Nova man off the floor and smashed his head into the ceiling twice. Brain matter rained down on the biomech as he continued his rampage.

When most of the Nova force lay dead or badly wounded, Angard had barely broken a sweat. He stepped over them. At the same time, Rane emerged from one of the junctions and threw aside the uniform he had been wearing.

Kurcher found himself being scooped up by one enormous hand and looked into Angard's one good eye. When he saw how dilated the crim's pupil was, he knew he wasn't the only one suffering withdrawal.

'I can walk,' Kurcher told him. What he meant was he needed to regain some dignity and being carried back to his ship would have been difficult to live down.

Angard didn't respond, but placed him down nonetheless. As he did, a metal bolt struck the biomech in the side of the neck and a surge of electricity burst from it. Angard roared and reeled backwards, clutching his head.

'Seems freaks like him are easily subdued by shock treatment.' Espina appeared from a nearby junction, flanked by two soldiers. Both were holding heavy tasers.

'I wouldn't recommend it,' Kurcher told her, fighting off the nausea again.

Angard lunged towards the commander. A second bolt hit him in the chest and stopped him in his tracks. Four more soldiers stepped into view behind Espina. A moment later, another squad turned the corner behind Kurcher, blocking in the enlister and the crims.

'Working with crims, Davian,' tutted Espina, raising her pistol. 'And quite infamous ones too. I didn't think I'd ever see the day.'

'Trin, you need to let me go.' Kurcher allowed his instinct to take over. 'No more bloodshed.'

'Unfortunately, you've just added to your list of crimes by killing more of my men, so I'm not feeling particularly warm-hearted right now. Plus, your crims here planted explosives on my ship coincidentally near key systems.'

'You need that code.'

'I'll work it out once you're gone.' Venom was beginning to seep into her tone.

Rane stepped forward. 'Commander, you need to understand what is truly going on here. If you kill Davian, you lose the opportunity to return home. Are you happy condemning your crew to that fate?'

Espina eyed him warily. 'I've heard a lot about Edlan Rane, including the fact you're full of shit. You've killed quite a number of Sapphire Nova men and women, so I'm glad Davian brought you here. I get to kill several birds with one stone.'

'Are we going to get this over with?' asked Hewn impatiently. 'Or do I have to listen to this bullshit much longer?'

Angard finally wrenched the first bolt free of his neck, spasming as the second shocked him again.

'Put that beast down,' Espina ordered two of her soldiers.

A wiry figure limped between the Nova men and Angard. 'You must lay down your arms, all of you, for the Lord is watching and knows your sins.'

Kurcher groaned. 'Fuck's sake. Who let him out?'

Rane shrugged. 'Choice had managed to escape his bonds and was working to hack the *Kaladine* again. I thought it best to keep an eye on him rather than let him hijack your ship finally.'

'Only that's not Choice,' muttered Broekow.

Espina laughed. 'This must be the preacher from Harper.' She looked to her men. 'Fine, shoot him too.'

Maric waved his book in the air and pointed at her. 'You are weighed down by your sins. It is you who must repent first and be cleansed in the eyes of the Lord.' He then cast his eyes over the approaching Nova soldiers. 'Whoever pulls their trigger condemns themselves to an eternity in Hell.'

When they hesitated, Espina's face reddened. 'What are you fucking waiting for?'

At that moment, two things happened: Angard pulled the second bolt from his chest with an agonising cry; a single shot was fired from the airlock, the bullet driving deep into the neck of one of the Nova men.

Kurcher saw Frost, Oakley and D'Larro emerging from the *Kaladine*, weapons in hand. He didn't realise his pilot was such a good shot.

As Espina and her men took a few seconds to react, the crims seized their opportunity. Hewn opened fire on the soldiers behind, sending them diving for cover. Broekow fired a shot almost from the hip that took one man in the centre of the chest. Angard lashed out and knocked two off their feet. Maric's expression melted into a grin as he pulled a knife from beneath his dirty jacket and plunged it into the throat of the nearest soldier.

Kurcher saw Espina take aim at Angard. As she pulled the trigger, Rane's sword swept up and sent the pistol spiralling into the air. Before she could react, he slashed the blade through her upper thigh and she let out a piercing scream as she toppled backwards.

The enlister shot one Nova goon in the back as the unfortunate man turned to face a raging Angard. He then saw Frost and D'Larro walking side-by-side up the corridor, letting off random shots at the nearest blue uniforms. The medic was using a razepistol, but was not the best shot.

283

Occasionally his shot struck someone in the shoulder or arm, spinning them around and instantly setting the limb on fire. Most of the time though, bursts of heat seared past them, scorching the walls or floor.

With Hewn and Broekow keeping the soldiers behind at bay, Kurcher and Rane made their way to where Angard was pummeling the Nova men into a sickening red pulp. The biomech had been grazed by several bullets and blood was running down his face from a gash across the forehead. It just made him look more fearful.

Kurcher hesitated when he saw Espina slouched against the wall, her face pale as she clutched the deep wound. Maybe he should take her with them. D'Larro could patch her up and then he would be able to spend time persuading her to leave Nova and join him. As he headed for her, a particularly bold soldier leapt from the corner behind them and opened fire, narrowly missing Kurcher and forcing Broekow flat against the wall to avoid being hit. One rogue bullet found its way through the carnage, passing Choice as he drove his knife into another man's groin and then speeding between Frost and D'Larro. Oakley shrieked as it struck her in the lower right abdomen and Angard instantly froze, watching her fall to the ground.

The brave Nova man's success spurred his comrades on and they pushed forward. Behind them, more soldiers were arriving.

Kurcher couldn't see any way out of the situation now. There were too many to take down. Hewn and Broekow were retreating towards him, aware that the soldiers' confidence had suddenly risen, and Rane was already heading back towards the airlock.

He checked his ammo. Enough to take another couple of Nova pricks with him.

There was a bestial roar as Angard charged along the corridor, nearly knocking Choice flying. The giant crim's teeth were clenched and his eye was wide. There was no mistaking the furious frenzied state of a deranged biomech.

As he thudded past Kurcher, the soldiers instinctively opened fire. Despite being hit several times, Angard launched himself forward and began tearing into them with a terrifying bloodlust.

Kurcher looked down at Espina, who shook her head at him. 'I have to do my job, Davian. You don't understand what the Nova board are like. I can't...'

Behind him, Broekow shot the only soldier left standing between them and the airlock.

'If they're anything like the Taurus board, then I do understand,' Kurcher told her. 'All a bunch of pompous pricks.'

'No, they're worse. They won't stop until the other corps are dead and buried. They want total control at any cost. The fleet is growing...' She flinched as she tried sitting up straight. 'More ships than you realise. Libra aren't the only corp lurking in the shadows.'

Kurcher could feel the nausea coming on again; his head was starting to swim badly. Angard's feral yells and his victims' dying screams lanced through his skull.

'Listen, Trin. One last chance. Come with us now and leave all this shit behind.'

She gave him a scathing look. 'You always were a persistent little fucker.'

'So?'

'I have to do my job,' she repeated. 'Going against them would be...'

A pistol fired just behind him and Espina's head snapped back before she crumpled lifelessly to the floor.

'Enough talk, Davian,' Frost said decisively, lowering her gun and turning to walk away.

Espina's dead eyes stared through Kurcher as he swept her fringe over to cover the bullet hole in her forehead. No time for sentiment. She certainly wouldn't have been too bothered had their roles been reversed.

Kurcher glanced back to see Angard disappear around the corner in pursuit of the Nova squad, leaving a pile of mangled corpses in the corridor. When he headed for the *Kaladine*, he saw D'Larro and Rane carrying Oakley through the airlock, with Frost following. Broekow and Hewn were covering their escape.

He suddenly realised something was amiss. 'Where the fuck's Choice?'

~

'This is not the path we should be treading.'

Maric had no idea where he was. The corridors all looked the same and panicked voices were calling out from all areas of the ship. He could smell smoke in the air too and that only served to remind him of Earth, when Taurus Galahad flushed out the Revenants with fire. He had been lucky to survive. His mother was perhaps lucky *not* to survive.

'Shut your mouth, preacher.'

Choice wished he could stab the weakling and end the constant whining, but he needed to focus on the task at hand. The *Huntress* was not unlike other assault vessels he had studied the schematics of over the last few years. He knew it had both small escape pods and much roomier lifeboats, the latter reserved for officer use. He was having trouble recalling which level they

285

were on.

'If we jettison into space, we will starve and die,' Maric said. 'I don't understand what we are doing here. If we had stayed on the *Kaladine*, Enlister Kurcher would have ensured our safety.'

Choice had to laugh at that. 'He would have given us to Taurus or killed us eventually. I was only useful in keeping that freak Angard subdued if he went off his rocker again and you... well, you were good for a distraction back there, but that's it.'

Nova soldiers rushed past the end of the corridor. There was the sound of distant gunfire.

'You are mistaken.' Maric leant against the wall for a moment as his knee threatened to buckle. 'By losing us in this maze, you are condemning us to certain death.'

'No, I'm not. All I have to do is get off this ship and I'll survive.'

'*We'll* survive.'

Choice rolled his eyes. 'Whatever. Just pipe the fuck down until I locate a lifeboat.'

He stumbled on, occasionally hiding to avoid those in blue uniforms. He wished he had taken one from a body before he had hobbled away from the fight; there hadn't been time.

'Rane knew you'd run.'

Choice sighed. 'Jesus, for someone who hardly utters a word, now I can't shut you up. Listen, that bastard freed us only to use us as fodder in that free-for-all back there. He clearly expected them to shoot both of us. If I'd been closer to him, I would've gladly severed his spine.'

Maric shook his head. 'No, he is a better man than you believe. He gave us a chance to decide our own fate, but you took the wrong path. It's not too late. The Lord will forgive you.'

'Enough of the God shit.' Choice pointed at a junction. 'That's our path and it leads to your fucking salvation.'

He grinned when he saw the escape pod airlocks. 'Not exactly the comfort of a lifeboat, but it'll do for one.'

'For two,' Maric reminded him.

After a few seconds, Choice had opened a pod up and was settling into one of four seats inside. A moment later, he hacked the surrounding systems and managed to activate the launch sequence. At the same time, the *Huntress* listed slightly, signalling that one of the explosives the crims had planted had caused more damage than expected.

'What happens next?' asked Maric, feeling completely lost.

'We take our chances,' Choice replied.

'I'll pray for us both.'

The preacher's words made him smile yet again as he accessed the files locked away in the depths of his app tech. As data began scrolling at the top of his vision, he issued the command to launch the pod and soon found himself hurtling away from the *Huntress*. He had to make sure he didn't get too close to the battle raging further out in the system, where the second assault ship was struggling to repel their unknown attacker.

'What is this I'm seeing?'

Choice shrugged. 'Just some data I managed to download a few days ago. Thought it might come in handy.'

Maric turned to peer out of one of the tiny windows. He found he couldn't stomach the spinning stars. At least the pod's artificial gravity kept him from vomiting.

'Lord, watch over us as we venture into the unknown,' he began, closing his eyes. 'I fear we shall not see familiar suns again, but I trust in you to protect us.'

'Try praying silently,' Choice suggested, finding the preacher's frequent interruptions more irritating than he ever had before. 'Besides, it's me who will save you, not that joke of a God.'

'Say what you will.' Maric remained calm. 'I fear you and I will remain lost together as we have been for so many years already.'

The thought gave Choice a jolt. 'Eternity with you? I'd rather shoot myself in the head.'

'Do you have a gun?'

'Shut the fuck up.'

'Did you bring any food or water?'

'You know I didn't.'

'Then I will continue praying for our souls and for your sins to be forgiven when the time comes.'

Choice looked out of the window. He didn't get queasy like the preacher. He caught sight of the *Kaladine* still attached to the *Huntress*, then his attention was snagged by the vast machine that came into view. At that moment, he wondered whether he had made the right decision. If his instincts proved to be his undoing, nobody would ever find the escape pod and he would die listening to Jaroslav's ramblings.

Maric patted his own hand. 'At least I am not alone.'

~

Kurcher slammed his hand against the mechanism, the resulting vibration shuddering through his body and only aggravating his aches.

'Are you listening to me?' came Frost's voice in his ear. 'It won't seal from this side. The *Huntress* locked it when it first opened.'

'So what's the best course of action?' His voice came out as a feeble croak.

'You're going to have to break the lock. Go through to the *Huntress* and blow it.'

Even his drug-starved brain knew what that meant. 'If I plant an explosive on the lock, it could blow a hole in our inner seal. I'm not about to be sucked out into space after going through all that.'

'It's the only way,' she stated. 'Either that or we stay attached to them for the foreseeable future. We still have work to do on the engine, but it shouldn't take long with Rane down there already. I'll head down to help him once I've finished in the cockpit.'

'And our *friend* out there?'

'Looks like he or she has done enough to leave the *Kaban* floundering. No doubt they'll be heading our way soon.'

Kurcher scratched at an internal itch. 'I don't trust whoever it is. If Santa Cruz sent them, chances are they might just destroy us.'

He tried to focus on what exactly would happen if he blew the airlock seal on the *Huntress*. It would definitely damage the *Kaladine*'s outer door. As long as the inner seal held, they would survive.

'I'm on my way,' he muttered, shuffling as fast as he could along the corridor.

He located several of the small Taurus explosives and recalled how just a single device had blown apart the *Beck's Fire*. After he left storage, he glanced into the rec room and saw D'Larro tending to Oakley. The medic spoke calmly to her as he continued to wash her wound.

'Alive then.'

D'Larro looked over his shoulder. 'She was lucky it passed straight through and didn't hit anything vital. You on the other hand look worse than she does.'

He didn't dignify that with an answer and headed back to the airlock. As he stepped through to the *Huntress*, making sure he had his revolver to hand, he cast his eyes over the remnants of the fight. Bodies were scattered near the first junction and at the far end, their blood streaking the walls and pooling across the floor. The odd limb could be seen detached from its body. For a split second, Kurcher felt lucky to be alive; the bile rose in his throat at that

288

moment and he vomited again, only just missing his boots.

Wiping his mouth, he began trying to attach one of the explosives to the airlock mechanism. As he fumbled with the explosive, a gunshot echoed along the corridor. He nearly dropped the device in surprise.

A huge figure trudged into view, blood dripping from his hands. As he got nearer, the enlister could see Angard's entire torso was covered in gore and viscera. The biomech's face was red, his cloudy eye standing out white against the blood.

'Oakley?' Angard's voice was almost a whisper.

'She'll be fine. Bullet went through her. D'Larro's patching her up.'

Angard nodded and leaned against the nearest wall. Kurcher then realised how much of the blood belonged to the giant, seeping from more bullet holes than he could count.

'There are more coming,' Angard told him. 'You need to go.'

Kurcher had no idea how the crim was still standing. 'I have to blow the lock. Get onboard and I'll...'

'No.' Angard pointed a broad finger at the airlock. '*You* need to go. Give me the explosives.'

'Don't be a fucking hero.'

Angard gave a deep rumbling laugh. 'Don't be a fucking idiot. Look at me. My drug supply has run dry so my brain will shut down shortly and leave me like some rabid animal. Besides, my body will succumb to these wounds once the final dose in my veins is spent. Just get Tara to safety.'

Kurcher finished attaching one explosive to the lock before priming all of the devices and handing the rest to Angard.

'Set to go off at the same time,' he said. 'Make sure you're far enough away from the airlock, otherwise you'll take us with you.'

Angard grunted. 'Understood.'

'I know you and I never saw eye-to-eye, but...'

'That some sort of joke?' growled the crim. 'I don't need comforting. Just fuck off.'

Kurcher wasn't sure what he was about to say. Comfort was not something he gave to anyone. With a shrug, he headed swiftly through into the *Kaladine*. As he turned to close the inner door, he saw Angard already striding back up the corridor.

'Any message for Oakley?' he called.

Angard didn't look back. 'Just that this was what I wanted. No more pain, no more drugs, no more freak.'

Kurcher closed the door and made his way to the cockpit, activating his

289

comms app as he slumped into his seat. 'You may want to hold on to something.'

The explosion tore a hole in the hull of the *Huntress* where the airlock had been and the force sent the *Kaladine* reeling away as hoped. Warnings flashed on the screens around Kurcher, stating that the outer door would not seal properly. Fortunately, the inner door was holding firm.

Angard's explosives devastated the interior of the assault ship as the starboard hull buckled and a great rip opened up. As the *Huntress* drifted away, listing badly, Kurcher could see bodies spinning through space among the debris.

The *Kaladine* steadied itself, but was still too close to the doomed Nova vessel for Kurcher's liking. The only thing he did like was the fact they were two more crims lighter. Was Choice floating out there too somewhere?

'Justyne, the engine?'

'Any minute,' she replied.

As he rubbed at his eyes and tried to shake the feelings of withdrawal, Kurcher caught sight of the alien library still silently waiting nearby. His mind raced. Everything they had just gone through on the *Huntress* was because of this machine. All he could think was that it had better be worth it.

Before he could take stock of what he was doing, he had entered the activation code given to him by Santa Cruz.

As the *Kaladine* received a torrent of indecipherable data, the machine's slow spin came to an abrupt halt. Kurcher's jaw dropped open as the dark fishbone began moving away from them. There were still no apparent engine ports; no lights flicking on.

Santa Cruz had said it would remain where it was and open the wormhole to Berg. Why the fuck was it suddenly moving with purpose and where was it going?

'We've got to move, Justyne.'

The machine picked up speed, hurtling away from both suns. It faded in and out of view, camouflaged against the void, before its hull caught the faint glow of the binary stars.

'We still aren't a hundred per cent,' stated Frost. 'But we have enough power for now.'

'I need manual control.' Kurcher leapt across to her seat.

'I'll be there in...'

'Now,' he snapped.

As he engaged the engines and turned the *Kaladine* to follow the machine, another wave of nausea struck him and his stomach twisted painfully. His

290

eyes watered as he was forced to swallow what had just bubbled up into his mouth. When he wiped them clear, he saw a wormhole opening just ahead of the library.

Santa Cruz had no intention of letting them return, the lying prick. It looked like Kurcher had signed their death warrants after all.

The new gateway stretched to accommodate the machine, forming a perfect circle in space; a hungry mouth eager to swallow the fishbone whole. No jump point Kurcher had ever seen even came close to the size of the monstrous portal ahead, and yet it seemed extremely stable.

As the machine entered, Kurcher pushed the engines as hard as he could. The edges of the wormhole began to dissipate quickly, signalling its imminent collapse.

'You're going to pull her apart,' cried Frost angrily, storming into the cockpit.

When she saw the dark structure vanish through the wormhole, her demeanour changed and she leant on the back of the seat.

'We going to make that?' Kurcher wiped a bead of sweat from his forehead.

'Give me control and we might,' she replied, noticing his ashen complexion.

Kurcher didn't let on just how relieved he was when Frost took back control of the ship. He almost fell into the other seat as he fought to battle the continuing withdrawal. Frost said something to him, her voice sounding distant. When he turned to look at her, the cockpit spun and he plunged into unconsciousness.

~

The whole situation was too messy for Winter.

He prepped his stalker to engage the fusion kick the engineers had warned him about, making sure he was buckled tightly into the seat. He had not anticipated purposefully inducing the kick; it was the only way he could possibly reach the closing wormhole. The machine had long gone and the *Kaladine* had somehow found the power to get through. He *had* to make it. There was no way he would end up stranded in some rogue system. The fact his ship had no cryo capability was playing on his mind.

Behind him, the *Kaban* had begun to slowly follow. The assault ship would be lost. The Nova officers and soldiers on board would then have the inevitable discussion as to how the hell they would get home. Perhaps they would try to salvage what was left of the *Huntress*, stealing her cryo equipment and fusion cells. Perhaps they would simply lie down and accept their fate.

As his secondary systems shut down temporarily and the short countdown to the kick began, Winter tried and failed to relax. He was too tense. He could sleep in the ruins of a city while Revenants roamed the streets, he could rest while gunfire rang all around him, but there was no way he could relax until he was back among the systems he knew.

The fusion kick catapulted the stalker forward, pushing Winter back hard into his seat. All he could do was watch as the rapidly fading wormhole loomed and hope that Santa Cruz wouldn't soon be explaining to the Taurus board why Saul Winter had not returned.

Enlister-class vessel *Kaladine*
Alscion system

'I'm surprised he hadn't passed out before.'

'He's a tough son-of-a-bitch, I'll give him that.'

'Why did he activate it?'

The voices swam through Kurcher's head. They sounded familiar but distant. One sounded like Trin, another like Beck. He already had the screams of the Cobb victims bouncing around his skull. He didn't need other voices haunting him.

'Has he come through the worst of it?'

'He'll probably suffer symptoms for some time yet. That Parinax is nasty stuff.'

Was that his mother talking to his father? He could hardly recall what their voices even sounded like.

'We need a plan.'

'The plan is to get the fuck out of here.'

'Davian needs to see this.'

Why wouldn't they just shut up and let him rest? The Parinax always kept them at bay. He needed a hit. That would silence the dead nicely.

'I think he's awake.'

Fuck. He knew whose voice that was.

He forced his heavy eyelids open and found himself squinting up at the ceiling. A bright light did its best to blind him. A youthful face appeared over him.

'Welcome back,' D'Larro smiled.

'Fuck you.'

'He's fine,' came Broekow's voice from somewhere nearby.

As he sat up, Kurcher felt as though he had just had ten shades of shit beaten out of him. His mouth was dry and he could taste something rancid.

'How long was I out?' he asked, swinging his legs off the rec room table.

D'Larro moved to help him but was shrugged off. 'An hour or so.'

Kurcher looked around at the faces surrounding him. 'What're you all staring at?'

Rane wore his usual wry smile. 'Glad you've pulled through, Davian. Your expertise is needed again, I'm afraid.'

'Fine. I've got enough ammo left for everyone.'

D'Larro handed him a glass of water. 'Here. You need a lot of this to make sure your symptoms don't get worse again.'

Kurcher glowered at the medic. All of them knew by now that he was an addict, but he still didn't like them watching as he suffered. He was more pissed off at himself for showing weakness in the first place.

He downed the water. 'Where are we?'

'We made it back,' Broekow told him. 'Just not where you thought. We're in Alscion.'

Kurcher saw concern in the sniper's eyes. 'Why the fuck are we in Sigma Royal's home system?'

The crims glanced at one another. He realised Oakley was the only one not present. No doubt she was resting in the hold. He wondered whether anyone had told her about Angard's demise.

'Well, it looks like we're late to the party,' Hewn said, his expression hard to read.

Kurcher jumped off the table and stumbled out of the room. There was only one person who wouldn't be quite so cryptic when all he wanted was a straight answer.

Frost gave him a disappointed look. 'Not going to pass out on me again, are you?'

'No.' He was aware the crims had followed him. He couldn't be bothered to send them away. 'Give me the facts.'

'The machine jumped to Alscion. We made it through but it sped up and, as the *Kaladine* is running on a jury-rigged engine, we're lagging behind quite a way now.' She hesitated and took a long drag on her cigarette. 'Davian, it's on approach to Meta.'

Kurcher rubbed at his temple. Why would Santa Cruz give him a code that sent the library to Sigma Royal's homeworld? Something must have gone wrong.

'I don't want to stick around here. Especially after what happened on Kismet.'

'There's something else.'

He heard uncertainty in her voice. 'Go on.'

'I detected an unusual amount of chatter coming from Meta, so I picked some of the long-range comms up. They were calls for help. Someone attacked the planet's defenses.'

Kurcher hid his surprise well. 'Even more reason for us to leave the system. If Meta sent out a distress call, it won't be long before the entire Sigma fleet arrives. I'll send a report to Santa Cruz and we can get the fuck

294

out of here.'

'It *is* Santa Cruz,' announced Rane calmly. 'Don't you see what's going on here, Davian? He sent you out there to activate something completely alien; something we know absolutely nothing about. When you transmitted the code, it came straight here. At the same time, someone coincidentally attacks Meta. The commander has used you. No doubt he never expected us to return from that rogue system.'

'Taurus wouldn't target Meta,' said Kurcher, dismissing the notion. 'If they were going to strike out at Sigma, they would take the outer colonies first and reduce their fleet before even considering coming here.'

'So why is that machine heading there?' Hewn asked. 'Doesn't make sense, unless it isn't a library after all.'

Kurcher turned to Frost. 'How long before it reaches Meta?'

'Less than an hour.'

'Get us in range so we can see what's going on.'

'You can't be serious.' Hewn's metal fingers wrapped around Kurcher's forearm. 'I was all up for trying to use that thing for our own benefit before, but we should cut our losses and go. You just said that Sigma's fleet will be on their way.'

'Take your fucking hand off me,' Kurcher growled. 'I need to know who attacked Meta before we leave. We don't have to get near the planet to find that out. I hadn't thought you to be a coward.'

Hewn bristled. 'We're all still armed. If you're incapable of making sound decisions thanks to that drug-fucked brain, maybe someone else should step up.'

'Pipe down.' Broekow pulled the Echo pirate away. 'Let's not spiral back into name-calling and threatening.'

'Sieren's right,' Rane said. 'As is Davian. It makes sense to find out who's behind the attack and perhaps discover just why the machine has gone there. We've survived this long by working together, even if nobody particularly likes each other.'

'That's an understatement,' muttered Hewn.

Rane scowled at him. 'You need to know just as much as we do, Jaffren. We've come this far and lost Bennet, Horsten and Maric on the way. They died so we could get to this point.'

'Ercko was murdered by Choice and Angard chose to go berserk on the *Huntress*,' stated D'Larro. 'All three were fucked up in the head and that's what got them killed.'

'If Bennet hadn't tried raping Tara and been knocked unconscious by

Horsten, Choice wouldn't have had the opportunity to extract the data implant.' Rane waved his finger at Kurcher. 'Data that Davian then got his hands on, leading us to that excursion out beyond the edge of the Milky Way. Choice played his part on the *Huntress*, believe me, and Horsten gave his life quelling the flow of Nova soldiers, helping us escape. Now do you see?'

D'Larro shrugged. 'You have a way of making a bleak situation seem poetic.'

'Fuck's sake.' Kurcher spun to face them. 'You're not my crew. You're not here to offer advice. D'Larro, go look after Oakley. The rest of you can leave too.'

All the crims except Broekow vacated the cockpit. The sniper crossed his arms and leaned against the wall.

'I'm staying. I want to see.'

As the *Kaladine* pursued the machine, Kurcher returned to his seat alongside Frost, neither of them uttering a word. They both knew that whatever was happening at Meta was big. Maybe not bigger than finding an alien structure lurking in deep space, but the ramifications were still huge.

'Not only is it the Sigma Royal homeworld,' Kurcher began suddenly. 'There is also a high military presence on Meta. They train soldiers there and have a number of shipyards. Seems a bad place to target for a surprise attack.'

'I heard Sigma had at least three guardians in orbit,' added Broekow. 'Plus there are frequent transport journeys to and from Cenia.'

Kurcher had always wanted to fly past Meta's frozen twin; a ball of gleaming white with veins of blue ice reaching out across the surface. Frozen worlds like Cenia were beautiful to behold and often too dangerous to visit.

When Frost finally announced they were in scanning range, all three leaned forward in anticipation as an image appeared on the screen before them.

'Jesus.' Broekow shook his head in disbelief.

Meta was a small sphere of green, brown and blue near the centre of the display. The scans highlighted several ships in orbit and listed their names: *Ravenedge, Tucana, Mantheus, Exodus, Arcturus, Requiem*.

There was no need to highlight the vast black fishbone shape which had settled into a higher orbit, like some hellish moon.

'What the fuck is Santa Cruz doing?' Kurcher knew nobody would have an answer, although Rane would probably have something to say if he was there.

Dense fields of debris were also spotted in orbit of Meta. The *Kaladine* was quick to confirm they were the remains of hull plating; the question of where Sigma's guardians were was answered.

'Six assault ships would struggle to take out three guardians,' Broekow pointed out.

Frost took a final drag on her cigarette. 'If there were three. Some of the data I'm receiving about the Taurus ships shows minimal damage. They must have had the element of surprise and hit the guardians with something powerful.'

'He's an intelligent prick,' said Kurcher, studying the screen closely. 'Santa Cruz would have timed this to perfection. Maybe one of the guardians was undergoing maintenance or maybe he arranged some distraction in another system to make sure Meta was left relatively unguarded.'

'There are still missiles being fired from the surface,' noted Frost. 'Coming up from Gibson most likely, but the assault ships are in such close proximity to one another that they can just swat them away.'

Kurcher's vision swam for a moment. He shook his head, as though that would sort out his problems. 'Mitchell would never have agreed to this. If the order had come from the board, why aren't there more Taurus ships here? At last count, there were just over a hundred assault vessels in the fleet and yet there are only six here.'

'Surely he wouldn't go behind their backs with something this huge?' Frost looked to both men for an answer.

Broekow could only offer a weak shrug. 'He's not exactly a balanced individual. Maybe he's trying to force their hand in the war.'

'No.' Kurcher got shakily to his feet. 'He's got his own agenda. We need to go now and leave Taurus to deal with him, or Sigma when their fleet arrives.'

'Something's happening.' Frost's voice had taken on the shrill edge it so often did when she was nervous.

They watched as a soft blue glow began emanating from the two prongs of the machine, pulsating slowly. As the light intensified, there was an odd greyness among the blue. This continued for less than a minute until, in the blink of an eye, it shot down the black body and a silent beam was cast from the ridged cone directly at Meta. It was as though a gigantic torch was being switched on to illuminate the planet. When the sickly light hit the atmosphere, it began seeping in all directions.

Kurcher couldn't tell what the hell was happening, but he knew one thing for certain: that machine wasn't a library.

As the light spread alarmingly fast across Meta, the alien structure

297

powered down and hung over the planet like a sinister satellite.

'Are you getting anything from Meta?' Kurcher asked Frost.

The pilot found it hard to tear her eyes away from the screen. 'Comms have just ceased. You're going to want to hear this though. It's all we could get from the last message.'

Kurcher wasn't sure he did.

... lit up the sky... trying to get grounded ships off the surface... what the hell?... reacting with oxygen... how is this possible?

'This is bad,' muttered Broekow.

Kurcher felt like puking again, but he wasn't sure it was down to his withdrawal. He knew they needed to leave Alscion; a part of him wanted to know what they had just witnessed.

'Davian.' Frost interrupted his thoughts. 'Santa Cruz is requesting to speak with you now.'

'Be ready to get us the fuck out of here,' he told her. 'I'll speak to him but no visuals.'

Frost glanced at Broekow before opening the link.

Kurcher wasn't feeling much like holding back. 'Care to explain what's really going on, commander?'

'I have to say I'm impressed.' Santa Cruz sounded elated. 'I never thought to hear from you again.'

'You sent us out there to die, you fucking bastard. I should've realised, but you're obviously adept at spinning lies. We made it back though, which is more than I can say for the Nova ships who pursued us.'

'Two fewer to destroy later.' Kurcher could tell the commander was smiling. 'Actually, I'm glad you survived. It gives me the opportunity to thank you for delivering the *Grail* to me. You should feel proud.'

'Of what?'

'This moment right here is the beginning of the end for the other corps. It starts with Sigma Royal and the others will follow suit.'

'What have you done?'

Santa Cruz laughed. 'You didn't really think I'd send you to activate a data library, did you? Our finds in Coldrig and across the known systems weren't lies, but when I found out that such a powerful weapon was just waiting out there somewhere, I had my research teams focus on working on the activation and command codes.'

Kurcher glanced at the screen. Meta was now pale blue and grey.

'Mitchell didn't authorise this,' the enlister said.

'Of course not. He and the rest of the board are weak. While they sit and

298

discuss how to secure the future of Taurus Galahad, the other corps are growing in strength and poised to attack our outer systems. My find will win the war for us and show that we need decisive action to take control of the galaxy.'

Frost waved to get Kurcher's attention and pointed to one of her screens. It showed two of Santa Cruz's fleet breaking orbit, accompanied by a number of smaller ships. Frost indicated silently that they were heading in the direction of the *Kaladine*.

'Congratulations, Kurcher.' The commander's tone was almost mocking. 'Your actions have just cleansed Meta. Now it's ripe for recolonisation.'

'What?' Kurcher's eyes widened. He was starting to shake again.

'It took Sigma Royal decades to populate the planet. We've wiped it clean in minutes. It's quite mesmerising to watch actually, poisoning a planet. In a few more minutes, that alien poison will begin to break down, returning the air to normal. The race that created it were ruthlessly efficient. I respect that.'

Kurcher staggered away from the controls, suddenly needing to get out of the cockpit. At the same time, Frost severed the comms link.

'I'm heading for the jump point,' she announced.

Kurcher didn't hear her. He barged past Broekow and out into the corridor. Rane and Hewn appeared but couldn't get anything from him so ran for the cockpit. As he neared his quarters, Kurcher found D'Larro standing before him.

'You look terrible.' The medic reached out for his arm. 'Nausea? Headache? How're you feeling?'

Kurcher pulled away. 'I've just been tricked into committing genocide. How do you think I feel?'

D'Larro frowned, then reached into his pocket and produced a small needle. 'You're feverish. Here, this will calm you down so you can rest.'

Kurcher caught his hand. 'Don't come near me, you murdering piece of shit.'

Before D'Larro could react, the enlister slammed his other fist straight into the medic's face, knocking him to the floor. The needle slid away as Kurcher pounced on the stunned crim and began raining down punch after heavy punch.

'I should never have brought you all on board,' roared Kurcher. 'You should all be dead.'

He continued beating the medic, trying to drown out both the voices that had haunted him for so long and the several million new screams now echoing in his head.

299

'My mercs are the best the corp has to offer, sir.'

Santa Cruz tapped a finger against his bottom lip. 'Prove it then.'

Byrne gave a curt nod. 'They will catch up with Kurcher and destroy the *Kaladine* before you have broken orbit.'

'That I doubt. We will soon be leaving Meta behind, then will replenish fuel and ammunition before moving on to our next target. Both yourself and Thomadakis will rendezvous with the rest of us before we jump.'

'Jump?' Byrne grimaced, which made him even uglier. 'I thought we would target Cenia, sir.'

Santa Cruz raised an eyebrow. 'Wait in Alscion much longer and we run the risk of being attacked by Sigma forces. You have your orders, commander.'

'Yes, sir.'

When Byrne's image vanished from the monitor, Santa Cruz turned to peer out at Meta. The poison delivered into the atmosphere by the *Grail* had gone, leaving the world looking healthy from their vantage point in orbit. On the surface though, bodies would be lining the streets of the various colonies and no doubt the local fauna would have died too. Santa Cruz hadn't really considered that before now, that his weapon would also wipe away the indigenous species. In fact, the entire ecosystem of Meta had been obliterated. That may mean it would end up being classed as a quaran.

The most important fact was that Sigma Royal's board were gone. Panic would set in throughout the mourning corp shortly, weakening them even further. Their fleet may have still been out there, but with no orders coming through, their highest-ranked officers would try to take charge.

Apart from Kurcher making an unexpected reappearance, the plan had gone relatively smoothly. He had seemingly lost Winter, but there were plenty more agents to utilise. The difficulty now would lie in jumping from system to system and using the *Grail* before retaliation. He was sure to receive a summons from the Taurus board too at some point. That would be easily ignored.

He stepped so close to the window in his quarters that his nose was nearly pressing against it and looked across to the alien machine. He had named it *Grail* as the term had been used so many times it just seemed apt. It was the most beautiful thing he had ever seen; a unique structure capable of killing his enemies swiftly. What other secrets it might hold, he had no idea. They had only really scratched the surface of what it was capable of. There were

300

questions, of course. Why would the race who built it make it so massive? Before they disappeared, had they used it on other worlds to conquer and colonise? It seemed likely that someone capable of building such a weapon would be ruthless, cold and eager to wipe planets clean of life. It made him wonder why they vanished, if that was the case.

Some of the dialect still being deciphered pointed to this race using an expansive language, the human vocabulary seeming miniscule in comparison. It also told him the *Grail* was something more than just a weapon, but the research continued. He planned to try boarding the machine once the initial cleanse was complete and hoped it would ultimately show him where to find more artefacts. One thing he did know was that the poisonous material created within it could be calibrated to affect different atmospheres, reacting with a number of elements as it had with the oxygen on Meta.

His mind wandered back to Kurcher eventually. The enlister had been useful, fulfilling his mission to activate the machine. The fact Sapphire Nova had sent two ships after him and both had been lost was just an added bonus. Now though, he had to ensure Kurcher did not escape and blab what had happened to others. The enlister had probably already sent a message to the Taurus board. Santa Cruz could handle them.

With the *Exodus* and *Arcturus* in pursuit, and Byrne's mercenary ships quick enough to catch up with the *Kaladine*, he hoped that was enough. Kurcher had proven more resourceful than he had given him credit for, after all.

'Commander.' Connolly's voice was as grating as ever. 'You have a comms link coming through.'

'From who?' He hoped it wasn't already Mitchell or Lenaghan.

'Saul Winter.'

A broad smile spread across his face. 'Patch it through.'

~

Frost ended the kiss abruptly and gave Broekow a shove.

'Not the right time,' she scowled, returning her focus to the task at hand.

If it hadn't been for Hewn and Rane standing directly behind them, she probably would've been more receptive. She knew it was just a reassuring kiss anyway. Broekow knew better than to distract her while they were being pursued by two assault ships and a swarm of mercs.

'Are you sure about this?' she asked, checking their time to the jump point.

'Absolutely,' replied Hewn confidently. 'Phoris is nice and close.'

301

Broekow turned to the two crims. 'Yeah, but Cerberus? I've only heard bad things about it.'

Hewn offered a crooked smile. 'All true. That's why it was the perfect place to hide a supply cache.'

'Remnants of the colony,' assumed Rane, nodding.

'Actually, no. Several miles from the ruins.' Hewn gave the killer a wary look. 'Is there anywhere you don't know much about?'

'I recall hearing the stories about Cerberus when I was young. The destruction of a Sigma colony there and the hundreds of people who died. In fact, my father once told me that, if I didn't behave, he'd send me there.'

'The reports never covered everything,' stated Hewn, peering over Frost's shoulder at her screens. 'We can hide there for a short while, but mustn't linger.'

'No sign of Kurcher yet?' Broekow asked them all.

Frost reached for her pack of cigarettes, finding just two left. 'He'll surface soon, I'm sure. Just needs to get his head straight.'

'I've been guilty of a lot of things throughout my forty-one years,' Hewn remarked. 'But I can't comprehend being responsible for killing an entire world. That's hard to come back from.'

Frost shook her head. 'Santa Cruz killed those people, not Davian.'

'Justyne's correct,' Rane agreed. 'Davian will realise this soon enough and then he will be thinking clearly again. It shouldn't be long before the Parinax is out of his system.'

Frost hated it when Rane backed her up. Several weeks ago, the mere thought of any crim standing in her cockpit with weapons at their side would have been laughable. She was surprised they hadn't already cut her throat and taken control of the ship, but Broekow might have had something to say about that. She was glad he was there and couldn't wait until they could be alone together again.

'How's D'Larro doing?' She blurted the question out as she lit a cigarette.

'He won't be quite as pretty anymore,' replied Broekow. 'Kurcher worked him over pretty good.'

'And Oakley?'

The sniper shrugged. 'Haven't looked in on her, but I'm sure she and D'Larro are licking their wounds in the hold. Just as long as they don't hold any grudges.'

Frost took a drag. 'What do you mean?'

'Kurcher was the last of us to see Angard alive,' Broekow explained. 'For all she knows, he put the big guy down and left him behind. As for D'Larro, there's something still not right about him.'

'There's nothing right about any of us,' muttered Hewn. 'Why worry about him?'

Broekow glanced at the pirate, noticing how their beards were starting to look scarily similar. 'He murdered patients in order to study death and yet, since being caught by Kurcher, he hasn't displayed any of the psychotic traits we were led to believe he has. In fact, he has been more than willing to help tend to our wounds.'

'He's not stupid,' said Rane. 'Regan knows that he has to behave, otherwise Davian will just execute him. He's curious, not psychotic.'

'Well he certainly can't shoot for shit.' Hewn gave an amused snort. 'Twice I had to duck when he was firing that razepistol.'

Rane could see the concern on Broekow's face. 'I'll keep an eye on him.'

'Like you kept an eye on Ercko?' Frost blew a cloud of smoke into the air. 'Or Choice?'

Rane tilted his head as he regarded the pilot. 'They had their uses before the end.'

An alert appeared at the top of Frost's vision. 'Oh fuck. There's a guardian at the jump point.' A tiny emblem dropped into view. 'It's a Taurus ship.'

'Course it is.' Broekow sighed loudly. 'Santa Cruz thought of everything.'

'Well we'd better think of something,' Frost stated bluntly. 'I'm not pitting the *Kaladine* against it.'

'No secret weapon?' Hewn was grasping at straws.

'A single fusion cannon and a pair of gats won't help us,' she replied.

Rane straightened his jacket, picking a random hair from the sleeve. 'You've piloted this ship through worse situations, Justyne. We have faith you can get us past another guardian.'

Frost looked back at the killer, who gave her one of his confident smiles. Perhaps she wasn't giving herself enough credit. The *Kaladine* had survived several tough encounters during their fucked-up job, but she was at the helm each time. She wasn't just some co-pilot on a planethopper anymore.

Then again, Rane was a master manipulator and she was loathe to listen to anything coming out of his mouth. He had *watched over* Ercko, whispering in the sadistic rapist's ear, and the man wound up dead. He had persuaded her to let Maric out just before they rescued Kurcher on the *Huntress* and she had seen him speaking with the preacher before leaving. Now Maric and Choice were gone too. He had even given himself up to Kurcher on Rikur, despite the horrific crimes they had been pursuing him for. Everything he did had some greater purpose, but those he manipulated tended to end up dead. What

303

exactly was he after?

She turned back to her console. 'Best you all go strap in then.'

~

D'Larro prodded at the bruising around his eye, flinching as a bolt of pain shot along his nerves.

'I'd have thought a medic would know better.'

He glanced at Oakley and shrugged. 'Pain is a strange symptom really. Was it not for the receptors in our brains, we wouldn't feel anything. An anaesthetic numbs the pain by blocking the signals being sent to the brain. Some people actually like certain types of pain. It's all very interesting.'

'To you maybe.' She flinched as she shifted on her bedroll. 'I could do without it though.'

'Sorry, here's me complaining after you've been shot.'

'Seems I'm your best patient. Not sure I ever thanked you after the Eidolon overdose.'

'No need.' He looked around the quiet hold. 'We're both in the same boat, so to speak. It'll do you good to walk around, by the way.'

Oakley cast her eyes to the vacant bedroll alongside her own. 'Did you see him?'

D'Larro knew exactly what she meant and had been waiting for her to bring it up. 'When you were shot, he went berserk. He ploughed through those Nova soldiers like they were made of paper.'

'And at the end?'

'I'd returned here with you by then.' The medic considered his next words carefully. 'He was a greatly misunderstood man and he cared for you deeply.'

'He lived every day with that pain you talk about,' she explained. 'I knew he had grown tired of it, but I was selfish and wanted him to stay alive so he could keep protecting me.'

D'Larro couldn't show his disappointment. He had wanted so badly to be able to examine what made Angard tick; to see how the scientists on Shard had effectively taken him apart and pieced him back together with the biomech tech. He had been gutted when he realised there wouldn't even be a body to study. Still, he wondered how many more like Angard there were locked away back on Shard and how he could ingratiate himself with the medical community living there.

He suddenly realised Oakley was watching him with a suspicious eye. 'He had his own mind. Looking after you gave him some sense of purpose I

304

suppose.'

She shuddered and rubbed at her arms for warmth. 'He's the only man I will ever truly miss. Probably because he never looked at me in *that* way.'

D'Larro nodded but looked away. Most men on the *Kaladine* had the willpower or the sense to know better than to look at her with lust in their eyes. Ercko had and he ended up a corpse with no penis, jettisoned into space wrapped in a bloodied sheet.

As Oakley closed her eyes, trying to get some more rest, he went back to prodding at the bruises Kurcher had given him. He remembered Hewn and Rane hauling the enlister off him, but it had taken a while for his senses to return fully. When they had, he mentally noted how Kurcher had looked in his state of withdrawal.

For D'Larro, everything that was happening was now a learning experience. He had not seen many addicts up close before so watching Kurcher's struggle to keep his demons at bay with Parinax had been fascinating. The withdrawal symptoms were even more interesting.

Getting to examine Ercko's body had made him happy too. Understanding exactly how the man had died, studying the tissue and blood. It was work that gave him a chance to continue his research into death.

Even tending to wounds sustained by Oakley, Kurcher and Maric had brought a smile to his face. He understood that not everyone could grasp the motives behind his past crimes; eventually he hoped his findings would broaden the minds of all.

'What're you thinking about?' Oakley's eyes were open again.

'Home,' he lied.

'Titan?'

'Titan station. Wondering how the research is going there.' Seeing her inquisitive expression, he continued. 'It used to be a hub for geological teams, but the medical facilities were getting better year-on-year. Before I left, they were studying the effects some med apps had on the human body. A couple of years ago, defibs were still occasionally malfunctioning and shocking people while their hearts were still beating. Titan Station took on a project to study why. At the same time, they were looking into upgrades for painkill apps. It was slow going. I often wonder how everyone is getting on back there. Then I remember there's no way I could ever return, so there's no reason to dwell on it.'

He looked across and saw Oakley's eyes were closed again. Was she pretending to be asleep to avoid his ramblings? He couldn't blame her.

This time, he watched her for a while. Here he was, sleeping in the same room as the highborn daughter of the Oakleys. She was certainly a privileged killer, but scarred just like everyone else on the *Kaladine*.

Since Kurcher picked him up on Summit, he had often thought just how surreal the situation was. It was even stranger that he felt almost at home on the enlister's ship, among a group of crims like this. Admittedly Kurcher made life on board difficult, but he preferred it to the panicked colonies of Amity or the claustrophobic station orbiting Titan.

Hewn's voice echoed down the stairs, followed by Rane's soft tone. Those two couldn't have been more different and yet they too were now working together. A pirate known for establishing a fast-growing organisation whose network of smugglers, drug runners and mercenaries had now expanded far beyond their humble beginnings, and a serial killer who tortured his victims before murdering them.

D'Larro closed his eyes, concentrating once more on the painful twinges across his face. It wasn't long before he was asleep, experiencing the same dream he so often did of delivering a speech on the findings of his research to the leaders of the five corporations and receiving a standing ovation from the medical community for his work.

Enlister-class vessel Kaladine
Phoris system

Finding out that a guardian was lurking near the jump point had been a surprise. The three Sigma Royal assault ships suddenly appearing had been an even greater surprise, and a welcome one.

Frost gave Kurcher a sideways glance. The enlister had resurfaced just after they managed to make the jump to Phoris and, despite his pallid appearance, he seemed to be back in the land of the living.

'How long?' he asked.

'Just over an hour.'

They were on the final approach to Cerberus. Kurcher had kicked up a stink when he heard what they were planning. He bluntly told them he had no desire to visit another quaran, but when Hewn explained what was there, Kurcher grudgingly agreed. He knew the benefit of raiding an Echo supply cache and Cerberus was also the best place to hide, until they were satisfied nobody was pursuing them.

Kurcher rubbed at his sore eyes. 'I still can't believe you didn't wake me. I'm the one in charge here.'

'Well, I knew that beating up D'Larro and sweating out that poison in your system would have worn you out.' The corner of Frost's mouth curled. 'I don't think you were in any state to be making decisions.'

'So instead you took orders from Hewn. For all we know, he's got men on Cerberus.'

'Doubtful,' she muttered. 'Besides, I didn't take orders from him. What he said made sense and it was a better option than staying in Alscion and getting blown apart.'

Kurcher drew in a deep breath and choked on it. 'Did you get the message off to Taurus?'

She nodded. 'Whether or not the board choose to believe us is debatable.'

'Still no sign of pursuit?'

'None.'

Kurcher looked as though he couldn't believe it. If he had been coherent when the *Kaladine* approached the jump point though, he would be somewhat less concerned.

Frost recalled the feeling of relief as the red and black assault ships arrived in Alscion. The Taurus guardian had positioned itself so that the

307

Kaladine had a narrow gap to pass through and, despite the crims telling her to take the risk, she wasn't prepared to try it. As they began veering away, the Sigma Royal vessels arrived and the guardian seemed to hesitate. A moment later, there was a barrage of fusion fire and missiles that caused the guardian to turn away from the *Kaladine* so it could retaliate.

As Frost had guided the ship past the battle, the guardian focused its multiple weapon ports on one assault vessel and punched a hole through it that would have surely killed everyone on board. Some of the crew may have managed to seal themselves in a corner of the burning ship, hoping to survive, but when the fusion cells ignited and tore it in two, Frost knew they were all dead.

The sheer power of the guardian had been terrifying to behold. Perhaps that was why Santa Cruz had chosen that particular ship. It was clearly not standard spec. The *Sentinel*. She would remember that name for the rest of her life.

By the time they jumped, the guardian had taken damage but the reinforced hull plating was holding firm and it was still lethal. She wondered whether the other two assault ships were now just pieces of debris floating in space near the gateway.

'I need to prep,' announced Kurcher, getting out of his seat.

'Prep what exactly?'

'We're about to land on one of the most dangerous worlds in known space. I need to take stock of ammo and I need to understand from Hewn exactly what we can expect to find down there.'

'Fair enough.' She gave him an approving nod. 'Good to have you back.'

'Whatever.'

As Kurcher left the cockpit, Broekow stepped inside and immediately placed his hands on her shoulders. This gave her reason to smile. An hour after they had reached Phoris, those hands were busy in her quarters.

'He seems better,' noted the sniper. 'He can stand at least.'

'With the drugs all but worn off now, his stoic resolve is back in place. What happened on Meta will still be eating away at him though.'

'It's not the sort of thing you can just forget about.' Broekow leant down and kissed the top of her head. 'Have you considered what we'll do after Cerberus?'

'I haven't even considered what to do when we land yet.'

'Taurus aren't just going to let us walk away,' he said, sadly. 'You know that.'

Frost looked up at him. 'One situation at a time. First we survive Cerberus,

308

then we go see Solomon Rees. He'll protect us.'

This time, Broekow's lips met her own. 'Yes, ma'am.'

She playfully tugged his beard. 'Don't call me that. Go keep an eye on Davian, will you? I'd hate him to go suicidal on us.'

'He's stronger than that.'

'He used to be.' She returned her attention to piloting the ship. 'I'm not sure he'll ever be his old self again.'

'His old self was drugged up most of the time,' Broekow reminded her. 'Maybe the clean Kurcher will be an improvement.'

He squeezed her shoulder one last time and then headed for the door.

'Oh, and by the way,' she called after him. 'Trim that fucking beard. It's starting to give me a rash.'

'Yes, ma'am.'

He was gone before she could respond. The smile returned to her face as she thought about how to make him pay later. The situation may have been dire, but allowing herself moments of pleasure ultimately helped her focus. Not that he was just there to be her sex slave.

As Cerberus grew larger before them, she enjoyed the time alone in the cockpit. When they had first headed off to apprehend the seven crims, the rules were simple: nobody except herself or Kurcher in the cockpit. Now the remaining crims came and went as they pleased. Whenever she considered this, fear clawed at her gut. She was allowing serial killers inside her personal space; deranged people who could surely snap at any time.

The thought made her shudder. Instinctively, she locked the door. Broekow was sane and Hewn seemed to be too, unless he was an excellent actor. Still, the pirate wouldn't hesitate in leaving them behind to get back to Echo and she fully expected him to do so once they reached his supply cache. He wouldn't risk the organisation he had built up over the last nineteen years and would know that Santa Cruz could turn his new play thing loose on the Echo Expanse.

Oakley had seemingly been quite affected by what had happened since they picked her up. Her usual response to what Ercko did would have been to make the man suffer before killing him, but Choice had stolen that opportunity away from her. Angard's death was more her fault than anyone else's as her being shot had caused him to fly into that rage. Maybe she was blaming herself and that was why she was so quiet. Then again, she was nursing a wound that must have hurt like hell. Without Angard around to watch over Oakley, Frost worried that one of the men on board might end up sliced open.

D'Larro seemed only too eager to help and she had to agree with Broekow. There was still something off about the disgraced medic. She didn't trust him. It was the eyes. They were cold, even when his smile was warm. She had half expected them to find Oakley dead after he treated her, but again Rane had vouched for D'Larro.

Rane troubled her more than any of the others. When he had vouched for her to get them past the *Sentinel*, she realised just what he was doing to all of them. His manipulations had dictated events and nobody had given much thought to his occasional whispers. He had started breaking down Kurcher's defences from the moment he had saved the enlister and given himself up. The beatings he had suffered at Kurcher's hands were probably planned too.

She lit a cigarette, having started on her final pack. The irony wasn't lost on her that she was as addicted to smoking as Kurcher had been to Parinax. She too was about to run out of her drug.

As the *Kaladine* closed on the side of Cerberus facing away from the Phoris sun, Frost blew smoke rings into the air and couldn't stop her mind returning to Rane.

He had persuaded Kurcher to keep him alive and had proved some worth when it turned out his information on the missing Taurus personnel was true. He hadn't fought back when Kurcher struck him. Instead, he kept speaking softly to the enlister, sowing the seed of doubt in his mind.

When they went to apprehend Hewn, it was Rane who persuaded Kurcher to take Ercko and Angard with them. Rane had ensured Ercko never left his side as the two of them caused havoc in Hewn's facility. If so, how did Ercko manage to get his hands on the Eidolon, allowing him to drug Oakley later on? That chain of events led to Ercko getting himself knocked out by Angard and gave Choice the opportunity to extract the implant.

Realisation struck Frost like a slap across the face. Rane had said the dead crims had their purpose before the end. She had almost forgotten that the killer had forced Kurcher's hand too by telling the rest of the crims the truth behind their enlisting, leading them to be ordered to the rogue system and the eventual activation of the alien machine.

Rane had manipulated everything from the start and was still doing so, but why?

'Fuck.' She had to speak with Kurcher.

As she went to stub the cigarette out, her pilot app alarm shrieked. A second later, a small but familiar ship came into view and the cockpit lit up green as it opened fire.

310

Earth
Sol system

Rees had read the message six times and still couldn't quite believe his eyes.

He poured himself a shot of brandy and downed it before turning to look out into the illuminated compound. Beyond the walls of the headquarters estate, darkness reigned, hiding the rest of the world and the horrors lurking in the shadows.

He checked his watch and wasn't surprised to find it was nearly midnight. The message had arrived on a secure personal link for his eyes only less than an hour ago, but time had lost all meaning as he pondered what was happening out in the Alscion system.

With Lenaghan having left for Galt just that morning, Rees was the most senior member of the board still on Earth. He had to make a decision on what action to take.

He started reading the message once more, paying particular heed to Kurcher's description of the machine Santa Cruz had sent him to find. If true, the commander had kept the single most important find in the history of the human race a secret, taking it upon himself to attack the rival corps in a bid to knock their very foundations from beneath them. And he did it all wearing the proud colours of Taurus Galahad.

As he finished reading it again, noting Kurcher's risky move to hide on Cerberus, Rees threw down his data unit in disgust and strode to his console. After studying the logistics of their entire fleet for a few minutes, he located the *Victory* in Lincoln. No wonder Lenaghan felt safer on Galt, with their flagship patrolling the system.

Rees requested a secure comms link with Mitchell and tapped his finger on the table as he waited. When he received a decline from the *Victory*'s system, he cursed and went to another screen.

'Where the hell are you?' he asked, studying the list of enlister ships.

They were all out on assignment and were so widespread that he opted to send them the same message. He waited until his console gave him the command to start recording.

'This is Solomon Rees. You are ordered to cease your current assignments and return to Sol immediately for an urgent briefing. I appreciate you may be close to catching your intended target, but this has to take priority. Make all haste in getting back.'

He didn't know how Mitchell would react to the news. His first thought was that the general would take his fleet to intercept the *Requiem* and order Santa Cruz to stand down. Would Mitchell risk stepping into an enemy system though and potentially being drawn into a fight?

While the military minds decided how best to deal with their rogue officer, Rees would take his enlisters and rendezvous with Kurcher. He had to protect his assets and Kurcher had just become his most important.

Enlister-class vessel *Kaladine*
Phoris system

The *Kaladine* was being drawn in by Cerberus, the dark red and brown surface looming before them like the jaws of the hellhound itself.

Kurcher clutched at the wall of the corridor as his ship continued to thrash violently from side to side, like some fish out of water. It was clear that the attacks had destabilised their propulsion and the engines were barely managing to register now. He had seen ships left for dead in a planet's gravity well before. None of them survived.

'Justyne, report,' he yelled over the rattling hull.

There was still no answer. He continued clawing his way along the corridor, fighting to stay upright each time the ship spun.

The initial attack had been focused on the front of the *Kaladine*, damaging key sensor bundles hidden beneath the plating. The fusion beams from their assailant licked at them like a whip instead of blasting them open. It was precise and planned; how could they have closed on them without Frost knowing?

Ahead, Broekow staggered from the rec room, a trickle of blood running down his chin from a cut to his cheek. His forehead was bruised. Rane and Hewn appeared a moment later, neither seemingly injured.

'If Cerberus pulls us down, the ship will go into a death spiral,' Hewn cried.

'Frost will steady us.' Kurcher hoped her silence meant she was busy regaining control.

Rane brushed past the enlister, heading the opposite way. 'I'll fetch Regan and Tara from the hold. I suggest you get the lifeboat ready.'

Kurcher watched him go, cursed, then carried on to the cockpit. Behind him, Broekow and Hewn eagerly followed.

Finding the door sealed, he entered the access code. It started to slide open, then came to an abrupt halt less than a third of the way along. The smell of smoke drifted from within, but it wasn't from any cigarette.

'Help me,' he called, steadying himself as the floor shifted again.

Hewn's metal fingers grasped the edge of the door and his bionic arm did the rest, allowing Kurcher and Broekow to rush inside.

The cockpit was a mess. The control console flickered where an explosion had torn up through it from the destroyed sensors below. The force had snapped the seat Kurcher so often sat in and that was now rolling on the floor. Pungent smoke had filled the room, meaning the *Kaladine*'s emergency ventilation systems were no longer working either. Even the swaying view of Cerberus was distorted by a crack down the screen. Fortunately, it had held so far.

Frost was still in her seat, tapping frantically at controls that were still operational while talking to the ship through her app.

Kurcher grabbed her arm. 'Can you...?' His voice faltered as he looked down.

The explosion from the sensor cluster had wrecked part of the console directly before the pilot, but the sheer jolt of the attack had brought down one of the supports from the ceiling. That support had landed on her legs. Blood was oozing out onto the floor.

When Frost turned her head, her eyes were drowning in tears, her face blackened by the smoke. Her bottom lip was trembling, as though she were freezing.

'Hewn, help move this beam.' Kurcher gave the pirate a scathing look. 'Now.'

'No,' she cried out, grabbing his hand and pushing it away. 'The *Kaladine* is fucked. In a few minutes, it'll enter the atmosphere and plummet to the ground.'

Kurcher gave her an incredulous look. 'So then, more reason to get you out.'

'Listen to me, you frustrating prick. I'm holding the ship together through auxiliary systems but they're failing. You need to get away before they do and I have to keep them in check until then, otherwise you wouldn't even be able to peel yourself off the walls.'

'Use your app,' he ordered, making another attempt to grab her.

Frost recoiled, grimacing in pain. 'I said no. Jesus, you're the most stubborn man I've ever known. I can't hold it just using the app. Besides, you move that support and I'll bleed out fast.'

Kurcher froze. If it were anyone else in that seat, he wouldn't hesitate leaving them behind. He couldn't lose the only person he truly trusted.

'Sieren?' called Frost, holding up her hand.

Broekow, who had been in stunned silence until that moment, pushed Kurcher aside and grasped her hand. 'We can work together to get you out. With D'Larro's help and Hewn's strength, we could...'

'Don't.' She squeezed his hand. 'I was attracted to you because you're not an idiot, so don't prove me wrong. If you don't leave the ship now, you all die.

314

I can't let that happen.'

'You could still land this shitheap,' he said, forcing a smile.

Frost scowled. 'I need you to get them away now.'

'She's right,' came Hewn's voice behind them. 'Leave her to do her job.'

As the pirate left the cockpit, Kurcher shook his head and pushed Broekow out of the way. 'You don't get to give the orders, Justyne,' he growled, trying to pull the support off her.

Frost gave Broekow a knowing look and the sniper wrenched Kurcher around to face him.

'Prep the lifeboat,' he told the enlister. 'You have always listened to her so hear what she's telling you now. She's not going to survive this, but she can make sure we do.'

Kurcher wanted to swing a fist at him. Instead he nodded and gave Frost one last lingering look. 'I'm sorry. You deserve better than this.'

'Just another day as Davian Kurcher's pilot,' she said through gritted teeth. 'Now fuck off.'

He made his way to the door. Glancing back, he saw Broekow kiss then embrace her. She whispered something in his ear, then pushed him away too as the *Kaladine* once again shuddered violently.

Kurcher and Broekow reluctantly left the cockpit, finding the others waiting by the lifeboat airlock. Once Kurcher had let them in, he settled into the pilot seat and drew a sharp intake of breath before releasing the clamps.

The lifeboat would have spiralled into oblivion was it not for Hewn stepping up to offer a strong hand in stabilising it. Kurcher had to admit the pirate was better suited to getting them to the surface, so he relinquished the seat.

They were greeted by angry storm clouds and the occasional bolt of red lightning as they descended. Twice Hewn had to give them a steeper angle of trajectory to avoid ploughing straight into lethal layers of swirling grey and red. Both times, Kurcher noticed Oakley and D'Larro grasp the arms of their seats in sheer terror.

After what felt like an eternity battling the storm, the lifeboat broke through the clouds and levelled out. Feeling the ride become smoother, Kurcher dared a glance out of the screen and could only see a brown mass below. He couldn't even tell what he was looking at.

'Cerberus is covered with several species of plant that forms those vast forests,' Hewn informed him. 'A delightful blend of brown and red flora that looks as horrible during the daylight hours as it does at night. It's going to be dark for another few hours yet around the cache.'

315

'That good?'

Hewn shrugged. 'Good for hiding from those corp fuckers. Not so good for staying under the radar of the indigenous species.'

Kurcher rubbed his eyes. They were still sore from the smoke billowing into the cockpit of the *Kaladine*. He looked back at the underside of the clouds, wondering whether Frost had managed to stabilise the ship after all. He had tried to reach her via the comms app since they left her behind, but was only greeted by an ominous static. He still couldn't believe they had actually left her. Surely there was something more he could have done.

'There.' Hewn pointed at a mountain to the east, its peak barely visible through the gloom. 'We're setting down at the base.'

Rane stood, patting a devastated Broekow on the shoulder. 'Can we expect to see any mawhounds there?'

Hewn shook his head. 'Not unless I call them.'

'Mawhounds?' D'Larro sounded less than impressed with the name.

'Imagine large dogs with a head like a huge Aridis rock grub.' Rane smiled as he painted the mental picture. 'They wiped out the colony Sigma Royal created here in one fell swoop.'

The medic looked uncomfortable. 'And how many of these things are there on Cerberus?'

'They're the dominant lifeform here,' Hewn remarked. 'They've bred across most of the land masses. Eaten damned near everything else.'

They reached the mountain quickly, circling it once so that Hewn could face the lifeboat west. This, he explained, would allow him to fit the ship through a tight gap in the rocks that led to the supply cache.

As they neared the entrance, Kurcher caught sight of something in the distance. 'Holy shit.'

The others gathered alongside him and together they watched as a fireball hurtled through the night sky, trailing a dark smoky tail. The flames spluttered out suddenly, revealing the red-hot hull of the *Kaladine* as the ship plummeted to the surface. Far to the west, she disappeared from view. An orange glow lit the horizon moments later.

Kurcher turned away. That was it then. The *Kaladine* was gone, as was Frost. She had held it for as long as she could and perhaps had even hoped to recover from the attack for a time. He wondered whether she had died at the same time as her beloved ship.

By the time Hewn had guided the lifeboat safely through the alarmingly narrow fissure in the rocks and set it down, a grim silence had fallen. Even Rane chose to remain quiet. Surprisingly, it was Broekow who spoke first. 'It won't be long before those Taurus mercs arrive and start searching for us.'

'I've got some customised conflector tech among the supplies,' Hewn stated, heading for the airlock. 'That should keep them at bay.'

'They will go to the crash site first, so it gives us some time to prepare,' added Rane.

'Can I ask an important question?' Oakley stood with some help from D'Larro. 'What exactly *is* the plan now?'

Kurcher looked around at the faces of the five crims. How the fuck did he end up in some hole on a quaran world with them?

'I haven't got much else to lose,' he said, tapping the grip of his revolver. 'I aim to get to Santa Cruz and wipe the insane smile off that sadistic fuck's face.'

~

Winter was pissed off.

The harsh Cerberus wind was biting at his face, bringing with it tiny sharp fragments of the resilient plants making up the nearby forest. The sky was evil; jagged red forks tearing through the grey. He almost expected to see brimstone raining down on them.

As he scanned the darkness around the site for any sign of movement, the mercs from the *Exodus* were making their way back towards him. Twenty-one men and three women had been sent after the *Kaladine*. All were just hired thugs, only interested in money. Winter had met them for the first time when they all landed and he already disliked the selfish pricks.

'No sign of anyone,' grunted the merc leader, a brawler named Vokes.

Winter was barely able to hide his contempt for the man. 'You checked the entire area?'

Vokes glanced back at the burning wreckage of the *Kaladine*. 'No tracks in or out. Nobody came to check for survivors.'

'No tracks out?' Winter wanted to laugh in his face. 'You really expect anyone to walk away from that?'

'Careful now,' bristled Vokes. 'You don't want to go upsetting us.'

Winter turned his back on the mercs, looking towards their ships. He didn't want to be out in the open much longer. The crash would have caught the attention of the local wildlife and he didn't plan on hanging around when they showed up.

'The lifeboat landed somewhere nearby,' he said, having to raise his voice to be heard above the howl of the wind. 'It'll be best to split your ships up to search the region from here to that mountain in the east.'

317

'We'll find them.' Vokes carried an air of arrogance when he spoke. 'We've tracked people in worse conditions than this.'

Winter's cold eyes turned to the *Kaladine* once more. His attack had managed to bring it down, but he was still angry at himself for being so distracted by Vokes' message that he failed to notice the lifeboat until it had gone. Then again, there was no way he was going to land on Cerberus on his own, so he had to wait for the mercs to catch up.

He blinked, trying to moisten his sore eyes. He was exhausted, having only managed sporadic sleep since returning from the bizarre trip beyond the edge of the galaxy. He could still see that alien machine when he closed his eyes. He wished he had been in a position to determine what it was doing in orbit of Meta, but Santa Cruz had ordered him after Kurcher immediately. The commander had a lot of explaining to do when he finally returned to the *Requiem*.

Something in the *Kaladine* reacted to the flames, sending a burst of orange and blue into the air with a loud crackle. The fusion cells had already exploded when it hit the ground, rending the hull apart from the inside.

'Pity.' Vokes was standing alongside him. 'Quite a nice ship.'

'Unique,' Winter muttered, too quiet for the merc to hear.

As they headed for their respective ships, eager to be away from the wrath of Cerberus, Winter's comms app picked something up. As he studied the data, he peered to the east. A buoy had been activated some distance from their position and it carried the lifeboat insignia.

It didn't take long to get to the site. Winter saw the faint light emitted by the buoy well before they reached it. A quick circle of the region picked up debris nearby too, scattered among the brown flora at the base of the mountain.

After signalling Vokes to investigate the site, Winter pondered the situation. If the lifeboat had been destroyed, was the buoy activated automatically as a distress beacon or did someone survive to switch it on? Kurcher wouldn't have done so as he knew he was being hunted. Perhaps it was one of the criminals desperate to be saved.

A thin strip of light had appeared on the horizon, signalling that whatever dawn broke on Cerberus wasn't far off. He wanted to be away from the quaran before anything woke up and found them poking around.

By the time he landed his stalker, Vokes' mercs had spread out from the buoy in all directions. Some were picking through the waist-high plants, trying to avoid the barbs that jutted from thick stems like small knives. Others were walking across the brown, unhealthy-looking grass, kicking at

318

the scrap lying around. Vokes and one of his mercs had clambered up onto the rocks, peering into cracks in the mountainside.

Winter had his rifle in hand as he made his way to the buoy, which was lying on its side surrounded by scorched metal fragments. When he crouched down to examine it more closely, he realised the wind wasn't quite as bad and he had to be thankful for that. Still, the stormy sky continued to roil overhead and he wondered whether Cerberus ever enjoyed a day of tranquility.

He heard the odd noise first. A steady thumping had begun somewhere near the site. To begin with, he thought it was the sound of some monstrous denizen making its way towards them, but it was too rhythmic; too artificial.

'What the fuck's that?' he heard one merc ask.

'It's coming from over here,' cried another from among the foliage.

Winter looked back down at the buoy, then at the debris. *Clever bastards.*

'Vokes, get your people back to the ships,' he called, hoping the merc could hear him.

An eerie howl echoed from the darkness around the site, quickly answered by others. Winter immediately sprinted for his ship as the mercs slowly realised what was happening.

The first mawhound loped into view, moving with such speed that the closest man didn't even have time to be terrified. He managed to fire off one shot before the beast smashed him to the ground and its horrific jaws clamped over his head. There was no muffled scream, no thrashing. Just a sickening, dull crack as it crushed his skull and devoured the contents.

The mercs opened fire as more of the creatures slunk from the shadows. The hungry roars of the mawhounds drowned out all other noise as they homed in on their prey.

Winter reached the rise where his ship sat and dared a look back. His breath caught in his throat when he saw just how many of the predators had been drawn to the site. They were emerging from all sides, ensuring the mercs couldn't flee into the night, their heads snapping open wide as they bellowed their intent.

Winter saw Vokes on the rocks running along a narrow ridge, occasionally firing down into the swarm of beasts below. The other merc who had been up there was nowhere to be seen; there was a bloody smear where he once stood.

A woman screamed and Winter saw her being dragged into the night by two mawhounds, one on each leg. One of her associates stood too long watching this and was savagely torn apart by three more beasts.

Winter had seen enough. As he turned, two mawhounds appeared,

319

stepping between him and his stalker. He hadn't appreciated just how formidable the creatures were until they were so close. Standing almost as tall as him, their bodies were covered in a thick reddish hide. Four strong legs each ended in a set of talons that reminded him of the lions found on Earth. Their heads were completely alien though, folding open four ways to reveal one great maw complete with serrated teeth. He couldn't see where their eyes were, if they had them at all.

With the screams of the dying mercs ringing in his ears, Winter prepared himself as the two mawhounds leapt forward.

~

'How do I know you'll be true to your word?'

Hewn flashed Kurcher an amused look. 'You don't. For everything you've put me through, I should be leaving you here to die like those poor bastards outside. I would too was it not for the fact that Santa Cruz and that fucking alien weapon pose a huge threat to Echo. Who do you think he would go after once he had wiped out the other corps?'

Kurcher couldn't argue with that and watched as the pirate prepped one of the two dusty ships they discovered waiting patiently inside the supply cache. Both were originally courier vessels, built with speed in mind, but Echo had kitted them out with small weapon ports.

'It's going to be a tight squeeze,' D'Larro stated as he finished changing Oakley's wound dressing. 'Five of us in one of those.'

'You don't want to go where I'm going,' Hewn told the medic. 'Bad people, bad attitudes. Hopefully the threat of a madman wielding a massive fucking planet killer might persuade them to help though.'

'Or maybe they'll just decide to cut your throat and go hide in a corner of the galaxy somewhere.' Kurcher wouldn't put it past them. 'A chance to get rid of Jaffren Hewn once and for all.'

Rane emerged from the second ship, a light layer of dust covering his hair. 'Relatively sound little ships. Should get us where we need to go.'

Kurcher listened to a howl from outside the cave. Hewn had reassured them that no mawhound would get past the defences set up at the various entrances to the cave system, but he wasn't feeling particularly confident.

He had to admit though that the pirate was much more useful than he had anticipated. Removing the buoy from the lifeboat, scattering the debris and placing the device to draw the beasts had all been the pirate's idea. Hewn had even built the device himself years back.

'So where do we *need* to go?' Broekow asked Rane.

320

'We aim to help Davian take down Santa Cruz, do we not? We can't do that alone and I know people who will help. People who hate Taurus Galahad and would gladly jump at the opportunity.'

The corner of Broekow's mouth twitched. 'And why do we follow you? Why would you put your own life on the line?'

'Why would you?' countered Rane immediately. 'For the same reason. Santa Cruz holds the key to taking control of the entire galaxy, but that machine is an unknown entity. His researchers could find a way to unlock other facets, other ways to kill. Believe it or not, I value my life.'

'It's just everyone else's lives you don't value.' It was a statement that turned all eyes on the sniper. 'Those who listen to your whispers tend to end up dead. I'm not going to be another of your fucking puppets.'

Rane held his hands up and smiled. 'Merely a suggestion, Sieren. Please, if you know someone who could help us get to and kill the commander, tell us.'

'We hardly have time to stand here debating,' Kurcher snapped. 'Hewn, get going. The rest of you get on board that ship. I'm done with Cerberus.'

Hewn gathered the last of his supplies and gave a nod of acknowledgement to the rest of them before climbing through the airlock.

'Wait.' Oakley pushed past D'Larro. 'I'm leaving on that ship too.'

'As he said, you don't want to go where he's going,' Kurcher reminded her.

Hewn's face appeared at the airlock. 'True. If I arrive with a beautiful woman on my arm, you can imagine what they'll say, or do.'

Oakley's expression darkened. 'Haven't you realised yet that what you see isn't the true Tara Oakley? She's a much uglier person who holds only contempt for every man she sees.'

'I know who you are.' Kurcher waved a hand at Broekow and D'Larro. 'I know that, under different circumstances, you would have seduced and killed them. I also know that you're not fucking stupid, so why go with Hewn?'

'I want no part in a war,' she said calmly. 'And that's what you're heading towards. Hewn can drop me off on Cradle and that's where I'll stay. I've seen enough in the past weeks to make me realise that the whole fucking universe is insane. I've been drugged and fondled by a rapist, shot during a gunfight on an assault ship out in some alien binary system and am now standing on a quaran where the wildlife wants to kill anything that moves. I want to go home.'

Kurcher's instinct was to say no. The enlister in him still struggled letting any crim go, but she was right. Those sparkling blue eyes she tried to use on

321

him when they first met had dulled. She was exhausted and hurt. Why not let her disappear to tend to her wounds? She would be no use in the fight to come.

'Come on then,' Hewn called, once again vanishing into his ship.

Oakley offered a curt farewell to Broekow, Rane and Kurcher, but whispered her thanks to D'Larro before following the pirate through the airlock as the engines fired up.

'Maybe I can help once I get to Cradle,' she shouted just before the door closed.

Hewn and Oakley left Cerberus several minutes before the others. By the time Rane had piloted them into orbit, the pirate's ship had gone.

Kurcher found Broekow staring out at the planet as they began to break orbit. The sniper still looked lost and angry.

'Time to look forward,' the enlister said. 'She wouldn't want you dwelling on what could have been.'

Broekow gave a derisive snort. 'Could? She *would* still be alive if not for you activating that fucking machine. Her death is on your hands.'

'I had to activate it to get us back. Santa Cruz killed her, just like he killed those people on Meta. He killed Ercko, Angard, Maric, Trin... they all died due to his lies.'

'But *you* accepted the mission in the first place.' Broekow pushed the long fringe from his eyes. 'The payment was too enticing.'

'It was,' Kurcher admitted. 'For both Frost and I.'

'I can glean some satisfaction that the one who shot the *Kaladine* down was among those left behind on Cerberus. I'll find further satisfaction when Santa Cruz is dead and when you...'

Kurcher knew what he was going to say. 'Don't worry. I'm sure karma will make sure I get what's coming to me.'

They watched quietly as the quaran slipped from view.

'Who was he anyway?' asked Broekow. 'One of Santa Cruz's assassins?'

Kurcher gave a weak shrug. 'I'm guessing he had been tracking us from the start, hired by the commander to ensure I succeeded.'

'And to ensure we all died.'

Kurcher nodded. He wondered whether it had been the same man who helped him on Summit when Trin's goons attacked and who had fed them anonymous information at key times during the mission. He must have been a cold-hearted bastard to do all that and then shoot them down.

'Well he's dead now,' the enlister stated. Another corpse rotting on Cerberus.

With the quaran behind them, Rane opened up the full power of the engine and aimed the ship for the jump point.

~

The sky had turned a fitting blend of putrid pink and grey as the Phoris sun was on the rise, casting its light onto the remnants of the massacre.

Winter managed to limp the last few metres before leaning against the hull of his ship and looking nervously for any more signs of movement. His hand left a bloody imprint on the cool metal, smearing slightly as he turned left and right.

Behind him, the bodies of half a dozen mawhounds lay in a nightmare heap. Beyond that, the gruesome remains of the attack had already started to attract insects that were unfazed by the feeding beasts.

Winter stumbled inside his stalker and cursed the airlock for closing so slowly. When he fell into his seat, it was then the pain started its steady throb. Grabbing a nearby medkit, he set to work trying to bind his wounds.

His left hand had narrowly avoided being caught in one of the maws, but a tooth had sliced one finger nearly off and cut deep into his palm. His leg was probably fractured when another beast swiped him with a huge paw and sent him reeling. Luckily, he had managed to fire a single shot into the looming mouth as it moved to finish him. Pity that his rifle had been broken in the process.

Outside, he heard two mawhounds fighting over a piece of merc. None of Vokes' people had survived, not even the arrogant thug himself. Winter recalled seeing him being pulled apart by two of the creatures.

After bandaging his hand and tying a support to his leg, he administered a painkiller shot. When he reached down to his belt, he found that all his weapons had been lost. Even his knife was lodged in the belly of one of the dead mawhounds. He wasn't about to go retrieve it.

As his stalker rose from the surface, he had to consider his next move carefully. He had seen the two ships leave Cerberus and could try following, but his wounds needed to be looked at by a medic and couldn't be left to fester.

Seconds after he broke orbit, a confidential message arrived. The Taurus Galahad insignia indicated it was from the board. He couldn't help but laugh as he read it through. If only it had arrived a few hours previously.

Solomon Rees' rank meant that the orders issued by Santa Cruz were now defunct. That was quite the relief. Still, his business with the commander was not at an end yet, it seemed.

323

When he finally arrived back in the Alscion system, he found Santa Cruz's fleet there to greet him. Just behind them lurked the alien machine, making the assault ships seem tiny and insignificant. Winter noted fields of debris floating nearby; remnants of the Sigma Royal vessels. The *Sentinel* was there too, scorched and battered in places but still formidable.

Winter docked with the *Requiem*. Despite being ordered to the medical bay, he made his way to the command deck. He found Santa Cruz in discussion with his fleet officers via comms.

'Actually, Saul Winter has just arrived back,' the commander announced. 'I'll admit he's looked better.'

'Where are my mercs then?' came Byrne's voice.

Santa Cruz beckoned Winter over. 'What happened?'

'Cerberus happened,' he replied, bluntly. 'I shot the *Kaladine* down there and waited until the mercenaries caught up so we could survey the crash site. Unfortunately the native predators attacked us and I was the only survivor.'

'Kurcher?' The commander's eyes glinted as a smile began to spread across his face.

'Dead.' Winter hoped he sounded convincing. 'So are his pilot and the crims.'

'I sent over twenty mercs,' Byrne cried.

'They never stood a chance,' Winter said, shifting uncomfortably. 'I was just lucky to be near the ships when they attacked.'

'You have your orders,' Santa Cruz said, addressing his officers. 'Restock at Haskell then we jump to Flint.'

'Flint, sir?' Winter needed to remain bold if he was to get what he needed. 'I don't understand.'

Santa Cruz led him away from the command deck. 'You need those injuries seen to. I'll fill you in on the way to medical.'

When the commander didn't immediately volunteer any additional details, Winter reminded himself that he was in the presence of a dangerous individual. Santa Cruz could not be taken lightly.

It was a relief when he finally spoke. 'You know the importance of Straunia. Imagine the advantage we would have if Sapphire Nova's entire board no longer existed. Imagine the chaos in Nova's ranks if their homeworld was left as a clean slate, ripe for recolonisation.'

'It would tip the war in our favour.' This man wasn't just dangerous, he was mad. 'You've discovered information from that machine on how to do this?'

'You could say that.'

324

A creeping horror slowly began to take hold of Winter as he listened to Santa Cruz explain everything that had transpired on Meta. The broad smile on the commander's face was unsettling too.

'You killed innocent people,' Winter said, unable to hold his tongue. 'I get that you saw the Sigma board as a suitable target, but the colonists down there were nothing to do with the corp wars.'

'They were *all* part of it, whether they knew it or not.' The smile vanished. 'Loyalists dedicated to a Sigma Royal rule.'

Winter came to an abrupt halt. 'Even the children?'

'They would have grown up to be Sigma men and women, taught from an early age to hate the other corps, especially Taurus. With the *Grail*, I will eliminate the population of each corp's homeworld and win us this war within the next few weeks.'

'The Taurus board won't stand for this.'

'That's why I decided to do this myself,' Santa Cruz said, placing a supportive hand on Winter's arm and guiding him along the corridor. 'They're too slow to act. Our enemies will have increased their military resources tenfold by the time Taurus went on the offensive.'

'You realise that you'll be considered a rogue officer now... sir.' Uttering that last word felt wrong. 'A wanted man.'

Santa Cruz seemed to genuinely find that amusing. 'Nobody would dare take me on while the *Grail* is in my control.'

'They will try. They may even attack the machine itself or find a way to access it and sever your control.'

'There are several ways into the interior of the *Grail*,' stated Santa Cruz. 'All protected by defenses designed by those who built it.'

Winter took a chance. 'So how can you hope to fully control it if you can't get inside?'

'I never said I couldn't get inside,' replied the commander. 'In fact, once we have cleansed Straunia of all Nova presence, I intend on being the first person to ever set foot in an alien construct.'

'You don't know what might be in there. You'll need someone to help secure it.'

Santa Cruz looked pleased. 'I didn't think you shared my enthusiasm. If you join me, I'll see to it you reap the rewards. Your talents are wasted killing revenants on Earth anyway.'

Winter had to swallow his true feelings on the matter for now. The thought of all those lives being snuffed out so suddenly was one that would haunt him forever.

'I understand your reasons.' He had to tread carefully. One misplaced word could mean his own demise. 'I don't like that so many innocents have to die, but if it means an end to hostilities across the known systems, I'll stand with you.'

'Good.' Santa Cruz pointed to an approaching junction. 'Once you've been patched up and rested, I'll have a list of tasks for you.'

Winter just wanted to return to his ship and get off the *Requiem*. He felt like an insect flying too close to a web, with Santa Cruz the arachnid just waiting for him to make a mistake.

'Damn.' The Taurus agent blinked and put a hand to his eye, stopping again. 'Do you have people here who can repair implants?'

'Yes. What's the problem?'

'When I was struck by one of those beasts on Cerberus, it must've damaged my sight apps.' He made a show of wiping his eyes and grimacing before they continued. 'I have to admit that I am intrigued by your *Grail*. I take it your research team found a safe way inside then.'

Santa Cruz nodded. 'Whoever built it locked it up tight before leaving it in that rogue system. There are many aspects of the alien dialect we still don't understand. Activation, navigation and targeting have been our priorities.'

'When we finally enter it, will there be a command deck of some sort? Does it have docking pylons?' Winter delivered the questions with an excited tone.

'It's nothing like man-made structures,' Santa Cruz replied. 'No pylons, no well-defined airlocks. I can't even guess what the technology inside will look like.'

'How can you know where to enter then?'

'Just under the dome is...' The commander hesitated. 'Well, you'll see in time.'

Winter saw the door to medical at the end of the corridor and clutched suddenly at his eye again, this time faking a painful cry. He made sure he twisted his head away from Santa Cruz as they came to an abrupt halt.

'It'll pass,' he muttered. 'Just give me a minute.'

Santa Cruz was clearly getting impatient with the frequent stopping. 'I'll have the medics remove your implant. You don't want malfunctioning tech in your head.'

Using his visual sensors, Winter managed to key a basic message into his comms app. It was an upgrade not used by many, but useful when unable to utter a command. The message was sent to his stalker with an order to forward it to the confidential link Rees had used.

He turned back to face Santa Cruz, even managing to force some tears to wipe away. 'Apologies, commander.'

As they reached the door to medical, Winter hoped his message would be received and understood. He had no doubt that Santa Cruz would have him fitted with some sort of tracking implant once he was at the mercy of the med staff, monitoring his every move, so he needed to get something to Rees before that happened.

Santa Cruz guided him through the door and shoved him forward. 'Hold him.'

Winter found himself immediately grabbed by four uniformed guards. Behind them, med officers did their best to ignore what was going on.

'Commander, this is not necessary.' He tried to pull free; it seemed the four strongest guards had been chosen for this duty.

Santa Cruz closed the door. 'I'm afraid it is. You carried out your assignment for me without question and I sincerely appreciate that, but I can't be certain of your loyalty moving forward, especially in light of recent events.'

Winter took a deep breath to calm himself. 'I went beyond the edge of the galaxy to see this task done. I even travelled to Cerberus as soon as I returned, barely managing to escape the horrors there. I have fought assault ships and killed a lot of people for you. Surely this shows I can be trusted.'

'Perhaps, but it's vital there are no loose ends.' Santa Cruz pulled a knife from beneath his jacket and drove it deep into Winter's chest.

The agent stared in disbelief, shock alone keeping his pain receptors from going haywire. He had flown too close to the web after all.

'You said... you said...'

Santa Cruz wrenched the knife back. 'We both had to tell lies.'

Now the pain gripped Winter. 'You traitorous bastard. I'm an agent of Taurus Galahad.'

'And a supremely talented one too.' The commander smiled sadly. 'Another casualty of war though.'

Winter could feel the room spinning as his legs buckled. The guards released him and he crashed to the floor, gasping for breath. As darkness began creeping in at the edge of his vision, Santa Cruz's voice sounded distant.

'What a pity that Saul Winter died on Cerberus too.'

Cobb
Kalbrec system

Fuller couldn't stop grinning as he watched the awestruck faces around him.

'How many more storage units do you reckon are out there?' Marie asked eagerly.

He shrugged. 'Could be tens, could be hundreds.'

A pilot named Jennaut stepped forward to study the haul. 'Could be one.'

Fuller rolled his eyes at Marie. 'Ever the pessimist. You were part of the team when we found it.'

'Funnily enough, I know that,' Jennaut huffed. 'I'm just saying that we can't let ourselves get too hung up on the idea that Taurus had a load of hidden underground units they seem to have forgotten about.'

Marie waved a hand at the pile of goods. 'Even if there aren't any more, this is a hell of a find. Food, weapons, ammo, parts that can be used for ship repairs.'

'Not to mention filters we can customise for the water tanks,' Fuller added.

Jennaut held up an apologetic hand. 'Okay, okay, no need to go on. It's a good haul. A great haul. Cal's a bloody genius for spotting it.'

'Let's not go overboard.' Fuller still felt immense pride at being able to show something for the hard work they were putting in. 'Make sure it all gets used sensibly please. Keep thinking of the long-term plan.'

As engineers began taking the goods away, Fuller scratched at the thick stubble under his chin. He was in desperate need of a shower and shave, but there were more pressing matters to attend to, such as deciding on their next recon run.

Since testing out their fleet, they had managed to locate several small stockpiles of equipment left behind by Jefferson colonists, plus had recruited nine people found barely surviving on the surface. The Taurus supply unit gave them renewed hope and he was thankful that his ship had alerted him to its presence. It would have been easy to overlook otherwise.

'All I'm saying is that we need to watch them closely,' came Jennaut's concerned voice as the pilot walked alongside Marie.

Fuller knew he was talking about the recently-discovered recruits. Jennaut always had a problem trusting new arrivals. There was a good reason for that.

Four years back, one man had been found out among the nearby ruins and brought below ground. That same man attacked a group of engineers later that week, injuring Jennaut's son before being put down like some feral dog.

'They've gone through the psych tests and passed with flying colours,' Marie assured him. 'Don't think they've got a bad bone in their bodies.'

Jennaut gave her a wary glance as they approached Fuller. 'Yeah, sure.'

'Armed guards around the clock,' Fuller stated. 'As protocol dictates.'

'So what's the next move?' Marie asked. 'When exactly are we going to strike out from Cobb and find a *real* Taurus depot?'

'What's the point if we're finding things like this?' Jennaut waved a hand at the now-diminished stack.

'I have to agree with him,' Fuller said, expecting the sour face Marie pulled. 'When we do venture from Cobb, we'll need all the help we can get. Extra people, weapons and ammo will go a long way. Now we just need to find more fusion cells.'

Marie spied someone heading for them. 'Cal, be nice now.'

He knew exactly who it was before he even turned. 'I'm always nice.'

Rettin was wearing his usual stupid smirk and had greased his hair back. The cigarette hanging from his lips completed the look, which was classic Cretin.

'So, I'm going to have to steal the mother of my child away from you for a while,' the engineer told them.

Fuller hated the way he began most sentences with *so*. 'Hello to you too, Dale.'

Rettin winked at him. 'We know each other too well for pleasantries, old man. Hell, we'll pretty much be related soon once I marry Marie.'

Except he wasn't her father. 'What could be so important that you have to pull my partner-in-crime away at such a key moment?'

'Medical check.' Rettin held his hand out to her. 'Don't tell me you'd forgotten.'

Marie shrugged. 'Sorry, Dale. I got swept up in the excitement.'

'So the welfare of our unborn child isn't as exciting as a load of old supplies?'

Fuller wanted to knock the idiotic expression right off his face. 'Go on, Marie. Cret... Dale's right. Your baby is more important than anything.'

As she took Rettin's hand, she gave Fuller a mischievous wink. 'Don't make any decisions without me.'

'Don't worry. This *old man* knows his place. We'll convene at...'

A shout echoed across the room as two men sprinted through the door.

Seeing Fuller, they waved frantically.

'A ship,' cried one. 'Must've been using some sort of conflector tech as we didn't pick it up.'

Fuller moved as fast as he could, realising as he reached the men that Marie and Jennaut had followed him. Rettin had been left behind with his now-empty hand still outstretched.

'Where is it now?' he asked, concern edging into his voice.

'Landing just above us.'

By the time they reached the hatch to the surface, a long line of men and women had joined them and all were armed. Fuller had tried to persuade Marie to remain behind. She was as stubborn as ever.

'Could be a merc with supplies,' suggested Jennaut.

'They would have contacted us before landing,' Fuller said, dismissing the notion. 'It could be an unmarked vessel sent by Taurus to scout the area. If so, it doesn't lift off again. Understood?'

There were nods all along the line.

'How would they know to land right here though, Cal?' Marie asked. 'I doubt it's just coincidence.'

'Maybe someone sold us out for the right price,' Jennaut remarked. 'I wouldn't put it past those merc bastards.'

They listened to the muffled engine as the unknown ship landed nearby and waited until the noise had ceased. Fuller allowed another five minutes before leading the Cobb Resistance out of the safety of their bunker and into the dreary light of the morning.

The ship was smaller than he had expected and he was surprised to find that the pilot had managed to manoeuvre it under one of the overhanging structures the mercs used when they visited, so they could be scanned before being allowed below. Perhaps Jennaut's first thought had been right.

The airlock opened with a squeak. Fuller's people took up positions a suitable distance away, weapons ready to fire on his command.

A man appeared in the airlock, grimacing slightly at the foul air, but then holding up his hands when he saw his greeting party.

'You've got to be fucking kidding me,' Fuller muttered, suddenly striding forward with his pistol aimed at the new arrival.

Rane smiled. 'Hello, Cal.'

'I don't know why you've come back here.' Fuller noticed another face peering from the airlock. 'I should just put a bullet in you right now.'

'And you would be entitled to,' admitted Rane, stepping off the ship. 'But I hope you'll hear me out.'

'I thought you'd be rotting in some cell by now.'

'If I had been caught, I'd be dead.'

Several weapons were trained on the next man to emerge – a grizzled, unkempt individual with anger in his eyes.

'I can't understand why you'd risk coming here,' Fuller said, caught in two minds.

Here was a man whose talents as an engineer had earned him respect among the Resistance, such as it was back then. When he was revealed to be a wanted killer though, Fuller had struggled to accept that someone so likeable could hide such a secret.

'Let me ask you a question, Cal.' Rane's smile broadened. 'How much do you hate Taurus Galahad?'

Taurus Galahad Assault Ship Requiem
Flint system

The assault ship split apart, tearing the Sapphire Nova emblem straight down the middle.

Santa Cruz gave a quiet sigh of relief as he watched the death throes of the final enemy vessel. He had expected resistance when they reached the system, but Nova had sent their closest assault ships later than expected. Straunia was just less than two hours away.

'How are the others faring?' he asked his command officers.

Connolly was stood over one of the consoles. 'No damage to the *Ravenedge* or the *Exodus*. Commander Fernandes reports significant damage to the port hull plating of the *Tucana*. Both the *Mantheus* and *Arcturus* received glancing strikes – nothing serious.'

Santa Cruz cursed beneath his breath. 'Tell Fernandes to bring up the rear as we approach Straunia.'

He had hoped to avoid any of his fleet sustaining heavy damage from the first wave of Nova defense. It could have been worse. He momentarily considered sending an order for the *Sentinel* to leave its position back at the jump point to join them. Then he realised the *Grail* meant they wouldn't need the guardian.

'Get us back on course,' he ordered.

As the *Requiem* continued to lead the fleet deeper into the heart of the Flint system, Santa Cruz took the time to study the latest data on what he could expect to find at the Nova homeworld. Three guardians were in orbit of the verdant world along with four more assault ships. They would have been a daunting prospect was it not for the fact the *Grail* would reach them first. He would let them fire on it. The retaliation would be a sight to behold.

Still, his fleet would once again engage the enemy and he was glad they had jumped to Haskell before heading to Flint. It may have delayed the outcome by five days, but at least they were ready for the offensive.

With the *Grail* half-an-hour out from Straunia, the commander sat watching the screen intently. He hadn't failed to notice the nervous glances from his officers and the occasional hushed conversation between them. He couldn't blame them for being so anxious when they were about to lay siege to such a well-protected planet. He had already shown what happened to those who doubted him, cutting down his command crew by nearly a quarter.

He needed unquestioning loyalty now as they executed the most important part of his plan.

Connolly's voice broke him from his thoughts. 'Sir, we're receiving a comms link from Solomon Rees.'

Santa Cruz stood and straightened his jacket. 'From Earth?'

'No, sir. From this system.'

It was a brave move from Rees, but too late. 'Put it through.'

'Commander Santa Cruz,' came Rees' stern voice. 'You are ordered to cease your attack on Sapphire Nova territory and surrender your fleet, including the alien weapon.'

'As you're already here in the *Nova territory*, I suggest you stand back and watch us win the war.' Santa Cruz tapped at his command console. Scans weren't finding any Taurus ships. 'You crept into Flint using conflector technology? Is that not a breach of protocol in itself?'

'Listen to me very carefully, commander.' Rees was clearly in no mood for games. 'You betrayed your own corporation when you took it upon yourself to wipe out the entire population of innocents on Meta. It is my job to ensure murderers are brought to justice. Stand down *now*.'

'News travels fast,' said Santa Cruz, still studying his console. 'I'm assuming you heard from Davian Kurcher before he was killed.'

Rees was silent for a moment. 'Your time is running out, commander. Consider the lives of your crew. I'm sure they don't want to die for your insane cause.'

'Listen to yourself, Rees. The cause is not insane. It is the logical plan of action considering the power I now control. If we had waited, the other corps would have made efforts to take the *Grail* from us. You know that.'

'We have contacted Sapphire Nova,' Rees stated. 'They are aware that you are now considered a rogue fleet and are a major threat to all corporations.'

Santa Cruz laughed. 'Distance yourself all you like. If it were Nova who had found the *Grail*, do you not think they would be wiping out Taurus as a priority?'

'Commander, surrender your fleet now.'

'I will not. As you are hiding in the shadows somewhere in Flint, I can assume that Mitchell and the rest of the fleet are not here too. He wouldn't risk entering enemy space for fear of stirring the hornets' nest further, but he can also probably see my reasons for doing this and is secretly hoping you fail.' He let his words sink in for a moment. 'I am intrigued though how you knew I would be here. It was either an extremely lucky guess or somebody got the intel to you.'

'You will not reach Straunia.' Rees' voice was quieter this time.

The answer dawned on Santa Cruz. Winter really had been a talented agent.

'Sir, ships ahead,' warned Connolly.

Santa Cruz couldn't see anything on the screen initially. Then tiny specks began glistening in the darkness. The line of ships had spread out before his fleet in some laughable attempt at bringing him to a sudden stop. As they closed, he chuckled to himself. They were possibly the sorriest looking collection of vessels he had ever seen.

He instantly recognised the five at the centre of the line. Rees had brought his enlisters with him. Was it some bizarre attempt at revenge for what happened to Kurcher? Surely people like that weren't led by a desire to get themselves killed for such an idiotic cause.

A number of ships bore an insignia he didn't recognise; a multi-limbed tree of some sort. Some of these were approximately the same size as the enlisters but two were larger, resembling a shrunken assault ship. All were heavily customised and looked as though they had been built from scratch.

The remaining ships had no insignia of any kind and looked as though they had been repaired so many times that they were just held together by random welded plates. They must have been a mercenary outfit, but who? He was slightly unnerved by their presence, but none of the junk armada before him would be a match.

The *Grail* wouldn't slow down for anything. He watched as it closed on the line. He was willing one of the ships to try stopping it when to his surprise and annoyance, they moved aside and the alien machine simply glided past. As the line reformed, he calmly returned to his seat.

'Have Byrne set his dogs on them.'

Despite losing so many mercs on Cerberus, the *Exodus* still spat out an impressive number of wasps, as Santa Cruz had come to think of them. Thin fusion pulses flashed in the void as the mercs opened fire. The defensive fleet was ready, reeling away to avoid the vicious licks.

The first ship to be destroyed in the opening few seconds of the dogfighting was one of the wasps, hammered on the starboard side by a fusion beam from an enlister but ripped apart when one of the tree vessels followed up swiftly.

The lethal dance soon became frantic as the losses began stacking up on both sides. Some of the unmarked ships made a bold move, breaking from the fight to take on the *Requiem*.

Santa Cruz saw the *Grail* beyond the battle continuing on course for Straunia and realised he couldn't allow any more delays.

'Lieutenant, tell the other assault ships to blow through and follow us.'

As Connolly began relaying the message, Santa Cruz noticed a lone vessel following the *Grail*. It was small and sleek, hence the reason he hadn't spotted it sooner. As he went to give the order to open fire on the approaching ships, he saw that the five enlisters had veered from the battle and were settling in behind the loner, heading also for Straunia.

'Take us through.' He glanced to his weapons officer. 'Destroy anything in our way.'

'Sir, there's something...' Connolly suddenly spun to face the commander. 'More behind.'

'What?' Santa Cruz looked down at his console. 'That's not possible.'

Multiple ship signatures had appeared at the rear of his fleet. His eyes widened as the data highlighted familiar insignias: Fortitude, Schaeffer's Nine and Echo. It was the final emblem that made his stomach twist though. What the fuck were Libra Centauri assault ships doing there and how had they managed to integrate conflector tech strong enough to mask their approach? How the hell had they managed to slip past the *Sentinel*?

'All ships fire at will,' he yelled.

It was at that moment the *Tucana* exploded.

~

'The aim was to try stopping it *before* it reached Straunia.' Kurcher had decided to focus his anger on Rane yet again.

'The machine is faster than anticipated,' came the response. 'Hopefully the defenses at the planet will delay the attack.'

Kurcher knew he should have transferred to the enlister ship Rees was on. The judicial officer had requested his presence, but the fact Hewn's customised courier ship was quicker had made his mind up. He had to reach the alien weapon and at least try to disarm it somehow. His revenge against Santa Cruz would have to wait, unless of course the commander had already been killed.

The ships belonging to the Cobb Resistance and the Oakley family had achieved their primary objective: delay the rogue fleet long enough to separate them from the machine and allow Hewn's associates time to reach them. It was a plan that could have failed spectacularly. Somehow it had prevailed.

'Can you tell what's happening back there?' It seemed the battle was also

335

on Broekow's mind.

In the pilot seat, Rane checked his data. 'Hard to distinguish. The scans are struggling to cope with the sheer number of ships caught up in the fight, such is the old tech we're relying on, but I can say with confidence that the *Requiem* has managed to get through and is now in pursuit.'

'And you didn't think to announce this before now?' snarled Kurcher.

'It only just happened, Davian.' Rane shot him a confused look. 'Surely our focus has to be what is in front of us, not behind.'

'When it's an assault ship commanded by a fucking madman, I like to know.'

Kurcher peered at the main screen and could see the blue and green orb that was Straunia growing ever larger ahead. The weapon would soon settle into orbit as it did at Meta. He wondered whether it had already been set to fire on the Nova homeworld or whether Santa Cruz needed to send an activation code. The latter would give them more time to try finding a way inside it.

'I'm not sure the Cobb Resistance truly appreciated what they were getting into,' D'Larro commented from the back of the tight cabin. 'I hope some of them survive.'

Kurcher opened his mouth to reply with another cutting remark, then thought better of it. Cal Fuller and his people were given all the facts about what they would be facing and had taken a fair amount of persuading. After all, why would they potentially throw away everything they had worked towards since Cobb was left to die?

It was Rane who had finally convinced Fuller to fight against Santa Cruz, warning him that eventually the weapon would likely be turned on Cobb to eradicate any remaining pockets of civilisation before being recolonised.

It was just a pity that the ships belonging to the Cobb Resistance would be nothing more than cannon fodder. It was highly likely that Fuller and his fighters were all dead by now. Kurcher just hoped they weren't relying on being seen as martyrs, sparking some uprising against Taurus Galahad. The harsh reality was that the Cobb Resistance would be stamped out and nobody would ever remember their names.

It was slightly different for the handful of ships sent by the Oakleys. The vessels were hardier and packed more of a punch but were crewed by inexperienced, naïve men and women. Tara Oakley had been good to her word; her family had spent a lot of time and money building their fleet only to see it ripped apart. They had taken less persuading though it seemed and were only too eager to help take down some rebel Taurus vessels. Perhaps they hoped that helping the corp would make them appear trustworthy, giving them an advantage in the future. Perhaps they just wanted to kill some Taurus pricks.

'Some of Hewn's support is following too,' Rane told them. 'Although the Libra Centauri ships aren't among them.'

Kurcher gave a quiet snort of derision. That was no surprise. Hewn's alliance with a specific arm of Libra had drummed up some assistance, no doubt ensuring that both Taurus and Nova saw a willingness to help from their rival corp. There was no way their assault ships would risk getting too close to Straunia though.

As for the others that came to Hewn's aid, Kurcher was forced to feel something akin to respect for the leader of Echo for getting them to fight alongside each other. He had only brought a few Echo vessels, wisely ensuring he wouldn't lose too many of his growing fleet, but managing to persuade Schaeffer's Nine to join the fight was a feat in itself.

The pirates didn't often risk fighting in the open and preferred skulking in the shadows as they smuggled goods from one side of the galaxy to the other. Kurcher doubted though that any of the Nine would actually be commanding the ships that had arrived with Hewn.

He was probably most surprised to see Fortitude ships among them. Not known for taking sides, the merc organisation would probably ask for something in return from Taurus or Nova. They never did anything for free.

Kurcher was not so surprised that there were no ships with Hewn belonging to the Knights Templar or Jericho's Bold. The former were probably still keeping their heads down after what happened to Rolan Cairns on Temple, whereas the Bold were too unpredictable and would have most likely tried boarding every ship around them as the battle raged. They were opportunists.

'Davian, Solomon Rees is asking to speak with you.' Rane was staring at him again with those unnerving eyes of his.

Kurcher nodded, waiting until the link was active. 'This is Kurcher.'

'Enlister, good to hear your voice again.' Rees sounded understandably nervous. 'Have you located the entrance?'

'We're working on it.' Kurcher didn't feel like an enlister anymore and kept wondering what would happen to him if he survived. Would Rees remain good to his word? 'It'd help if we knew exactly what we were looking for.'

'I'm sure you'll find it. We will protect you for as long as we can.'

'If the *Requiem* catches up, I doubt five enlisters will be able to hold it off.' Kurcher was amazed that his counterparts were so willing to give up their lives to protect him. He had purposefully avoided any meetings with them. 'There's no guarantee we could even stop this thing if we were to get inside it.'

Rees was silent for a moment. 'Understood, but we have to try.'

Kurcher knew the board member was on the *Skylan*; why he had chosen that particular ship was a mystery. If anything, it was less impressive than the other four. Maybe Rees hoped Santa Cruz wouldn't think him to be on a weaker vessel. The commander would jump at the chance of getting rid of him after all.

'Good luck, enlister,' said Rees, ending the link.

Kurcher looked up and saw Broekow and D'Larro watching him. He wished Frost was with them, offering her special brand of advice and filling the cockpit with smoke.

'This is fucking ridiculous,' he mumbled, tapping at his forehead as if to jolt his brain back into gear.

'Agreed,' Broekow nodded. 'If we fail though, at least we won't give a shit what happens next.'

D'Larro looked like he was about to vomit. 'Morbid way of looking at it.'

'You might want to see this,' Rane told them.

The *Grail* arrived at Straunia and was fired on by the three guardians protecting the planet immediately. The four assault ships in orbit moved to intercept it too, their fusion beams leading the way and seemingly doing no damage. There was a pale blue pulse from the prongs of the machine. Nothing emerged from the cone at its base. As the ships closed, continuing to bombard the *Grail* with fusion and missiles, the prongs pulsed again. This time, a wide arc of sickly light was cast out directly at the assault vessels. It swept through all four, passing on towards the nearest guardian. At first, nothing seemed to happen. Then the ships ceased their attack and two pitched suddenly downwards, disappearing into the upper atmosphere of Straunia. Another simply passed the alien weapon, as though the crew had decided to flee instead. The final assault ship, however, ran a collision course straight into the shaft of the *Grail*, crumpling against its black hull and breaking apart violently.

'What the fuck just happened?' asked Broekow as they watched the remnants of the assault ship orbiting the planet.

'Unknown,' replied Rane, fascinated at what was happening before them. 'But I would suggest not firing on it at any time. Pity those guardians aren't heeding what just happened.'

338

The full might of the planet protectors was unleashed on the *Grail*, which just absorbed the strikes again and settled into orbit alongside them. The dark hull of the leviathan remained unblemished, though an occasional hint of grey and blue could be seen passing along the surface.

'It's time,' Kurcher announced as he saw the same arc of light emanate from the *Grail* towards the guardians. 'We need to locate that airlock... door... whatever the fuck it is.'

Rane guided them into Straunia's orbit and got them so close to the machine that it looked to be within touching distance. His eyes scanned the screen on his console intently for several minutes.

Kurcher and Broekow made sure that the explosives they had acquired from the Cobb Resistance were secure and checked their ammo. D'Larro took a deep breath and studied the razepistol he had chosen to carry.

'How do you check the ammunition for this?' the medic asked sheepishly.

'Maybe you shouldn't use that,' Broekow suggested.

'Maybe you shouldn't come with us, if we can get inside,' Kurcher said. 'You're not a soldier.'

'Neither is Rane,' pointed out D'Larro.

Kurcher holstered his revolver. 'No, but he is useful in a fight. Besides, I don't trust him enough to leave him here.'

There was still a strong part of him that wanted Rane dead and it wouldn't be a tragedy if the killer didn't come back from the *Grail*.

'Thank you for the vote of confidence,' Rane called. 'I've found the way in.'

The men gathered behind him, looking out at the darkness beyond.

'I don't see anything,' D'Larro remarked.

'Look.' Rane pointed to where the strange symbols of the alien dialect were scrolling down one of the screens.

Kurcher recalled something similar happening when they had first approached the machine. He produced the adapter that Choice had created and checked that the tiny implant was still in place. Reluctantly, he handed it to Rane.

They all knew gaining entry this way was a long shot. If it failed, chances were they would get to witness the alien defenses first-hand. Breaths were held as Rane slotted the adapter into a port and used the comms link to send data from it directly at the *Grail*.

After five long minutes, the link suddenly closed. To their amazement, the hull of the machine began to shift. As they watched, the surface seemed to bend inwards and a dark shape protruded from the hole; three black fingers reaching awkwardly for their ship.

Then they were in its grasp.

'This is fucking ridiculous,' repeated Kurcher as they vanished inside the *Grail*.

~

Santa Cruz managed a weak smile as he saw the orbiting debris around Straunia. Some positive news at last.

'The assault ship and the two guardians are non-responsive, sir,' reported Connolly.

'I can see that,' snapped the commander, moving to stand near the main screen. 'Where is the other ship that followed the *Grail*?'

Connolly exchanged words with both the comms and navigation officers. 'It must have been destroyed.'

Santa Cruz bit nervously at his lip. 'No, it's hiding somewhere out there. Rees and his enlisters are aiming to distract us again.'

He wondered who was on that small ship he had seen pursuing the *Grail*. Special forces perhaps aiming to try finding a way into the machine, or it could even be a demolition crew brought in to try setting explosives.

No matter. 'What's happening on the surface?'

'The chatter is manic, sir,' replied the comms officer. 'More so than Meta. It's hard to distinguish any one link, but it sounds like they are activating defenses. Many ships are being launched too, including transports and fighters.'

Santa Cruz gave the *Grail* a quick scan, narrowing his eyes. 'If any of the launching ships come into range, destroy them.'

'Even the transports, sir?' Connolly regretted asking that as soon as the words left his mouth.

'*Any* ships.' Santa Cruz glared at the lieutenant. 'And get rid of those enlisters too.'

As he returned to his seat, the numb feeling returned. It had crept into his skull when he saw the *Arcturus* destroyed. It had been hammered by numerous beams of fusion during a combined attack by Echo, Schaeffer's Nine and Fortitude; a Libra ship had finished it off. The resulting explosion had been so violent that it seared the starboard side of the *Mantheus*.

Fernandes and Thomadakis were both dead. The other commanders were likely gone too. He felt a pang of guilt for leaving them behind, but ensuring the *Grail* completed its mission was more important.

'There is a recorded message coming across from Solomon Rees,

340

commander,' the comms officer told him.

Santa Cruz signalled to put it through.

'To the crew of the *Requiem*, stand down or suffer the same fate as your other ships. This is your final warning.'

Arrogant bastard, thought Santa Cruz. 'I want those ships joining the rest of the debris in orbit now.'

Santa Cruz sat back to watch. He would enjoy seeing Rees' beloved enlisters wiped out. When he took control of Taurus, he would disband any that were left. They were a blight on the reputation of the corporation and were better off dead. He would recruit loyal officers to take their place. After all, enlisters were just glorified bounty hunters with a penchant for betrayal.

As the *Requiem* opened fire, Santa Cruz shrugged the numbness off and sent the activation code to the *Grail*.

~

Kurcher had no idea what he was looking at.

The docking bay, for want of a better term, had been disappointingly mundane. A dark chamber leading to a dark corridor, surrounded by dark walls. All very gothic but not what he would call *alien*.

Soon though, the unwelcoming gloom gave way to a vast space deep inside the structure and the mundane became the extraordinary. They had traversed a lone walkway that spanned a frighteningly deep chasm and the chamber also rose so high above that they couldn't even see any ceiling. The walls were dotted with odd white and grey cylinders, or *pods* as Rane referred to them. The entire space was illuminated with a pale blue glow despite no light sources being seen.

The air inside the *Grail* was difficult to inhale. It left a metallic taste in the mouth and Kurcher's throat became sore just seconds after stepping off their ship. They had initially been afraid that the poisonous substance used to wipe the life from planets would be seeping throughout the interior, but scans before they opened the airlock showed surprising levels of oxygen. It was as though the machine was welcoming them inside. There was even artificial gravity, albeit one that made it feel like they were walking uphill.

The walkway had ended at a black pillar that stretched both ways vertically as far as the eye could see. Inside this, they had discovered a smaller chamber with curved walls covered completely with some sort of tech. A hole in one wall led into a similar room, also filled with the alien equipment.

Kurcher found himself standing alongside Rane at what they had guessed

341

to be a control console, while Broekow and D'Larro explored the adjacent chamber.

'You can't possibly know what this is or what it does,' the enlister said quietly. His voice echoed off the surfaces, whatever they were made of.

Rane tapped a finger against his lips before pointing at the console. 'This large surface here is the screen, I believe. They had to have a way of monitoring power, or keeping an eye on energy levels.'

'We don't know what they monitored or whether they even had eyes.' Kurcher frowned as he leaned forward to examine the tech. 'We could be looking at a fucking table for all we know.'

Rane smiled at that. He ran a hand over the surface. Beneath his hand, the console erupted into life as the familiar pale lighting highlighted what looked like various control panels. At the same time, the alien dialect began appearing on the screen Rane had pointed to, although it almost looked as though the symbols were rising into the air.

'That looks like the pods,' Rane said, managing to remain unnervingly calm throughout their journey into the alien structure. 'Perhaps they are the power source that creates the poisonous material.'

'Fuck knows.' Kurcher studied some of the panels, recognising the occasional symbol from previous data. 'This is like us arriving at Sullivan's Rest and walking to the initial hub. We've seen only a tiny part of this structure. There could be anything on the levels above or below.'

Rane's mellow exterior suddenly threatened to crumble as he pulled his hand back. 'It wasn't me that activated the console.'

'What're you talking about?'

'The *Grail* is preparing to fire on Straunia. Santa Cruz must have activated it.'

Kurcher could feel a change in the air. There was a strange buzzing sensation rattling his bones. What the fuck would happen if it fired while they were inside? Would they join the millions about to die?

'So set the explosives and let's go.' He hadn't heard Broekow return. 'As awe-inspiring as this place is, I don't want to stay any longer.'

Kurcher cursed himself for almost forgetting he was carrying the explosives and began carefully unpacking them. 'How long do we have?'

'Hard to say,' Rane replied, still studying the console. 'We saw it fire quickly at Meta once the prongs lit up, but I couldn't possibly guess how long it takes the internal tech to activate.'

'Did you find anything through there?' Kurcher asked the other two.

'Just more bizarre shit.' Broekow held out his hand. 'Here, give me a

342

couple and I'll go plant them in there. The more we destroy, the better.'

'The wiring reminds me of veins and arteries,' D'Larro told them. 'It's possible this other race used a form of biomech technology.'

'That might make it easier to kill it then.' Kurcher planted the first explosive. 'There's no time for meticulous surgery now though. Go help Broekow.'

The medic looked around sadly. 'Understood.'

'No point trying to learn much about it,' Kurcher said to Rane, seeing the crim deep in thought as he watched the symbols float from the screen. 'Why don't you do something useful?'

Kurcher quickly distributed the rest of the explosives around the room, attaching them to anything that looked important. The final cluster he placed around the console, hoping that destroying it would at least create a malfunction in the system.

'Davian.'

'I don't want to hear anything more about this thing, Rane. I just want to blow the fucker up.' He never thought he would be trying so desperately to save Nova's homeworld. Then again, it was more about avoiding having their screams join the others. All those deaths he'd witnessed, so many he was directly to blame for...

'Davian.' Rane's tone had more urgency this time.

Perhaps he should take the opportunity to get rid of the killer finally. Chasing him down through Monarch City seemed like such a distant memory now.

'Right, let's prime these and get the fuck...'

'I'm impressed.'

Kurcher flinched at the unexpected voice, pulling his revolver quietly from its holster as he lifted his head to peer over the top of the console.

'Winter was an accomplished liar,' boomed Santa Cruz, the echo lasting for a few seconds as it bounced from surface to surface. 'I should've known you'd survive. You adapt. That's your greatest talent.'

Kurcher eyed the squad of soldiers flanking the commander. 'I wish I'd known how fucking insane you were when we first met. Killing you then would have saved a lot of people.'

Santa Cruz tutted. 'And got you killed at the same time. Nonetheless, here we all are.' The commander looked to a motionless Rane. 'How *did* you get onto the *Grail* anyway?'

'Via a lucky guess.'

Santa Cruz chuckled at the crim's answer before turning his attention back to Kurcher. 'You must be the first enlister to work alongside a murderer like him. I do have to commend you though. Cooke simply tried running. I should've guessed you wouldn't.'

'All very fascinating,' Kurcher said, raising his voice on purpose. 'But I'm not really much of a talker. Save your pompous fucking words.'

Santa Cruz regarded him coldly for a moment. 'This was supposed to be an exhilarating experience, entering the *Grail* for the first time. Your presence here threatens to ruin that.'

Kurcher prepared himself, noting that Rane's hand had crept to the hilt of his sword. Rane was skilled with the blade, but Kurcher doubted he could deflect bullets. Silver lining in a bleak situation though.

'Kill them both,' came the order.

The Taurus soldiers had been glancing around the chamber, some of them clearly in awe of the alien structure they found themselves in. The slight delay before they raised their weapons gave Broekow his opportunity, swinging from the opening to the next room and firing his rifle. His first bullet took the man to Santa Cruz's left in the shoulder, spinning him round before he fell. A second snapshot whistled an inch past the commander's ear, striking the soldier directly behind him and blowing half his skull apart.

As the Taurus men hesitated, Kurcher fired over the top of the console, hoping to hit Santa Cruz. To his chagrin, the commander stepped back behind his men and the bullet instead caught one of his human shields in the chest.

Rane danced into action, moving so quickly he took the nearest soldiers by surprise. His sword sliced through the neck of one and he knocked the rifle from another's hands with the flat of the blade.

The soldiers split – some moving back into the corridor for cover and others boldly stepping further into the chamber. Assault rifles blazed, missing Broekow as he darted back into the adjacent room.

Kurcher ducked behind the console again as bullets passed over his head and struck the wall.

'Don't shoot the tech,' screeched Santa Cruz.

When Kurcher dared to peer out again, he could see the commander striding back into the chamber, his pistol raised. His men charged forward too, three heading for Broekow's position and three for the console. Another two opened fire at Rane, who swiftly grabbed the unarmed soldier and pulled the poor man in front of him to take the bullets. Kurcher saw one bullet pass straight through the soldier and graze Rane's thigh.

As the three headed through the opening and the sound of gunfire rang out

344

again, Kurcher slid his revolver around the edge of the console and opened fire blindly. If he raised his head again, he knew at least one bullet would blow his brains all over the alien tech behind him.

'Commander.' The sound of Broekow's voice came as a relief.

Kurcher knew he only had one bullet left in the clip. There was no time to reload. When he looked past the console, he saw Santa Cruz staring at the sniper, who had emerged from the doorway with one of the soldiers. The barrel of Broekow's pistol was against the man's temple.

The three who had been approaching his own position had met with differing fortunes. One was stood unhurt, watching the sudden exchange between the commander and the crim. Another was struggling to get back to his feet thanks to the wound in his lower leg. The third was lying lifeless.

Rane had been knocked on his backside after a tussle with the two gunmen before him. Both assailants now had deep cuts, but they had obviously managed to get in a telling blow. From the mark on Rane's cheek, it looked like the butt of a rifle.

'Time to lower your weapons,' Broekow told the fuming commander, pushing the pistol barrel hard against the soldier's skull. 'Nobody else has to die.'

Santa Cruz lifted his own pistol and put a bullet in the soldier's chest. As the man fell, the pistol fired twice more, hitting Broekow both times and sending the sniper reeling back into the adjoining chamber.

There was a stunned silence as the remaining soldiers looked at one another, trying to gauge what had just happened.

Kurcher stood and saw Santa Cruz step into the doorway, aiming his pistol down at a stricken Broekow. When the enlister raised his own weapon, looking to put his final bullet in the commander's back, Santa Cruz turned his head and offered a cruel smile.

'Shoot me and you'll never be able to stop the *Grail*. I've given it orders to move on to the remaining corp homeworlds and obliterate them before heading to its final destination. Once Earth has been cleansed of Revenants and those loyal to the old Taurus Galahad, it will pave the way for our new regime.'

Kurcher could feel the floor vibrating. There was a strange smell in the air, as if a storm was brewing. 'You're bluffing. Why would you kill everyone on Earth? Doesn't make sense.'

'Of course it does. It'll create a clean slate to work with.'

'Bullshit. Just words again. You're buying time.'

'I don't need to bluff,' Santa Cruz scoffed. 'Or buy time.'

345

Kurcher returned the smile. 'I do.'

D'Larro's knife plunged into the commander's back between his shoulder blades. Santa Cruz howled in pain before striking the medic across the face with his pistol.

Rane took the opportunity and leapt to his feet, bringing his sword up with so much momentum that it entered through one soldier's groin and exited from his guts, spilling the entrails. The second soldier didn't react fast enough and his head rolled.

As Santa Cruz turned his gun on D'Larro, Kurcher fired the remaining bullet, which blew through the rogue officer's hand and sent the pistol flying.

'Davian, we don't have long.' Rane had rushed back to the console. Kurcher saw he had dispatched the only surviving soldiers silently too. 'The explosives would need more time. I'm afraid we're going to need the code to deactivate the *Grail*.'

Kurcher watched as Santa Cruz slumped against the opening, D'Larro's knife still protruding from his back. The medic had shaken off the strike to the face and was crouched next to Broekow, who remained prone on the floor.

'Don't die on us yet, commander.' Kurcher began reloading his revolver as he hurried across the chamber.

A resonating thrum could be heard as the sickly alien light filled the room and Kurcher's head immediately started hurting. All their efforts could have been in vain. *Fuck.*

As he reached for Santa Cruz, aiming to drag him to the console and twist the knife until he gave them the code, there was a surge of energy through the surrounding tech. It felt as though the artificial gravity was cut for a split second. All of them were lifted from the floor and plunged back down heavily, Kurcher stumbling as he landed.

Before he could recover, a fist connected with his chin, throwing his head back. There was a flash of pain through his wrist. He felt the revolver slip from his hand as he fell backwards.

'Wait,' he heard someone shout, followed by a muffled cry.

When his vision cleared, he saw Santa Cruz wrench a knife bearing the Taurus insignia from the side of D'Larro's neck before throwing the medic aside. Kurcher tried to push himself up, but his right wrist gave way agonisingly. Looking down, he saw that a blade had bitten deep and he couldn't flex his thumb or index finger.

Santa Cruz spun, his expression of pure hatred giving him a feral look. He seemed not to feel the knife in his back or the hole in his hand. His teeth

346

gritted, the commander lunged towards Kurcher, who raised his good hand to try deflecting the blow. A shot rang out above the thrumming as Santa Cruz pitched forward, tripping over Kurcher and landing face-first on the cold floor.

Broekow slumped back again, dropping the smoking pistol. Kurcher saw it was Santa Cruz's own weapon. Surprisingly, that gave him a modicum of satisfaction.

By the time he got to his feet, he saw Rane had dragged the commander to the console and was leaning him against it. Broekow's shot had taken the bastard in the base of the spine and Santa Cruz's face was ashen as he shook his head at Rane.

'I won't help you deactivate it. We can all die here today along with those on Straunia.'

Rane drew in a deep breath and glanced at the alien controls before slowly stabbing his sword into the doomed man's leg. 'The code please, commander.'

'Go to hell, Rane.'

'Oh, I think we'll all be heading there eventually.' The sword twisted. 'The code please.'

Santa Cruz tried to remain stoic. Tears welled in his eyes. 'I'm an... interrogator, you piece of shit. I know what makes men talk and... there is nothing that will get me to give you that code.'

Kurcher watched as Rane leant down and spoke softly into the commander's ear. When he finished, the blade was yanked free. Rane placed the tip against his shoulder instead.

'The nerve cluster there will allow you to experience exquisite pain, but you already know that.' He slowly pushed the hilt, breaking the skin. 'The code please.'

Kurcher knew Santa Cruz would not relinquish the data. The *Grail* would fire any minute and they would have failed. If being inside the machine when it released the pale beam meant they died too, so be it. Maybe someone else could stop it, maybe not.

He looked over his shoulder into the adjoining chamber, at the bodies littering the floor. Broekow had killed the soldiers who went in after him. His sniper rifle was lying broken alongside one of the corpses. Broekow himself was barely alive, his breathing shallow. Both bullets had hit him in the chest. He had saved Kurcher's life, but the enlister doubted he would wake up again if he fell into a coma.

D'Larro was lying near to the sniper, his eyes staring lifelessly up at the ceiling. Kurcher couldn't feel sorry for the medic. For all his demented research, D'Larro couldn't fully understand death until he faced it.

The thrumming suddenly ceased and the chamber dimmed once more. At the console, Rane grinned triumphantly; the sweat across his brow betrayed the confident façade for once.

'That's it?' Kurcher asked, incredulously.

'The commander made the right choice.'

Santa Cruz looked small and frail now, sitting in a pool of his own blood. There would be no trial for him; no court martial. He would die on his beloved *Grail*.

'Davian, you need to get Sieren out of here now or he will die. There is a medpack in the ship which will help.'

Kurcher recovered his revolver, instinctively reaching out with his numb right hand before the blood dripping from his wound reminded him. 'We need to prime the explosives.'

Rane nodded. 'Let me do that. If you delay any longer, Sieren will bleed out. He doesn't deserve to die here. Just a pity Regan didn't survive too.'

'If you take him, I can...'

'Look at your wrist, Davian. If you don't get back, you'll end up passed out too. You both need that medpack. Besides, if something were to go wrong, I'm sure you'd rather I didn't make it back.'

Kurcher couldn't argue with that logic. Rane may have been useful in getting them to this point, but once the *Grail* was destroyed the killer needed to answer for his own crimes. Then again, Kurcher didn't feel like an enlister any longer. Perhaps dealing with Rane would be his final act for Taurus Galahad.

With Rane's help, he managed to get Broekow up. The sniper was a dead weight – it would be slow going.

'This may be farewell,' Rane called as Kurcher headed for the corridor.

Kurcher looked back, his eyes moving from the dying Santa Cruz to the smiling serial killer. 'I fucking hope so.'

He left the control chamber and made his way back through the interior of the machine, dragging Broekow along the walkway and back to the docking bay. When they reached the ship, Kurcher noticed the lifeboat from the *Requiem* that had transported Santa Cruz and his men. He considered checking it for any other soldiers and remembered time was of the essence.

Inside their ship, he secured Broekow and administered painkillers which knocked the sniper out cold. If he could get them to a vessel with a proper medical team, they would stand a much better chance. As he bandaged his wrist, he avoided giving himself any drugs. As much as he wanted to have some Parinax left in his boost app, he could hear Frost tutting him. That was enough to work through the pain.

It all seemed too quiet as he peered out into the gloom of the bay. Enough sitting around though: if Rane thought Kurcher would wait for him, the crim would get an unpleasant surprise. Settling into the pilot seat, he fired up the ship.

Fuck Rane, fuck Santa Cruz and fuck Taurus Galahad.

~

Rane primed the final device and casually strode back to the console. Santa Cruz had keeled over to one side, occasionally drawing in a sudden breath then choking as he let it back out.

'Stay awake, commander.' Rane stirred him with a kick to the wounded leg. 'I need you to do one last thing for me. Then you can die.'

Santa Cruz looked him up and down, disgust etched on his face. 'Just get on with it. What more do you want?'

Rane crouched before him. 'The *Grail* isn't just a weapon, is it?'

'It's many things, but none of that matters now.'

'I'm curious to know what exactly you were planning to do once you'd used it to get what you wanted. Were you hoping to wake them all up?'

Santa Cruz looked confused. 'How could you know?'

'I may be a cold-blooded killer with a penchant for inflicting pain and suffering, not unlike you, but I'm not stupid. I saw the pods for what they are and I saw the display on this console. The *Grail* may be a weapon, but it's also a structure designed to protect those asleep inside it.'

'It would have been glorious,' Santa Cruz stated. 'A unity the human race would never have dreamt of.'

'Unity? You could have brought about the *fall* of the human race. There was no way you could know how they would react when you woke them.'

'You don't understand,' said the commander. 'How could you?'

Rane jabbed a finger at the console. 'I understand they are alive inside those pods. I understand the risk cannot be taken waking them up. I understand that this machine somehow draws power from their pods to help create the poison and that means I understand the *Grail* needs to be destroyed.'

Rane stood and cast his eyes over the inactive controls. He had guessed that whoever built the structure had left some of their own behind. Whether or not they were simply to be used as an energy source was something he would never know. He was naturally curious to see what they looked like and whether there was any similarity between races, but they were intelligent and anyone who could create something capable of wiping all life off a planet had to be considered extremely dangerous.

With one last look around the chamber, he shrugged at the commander. 'At least you get to see it in action one last time.'

Remembering where the controls were from when he entered the deactivation code, Rane held his hand over the panel and the symbols began to illuminate, rising from the darkness of the surface. He quickly entered the second code Santa Cruz had given him and stepped back as the tech around the chamber sprang back into life.

'Thank you, commander. The explosives are set to go off once the *Grail* has fired. I thought it apt that you should meet your end at the same time.'

With that, Rane headed for the corridor. He looked back only once, seeing Santa Cruz wasn't even trying to move. It seemed the man had finally accepted his fate. It was more likely, however, that Broekow's shot had struck his spine and paralysed him.

As he headed back through the *Grail*, Rane felt elated. Everything had fallen into place for him almost perfectly. There would always be casualties, but all of them had played their part well.

His parents would be so proud.

~

Kurcher couldn't believe what he was seeing.

The *Grail* had reactivated. There was nothing he could do as the weapon cast its lethal beam down onto the planet below. Everyone on Straunia would be dead shortly; another world wiped clean.

When they left the machine, Kurcher had found himself staring straight at the *Requiem*. He guided the ship out of orbit and put some distance between them. There was no sign of the other enlisters and no response from Rees. By the look of the local debris, they had been destroyed as they tried protecting Kurcher and the crims. Yet more voices to keep him company.

It turned out that the *Requiem* was being held in check by a number of smaller ships belonging to Hewn's associates. There had been a battle, it seemed, above Straunia. Santa Cruz's officers had finally surrendered in the absence of their crazed commander.

Kurcher couldn't watch any longer and bowed his head. Why did he trust Rane to finish the job? He found it hard to believe Santa Cruz had got the jump on the accomplished swordsman, but what the fuck had happened?

350

Three ships arrived alongside, all of them showing the Echo insignia. The expected comms eventually came through.

'Kurcher?' Hewn's gruff voice was actually good to hear. 'You there?'

'Yeah.'

'I thought it'd powered down.'

'Me too. Broekow's badly wounded. Just the two of us left.' Kurcher grimaced. 'We left Rane behind to blow the fucking thing up.'

'Listen, there are ships heading here who survived the battle with the rogue fleet. Some of them have active med bays, if Broekow can hold on.'

Kurcher looked back at the unconscious sniper. 'Hopefully he can. How did the others fare in the fight?'

'We'll have to take stock once we're all together again,' said Hewn. 'There were a few Cobb Resistance ships left and some of the Oakleys, but both lost a lot of people.'

Kurcher noticed another comms request coming in. The Taurus insignia gave him cause for concern though. He managed to patch it through so that Hewn would also be able to join any conversation.

'Hello, Davian.'

Fucking bastard. 'What the hell have you done, Rane?'

'I'm afraid that I just couldn't pass up the opportunity to pull the trigger myself and eradicate the Sapphire Nova homeworld. I know there were innocents down there, but their allegiance to Nova signed their death warrant unfortunately.'

'You sound like Santa Cruz.'

Rane laughed. 'I guess I do. I'm sorry for betraying your trust, Davian, but now I am finally sated.'

'Rane, you sadistic prick, this is Hewn. I can see the ship you're on now and I can't think of one good reason not to blow the shit out of it.'

'Hello, Jaffren.' Rane sounded like he was greeting an old friend. 'You would have every right to do so, although I have fulfilled my end of the bargain. Just not straight away.'

Kurcher's attention was drawn to the *Grail* as the beam dissipated and the machine unexpectedly pitched downwards. It was a surreal moment as the alien structure plunged into Straunia's atmosphere and moments later crashed into the surface, sending clouds of dust into the air that masked the fallen giant from the eyes in orbit.

'Fuck me,' muttered Hewn.

'I feel I should explain,' began Rane, who had clearly been waiting for the right moment to continue. 'I told you I had a reason for killing, Davian.

351

Those people I went after were all part of Sapphire Nova. To start with, I found and killed those who stood by and did nothing as my parents were executed. You see, they were blamed for the rig accident on Rikur twenty-eight years ago, but those who really caused it chose to remain quiet. I killed soldiers, engineers, admin personnel. Once I had made my way through the real criminals, I went after others in Nova. Those who had given the orders, those who knew the truth but hadn't spoken up, even those who could lead me to someone higher up in the Nova hierarchy. I knew it would be hard to stop. I knew it was likely I would be killed before I could somehow get to the Nova board, but my parents deserved better. Sapphire Nova tore my life apart back then, so I dedicated the rest of my years to tearing theirs apart.'

'Portman,' said Kurcher.

'Yes. He was part of the team who arrested my parents and I saw a chance to remove him then help you.'

'Help?' Kurcher wished Rane was standing next to him so he could throttle the man and watch the life drain from his eyes. 'You used us all to get here.'

'And I thank you for that, Davian. I couldn't possibly have foreseen that I would get onto the *Grail* and stand before the controls that would kill Nova. That was just luck.'

'I think we need to get out of here,' Hewn said with some urgency. 'Nova forces will likely arrive soon and we need to leave them to clear up the mess.'

'It is a pity that the *Grail* didn't explode in orbit as we hoped,' added Rane. 'Shame we won't have time to make sure it was destroyed on impact.'

'It's not going anywhere.' Hewn cursed. 'Time for us to leave.'

Kurcher was caught in two minds. Rane had ensured the machine was now lying broken on a dead world but had killed millions, just as Santa Cruz had. The enlister in him screamed for Rane to be executed. All of the other voices urged him otherwise.

You deserve to rest now, said Frost.

Forget Rane, Trin advised.

Nobody else matters, D'Larro told him.

Stop being a prick, growled Angard.

Perhaps he needed to listen to them after all. 'If we cross paths again, Rane, I'll...'

'I know,' interrupted the Nova killer. 'I wish you all luck. Exile isn't so bad.'

Before Kurcher or Hewn could respond, Rane cut off. A distant Taurus lifeboat broke orbit and disappeared into the void.

'There will be some real fuck-off backlash from all this,' Hewn remarked. 'I suggest none of us are around for that. I can't believe I'm actually going to say this, but I could use men like you and Broekow in Echo. It'd be a good place to lie low while the corps recover or kill each other.'

'Okay.' It was no longer the enlister talking. 'Appreciate it.'

'Don't get me wrong. One foot out of place and I'll use you for boomer practice.'

'Fair enough.'

Kurcher set a course to follow Hewn's ships away from Straunia, to regroup with the surviving ships from the battle. Perhaps what had transpired in the Flint system would lead to other alliances. The Cobb Resistance needed help and there would be something almost poetic about him helping them after everything he did back on that dustball. No doubt the Oakleys might need protection too moving forward.

If there was any amnesty between the merc and pirate organisations, he knew it wouldn't last long. There was something about Hewn's Echo though. Maybe things would be different. Then again, maybe he would end up face-down on some distant world with a bullet in his skull.

Fuck it.

Uncharted world
Coldrig sector

The signal had finally reached its destination. Slowly, it worked its way into the machines hidden below the surface, rousing them from their centuries-old slumber. It marked its origin from the binary system, despite its source having moved since being activated.

As the signal finally delivered the data and announced its arrival with a deep repeating thrum, thousands of eyes opened simultaneously. The planet that had been silent for so long came alive with the forlorn cries of the awoken.

Corporations

Corporations	Other Factions
Taurus Galahad	Fortitude (merc)
Sapphire Nova	Knights Templar (merc)
Libra Centauri	Echo (pirate)
Sigma Royal	Jericho's Bold (pirate)
Impramed	Schaeffer's Nine (pirate)
	Cobb Resistance
	The Kindred

Taurus Galahad

Davian Kurcher - enlister
Justyne Frost - pilot of the Kaladine
Cmdr. Jorelian Santa Cruz - interrogation officer
Solomon Rees - judicial officer
Fraser Lenaghan - senior board member
Gen. Mitchell - head of military operations
Saul Winter - agent
Lt. Connolly - officer on the Requiem
Ged Cooke - enlister
Akeman - agent
Cmdr. Neri Ishlan - military officer
Cmdr. O'Brien - military officer
Cmdr. Fernandes - military officer
Cmdr. Byrne - military officer
Cmdr. Thomadakis - military officer
Vokes - merc leader working for Byrne

Sapphire Nova

Cmdr. Trin Espina - special forces officer
Devlin - acting head of Harper security
Cmdr. Rolan Cairns - military officer

Crims

Edlan Rane - serial killer
Sieren Broekow - Taurus Galahad sniper
Tara Oakley - part of ruling family on Cradle
Jaffren Hewn - leader of Echo
Regan D'Larro - Taurus Galahad medic
Horsten Angard - biomech test patient
Bennet Ercko - serial killer
Maric Jaroslav/Choice - Ex-Taurus Galahad electronics expert

Additional characters

Beck - Sigma Royal enlister
Coyle - Fortitude merc
Jenson Cassius - member of The Kindred
Pask - cargo worker on Sullivan's Rest
Flynn - leader of the Knights Templar
Cal Fuller - leader of the Cobb Resistance
Marie Butler - member of the Cobb Resistance
Aman Saib - Impramed officer
Kopetti - smuggler
Lars Hengeveld - Libra Centauri officer
Jos Chaplin - head of operations on Tempest
Dale Rettin - member of the Cobb Resistance
Jennaut - member of the Cobb Resistance

Other GBP Science-Fiction
www.gbpublishing.co.uk

The ordinary series Christopher Ritchie
SILVER WINNER
2015 IndieFab Book Awards Horror
Dante: "Fusing horror and new age religion, this winner repels as much as it fascinates with death, destruction and nuggets of ironic black humour."

GODS' Enemy Derek E Pearson
FINALIST
2016 Indies Book Awards Fantasy
Read2Write: "Texas 1883, a terrifying story that fuses sci-fi with history and theology. Pearson is in electrifying form"

Soul's Asylum trilogy Derek E Pearson
FINALIST
2016 Indies Book Awards Science Fiction
The Sun ☆☆☆☆:
"a weird, vivid and creepy book, not for the faint hearted. But its originality and top writing make for a great read."

Body Holidy trilogy Derek E Pearson
Surrey Life:
"Pearson's galactic-sized imagination delivers, with veiled gallows humour, a compelling image of a chic, high-tech society infused with a toxic strain that feeds on extreme violence."

357

Lightning Source UK Ltd.
Milton Keynes UK
UKOW05f2050060717
304790UK00014B/97/P